# "You're flirting with me? Why?"

Caleb debated for a moment before answering. But then he reminded himself he was in Colorado. People were forthright around here. And he owed Mandy no less than she was giving him.

"Because you're real," he told her. "When you laugh, it's because you're happy. When you argue, it's because you have a point to make. And when your eyes smolder, it's because you're interested in me."

"I'm not interested in you."

"But you are." He smoothed a stray lock of her hair and tucked it behind one ear. "That's what's so amazing about you. Your body language doesn't lie."

"And if my body language slaps you across the face?"

"I hope it'll be because I've done something to deserve it." Because then the slap would be worth it.

Dear Reader,

Welcome to the first book of the COLORADO CATTLE BARONS series from Desire. I have a deep fondness for cowboy heroes, and this series will allow me to indulge myself by writing a whole string of them.

In book one, millionaire Caleb Terrell returns to his family's Colorado ranch, following the death of his abusive father. There, he meets sexy, down-to-earth neighbor Mandy Jacobs, the key to finding Caleb's missing twin brother, Reed. While Mandy opens the door to painful childhood memories, she also shows Caleb the pathway to love and forgiveness.

I sincerely hope you enjoy *A Cowboy Comes Home*. And I hope you'll look for Caleb's brother, Reed, along with Mandy's siblings, in future COLORADO CATTLE BARONS books. I'd love to hear from you, so please feel free to drop me a line through my website, barbaradunlop. com.

*Barbara Dunlop*

# A COWBOY COMES HOME

BY
BARBARA DUNLOP

Published in Great Britain 2012
by Mills & Boon, an imprint of Harlequin (UK) Limited,
Eton House, 18-24 Paradise Road, Richmond, Surrey TW9 1SR

© Barbara Dunlop 2012

ISBN: 978 0 263 89186 7
ebook ISBN: 978 1 408 97770 5

51-0612

Harlequin (UK) policy is to use papers that are natural, renewable and recyclable products and made from wood grown in sustainable forests. The logging and manufacturing processes conform to the legal environmental regulations of the country of origin.

Printed and bound in Spain
by Blackprint CPI, Barcelona

**Barbara Dunlop** writes romantic stories while curled up in a log cabin in Canada's far north, where bears outnumber people and it snows six months of the year. Fortunately she has a brawny husband and two teenage children to haul firewood and clear the driveway while she sips cocoa and muses about her upcoming chapters. Barbara loves to hear from readers. You can contact her through her website, www.barbaradunlop.com.

For Carla Daum and Jane Porter
One-Hundred Books Later

# One

Dust plumes scattered beneath Caleb Terrell's loafers as he approached the front steps of his former home, looking for the brother who'd despised him for ten long years. A copy of his late father's will was snapped into his Bulgari briefcase, and a million, disturbing questions swirled inside his brain. The Terrell Cattle Company hadn't changed much. The two-story brick house had been meticulously maintained, while the crisp, northern-Colorado mountain air still held the familiar tang of wheatgrass and ponderosa pine.

The soles of his shoes met the smooth wood of the wide, front porch, and for a fleeting moment he wished he'd stopped in Lyndon and changed into blue jeans and boots. But he banished the impulse. He was a businessman now, not a cowboy. And the last thing he wanted to do was feel at home.

His brother, Reed, wouldn't be remotely happy to see him, but outrageous times called for outrageous measures. Reed would have to deal with it.

Caleb briefly toyed with the idea of bursting in unannounced. He owned the place, after all, and Reed had been dodging his calls for over a week. To be fair, Caleb hadn't tried to contact his fraternal twin brother in ten years. Then again, in all that time, Reed hadn't tried to contact Caleb, either.

But now, their father was dead. Caleb wouldn't have set foot on the Terrell ranch in any other circumstance. He'd probably have been shot if he'd tried. Which made the contents of the will that much more baffling.

He gave three short, sharp knocks.

In the moments of silence that followed, he glanced around the ranch yard, refreshing his memory and bracing himself for the conversation to come.

The main barn had been recently painted a dark green. The square horse corrals were still meticulously maintained, their straight rails gleaming white in the afternoon sunshine. He knew every angle was precisely ninety degrees, and the posts were exactly six feet apart, rail centers at twenty-four-inch intervals.

Beyond the yard, black angus cattle dotted the summer green, hillside meadows between groves of aspen and pine. And the snowy peaks of the Rockies rose up to the misty sky. Caleb blinked against the blinding sun, refocusing closer in.

Half a dozen pickup trucks were backed up in formation in front of the equipment sheds. A freshly washed combine, cultivator and hay truck sat on the far side of the barn, and a few dozen chickens were pecking the ground around the tires. In one of the pens, a black horse whinnied and bucked, tossing its glossy mane as it ran the length of the enclosure before stopping short at the fence, nostrils flaring in annoyance.

Caleb didn't recognize the animal. No surprise there. Though there had been a time when he'd been able to name every one of the fifty plus horses at Terrell. He inhaled once more, this time catching the sharp scent of manure. His spine stiffened with a latent memory of his father's quick temper. Yeah, most things had stayed the same around here, and he didn't care to revisit any of them.

As soon as he straightened out the mess with the inheritance, he'd climb back into his rented Escalade, head for the Lyndon airport and take the Active Equipment jet back to his corporate headquarters in Chicago.

Sayonara Colorado.

He turned back to the door and knocked again.

This time, there was a sound on the other side. But it was a light, quick step crossing the living-room floor—so, not his brother, Reed.

The door swung full open, and Caleb came face-to-face with a beautiful, brunette woman. She was maybe five feet five, dressed in a cowl-necked, navy T-shirt with four buttons leaving an open V-neck. Her hair was long and glossy, her lips a dark coral pink, skin smooth, brows gently arched and her moss-green eyes clear and assessing.

She looked vaguely familiar. Or maybe that was just wishful thinking. Even in faded blue jeans and scuffed brown boots, she definitely looked like someone Caleb would like to know. His instantaneous attraction was quickly tempered by the thought that she might belong to his brother—a girlfriend, maybe even a wife.

His glance dipped reflexively to her left hand. No ring. But that didn't mean she wasn't Reed's.

"Are you selling…something?" she prompted, glancing from his silk tie to his briefcase. Her melodic, slightly husky voice sent a vibration through the center of Caleb's chest.

It took him a moment to respond. "I'm looking for Reed."

Her delicate brows sloped closer together with curiosity. "Is he expecting you?"

"I called a few days ago," Caleb offered evasively. He hadn't spoken to his brother, only left voice-mail messages, and he wasn't about to discuss his personal business with a stranger.

She crossed her arms over her chest and canted a slim, denim covered hip to one side. "Are you saying Reed invited you here?"

Caleb gave into curiosity. "Who are you?"

"Who are you?"

There it was again, that feeling that he'd met her somewhere before. "You live here?"

"None of your business."

"Where's Reed?"

She stilled for a split second, her soft, coral mouth pursing into a sexy moue. "Also, none of your business."

He struggled to be annoyed, but he found himself intrigued. "Are you going to tell me anything?"

She shook her head.

"Have we met before?" he asked.

"Is that a line?"

"It's a question."

"It's been my experience that most lines are delivered in the form of a question."

Caleb felt himself crack a reluctant smile, and her green eyes sparkled in return.

He watched her for a few moments, then conceded defeat, shifting his briefcase from his right hand before holding it out to her. "Caleb Terrell."

Her gorgeous eyes went wide and round. "Caleb?"

Before he could react, she squealed and threw herself into his arms. "You came home!"

His free arm automatically wrapped around her slender waist, returning the hug and holding her lithe body against his own. He inhaled the sweet scent of her hair and found himself desperately hoping she wasn't Reed's girlfriend.

She pulled back and gazed up into his eyes. "You don't remember me?"

He was forced to shake his head, admitting he did not.

She socked the front of his shoulder with the heel of her hand. "It's Mandy."

Caleb felt his jaw go lax. "Mandy Jacobs?"

She nodded, and he pulled her into another hug. Not that they'd been particularly close. She'd been thirteen to his seventeen when he'd left home. He was twenty-seven now. And it felt astonishingly good to hold her in his arms.

He let the hug go on a little too long, then reluctantly let her go.

"You missed the funeral." Her tone was half regretful, half accusing as she backed her way inside the house, gesturing for him to follow.

"I didn't come back for the funeral," he told her soberly as he took a step over the threshold. Reminded of his reason for being here, his mood swung back to determination.

"He was your father," she chided, turning to walk around the corner from the foyer and into the big living room.

Caleb followed, letting his silence speak for itself. Unless Mandy was hopelessly naive, she knew the history of the Terrell family. Wilton Terrell might have been Caleb's father, but he was also the meanest son of a bitch in northwestern Colorado.

Inside the startlingly familiar room, he glanced around, attempting to orient himself. Why was Mandy here, and where was Reed? "So, you and Reed are..."

She shook her head. "He's not here."

"I can see that." It was a big house, two stories, four bedrooms, but if Reed had been around, Mandy's squeal would have brought him running. Now, Caleb found himself impatient to qualify her role. "You live here?"

Her look went blank. "Huh?"

He enunciated his next words. "Do you live here?"

"Are you asking me if I'm sleeping with your brother?"

"I'm asking if you're in a relationship with him, yes." That was the most obvious answer for her presence.

"I'm not." Her left eye twitched. "Either of those things."

"Okay."

Good. Very good. Not that it mattered to Caleb. Nothing about Lyndon Valley or the Terrell ranch mattered to Caleb. This was a temporary glitch on the thoroughfare of his life. Mandy was irrelevant.

Her tone turned tart. "But how very polite of you to inquire about my sex life."

"You're here, and he's not," Caleb reasoned. She'd answered the front door, appeared very much at home. It wasn't such a stretch to think she lived here.

She traced a finger along the beveled edge of a polished cedar side table. "I came up here to check things out." Then a cloud of concern darkened her expression. "I got worried."

"Why were you worried?"

"Because nobody's seen Reed since the funeral five days ago."

Mandy Jacobs had been Reed's close friend for nearly ten years. Before that, she'd felt something close to hero worship for him in high school, ever since the day he'd rescued her when her bikini top flew off as she dove into the Stump Lake swimming hole. The boys in her own grade had howled with laughter, stopping her girlfriends from coming into the water to help her, waiting with wide-eyed anticipation for the numbing cold to force her from the lake.

Just as she was about to give in and cover her dignity as best she could manage, Reed had come along and read the younger boys the riot act. He'd stripped off his boots and waded up to his waist, handing her his own T-shirt. He'd never even peeked while, teeth chattering and toes tingling, she'd struggled her way into the shirt while under water. And then he'd threatened the younger boys with dire consequences if they dared to tease her about it in the future.

When she came home after two years in college in Denver, she and Reed had grown closer still. Over the years, she'd learned about his mother's death, his father's cruelty and the reasons behind his fraternal twin brother, Caleb, leaving the valley.

Reed had no siblings left at home, and Mandy's two brothers did nothing but tease her. Her oldest sister, Abigail, had been a bookworm, while her younger sister, Katrina, had gone away to boarding school when she was only ten. If Mandy could have chosen a brother, it would have been Reed.

This morning, genuinely worried and determined to track him down, she'd let herself into the familiar house, listened to his phone messages, hunted her way through his letter mail, even checked his closet before realizing she wouldn't know if some of his clothes were missing or not. She did know his wallet was gone. His watch wasn't lying around and his favorite Stetson wasn't hanging on the peg in the front entry hall.

She had to believe he had left the ranch willingly. The man was built like a mountain. She couldn't imagine anyone forcing him to do anything he didn't want to do.

Still, she was very glad Caleb had shown up when he did. Something definitely wasn't right, and she could use his help to figure out what had happened.

Caleb clunked his briefcase down on the hardwood floor, interrupting her musings as he straightened beside the brown leather couch that sat in front of the picture window.

His gaze pierced hers. "Define *missing*?"

"Reed left the cemetery after the funeral," Mandy explained, casting her memory back again to the events of last week, hunting for little details she might have missed that would give her a clue to what happened. "He drove off in one of the ranch pickup trucks. I assumed he was coming back here."

She focused on the row of pictures along the fireplace mantel, zeroing in on a recent one of Reed at the Lyndon Rodeo. "We all came over to the house afterward for refreshments. I didn't see him, but I didn't think that was particularly odd. He'd just lost his father and, you know, he might have wanted to be alone."

From behind her, Caleb's voice was cool. "Are you trying to tell me Reed was mourning our father?"

She turned back to face him while she framed her answer. She couldn't help contrasting the two brothers. They were about as different as two men could get. They'd both been attractive teenagers who'd grown into very handsome men. But where Reed was rugged and rangy, Caleb was much more urbane and refined.

Reed was nearly six-four, deep-chested, bulky in his arms and legs, and about as strong as an ox. His hair was dark, his eyes darker. While Caleb was closer to six-one, broad shouldered, but with leaner muscles, a chiseled chin and bright blue, intelligent, observant eyes. His hair was a lighter brown, his voice bass instead of baritone.

"Mandy?" Caleb prompted, and there was something about the sound of her name on his lips that made her heart thud an extra beat. Where on earth had that come from?

"I doubt he was mourning your father," she acknowledged.

If anything, Reed and Wilton's relationship had deteriorated after Caleb left. Wilton wasn't capable of anything but criticism, no matter how hard Reed worked. And no matter how much Reed accomplished on the ranch, his father wasn't satisfied and told him so on a regular basis.

Intimidated by the man, Mandy had visited the Terrell house only when Wilton was away. Thankfully, he was away quite often. The very definition of a crotchety old man, he seemed to prefer the company of cattle to humans, and he spent many nights in line shacks on the range.

She'd done everything she could to support Reed. When she was sixteen and Reed was twenty, Wilton had ended a particularly hostile argument by whacking Reed's shoulder with a two-by-four. Mandy had impulsively offered to marry Reed so he could move to the neighboring Jacobs ranch.

But he'd had laughed at her and tousled her hair, telling her he loved her like a sister, not a wife, and he wouldn't turn his back on his father ever again. And by then, he was big enough to defend himself against Wilton.

"He should have left when I did," Caleb broke into her thoughts again, his voice brittle.

"*You* should have stayed," Mandy countered, giving him her unvarnished opinion. If Caleb had been around, it would have been two against one, and Wilton would not have gotten away with so much cruelty.

Caleb's eyes crackled like agates. "And rewarded him for

killing my mother, by breaking my back for him day after day?"

"Reed saw it differently." Mandy understood just how differently Reed had viewed the situation. And she admired him for it.

The Terrell Cattle Company had been the merging of both Wilton Terrell's family holdings and those of his young wife, Sasha's. After her death, through thick and thin, Reed had vowed to protect his mother's heritage. He had plans for the ranch, for his future, ways to honor his mother's memory.

Which made his disappearance, particularly now, even more confusing. Where *was* he?

"Reed was a fool," said Caleb.

Mandy found herself taking a step forward, squaring her shoulders, hands curling into fists by her sides, her anger rising in her friend's defense. "I love Reed."

"I thought you said—"

"Like a *brother*."

"Yeah?" Caleb scoffed, blue eyes glaring right back at her. "Why don't you tell me what that's like?"

His mocking tone was at odds with the trace of hurt that flashed through his eyes, and her anger immediately dissipated.

"Why did you come?" she found herself asking.

Did she dare hope Caleb had reconciliation on his mind? She'd be thrilled to see the two brothers bury the hatchet. She knew that, deep down, Reed missed his brother, and she had to believe Caleb missed Reed.

Suddenly, she remembered one of the letters she'd sorted this morning. Her heart lifted, and her chest hummed with excitement. That had to be the answer. "He *was* expecting you."

"What?"

She pivoted on her heel and headed for the kitchen, beelining to the pile of correspondence that hadn't yielded a single clue to Reed's whereabouts.

Caleb's footfalls sounded in the hallway behind her as she

entered the bright, butter-yellow kitchen, with its gleaming redwood cabinets and granite countertops.

"Here it is." She extracted a white envelope with Caleb's name scrawled across the front. It hadn't made sense to her at the time, but Reed must have known his brother would be here. Maybe this was the clue she needed.

She strode back across the big, bright kitchen and handed the envelope to Caleb. "Open it," she demanded impatiently.

Caleb frowned. "I didn't tell him I was coming." The messages had been a cryptic "call me, we need to talk." He hadn't doubted for a second Reed would understand.

"Then why did he leave you a letter? It was sitting on the island when I got here this morning." She pointed out the spot with her finger.

Caleb heaved a deep breath, hooking his thumb beneath the end of the flap and tearing open the flimsy paper.

He extracted a single, folded sheet and dropped the envelope onto the countertop next to the telephone. He unfolded the paper, staring at it for a brief moment.

Then he uttered a sharp, foul cussword.

Mandy startled, not at the word, but at the tone. Unable to control her curiosity, she looked around the paper, her head next to Caleb's shoulder and read Reed's large, bold handwriting. The message said: *Choke on it.*

She blinked and glanced up at Caleb. "I don't understand. What does it mean?"

"It means my brother's temper hasn't changed one bit in the past ten years."

"Do you know where he went?" The cryptic message didn't help Mandy, but maybe Caleb understood.

Caleb growled at the paper. "You stupid, stupid idiot."

"What?" Mandy demanded.

He crumpled the paper into a tight ball, emitting a cold laugh. "He doesn't trust me. He actually thinks I'd screw my own brother."

"Screw him how?" She'd been telling herself Reed was off

on his own somewhere, reconciling what had to be conflicting emotions about losing such a difficult father. But now Caleb had her worried.

He stared down at her, blue eyes rock-hard, jaw set in an implacable line. She could almost see the debate going on inside his head.

Finally, he made a decision and spoke. "Wilton Terrell, in his infinite wisdom, has left his entire estate, including the Terrell Cattle Company, to his son...Caleb."

Mandy braced herself on the edge of the island, her breath hitching inside her chest. "He left it to *you?*"

"He left it to me."

A thousand emotions burst through her. This was colossally unfair. It was ridiculously and maliciously, reprehensibly... Reed had given his blood, sweat and tears to this place, and now Caleb was simply going to ride in and take over?

Her voice was breathless with disgust. "How could you?"

"How could *I*—" He gave a snort of derision. "Wilton did it."

"But you're the one who benefited."

"I'm here to give it *back,* Mandy. But thank you for the faith in my character. Your low opinion of me is matched only by my idiot brother's."

"You're going to give it back?" She couldn't keep the skepticism from her tone. Caleb was simply going to walk away from a ranch worth tens of millions of dollars?

"I live in Chicago now. Why in the hell would I want to come back to a place I hated, that holds nothing but bitter memories? And he's my brother. We hate each other, but we don't *hate* each other."

Judging by his affronted expression and the passion in his tone, Caleb truly was going to do the honorable thing. But Reed must have been as skeptical as Mandy. The anger in the note was plain as day, and he'd obviously hightailed it out of there before he had to watch his brother come in and take over.

Fresh worry percolated to life inside her. "We have to find him. We have to explain and bring him home."

"He's not a lost puppy."

"He's your brother."

Caleb seemed singularly unmoved. "What exactly does that mean?"

His brother's house was the last place Caleb wanted to be. He didn't want to eat in this kitchen or sit in that living room, and he definitely had no desire to go upstairs and sleep in his old bedroom.

He'd had enough déjà vu already.

The kitchen might as well have been frozen in time. A spider plant sat in the middle of the island, serving utensils upside down in a white container next to the stove, a bulletin board above the phone, a fruit bowl under the light switch and the coffeemaker beneath the built-in microwave.

He knew the sugar would be on the third shelf of the pantry, the milk in the door of the stainless-steel refrigerator and the coffee beans on the second shelf in the pantry next to the dining room. He'd kill for a cup of coffee, but there was no way he was making himself at home.

Mandy, on the other hand, seemed to feel completely at home. She'd perched herself on one of the high, black-cushioned chairs at the center island, one booted foot propped on the cross piece, one swinging in a small arc as she dialed her phone.

"Are you here often?" He couldn't help asking. He didn't remember anyone ever looking relaxed in this house.

She raised her phone to her ear and gave a small, wry smile. "Only when your father was away. Reed and I used to drink cheap wine and play poker."

"Just the two of you?" Caleb arched a brow. He didn't yet have a handle on the relationship between his brother and Mandy.

She raked her loose hair back from her forehead. "I told you

I wasn't sleeping with him." She left a deliberate pause. "When I stayed over, I slept in your bed. Oh, hey, Seth," she said into the phone.

Absurdly rattled by her taunt, Caleb withdrew into the living room to clear his head. This trip was not going even remotely as he'd planned.

It was two hours to the Lyndon airport. He could drive there and fly back to Chicago tonight. Or he could get a hotel room in Lyndon. Or he could stay here and figure out what on earth to do next.

His gaze strayed to the staircase at the opposite end of the living room. His old bedroom was up there. Where, apparently, Mandy had been sleeping. Of course, she could have been lying about that, simply amusing herself by messing with his head.

Then again, even if she had slept in his bed, why should he care? He didn't. The woman could sleep wherever she wanted.

Her footfalls sounded on the kitchen tiles. Seconds later, she strode through the archway between the kitchen and the living room, tucking her phone into the front pocket of her jeans. "Seth's going to send a couple of hands."

"Send them where?"

She did a double take. "Here, of course."

"Why?"

"To help you out."

"I didn't ask for help." Caleb didn't mean to sound ungrateful, but he didn't need Mandy waltzing in and making decisions for him. He didn't know what happened next, but he knew he'd be the guy calling the shots.

She blinked. "I know. I did it as a favor."

"Next time, please ask permission."

"You want me to ask for permission to do a favor?"

"I want you to ask permission to meddle in my business."

"Meddling? You call lending you two highly qualified hands to take care of your ranch while we look for your brother *meddling?*"

Caleb took in the determined tilt of her chin, the squared

shoulders that said she was ready for a scrap and the animated flash in her jewel-bright eyes. He decided it wasn't the right time for a fight.

"Next time," he told her more softly, "please ask first."

"I wouldn't worry about there being a next time."

Fine. No problem. He'd dealt with everything else in his life without help.

He'd find his brother. He'd find him fast and get his life back to normal.

He couldn't help thinking about how his financial lawyer, Danielle Marin, was going to react to him being stuck in Colorado.

Active Equipment was at a critical point in setting up a new division in South America. Danielle was wading her way through Brazil's complicated banking and accounting regulations.

Mandy moved in closer. "What are you going to do now?"

"Find Reed." And drag him home.

"And in the meantime? The ranch? The animals?"

"I'll deal with it."

A mocking lilt came into Mandy's voice. "Sure would be nice if you had a little help."

"Sure would be nice if you minded your own business."

"I'm only doing my duty as a neighbor."

"Are you going for the good-neighbor merit badge?"

She perked up. "There's a badge?"

"Were you always this much of a smart-ass?"

"You don't remember what I was like?"

"You were four grades behind me. I barely noticed you."

"I thought you were hot."

Caleb went still.

"Schoolgirl fantasy," Mandy finished smoothly. "I didn't know your true character back then."

"You don't know my true character now," he retorted.

But her words triggered some kind of hormonal reaction deep inside him. *He* thought *she* was hot, right here, right now, right this very minute. And that was a complication this situation definitely didn't need.

"You married?" he asked her hopefully. "Engaged?"

She wiggled her bare left hand in front of his face.

"Seeing someone?" he pressed, praying for the yes that would make him honor bound to quit thinking of her naked in his arms.

"Why do you want to know?"

"I wondered who I should pity."

Despite the insult, their gazes locked. They flared, and then smoldered. He couldn't seem to tamp down his unspoken desire.

"No," she told him flatly.

"I didn't ask you anything." He didn't want to kiss her. He *wouldn't* want to kiss her.

She tipped her head to a challenging angle, her rich, dark hair flowing like a curtain. "I'm helping you find your brother. Don't get any ideas."

"I didn't ask for your help." What he really wanted was for her to go away and stay away so he could keep him emotions on an even keel.

"You're getting it, anyway, neighbor."

"There isn't actually a badge, you know."

"I want him back, too."

It wasn't that Caleb had an interest in ferrying Reed back to Lyndon Valley. He had an interest in the Terrell ranch no longer being his problem. And there was more than one way to accomplish that.

"I could sell the place," he pointed out.

She stiffened, drawing back in obvious astonishment. "You wouldn't."

"I could."

"I won't let you."

The threat was laughable. "How're you going to stop me?"

She lifted her chin. "I'll appeal to your honor and principles."

"Fresh out," he told her honestly, his desire for her starting a slow burn in his body. There was certainly no honor in lusting after his brother's neighbor.

She shook her head in denial, the tip of her tongue touching her bottom lip. "You're here, aren't you? You came all the way out here to give the ranch back to Reed. You can't undo all those good intentions because you've been slowed down by a day or so."

Caleb hesitated. The faster the better as far as he was concerned. "You think we can find him in a day or so?"

"Sure," she said with breezy conviction. "How hard can it be?"

Caleb wasn't touching that one.

But the flash in her eyes told him she'd heard the double-entendre as clearly as he did. She held up a warning finger. "I told you not to get any ideas."

"You have a vivid imagination."

"And you have a transparent expression. Don't ever play poker."

"Well, not with you."

"So, you admit I'm right?" Her expression held a hint of triumph.

"I can control myself if you can."

"There's nothing for me to control."

"You think I'm hot," he reminded her.

"When I was thirteen and underage."

"You're not underage now."

She pointed to him and then back to herself. "You and me, Caleb."

Sensual anticipation shot through his chest.

But she wasn't finished speaking. "Are going to find your brother, give him back his ranch and then go our respective ways."

Caleb squelched his ridiculous disappointment. What had he expected her to say?

# Two

Having escaped to the Terrell's front porch and perched herself on the railing, Mandy tried not to think about the sensual awareness that flared inside her every time Caleb spoke.

And when he'd hugged her.

Hoo boy. She fanned herself with her white Stetson, remembering the tingling sensation that flowed across her skin and the glow that had warmed the pit of her stomach as he'd pressed his body against hers. Though the brothers were twins, she'd never felt anything remotely like that in a hug from Reed.

She heard the sound she'd been waiting for and saw a Jacobs ranch pickup truck careen up the driveway. She stuffed the hat back on her head as the truck caught air on the last pothole before spraying gravel while it spun in the turnaround and rocked to a halt. Two Jacobs ranch hands exited the passenger side, giving her a wave as they headed for the barn, while her brother Travis emerged from the driver's, anchoring his worn hat on his head and striding toward her.

"And?" Travis demanded as he approached, brows going up.

Mandy jabbed her thumb toward the front doorway just as Caleb filled the frame.

At six-two, with long legs, all lanky muscle, Travis easily took the stairs two at a time.

"Came to see for myself," he told Caleb, looking him up and down before offering his hand.

Caleb stepped outside and shook it, while Mandy slid off the rail, her boot heels clunking down on the porch.

"Good to see you, Travis," Caleb offered in a steady voice.

"Figured Seth had to be lying," said Travis, shoulders square, gaze assessing. "But here you are. A little uptight and overgroomed, but at least you didn't go soft on us."

"You were expecting a pot belly and a double chin?"

"And a pasty-white complexion."

"Sorry to disappoint you."

Travis shrugged. "What brought you back?"

Caleb's gaze slid to Mandy.

Travis glanced between them. "What?"

Caleb hesitated, obviously debating whether or not to reveal the information about the will.

"Travis can keep a secret," Mandy offered, moving toward them. Her family would be in a better position to help Caleb if he'd be honest with them.

Travis tipped his chin to a challenging angle, confronting Caleb. "What did you do?"

"Nothing," Caleb stated levelly. "I'm solving a problem, not creating one. But I remember gossip spreading like wildfire around here."

"Welcome home," Mandy put in, struggling to keep the sarcasm from her voice.

Caleb frowned at her. There was nothing salacious in his expression, no inappropriate message in his eyes. Still, the mere fact that he was looking at her sent a flush across her skin.

"Come back to dance on your daddy's grave?" Travis asked Caleb.

"You want a beer?" Caleb offered. Surprisingly, there was no annoyance in his tone at Travis's crass remark.

Mandy took the opportunity to escape from Caleb's proximity again, passing through the doorway and calling over her shoulder. "I'll get them."

She headed straight down the hall to the kitchen at the back of the house, shaking off the buzz of arousal. There was no denying the chemical attraction between her and Caleb, but that didn't mean she had to give in to it. Sure, he was a great-looking guy. He had an undeniably sexy voice, and he could pull of a Saville Row suit.

She had no doubt he'd look equally good in blue jeans and a Western-cut shirt. When they'd hugged, she'd felt his chest, stomach, thighs and arms, so she knew he was rock-solid with muscle. Whatever he'd been doing in Chicago for the past ten years, it wasn't sitting behind a desk.

She checked the wayward track of her brain and extracted three bottles of beer from the refrigerator, heading back down the hall.

When she arrived on the porch, Caleb had obviously brought Travis up to speed on the will. The two men had made themselves comfortable in the painted, wood-slat chairs. Mandy handed out the beers, her fingertips grazing Caleb's as he accepted his. She refused to look in his eyes, but the touch sent an electrical current coursing the length of her arm.

She backed away and perched herself on the wide railing, one leg canted across the rail, the other dangling between the slats.

"Just when you think a guy can't get any nastier," said Travis, twisting off the cap of his beer bottle.

Caleb took a swig of his own beer. "Only Wilton could screw up our lives from the grave."

Mandy had to agree with that. It looked as if Caleb's father had deliberately driven a new wedge between his two sons. The only way to repair the damage was to tell Reed about Caleb's offer to return the ranch.

"How are we going to find him?" she asked.

"We won't," said Travis, "if he doesn't want to be found."

"Probably doesn't," said Caleb. "Which means he's finally come to his senses and left this place in his dust."

"He thinks you're stealing his ranch," Mandy corrected, her voice rising on the accusation.

"Then why didn't he call me and talk about it? I'm listed."

"He probably thought you'd gloat," she guessed.

"Your faith in me is inspiring."

She hadn't meant it as an insult. "I was speculating on what Reed might think. I wasn't saying what I personally thought." She took a swig of the cold, bitter brew. It wasn't her favorite beverage, but sometimes it was the only thing going, so she'd learned to adapt.

"You thought I was going to keep the ranch," Caleb reminded her.

"But I believed you when you said you wouldn't," she countered.

"You want points for that?"

"Or a merit badge." The joke was out before she could stop it.

Caleb gave a half smile. Then he seemed to contemplate her for a long, drawn out moment. "I should just sell the damn thing."

"Well, that would be quite the windfall, wouldn't it?"

"You think I'd keep the money?"

She stilled, taking in his affronted expression. Oops. She swallowed. "Well…"

Caleb shook his head in obvious disgust, his tone flat. "I'd give the money to Reed, Mandy."

"Reed wants the ranch, not the money," she pointed out, attempting to cover the blunder.

"Then why isn't he here fighting for it?"

"Excellent question," Travis jumped in. "If it was me, I'd fight you tooth and nail. Hell, I'd lie, cheat and steal to get my land back."

"So, where is he?" Caleb's question was directed at Mandy. "I'm going to find out," she vowed.

Two days later, Mandy was no closer to an answer. Caleb, on the other hand, was moving his alternative plan along at lighting speed, having decided it was most efficient for him to stay on the ranch for now. He had a real-estate broker on retainer, an appraiser marching around the Terrell ranch and a photographer compiling digital shots for the broker's website. He'd told her that if they didn't find Reed in the next few days, the ranch was going on the market.

Trying to keep her activities logical and rational, despite the ticking clock, Mandy had gone from checking Reed's web-browser history for hotel sites, to trying his cell phone one more time, to calling the hospitals within a three-hundred-mile radius, just in case.

At noon, tired, frustrated and hungry, she wandered into the Terrell kitchen. She found a chicken breast in the freezer, cheese in the refrigerator along with half a jar of salsa, and some tomatoes, peppers and onions in the crisper.

Assuming Caleb and the appraiser would be hungry when they finished their work, she put the chicken breast in the microwave and set it to defrost. She found a thick skillet, flour, shortening and a rolling pin, and started mixing up a batch of homemade tortilla shells.

When Caleb walked in half an hour later, she was chopping her way through a ripe tomato on the island's counter, the chicken frying on the stove.

She glanced up to see Caleb alone. "Where's the appraiser?" she asked.

"On his way back to Lyndon."

"He wasn't hungry?"

Caleb snagged a chunk of tomato and popped it into his mouth. "He didn't know there was anything on offer."

"You didn't offer to feed him?" It was more than two-and-a-half hours back to Lyndon.

"I didn't think it was worth the risk."

She gave him a perplexed look.

"I don't cook," he clarified.

"Don't be ridiculous." She turned her back on him to flip the last of the tortillas frying in the pan. "Everybody cooks."

"Not me."

She threw the vegetables in with the chicken. "How is that possible? You said you lived alone. Please, don't tell me you have servants."

"I don't have servants. Does anybody have servants in this day and age? I live in a high-rise apartment in downtown Chicago. I'm surrounded by excellent restaurants."

"You eat out every night?" She couldn't imagine it.

"I do a lot of business over dinner," he told her easily. "But most of the restaurants in the area also offer takeout."

"It's hard to believe you survive on takeout." She turned back, returning to chopping the tomato on the island. How could he be so fit eating pizza, burgers and chicken?

"There's takeout. And then there's takeout." He spread his arms and rested the heels of his hands against the lip of the granite countertop, cornerwise from where she worked. "Andre's, around the corner from my apartment, will send up filet mignon, baby potatoes in a sweet dill sauce and primavera lettuce salad with papaya dressing."

Suddenly, her soft-taco recipe seemed lame. She paused. "You must make a lot of money to afford meals like that."

He was silent for a long moment, and she quickly realized her observation had been rude. It was none of her business how much money he made.

"I do okay," he finally allowed.

"Tell me something about your job." She tried to graciously shift the subject.

She also realized she was curious. What had happened to the seventeen-year-old cowboy who landed in Chicago with nothing more than a high school education. It couldn't have been easy for him.

"The company's called Active Equipment." He reached out and snagged another chunk of tomato.

She threatened him with her chopping knife.

But he only laughed. "We sell heavy equipment to construction companies, exploration and resource companies, even ranchers."

"So, like a car dealership?"

"Not a dealership. It's a multinational corporation. We manufacture the equipment before we sell it." With lightning speed, he chose another piece of tomato from the juicy pile and popped it into his mouth, sucking the liquid from the tip of his finger.

"There's not going to be any left for the tacos," she warned.

"I'll risk it."

"So, what do you do at this corporation?"

Caleb swallowed. "I run it."

"What part of it?"

"All of it."

Her hand stilled. "You run an entire corporation?" He'd risen all the way to the top at age twenty-seven? That seemed impossible.

"Yes."

"I don't understand."

He coughed out a laugh. "I'm the president and chief executive officer."

"They gave you *that* many promotions?"

"Not exactly. They let me run things, because they have no choice. I own it."

She set down the knife. She couldn't believe it. "You *own* Active Equipment?"

He nodded.

"How?"

He shrugged. "Hard work, intelligence and a few big financial risks along the way."

"But—"

"You should stop being so surprised that I'm not a loser."

He paused, but she didn't know how to respond to that.

"Though it's true that I can't cook," he allowed with a crooked smile. "I guess I concentrated on the things I was good at and muddled my way through the rest."

"With filet mignon and baby potatoes. Poor you." She kept her tone flippant, but inside she acknowledged he was right. She should stop being so surprised at his accomplishments.

"It wasn't always that way," he told her, tone going more serious. "In the beginning, it was cheap food, a crappy basement suite and two jobs."

Then he straightened his spine, squaring his shoulders. "But I was never coming back here. I'd have starved to death before I'd have come back to Wilton with my tail between my legs."

She found her heart going out to the teenager he'd been back then. "Was it that bad? Were you in danger of starving?"

His posture relaxed again. "No real danger. I was young and healthy. Hard work was good for me. And not even the most demanding bosses could hold a candle to Wilton Terrell."

She retrieved the knife and scraped the tomato chunks from the wooden cutting board into a glass bowl. "So now, you're a self-made man."

"Impressed?"

Mandy wasn't sure how to answer that. Money wasn't everything. "Are you happy?"

"Delirious."

"You have friends? A social life? A girlfriend?" She turned away, crossing the short space to the stove, removing the tortilla shell, setting it on the stack and switching off the burner. She didn't want him to see her expression when he started talking about his girlfriend.

"No girlfriend," he said from behind.

"Why not?" she asked without turning.

"No time, I guess. Never met the right girl."

"You should." She turned back. "Make the time. Meet a nice girl."

His expression went thoughtful, and he regarded her with obvious curiosity. "What about you? Why no boyfriend?"

"Because I'm stuck in the wilds of Colorado ranch country. How am I going to meet a man?"

"Go to Denver. Buy yourself a pretty dress."

She couldn't help glancing down at her simple T-shirt and faded blue jeans with a twinge of self-consciousness. "You don't like my clothes?"

"They're fine for right now, but we're not dancing in a club."

"I've never danced in a real club." A barn, sure, and at the Weasel in Lyndon, but never in a real club.

"Seriously?"

She rolled her eyes at his tone of surprise. "Where would I dance in a club?"

He moved around the island, blue eyes alight with merriment. "If we were in Chicago, I'd dress you up and show you a good time."

"Pretty self-confident, aren't you?" But her pulse had jumped at the thought of dancing with Caleb.

He reached out, lifted one of her hands and twirled her in a spin, pulling her against his body to dance her in the two-step across the kitchen. She reflexively followed his smooth lead.

"Clearly, you've been practicing the Chicago nightlife," she noted.

"Picture mood lighting and a crowd," he whispered in her ear.

"And maybe a band?" she asked, the warmth of his body seeping into her skin, forcing her lungs to work harder to drag in the thickening air.

"You like country?" he asked. "Blues? Jazz? There are some phenomenal jazz clubs in Chicago."

"I'm a country girl," she responded brightly, desperate to mask her growing arousal.

"You'd like jazz," he said with conviction.

The timer pinged for the simmering chicken, and they both halted. Their gazes met, and their breaths mingled.

She could see exactly what he was thinking. "No," she whispered huskily, even though she was definitely feeling it, too. They were not going to let this attraction go over the edge to a kiss.

"Yes," he responded, his fingertips flexing against the small of her back. "But not right now."

Caleb had known it was only a matter of time before Maureen Jacobs, Mandy's mother, extended him some Lyndon Valley hospitality. He wasn't really in a mood for socializing, but he couldn't insult her by saying no to her dinner invitation. So, he'd shut the ranch office computer down early, sighing his disappointment that the listing hadn't come up on the broker's web site yet. Then he drove the rental car over the gravel roads to the Jacobs ranch.

There, he returned friendly hugs, feeling surprisingly at home as he settled in, watching Mandy's efficient movements from the far reaches of the living room in the Jacobs family home. The Jacobses always had the biggest house, the biggest spread and the biggest family in the valley. Caleb couldn't count the number of times he had been here for dinner as a child and a teenager. He, Reed and Travis had all been good friends growing up.

He'd never watched Mandy like this. She had always blended in with her two sisters, little kids in pigtails and scuffed jeans, and was beneath his notice. Now, she was all he could focus on as she flitted from the big, open-concept kitchen to the dining area, chatting with her mother and sister, refilling glasses of iced tea, checking on dishes in the oven and on the stove, while making sure the finishing touches were perfect on the big, rectangular table.

Caleb couldn't imagine the logistics of dinner for seven people every single night. Tonight, one of Mandy's two sisters was here, along with her two brothers, Travis and Seth, who was the oldest. And her parents, Hugo and Maureen, who looked quite a bit older than Caleb had expected, particularly Hugo, who seemed pale and slightly unsteady on his feet.

"I see the way you're looking at my sister," Travis said in an undertone as he took the armchair opposite Caleb in the corner of the living room.

"I was thinking she suits it here," Caleb responded, only half lying. He was thinking a whole lot of other things that were better left unsaid.

"She does," Travis agreed, "but that wasn't what I meant."

"She's a very beautiful woman," Caleb acknowledged. He wasn't going to lie, but he certainly wasn't going to admit the extent of his attraction to Mandy, either.

"Yes, she is." Travis set his glass of iced tea on the small table between them and relaxed back into the overstuffed chair.

Caleb tracked Mandy's progress from the stovetop to the counter, where her mother was busy with a salad, watching as the two of them laughed at something Mandy said. He didn't want to reinforce Travis's suspicions, but his curiosity got the better of him "Did she and Reed ever…?"

Travis shook his head. "It was pretty hard to get close to your brother. He was one bottled up, angry man after you lit out without him."

Caleb felt himself bristle at the implication. He hadn't deserted Reed. He'd begged his brother to come with him. "It wasn't my leaving that did the bottling."

"Didn't help," said Travis.

Caleb hit the man with a warning glare.

"I'm saying he lost his mother, then he lost you, and he was left to cope with your father's temper and crazy expectations all on his own."

Caleb cleared his dry throat with a sip of his own iced tea. "He should have come with me. Left Wilton here to rot."

"You understand why he didn't, don't you?"

"No." Caleb would never understand why Reed had refused to leave.

"Because of your mother."

"I know what he said." But it had never made sense to Caleb.

Their mother was gone. And the legacy of the ranch land didn't mean squat to Caleb. There was nothing but bad memories here for them both. Their father had worked their mother to death on that land.

The sound of female laughter wafted from the kitchen again. Caleb couldn't help but contrast the loud, chaotic scene in this big, family house to his own penthouse apartment with its ultramodern furniture, crisp, cool angles of glass and metal, its silence and order. Everything was always in its place, or at least everything was sitting exactly where he'd last left it.

Maureen passed her husband, Hugo, giving him a quick stroke across the back of the neck. He responded with a secretive smile and a quick squeeze of her hand.

Here was another thing that wasn't in Caleb's frame of reference, relaxed and loving parents. He couldn't remember his mother ever voluntarily touching his father. And his father had certainly never looked at his wife, Sasha, with affection.

Travis shifted his position in the armchair. "Reed thought you were afraid to stay and fight."

Caleb straightened. "Afraid?"

Travis shrugged, indicating he was only the messenger.

"I hated my old man," Caleb clarified. "But I was never afraid of him."

That was a lie, of course. As a child, Caleb had been terrified of his father. Wilton was exacting and demanding, and quick with a strap or the back of his hand. But by the time Caleb was seventeen, he had a good two inches on his father, and he'd have fought back if Wilton had tried anything. Reed was even bigger than Caleb, and Wilton was no physical threat to Reed by then.

"Where do you think Reed went?" Travis asked.

"I couldn't begin to guess," Caleb responded, thinking Reed's decisions were finally his own. He honestly hoped his brother was happy away from here.

He'd thought a lot about it over the past two days. Reed was perfectly entitled to live his life any way he saw fit. As was Caleb, and Caleb had become more and more convinced that selling the ranch was the right thing to do.

Reed could do whatever he wanted with the money. And, in the short term, Caleb was in no position to hang around Lyndon Valley and run things. And he sure couldn't continue to depend on the Jacobses to help him out.

He supposed he could hire a professional ranch manager. But, then what? It wasn't as if he was ever coming back again. And Reed had made his choice by leaving. If Reed had any interest in keeping the ranch, all it would have taken was for him to jot down a contact number in his cryptic note. Caleb would have called, and they could have worked this whole thing out.

Mandy swished across the room, a huge bowl of mashed potatoes in her oven-mitt-covered hands. She'd changed from her usual blue jeans to a pair of gray slacks and a sleeveless, moss-green sweater. It clung to her curves and brought out the color of her eyes. The slacks molded to her rear end, while her rich, chestnut-colored hair flowed like a curtain around her smooth, bare shoulders.

"I see the way you're looking at my sister," Travis repeated.

Caleb glanced guiltily away.

"You hurt her," Travis added, "and we're going to have a problem."

"I have nothing but respect for Mandy," Caleb lied. While he certainly had respect for Mandy, he was also developing a very powerful lust for her.

"This isn't Chicago," Travis warned.

"I'm aware that I'm not in Chicago." Chicago had never been remotely like this.

"We're ready," Maureen announced in a singsong voice.

Mandy sent Caleb a broad smile and motioned him over to the big table. Then she seemed to catch Travis's dark expression, and her eyes narrowed in obvious confusion.

"She's a beautiful, intelligent, strong-minded woman,"

Caleb said to Travis in an undertone. "You should worry about her hurting me."

Travis rose to his feet. "I don't care so much about you. And I'm not likely to take her out behind the barn and knock any sense into her."

Caleb stood to his full height. "Does she know you try to intimidate guys like this?"

The question sent a brief flash of concern across Travis's expression. Caleb tried to imagine Mandy's reaction to Travis's brotherly protectiveness.

It was all Caleb could do not to laugh. "Stalemate."

"I'll still take you out behind the barn."

"I'm not going to hurt Mandy," Caleb promised.

Not that he wouldn't let Mandy make up her own mind about him. She was a grown woman, and if she offered a kiss, he was taking a kiss. If she offered more, well, okay, he didn't imagine he'd be around long enough for that to happen. So there was no sense in borrowing trouble.

He deliberately took a chair across the table from Mandy instead of sitting next to her. Travis grunted his approval.

As dishes were passed around and plates filled up, the family's conversation became free-flowing and boisterous.

"If there's a competing interest lurking out there," Mandy's sister Abigail was saying, "I can't find it. But it's important that as many ranchers as possible show up at the first meeting."

"We need a united front," Hugo put in, helping himself to a slice of roast beef before passing the platter to Travis. "It's suspicious to me that they're calling the review five years early."

"The legislation allows for a water use review anytime after thirty years and before thirty-five," Abigail responded. "Technically, they're not early."

Seth, the eldest brother, stepped in as he reached for a homemade bun. "When was the last time the state government did anything at the *earliest* possible date? Dad's right, there's something they're not telling us."

"I've put in an access to information request," said Abigail. "Maybe that'll solve the mystery."

"That won't get you anything," Hugo grumbled. "The bureaucrats will just stonewall."

"You should catch Caleb up," Mandy suggested.

"This is important to you, too," said Travis, and Caleb waited for him to elaborate.

"Any decrease in the flexibility of our water licenses, will devalue the range land."

"Devalue the range land?" Seth interjected. "Who cares about the land value? It'll impact our grazing density. There are operations up and down the valley that are marginal as it is. The Stevensons, for example. They don't have river access anywhere on their land. A couple of tributaries, but they depend on their wells."

"Seth," Maureen put in, her voice stern. "Did anyone ask you to bring your soapbox to the dinner table?"

Seth's lips thinned for a moment. But then he glanced down at his plate. "Sorry, Mom."

Maureen's face transformed into a friendly smile. "Now, Caleb. How long do you expect to be in Lyndon?"

Caleb swallowed a mouthful of potatoes smothered in the best gravy he'd ever eaten. "A few days. Maybe a week."

"We're sorry you missed the funeral, dear." Maureen's tone was even, but he detected a rebuke. One look at Mandy's expression told him he'd detected correctly.

"I was tied up with work," he said.

"Did you know Caleb owns his own company in Chicago?" Mandy asked.

Caleb appreciated the change in topic, and silently thanked Mandy. The Jacob family would learn soon enough that he was planning to sell the Terrell ranch. Just like everyone would soon learn about Wilton's will. But he was in no hurry to field the inevitable questions.

"Active Equipment," he told them. "Heavy machinery. We're

making inroads into Asia and Canada, and we hope to succeed in the South American market soon."

"That's lovely, dear," said Maureen, her quick gaze going from plate to plate, obviously checking to see if anyone was ready for seconds.

"Active Equipment?" asked Hugo, tone sharp and vaguely accusing. "*The* Active Equipment, loaders and backhoes?"

"Yes," Caleb confirmed.

"So, you can get me a discount?"

Maureen scowled at her husband. Travis laughed, and Mandy's eyes danced with amusement.

"Absolutely," Caleb answered, unable to look away from Mandy. Her green eyes sparkled like emeralds under the chandelier, and he didn't think he'd ever seen a more kissable set of lips. "Just let me know what you need."

"Seth and I will come up with a list," said Hugo.

"Happy to help out," said Caleb.

Mandy's lashes swept briefly down over her eyes, and the tip of her tongue moistened her lower lip. He didn't dare glance Travis's way.

# Three

Mandy couldn't help but stare at the tall, elegant, brunette woman standing on the porch of the Terrell ranch house. She wore a chic, textured, taupe jacket, with black piping along the neck, lapels and faux pockets. It had a matching, straight skirt, and the ensemble was layered over a black, lace camisole. Her black, leather pumps were high heeled, closed toed with an open weave along the outsides.

Her earrings were large—a woven, copper geometric pattern that dangled beneath short, stylishly cut hair. Her makeup was subtle, coral lips, soft thick lashes, sculpted brows and dusky shadow that set off her dark, hazel eyes. She held a black, rhinestone purse tucked under one arm, and a leather briefcase in the opposite hand.

How she'd made it to the porch dust-free was beyond Mandy.

"Can I help you with something?" Mandy belatedly asked.

"I'm looking for Caleb Terrell." The woman's voice was crisp and businesslike.

"I'm afraid he's not here at the moment."

The woman's lips compressed in obvious impatience.

"Was he expecting you?" Mandy asked, confused and curious in equal measure.

"*I* was expecting *him*. Two days ago in Chicago." The woman clearly had a close enough relationship with Caleb that she had expectations, and she was free to express frustration if he didn't meet them.

A girlfriend? A lover? He'd said he had none, but evidence to the contrary was standing right here in front of Mandy.

"Would you like to come in?" she offered, remembering her manners, telling herself Caleb's personal life was none of her business. "He should be back anytime."

Sure, he'd made a couple of flirtatious allusions in their conversations. But they were harmless. He hadn't even kissed her. She certainly hadn't taken any of it seriously.

The woman smiled, transforming her face, and she held out a slim, perfectly manicured hand. "Forgive me. I'm Danielle Marin."

Mandy hesitated only a brief second before holding out her own, blunt-nailed, tanned and slightly callused hand.

She couldn't help but wish she was wearing something other than a plain, blue cotton blouse and faded jeans. There was some eyelet detail on the collar, and at least she didn't have manure on her boots. Then again, she'd been sweating in the barn all morning, and her casual ponytail was certainly the worse for wear.

"Mandy Jacobs," she introduced herself. "I'm, uh. I've been helping out on the ranch."

"I'm sure Caleb appreciates that." Danielle waved a hand in the air as she stepped into the house. "I have to say, this whole situation borders on the ridiculous."

Mandy closed the door behind them. She couldn't disagree. "Once we find Reed, things will smooth out."

"Any progress on that?" Danielle asked, setting her purse on the side table in the entryway and parking her briefcase beneath. "Caleb told me you were spearheading the effort."

Mandy didn't know what to say to that. She didn't want to share details with a stranger, but she couldn't very well ask about Danielle's relationship with Caleb without being rude.

Danielle strolled her way into the great room, gazing at the high ceiling and the banks of windows overlooking the river. "I assume you've already checked his usual hotels."

Mandy followed. "Reed never traveled much. But I have checked hotels, hospitals and with the police as far away as Fort Collins."

"Car-rental agencies?"

"He took a ranch truck."

Danielle nodded. "Have you tried checking his credit-card activity?"

Mandy tried to figure out if Danielle was joking. Judging by her expression, she was serious.

"I wouldn't know how to do that," Mandy said slowly. Was she even allowed to do that? It sounded like it might be illegal.

"It's not a service we could provide, but I do have some contacts…" Danielle let the offer hang.

Mandy didn't know what to say. Was Danielle suggesting she could help Mandy break the law?

The front door opened, and a pair of boots sounded in the entryway. Mandy took a couple of steps back and crooked her head to confirm it was Caleb. Thank goodness.

He gazed quizzically at her expression as he strode down the short hall. Then, at the living-room entrance, he halted in his tracks. "Danielle?"

"Yes," Danielle answered shortly as she moved in on him.

"What on earth are you doing in Colorado?"

"What on earth are *you* still doing in Colorado?"

"I told you it was going to take a few days."

"That was a few days ago."

"*Two* days ago."

"Do you want this to work or not?"

Mandy scooted toward the kitchen, determined to get away from the private conversation. One thing was sure, if Caleb kept flirting with other women, his relationship with Danielle was definitely not going to work out.

"We have to be in Sao Paulo by the sixteenth," Danielle's voice carried to the kitchen. "We've made a commitment. There's no cancellation insurance on this kind of deal, Caleb."

"Have I done something to make you think I'm stupid?" Caleb asked.

Mandy wasn't proud of it, but her feet came to a halt the moment she was around the corner in the kitchen, intense curiosity keeping her tuned to what was happening in the living room.

"You mean, other than moving to Colorado?" Danielle asked.

"I haven't moved to Colorado."

There was a moment of silence, and Mandy found herself straining to hear.

"You have to come back, Caleb."

"I can't leave yet."

"You said you were going to sell."

"I am going to sell."

Mandy was forced to bite back a protest. For years, she'd fantasized about the two brothers reconciling, and they were so close right now. Whatever hard feelings were between them, she was confident they loved each other. And they were the only family each of them had.

"You can look at offers just as easily from Chicago," said Danielle.

"And who runs the ranch until then?"

"What about that Mandy woman?"

"She's doing me a favor just by being here." There was another pause. "Mandy?" Caleb called. "Where did you go?"

"Kitchen," she responded, quickly busying herself at the counter. "You two want coffee?"

"You don't need to make us coffee," Caleb called back.

"It's no problem."

She heard him approach.

Then his footfalls crossed the kitchen, his voice lowering as he arrived behind her. "You *don't* need to make us coffee."

She didn't turn around. "You and your girlfriend should sit down and—"

"My *girlfriend?*"

"Talk this out," Mandy finished. "But, can I say, I really hope you'll give it some time before you sell, Caleb, because I know Reed—"

Caleb wrapped a big hand around her upper arm and turned her to face him. "She's not my girlfriend."

"Oh." Then what was she doing here? Why were they making plans for a vacation in Brazil?

"She's my financial lawyer."

"Sure." Whatever. It didn't mean they weren't romantically involved.

He lowered his voice further. "And why did your mind immediately go to a romance?"

"Because she's gorgeous," Mandy offered, counting on her finger. "Because she's here. Because she just told you if you didn't come back to Chicago, things weren't going to work out between you."

Caleb's voice lowered to a hiss. "And what exactly do you think I've been doing with you?"

She was slow to answer, because she really wasn't sure what the heck he'd been doing with her. "A harmless flirtation. I assumed you didn't mean it the way—"

"I did."

"I'd love some coffee," came Danielle's sultry voice from the kitchen doorway.

"Coming up." Mandy quickly turned away from Caleb.

"She thinks you and I are dating," he said to Danielle in a clear voice.

Danielle's response was a melodic laugh. "Like I'd get you to sit still long enough for a date."

"See?" Caleb finished before backing off.

"I'm setting up a corporation for him in Brazil," Danielle

explained. "Do you by any chance have an internet connection? A scanner?"

"In the office," Caleb answered. "Up the stairs, first door on the right."

When Mandy turned around, two stoneware mugs of coffee in her hand, Danielle was gone.

Caleb was standing in front of the table in the breakfast nook. "I'm not dating her."

"Got that." Mandy took a determined step forward, ignoring the undercurrents from their rather intimate conversation. "Brazil?"

"It's a huge, emerging market."

She set the two mugs down on the table. "Are you, like a billionaire?"

"I've never stopped to do the math."

"But you might be." No wonder he could give up the ranch without a second thought. He wasn't quite the philanthropist he made himself out to be.

"The net worth of a corporation is irrelevant. All the money's tied up in the business. Even if you did want to know the value, you'd spend months wading your way through payables, receivables, inventory, assets and debts to find an answer. And by the time you found it, the answer would have changed."

"But you don't need the money from the ranch," was really Mandy's point.

Caleb drew a sigh. "I'm giving the money to Reed because he earned it." Caleb's hand tightened around the back of one of the chairs. "Boy, did he earn it."

"Then don't sell the ranch."

"I can't stay here and run it."

Mandy tried to stay detached, but her passion came through in the pleading note of her voice. "Reed doesn't want the money. He wants the ranch."

"Then, where is he?"

"He's sulking."

Caleb gave a cold laugh. "At least you've got that right. He's off somewhere, licking his wounds, mired in the certain and self-righteous anger that I'm about to cheat him out of his inheritance. Nice."

"Reed doesn't trust easily."

"You think?"

"And you've been gone a long time."

"When I left, I *begged* him to come with me."

"Well, he didn't. And you have a choice here. You can make things better or you can make them worse."

"No. Reed had a choice here." Caleb's voice was implacable. "He could have stayed."

"He'll be back."

Caleb shook his head. "I don't think so. And he'll be better off with the money, anyway. He can go wherever he wants, do whatever he wants. He'll be free of this place forever."

"If he wanted to be free," she offered reasonably, "he'd have left with you in the first place."

Caleb's eyes narrowed. "Why do you want him back here so badly?"

Mandy wasn't sure how to answer the question. What she wanted was for Caleb and Reed to reconcile. She wanted the ranch to stay in the Terrell family for Reed's children, for Sasha's grandchildren. Reed had sacrificed ten years to protect his heritage. Caleb had no business pulling it out from under him.

Caleb watched the last of the dozen pieces of paper disappear into the ranch house office fax machine. The machine emitted a series of beeps and buzzes that indicated the pages were successfully reaching the Lyndon real-estate office.

"You did it, didn't you?" Mandy's accusing voice came from the office doorway. It was full dark, and the ranch yard lights outside the window mingled with the glow of the desk lamp and the stream of illumination from the upstairs hallway. Danielle had retired to the guest room half an hour ago. Caleb thought Mandy had already left.

"The Terrell Cattle Company is officially for sale," he replied, swiping the pages from the cache tray and straightening them into a neat pile.

"You're making a mistake," said Mandy.

"It's my mistake to make."

She moved into the room. "Did you ever stop to wonder why he did it?"

"Reed or Wilton?"

"Your father."

Caleb nodded. "I did. For about thirty-six hours straight. I called Reed half a dozen times after I left my lawyer's office that day. I thought he might have some answers. But he didn't call back. And eventually his voice-mail box was full and I knew it was hopeless."

"Danielle's office?"

"Different lawyer."

"Oh."

Caleb set down the papers and turned to prop himself against the lip of the desk. "I guessed maybe Reed and the old man had a fight, and leaving me the ranch was Wilton's revenge."

"They had about a thousand fights."

Caleb gave a cold chuckle. "Wilton fought with me, too. A guy couldn't do anything right when it came to my old man. If you piled the manure to the right, he wanted it to the left. You used the plastic manure fork, you should have used the metal one. You started brushing from the front of the horse, you should have started from the back—" He stopped himself. Just talking about it made his stomach churn. How the hell Reed had put up with it for ten extra years was beyond Caleb. The guy deserved a medal.

"My theory," said Mandy, moving farther into the dimly lit room, "is that once you were gone, he forgot you were such a failure." An ironic smile took the sting out of her words.

"While Reed was still here to keep screwing up over and over again?"

"Got a better theory?"

"He found my corporation thanks to Google and decided I was worth a damn?" Even as he said the words, Caleb knew it was impossible. He'd spent the better part of his adult life warning himself not to look for his father's approval. There was nothing down that road but bitter disappointment.

Mandy perched herself on the inset, cushioned window seat. She was silhouetted now by the lights from the yard. "You have to know you are worth a damn."

"You're too kind."

"Reed's worth a damn, too."

"No argument from me."

She tucked her feet up onto the wide, bench seat, and he noticed she was wearing whimsical sky-blue-and-pale-pink, mottled socks. It surprised him. Made her seem softer somehow, more vulnerable.

"I don't understand why you're in such a rush to sell," she said.

"That's because you live in the Lyndon Valley and not in Chicago."

"Rash decisions are compulsory in Chicago?"

He moved across the room and took the opposite end of the bench, angling his body toward her and bracing his back against the wall, deciding there was no reason not to give her an explanation. "I've had two weeks to think about it."

"Reed had ten years."

"In many ways, so did I."

Mandy shifted her position, smoothing her loose hair back from her face. His gaze hungrily followed her motion.

"Did you ever wish you'd stayed?"

He hesitated at the unsettling question, not sure how to answer. Back then, he'd second-guessed himself for months, even years, over leaving Reed. But it all came down to Wilton. "He killed my mother," Caleb said softly. "I couldn't reward him for that."

"She died of pneumonia."

"Because it was left untreated. Because she was terrified of telling him she was sick. Because he would have berated and belittled her for her weakness. Terrells are not weak."

"I never thought you were."

"I'm not," he spat, before he realized it wasn't Mandy he was angry with.

She tossed back her hair. "Reed wasn't weak. Yet, he stayed."

"He squared it in his head somehow."

Reed claimed he wanted to protect his mother's heritage, since half the ranch had belonged to her family. Which, looking back, was obviously the reason Wilton had married her. The man was incapable of love.

"She was twenty years younger than him," Caleb remembered. "Did you know that?"

"I knew she was younger. I didn't know by how much. I remember thinking she was beautiful." Mandy's voice became introspective. "I remember wishing I could be that beautiful."

Caleb couldn't hold back his opinion. "You are that beautiful."

Mandy laughed. "No, I'm not." She held out her hands. "Calluses. I have calluses. Danielle has a perfect French manicure, and I have calluses." She peered at her small hands. "I think there might even be dirt under my fingernails."

"Danielle has never had to clean tack."

"No kidding."

"I mean, she lives a completely different life than you do."

Mandy's face twisted into a grimace. "She goes to parties and I shovel manure?"

"Her world is all about image. Yours is all about practicality."

"I'm just a sturdy, little workhorse, aren't I?"

"Are you wallowing in self-pity, Mandy Jacobs?"

She went silent, her glare speaking for her.

Caleb moved inches closer, fighting a grin of amusement. "Are you by any chance jealous of Danielle?"

Mandy tossed back her hair in defiance. "Jealous of a stunningly beautiful, elegant, intelligent, successful lawyer, who's flying off to Rio—"

"Sao Paulo," Caleb corrected, enjoying the flash of emotion that appeared deep within Mandy's green eyes.

"They're both in Brazil."

"It's a big country. One's a beach resort, the other's full of skyscrapers, banks and boardrooms." He fought the urge to reach out and touch her. "But I'd take you to Rio if that's where you wanted to go."

She cocked her head sideways. "You'd take me to Rio?"

"I would." He dared stroke an index finger across the back of her hand. "We'd dress up, and go dancing at a real club and have blender drinks on the beach. You could even get a manicure if you'd like."

"Are you flirting with me?"

He met her gaze full on. "Absolutely."

"You have women like Danielle in your life, and yet you're flirting with me?"

"I am."

"Why?"

Caleb debated for a moment before answering. But then he reminded himself he was in Colorado. People were forthright around here. And he owed Mandy no less than she was giving him.

"Because you're real," he told her. "You're not some plastic package, constructed to appeal to a man's anthropological triggers. When you laugh, it's because you're happy. When you argue, it's because you have a point to make. And when your eyes smolder, it's because you're attracted to me, not because you've spent days and weeks practicing the exact, right look to make a man think you're interested in him."

"I'm not interested in you."

"But you are." He smoothed a stray lock of her hair and tucked it behind one ear. "That's what's so amazing about you. Your body language doesn't lie."

"And if my body language slaps you across the face?"

"I hope it'll be because I've done something to deserve it." Because, then the slap would be worth it.

"You're impossible." But her voice had gone bedroom husky. Her pupils were dilated, and her dark pink lips were softened, slightly parted.

"It's not me you're fighting," he told her.

She didn't answer. Her breathing grew deeper while a pink flush stained her cheeks.

He moved the last couple of inches. Then he dared to bracket her face with his hands. Her skin was smooth, warm and soft against his palms. His pulse jumped, desire igniting a buzz deep in his belly.

He bent his head forward, his lips parting in anticipation of her taste. He hadn't even kissed her yet, and desire was turning his bloodstream into a tsunami.

She sucked in a quick breath, her jade-green eyes fluttering closed.

Caleb could tell stop signals from go signals, and this was definitely a go. Her head tilted sideways, as she leaned into his palm. He crossed the final inches, her sweet breath puffing against his face in the split second before his lips touched hers.

Desire exploded in his chest. He'd meant it to be a gentle kiss, but raw passion pushed him forward.

He'd known it would be good, guessed she would taste like ambrosia, but nothing had prepared him for the rush of raw lust that made his arms wrap around her and his entire body harden to steel.

He opened his mouth, deepening the kiss. She whimpered in surrender, giving him access, her small tongue parrying with his, while his broad palm stroked its way from her waist to her hip, to the curve at the side of her breast.

He shifted his body, pulling her into his lap, never breaking the kiss as her soft, pert behind settled against him. He raked the satin of her hair out of the way, his fingertips convulsing against her scalp. Her small hands clung to his shoulders, hanging on tight, while her rounded breasts pressed erotically against his chest.

He wanted to rip off her clothes, push her back on the seat, or down on the floor, and ravage her body until neither of them could see straight. He knew he couldn't do that, knew he was losing control, knew he had to drag them back to reality before their passion got completely out of control.

But then her hot hands slid the length of his chest, and he put sanity on hold. She freed the buttons of his cotton shirt, her palms searing into his bare skin.

His hand closed over her breast, feeling its weight through the fabric of her shirt and the lace of her bra. He kissed her harder, deeper, settling her more firmly on the heat of his need. Her kisses trailed to his chest, over his pecs, across one flat nipple, and he groaned in reaction.

"We can't," he whispered harshly, even as he buried his face in her fragrant hair and prayed she'd keep going.

She stilled, her breath cooling a damp spot on his bare skin.

They were both silent for a long moment, while Caleb tried unsuccessfully to bring his emotions under control.

"I'm sorry," she whispered, lips grazing his skin.

"Are you kidding me?" he breathed. He forced himself to draw back, tipping up her chin and gazing into her passion-clouded eyes. "I have never—"

The cell phone in her jeans pocket buzzed, startling them both.

"—ever," he continued, trying to hold her gaze, reluctant to let the moment go.

The cell phone buzzed again.

"Fortuitous?" she asked, seeming to regain her equilibrium.

"Not the word I would have used." He sighed.

She shifted off his lap, slipping her hand into her jeans pocket to retrieve the cell phone.

"Abigail," she announced while she pressed the talk button. "Hey, Abby."

Caleb couldn't believe she could sound so normal. He sure wasn't that capable of turning on a dime like that. Desire was still pulsing its way through his extremities. It was going to be long minutes before he would be able to do anything more than breathe.

"When?" Mandy asked into the phone, her voice going guttural.

Her gaze locked on to Caleb's, fear shooting through her irises. "I don't—"

She swayed on her feet, and he instantly leaped to his, holding her steady.

"Where?" she asked hoarsely, bracing herself by grasping his arm. "Yes. Of course." She nodded reflexively. "Yes."

She was silent for another moment, her hand squeezing his arm in a vice grip. "Right now," she told her sister. "I'll be there. Bye." Her tone was whispered as she lowered the phone.

"What?" Caleb prompted, his stomach clenching hard. Something had obviously gone terribly wrong.

"My dad," she managed, blinking back twin pools of gathering tears. "They think it was a stroke."

"Is he…" Caleb couldn't finish the sentence.

"The medical airlift is on its way."

"How bad?"

"Numbness, speech problems, confusion." She broke away from Caleb's hold. "I have to get home."

"I'll drive you."

"No, I can—"

"I'll *drive* you." There wasn't a chance in hell he was letting her speed down the dark, dirt ranch road all alone.

# Four

All the lights were blazing when Mandy and Caleb drove up to the ranch house. Caleb's rented SUV had barely come to a halt when she flung open her door, feet barely touching the dirt driveway as she sprinted across the porch. She rushed through the entry hall to the big living room.

There, she saw Seth first, his strong face pinched in concern where he sat on the sofa, holding her mother's hand. Her sister Abby was furiously hitting keys on the computer, while Travis paced in the middle of the room, obviously ready for action and obviously frustrated because there was nothing he could do to help.

"Mom." Mandy rushed forward, sliding down beside her mother and wrapping an arm around her slim shoulders. Her mother's face was pale, eyes red-rimmed and hollow looking.

"The helicopter left about five minutes ago," said Seth.

"They said there wasn't room for Mom." Travis sounded angry.

Mandy heard Caleb enter the house and cross the foyer behind her, but she didn't turn. She felt guilty for being attracted to him, guilty for kissing him, guilty as sin for getting lost in his embrace while her father fell ill and collapsed.

"I'm trying to find her a ticket out of Lyndon for the morning," Abigail put in.

"They're taking him straight to Denver," said Travis. "There's a specialist there, a whole team with the latest technology for early stroke intervention."

"That sounds good," Mandy said to her mother, rubbing Maureen's shoulder with her palm.

"Damn it. The connection is bogged down again," said Abigail.

Caleb stepped fully into the room. "My corporate jet's on the tarmac in Lyndon."

Everyone turned to stare at him.

Seth came to his feet. "How many of us can you take?"

"As many as need to go." He captured Mandy's gaze for a long second.

"I'll stay here," Travis put in, drawing everyone's attention. He glanced at his siblings. "I'm probably the least help there, but I'm the most help here."

Seth nodded his agreement with the suggestion.

Responding to Seth's concurrence, Caleb pulled out his cell phone. "I'll have the pilots meet us at the airport. Mandy, why don't you put together an overnight bag for your mother?"

Abby swiveled back to the computer. "I'm booking a hotel for us in Denver."

"See if there's an Emerald Chateau near the hospital," said Caleb as he pressed the buttons on his phone. "We have a corporate account. Call them and use my name." He put his cell phone to his ear and turned toward the foyer.

Mandy squeezed her mother's cool hand. "Did you hear that, Mom?"

Maureen gave a small nod of acknowledgment.

"Good." Mandy struggled to keep her voice even. Breaking down right now wouldn't help anyone, least of all her mother. "I'm going to pack you a few things. You just sit tight."

"He couldn't speak." Maureen's voice was paper dry, her hand squeezing Mandy's. "He tried, but his words were all muddled. Syllables sometimes, then nonsense."

Mandy swallowed the lump in her throat. "I think that's really common with a stroke. And it's sounds like they've got a great team in Denver. He'll get the best care." Her gaze met her brother Seth's and he motioned with his head for her to go pack.

She nodded in response, gently releasing her mother's hand. The sooner they got to Denver, the better.

As she headed for the staircase, she passed Caleb in the foyer, where he was talking on the phone to his pilot. "Two hours, tops," he said. "Right. We'll be there."

She stopped and turned back, reaching out to lay the flat of her hand on his chest, mouthing the words "Thank you."

He placed his hand over hers and gave one quick squeeze then pointed her toward the staircase.


Mandy had never been on a private plane. The flight to Denver was, thankfully, quick and smooth. The Active Equipment jet had room for eight passengers, and Caleb had arranged for a car to take them directly from the airport to the hospital. There, Mandy's mother was the only person allowed to see her father, and the nurse would let her into his room for only a few minutes.

The doctors were medicating him and monitoring him closely to watch for additional strokes. They told the family they needed to keep him calm. The initial prognosis was for a slow, potentially limited recovery. There was no way to tell how much of his speech and mobility he would regain. A doctor told them the first few days were critical.

Although Abby had booked regular rooms at the Denver Emerald Chateau, a word from Caleb to the front-desk clerk had Mandy, Abby and her mother in a luxurious, two-bedroom suite. Caleb and Seth had taken an identical suite at the opposite end of the twentieth-floor hallway.

It was nearly three in the morning before Mandy's mother finally got to bed. Thankfully, she fell asleep almost immediately, and Mandy joined Abby, Seth and Caleb in the suite's living room.

Abigail was handing Seth her cell phone. "Your brother wants to talk to you."

"Thanks, tons." Seth scowled as he accepted the phone.

The only vacant seat was on a small couch next to Caleb, and Mandy sat down. She felt his gaze on her profile, swore she could feel his energy through her pores, but she didn't turn.

"Must we do this *now?*" Seth was asking into the phone.

Mandy gave her sister a quizzical look.

"Seth was talking about dropping out of the Lyndon mayoralty race," Abby explained. "Travis disagrees."

Mandy disagreed, as well, strenuously. Her oldest brother had been planning this political move for over two years. "It'll be weeks before he even needs to campaign."

Abigail huffed as she crossed her arms over her chest. "That's what I told him. And that's what Travis's telling him."

Mandy shook her head. "Dad won't want him to drop out."

Their father had been totally supportive of Seth's decision to run for mayor. The ranching community was slowly being pushed out of the economic framework of the district as tourism operations and small businesses moved in and began to lobby for their own interests.

"Who's going to run the place?" Seth demanded into the phone. "You?"

He listened for a moment, then gave a cold laugh. "Don't make promises you can't keep."

Caleb leaned toward Mandy. "This is a terrible time for them to have this conversation. They have absolutely no perspective at all."

She knew he was right and nodded her agreement. They were all exhausted and their emotions were raw.

Caleb rose to his feet. He moved in front of Seth and motioned for him to hand over the phone. Seth scowled at him, but Caleb persisted. When Seth finally complied, Caleb put the phone to his ear.

"Travis? It's Caleb. You need to go to bed. So does Seth and so do your sisters."

There was a pause.

"In the morning. No. You listen. I don't care who started it. I'm the only one here who's not operating on grief and fear, and I'm telling you to shut it down."

Caleb paused again. "Yes. I will." His gaze slid to Mandy for a brief second. "Of course not."

Abigail rose from her chair to lean over and give Mandy a quick hug. "I'm beat," she whispered in Mandy's ear. "Mind if I use the bathroom first?"

"Go ahead." Mandy squeezed her sister tight, grateful to have her siblings close to her tonight.

"We're going to have to call Katrina in the morning." Abigail referred to their youngest sister who lived in New York City.

"It's almost morning there now," said Mandy.

"When we get up is soon enough. I'm sure it'll be early."

"Yeah," Mandy agreed on a sigh. It was going to be a long day tomorrow.

Abigail made her way to the second bedroom and its en suite bathroom.

Caleb put the cell phone on the coffee table.

Seth rose. "I'm ordering a single malt from room service," he told Caleb. "You want one?"

"Yeah," said Caleb. "I'm right behind you."

Mandy came to her feet to give her oldest brother a big hug.

"You okay?" he whispered gruffly in her ear, ruffling her hair.

"I'll let you know in the morning." Mandy dreaded having him leave the suite, having her sister fall asleep, leaving her alone with her thoughts and fears. She wasn't going to sleep. Her family had just turned on a dime. She had no idea what would come next.

Seth shut the door behind him, and Caleb turned to her. "You're not okay."

"I'm not okay," she agreed, her body turning into one big ache.

He stepped closer. "Anything I can do to help?"

"You already have." She drew a shuddering breath, trying to put the night's events in some sort of order. "You have a jet?"

"Active Equipment has a jet."

"But you own Active Equipment."

"True enough."

"Thank you for bringing us all here. I know my mom was terrified…" She swallowed, her throat going raw all over again. "I was so afraid he'd die before—"

Caleb drew her into his strong arms, cradling her against his body. "Of course you were. But he didn't. And you're here now. And there may very well be good news in the morning."

Mandy found herself lying her cheek against Caleb's chest, taking comfort in the steady thud of his heartbeat and the deep, soothing rumble of his voice.

He leaned in and kissed her gently on the temple, bringing all her earlier feelings rushing back. She felt off balance, out of sync, like she was floating in space without a lifeline.

"Caleb," she stuttered. "What we—"

"Shh. Not now. Nothing matters right now."

She closed her eyes. "Are you always this nice?"

"I'm hardly ever this nice." He paused. "You need to sleep now."

"I know." She wished she could lie down right there, right then and stay safe in Caleb's arms for the rest of the night. Deep down inside, she knew she was being foolish. She was emotional and vulnerable, and he seemed strong and safe. It was that simple.

These feelings would probably go away by morning, but right now, they were powerfully strong.

The next morning did bring positive news. Caleb was surprised, along with everyone else, by Hugo's rapid progress.

Hugo recognized all the family members. They were each allowed to visit him, and he was able to say Maureen's name, along with several other rudimentary words, enough to get his general meaning across. His meaning, Caleb noted, was that Seth should continue to plan his campaign for the mayoralty race, Abigail should stay in Denver with Maureen, while Mandy should go home and run the ranch with Travis.

Caleb had to admire the tough old man. Less than twenty-four hours after the stroke, Hugo was regaining movement in his right arm, and he also had some movement in his right foot and ankle. The doctors were very pleased with his progress and feeling optimistic about his eventual recovery, although they cautioned it would take weeks, possibly months.

Seth decided to stay in Denver for some political meetings, so Caleb and Mandy returned alone on the Active Equipment jet. Once in Lyndon, they exited down the airplane staircase and onto the tarmac outside a small maintenance building at the private area of the apron. It was late afternoon, and thick clouds were gathering as the sun made its descent and the air cooled down.

Caleb switched on his cell phone, and Mandy did the same. Hers immediately rang, and they picked up their pace to get away from the sound of the airplane engines.

She plugged one ear and called "hello" just as Caleb's phone rang. They made it around the end of the building, blocking the noise.

Caleb answered his phone with one hand, unlocking and swinging open the chain-link gate with the other. There were few cars in the parking area.

"It's Travis," came the voice at the other end.

"Just touched down in Lyndon," Caleb offered. "Did you talk to your mother?"

"Just got off with her," said Travis. "Dad's progress is still good. The doctors are amazed."

"Good to hear." With his free hand, Caleb hit the unlock button on his key fob and opened the passenger door first.

Mandy was focused on her own conversation as she absently accepted his offer and climbed inside.

"About Danielle," Travis continued.

"Were you able to reach her?" Caleb had tried Danielle's cell this morning and got her voice mail. Odds were good that she'd headed back to Chicago and was on an airplane. Still, he'd asked Travis to retry the call and check the ranch just in case. He'd rushed off so fast last night, he'd barely had time to explain. Danielle wasn't the most patient woman in the world.

"I drove up to your place," Travis confirmed.

"So, she's on her way back to Chicago?"

"Not exactly."

"She's not?" Caleb swung into the driver's seat and slid the key into the ignition.

"You know that hairpin turn where you come out at Joe Mountain?"

"What?"

"Where the rear wheels always break loose?"

Uh-oh. Caleb didn't like where this was going. "Is Danielle all right?"

"She's fine. Now."

"Give me the bad news."

Travis confirmed Caleb's fears. "She couldn't recover from the slide, missed the turn. Got stuck at the edge of the pond. She wasn't hurt, but evidently, there's no cell service at that particular spot."

Caleb groaned and thudded his head on the steering wheel. Mandy spared him a glance of confusion.

"How long was she stuck?" he asked Travis.

"A few hours. I have to give the girl points for moxie. She spotted the Eldridge barn and decided they might be able to help her."

"That barn's seventy years old. And it's half a mile from the road."

"Hard to judge, I guess. Miss Danielle may want to have

her distance vision checked. She climbed through the barbed-wire fence and started hiking."

Caleb groaned again.

"Didn't go well," Travis confirmed. "Apparently you owe her for a designer blazer that got torn. Oh, also the shoes that weren't made for hiking."

"Did she make it to the barn?"

"Barely. By the time she realized it was a derelict, a herd of cattle had cut her off from her car. I guess a bull made some threatening moves, and she ended up climbing into the loft. It's dusty up there and, apparently, there are quite a few spiders."

Caleb shouldn't laugh. He really shouldn't. "I'm in a lot of trouble, aren't I?"

"Hell, yeah. You and me both."

"Why you? I assume you rescued her."

"By the time I got there, she'd been trapped for a few hours."

"Do I by any chance need a new lawyer?"

"She was pretty desperate for a restroom."

Caleb rewhacked his head. Anything less than marble fixtures was considered slumming it for Danielle.

"I told her to go behind the barn," said Travis with an obviously suppressed chuckle.

"Are you laughing?"

"You also owe her for a pair of designer undies. There were nettles."

"Could you just shoot me?"

Mandy had finished her call, twisted her body in the passenger seat and was now staring unabashedly at Caleb.

Caleb met her curious gaze.

"We had to tow her car back with a tractor," said Travis. "Scooter says it needs parts. Hey, can you stop by the auto-parts store while you're in Lyndon?"

"Sure," Caleb agreed fatalistically.

"We'll text you a list."

Caleb braced himself. "She doing okay?"

"She's been in the upstairs bathroom for two hours. I don't

know what women do in there, but hopefully it'll improve her disposition."

"Hopefully," Caleb agreed, but he wasn't holding his breath. "Thanks, Travis."

"No need to thank me. That was the best entertainment I've had all month."

"Don't tell her that."

"Already did. See you, Caleb."

Caleb signed off, pocketing his phone.

"Were you talking to Abigail?" he asked Mandy.

She nodded. "The news on Dad just gets better and better. I'm *so* relieved."

"Good to hear," Caleb agreed.

"You were talking to Travis?" she asked him in return, raising her brows in a prompt.

"Danielle had some car trouble."

"She's still in Colorado?" Mandy was obviously surprised by the news. "I got the impression she was going to be on the first flight out."

"They're sending us a list of parts for the car." Caleb turned the ignition key and started the Escalade.

"Is she okay?"

"She's fine. Travis helped her out. But she's frustrated to be stuck in Lyndon."

His phone rang again, but he didn't recognize the number. He flipped it open. "Caleb Terrell."

"Mr. Terrell? It's Frank Cummings here, Mountain Real Estate. I have some good news for you."

"Hello, Frank."

"We have an interested buyer."

"This soon?" Caleb was surprised. It had been less than twenty-four hours since he'd listed the ranch.

"The gentleman has been watching for opportunities in the area, and he'll be in Lyndon tonight. I'm meeting him for dinner. I was wondering if we might touch base with you by phone in a couple of hours? If all goes well, we'll want to arrange a viewing."

"I'm in Lyndon."

"Right now?"

"Right now."

"Then you should join us for dinner." Frank sounded excited at the prospect.

"Sure." Why not? If it was a serious buyer, Caleb would like to look him in the eye and make his pitch. "I'm with someone," he told Frank, his glance going to Mandy.

"Up to you, but feel free to bring them along."

"Where and when?"

"Riverfront Grill at six."

"We'll be there." He ended the call.

Mandy arched a brown. "We'll be where?"

He pocketed his phone and pulled the shifter into Reverse. "Is there any chance I can trust you?"

Mandy buckled up. "To do what?"

"To behave yourself—"

She sputtered an unintelligible protest.

"Frank Cummings has a buyer," he finished.

She froze, jaw dropping. "For the ranch?"

He reversed the SUV out of the parking spot, tires slipping to a stop on the gravel scattered on top of the pavement. Then he shifted into Drive. "Only thing I'm selling."

"But… You… That's too fast!"

"I don't think there are any speed regulations."

"Who's the buyer? What does he want? Is he going to keep it as a working ranch?"

Caleb shot her a look of annoyance. "You can't ask him questions like that. It's none of our business."

She clenched her jaw.

"I mean it, Mandy. If you come to dinner, you have to behave yourself."

"You make me sound like a child."

"You're about as emotional as one."

"Can you blame me? Really, Caleb. Can you blame me for trying to protect your land and your family—"

"It's not yours to protect."

"—from someone so determined to make such a stupid mistake?"

"You're referring to me?"

"If the shoe fits."

He glanced sternly at her one more time. "You want to come to this dinner, or not? I'm serious, Mandy. I don't want to dump you off on the side of the road, but I'm not taking a lit stick of dynamite into a business meeting."

She seemed to have to think about it for a moment.

He waited.

"I won't ask him his plans for the ranch," she finally promised, folding her hands primly on her lap, staring straight ahead and looking for all the world like a mischievous young girl.

He squelched an urge to waggle his finger at her. "You are to say nothing but cheerful, positive things about Terrell Ranch and the Lyndon Valley."

She turned to him, tone dripping with sarcasm. "I *love* the Lyndon Valley."

"And if you could do that little pouty thing with your mouth, make the guy think he'll have a sexy, farmer's daughter living next door—"

Mandy socked Caleb soundly in the shoulder. "Watch your mouth."

"I'd rather watch yours."

"And you're worried about *my* behavior?"

He cracked a grin. "I'll be good if you will."

And then he found himself second-guessing the wisdom of that particular promise. Honestly, it might be worth letting her blow the sale if it meant they could flirt instead.

# Five

At a window table at the Riverfront Grill, Mandy plucked the cherry from the top of her hot-fudge sundae. She considered it consolation food, since Caleb's sales meeting was going so well. Frank Cummings had come prepared with everything from surveyors' drawings to photographs and climate charts. Nathan Brooks, a fifty-something man from Colorado Springs, was enthusiastic and obviously interested in the ranch.

She licked the whipped cream from the cherry and popped the fruit into her mouth, catching Caleb's gaze as she chewed contemplatively and swallowed.

"I'm sorry?" Caleb turned his attention back to Nathan. "Can you repeat the question?"

"The upkeep of the house?"

"Has been regular, thorough maintenance, from paint and fixtures to plumbing and electrical."

Mandy selected one of the dessert spoons. The waiter had provided four and set them in the middle of the table. She assumed it was to make her feel less self-conscious about being the only person at the table to order dessert. Not that she cared.

It was only a chocolate sundae. Caleb was about to sell his birthright.

She scooped up a mound of whipped cream.

"The house is on a separate well?" asked Nathan.

"A well for the house. One for the outbuildings, and a third for the staff quarters."

"Those cabins are all less than five years old," Frank put in. "They're a great draw for couples or families who are interested in working at the ranch."

"What about irrigation?" asked Nathan.

"Two-hundred acres are irrigated and seeded to hay," Caleb answered.

"Four-hundred," Mandy put in.

Everyone looked her way.

"They doubled it," she explained, seeing no reason to leave the man with a misconception.

"Thanks," said Caleb.

She waved her spoon in acknowledgment, then dug into the ice cream and warm fudge.

"There are water rights on the river." Frank produced a sheaf of papers. "Spelled out in the agreement with the state."

Mandy swallowed her smooth, cool mouthful. "You might want to tell him about the review."

Both Caleb's and Frank's eyes went wide. Nathan turned to look at her. "Review?"

"The water rights are up for review." She dug her spoon in again, going for a big glob of the thick, cooling fudge. "It's a provision under the regulations. The first stakeholders meeting is this weekend. Here. In Lyndon. You must have seen the notices."

"Well," Frank put in heartily. "I don't think it's so much a review of existing—"

Nathan's eyes narrowed across the table at Frank. "You knew about this?"

Mandy stopped midbite, taking in the men's expressions.

Nathan looked angry. Frank looked like a deer in the head-lights. While Caleb was glaring at her in obvious frustration.

Okay, can of worms, she'd own up to that. But surely they hadn't expected to keep the review a secret. The man deserved to know what he was getting into.

Nathan pushed back his chair and threw his napkin down on the table. "Thank you for your time, gentlemen. Ms. Jacobs."

Frank quickly hopped up. "It's not what you might think. If you'd like, I can email a link to the Colorado information site."

Nathan headed for the exit, with Frank hustling along behind.

Mandy finished the bite of fudge sauce.

"You did that on purpose," Caleb accused, as he waved a waiter over to the table.

"I did not." She brandished her spoon. "But I hope you're not going to sit there and defend a plan to keep Nathan Brooks in the dark about the water review."

"No one's officially served notice to the property owners."

"You *were* going to keep him in the dark," Mandy accused. She couldn't believe it. She never would have expected it of Caleb.

"And *you* were going to behave yourself at this meeting," he countered.

The waiter stopped beside their table.

"Glen Klavitt, on the rocks. A double," said Caleb.

"I can't believe you would intentionally keep a buyer in the dark."

"Hey, I'm not his nursemaid."

"But you know the water rights are under review."

"I also know it's a routine review. And we're talking about preliminary discussions to determine if there should even be an official review."

"You've been doing your homework." Despite her disap-pointment in his principles, Mandy had to admire that.

"Which is what Nathan Brooks ought to have done. And what he likely would have done, *after* he'd seen the ranch and maybe fallen in love with it. And at that point, he would have been far more interested in making a compromise and listening to reason."

Okay. Mandy had to admit, when you looked at it like that, Caleb wasn't completely amoral.

"You don't lead with your flaws, Mandy."

The waiter set Caleb's drink down on the table.

Caleb nodded his thanks. "Marketing 101."

"I never studied marketing," she told him, scooping up another bite of ice cream, feeling a little like celebrating now. The sale was dead. She had some more time to find Reed.

"Did you study manipulation?" Caleb asked.

"They didn't have it as an elective at Metro State."

"Too bad. You're a natural."

"Do you really think I did that on purpose?" She hadn't meant to scare Nathan off. Then again, her heart wasn't exactly on the side of selling, either.

"I think you were very effective."

She made a show of shaking her head. "You must have studied paranoia."

He took a swig of the scotch. "Are you trying to tell me, you had no idea telling him about the review might scare him off? None at all? It never occurred to you? Not for one second?"

Okay, so as the words were coming out of her mouth, particularly when she saw Caleb's expression, of course it had occurred to her. But it didn't seem prudent to admit that now. "I was simply providing information." She stuck to her original story.

"Serves me right," said Caleb, polishing off the drink. "I never should have brought you along."

Mandy battled a twinge of guilt, setting down her dessert spoon, deciding she'd had enough of the sweet concoction.

Frank returned to the table. "I'm afraid we lost him. Permanently." Then his affable expression hardened as he focused on Mandy. "And you. I trust you learned a valuable lesson—"

"Leave her out of it," Caleb immediately put in, tone dark.

"But—" Frank began. The he took in Caleb's expression and cut himself off.

"Win some, you lose some." Caleb tossed his credit card on the table. "Thank you for your time, Frank."

"I…" Frank snapped his mouth shut. "Right. I'll be in touch."

Caleb nodded a dismissal, and Frank deliberately straightened his suit jacket, tugged at the sleeves and headed for the exit.

"You didn't need to defend me," Mandy felt compelled to point out. Caleb standing up for her made her feel even guiltier than she had a few moments ago.

The waiter came by and smoothly accepted Caleb's credit card.

"It's none of his business what you do or do not say." Caleb swirled the ice cubes in his glass. "But it is my business. And it's my responsibility to make sure you're never in a position to do anything like that again."

The intensity of his expression made a shiver run through her. "That sounded like a threat."

He tapped his fingertips against the white tablecloth. "I don't threaten. It's a waste of time. I just deliver."

"In this instance—" she couldn't seem to stop herself from asking "—what exactly are you going to deliver?"

While she waited on his answer, he helped himself to one of the extra dessert spoons and took a scoop of the sundae. "You, Mandy Jacobs, are off the list."

Okay, that didn't sound too dire. "There's a list?"

He took his time savoring the mouthful of ice cream. "The list of people who are invited to my meetings with perspective buyers."

She took his lead and retrieved her own dessert spoon. "I thought I added value to the conversation. I was the one who knew about the four-hundred acres."

"I'll give you that," he allowed, scooping into a swirl of

whipped cream. "You were doing great, right up until you blew the entire deal."

"There's another way of looking at this, you know."

"And, how is that?"

"A second chance."

"Didn't you hear Frank? That buyer is gone for good."

She concentrated on mining a vein of the gooey fudge. "I didn't mean a second chance with the buyer. I meant, a chance to make the right decision."

"The right decision?"

"To change your mind about selling the ranch."

He rolled each of his shirtsleeves two folds up his forearms. "I can't wait to see how you try to sell this."

She licked her spoon, gathering her thoughts. "I don't think you can discount the possibility that this was fate."

"You telling Nathan Brooks he might not be able to water his cattle was fate?"

"Exactly."

"Please tell me that's not the end of your argument."

"First," she counted, "Nathan asks for a meeting with Frank. Second, you and I happen to be in Lyndon. Third, I happen to be free for dinner. And fourth, the subject of the water rights came up in conversation. Those are either four separate coincidences, or it's fate."

Caleb waggled his spoon. "Wow. You really had to reach for it, but that was a pretty good spin."

"Thank you." She took a bite.

"I'm not changing my mind."

"I'm only asking for a few more days, maybe a couple of weeks."

"I don't have a couple of weeks."

"Sure, you do. You've put this false sense of urgency on a situation that doesn't—"

"The Brazilian government is the one with the sense of urgency."

"I'll look after the ranch," she offered. "I can do it. You know I can. And then it'll be waiting when Reed—"

"Reed made his choice. And you have your own ranch to run."

"Travis's there to run—"

But Caleb was shaking his head. "Your family needs you, Mandy. And I'm not chasing after Reed like some preschool nanny. I've made my decision."

She set down her spoon, struggling to hold her temper, and struggling to stay calm. "Your decision is wrong."

He set aside his own spoon. "You might not like it, but it is the right thing to do. And there's nothing to be gained by prolonging it."

"Caleb—"

"No. I've listened. I've considered your perspective—"

"You're joking, right?"

The man hadn't considered anything. He was being closed-minded and reactionary. And he was going to destroy what was left of his family.

But Caleb's jaw went hard. "I've considered your perspective, Mandy. And I disagree. And that's that."

Now her temper was taking a firm hold. "And that's the end of the discussion?"

"That's the end of the discussion."

"I see." Mandy rose to her feet, and Caleb instantly followed suit.

She drew a sharp breath, looking him square in the eyes. "Then, thank you for dinner. I can find my own way back to the ranch."

"Is this your version of a temper tantrum?"

Mandy clamped her jaw tight.

"It's dark outside, Mandy. And it's starting to rain."

She didn't respond. She was an intelligent, capable, functioning adult. She didn't need a man to escort her home on a rainy night.

Before he could say anything else, she turned on her heel

and headed for the exit. At the very least, there were buses. She'd hop on a bus, and Travis or one of the hands could meet her at the end of the ranch road. They wouldn't mind.

"I'm getting us cottages at the Rose Inn," Caleb's deep voice came from behind her. "We'll drive back to the ranch tomorrow."

"Go away." He might be a sexy, intelligent, compelling man, but he was a stubborn jerk, and she didn't want anything more to do with him.

Mandy was still scowling when Caleb swung back into the driver's seat and handed her the key to cottage number six. He slammed the door shut behind him. The rain was now pounding down on the roof, and the wind was lashing the trees around them. Caleb's clothes and hair were soaked from the sprint to the small office building and back again.

"I'm in seven," he offered amicably. "We're down at the end of the river road." He pulled ahead, carefully maneuvering the SUV through the muddy ruts and around the deepest of the puddles.

"Thank you," she offered stiffly, eyes straight ahead.

"We should probably try to get away early in the morning," he continued, while the bright headlights bounced against the dripping, undulating aspen branches.

Mandy gripped the armrest and braced her feet against the floor.

"The restaurant opens at seven. That good for you?"

"I'll be ready," she said.

"Great." He supposed he'd have to be content with her agreeing to drive with him at all. Cordiality was probably still a fair way down the road.

The dark outline of a two-story cottage came into view. His headlights picked up the signs for numbers six and seven on the post out front. There were porches on both stories and a long staircase running between them.

"You're on top," he told Mandy as he brought the vehicle as close to the building as possible.

She reached for the car door handle.

"Hang on," he cautioned, opening his own door.

He quickly rounded the hood as she opened her door. His boots sank into the mud, and a river of water flowed over them.

"Hold still," he told her, putting a hand out to stop her progress. He reached into the vehicle to lift her from the seat.

"Back off," she warned him, holding up a finger.

"Don't be ridiculous." Undeterred, he slid an arm around the small of her back. "There's no sense in both of us ruining our shoes."

"I've waded through mud before."

"Bully for you." He wove his other arm beneath her jean-covered knees. "Hang on."

"This is ridiculous," she muttered, but her arms went around his neck, anchoring her to him.

He straightened and shoved the door shut with his knee. Then he ducked his head over hers and mounted the stairs.

"Key?" he asked, setting her down as they made it to the narrow shelter in front of the cottage door.

"Right here." With dripping hands, she inserted the key into the lock.

Caleb turned the door handle, yawing the door wide into the dark room. He felt for the light switch on the inside wall, finding it, flipping it, bringing two lamps to life on either side of the king-size bed.

The room was peak-ceilinged and airy, with a cream-colored love seat and two padded armchairs at the far end. The living room grouping bracketed a sliding-glass door that opened to a small balcony. The bed was covered in an English country floral quilt, with six plump pillows and a gauzy canopy. Candles and knickknacks lined the mantel above a false fireplace. And a small kitchenette next to the bathroom door completed the suite.

"They said the heater was tricky," Caleb explained to

Mandy, crouching down next to the propane unit, squinting at the faded writing on the knobs.

"I'm not cold," she told him.

He pressed the red button, turning the black knob to pilot. "If you do get cold, you can adjust it up like this." He turned to find her still standing next to the open door. "Will you come and look?"

"I'm sure it's not that complicated."

"You're behaving like a two-year-old."

"Because I won't roll over and play dead? I have to wonder what kind of people you employ, Caleb. Do you have a string of yes-men who follow you around all day, never questioning your infinite wisdom?"

"No," he answered simply, deciding he liked it better when she was giving him the silent treatment. "Do you want to know how to work the heater or not?"

"Not."

He shrugged and rose to his feet, dusting off his hands. "Suit yourself."

Refusing to cater to her temper any longer, he crossed the room, bid her good night and firmly closed the door behind him, trotting swiftly down the staircase to open his own cottage.

His suite was slightly larger than Mandy's, but with the same English country look, deep mattress, plump pillows and floral curtains. He adjusted his own heater, slipped off his wet leather boots and stripped his way out of his soaking clothes.

The cottage provided a health kit with a toothbrush, toothpaste, comb, shaving razor and cream, along with a few other necessities, including scented body wash, which he set aside in favor of the plain bar of soap.

Half an hour later, Caleb felt refreshed. He'd opened the minibar to find a light beer, chose a magazine from the selection on the coffee table and stretched out under the quilt in his boxers.

He entered the password into his phone and chose the email

icon. He scrolled through the messages, finding one from Danielle labeled *stranded*. With an anticipatory grin, he clicked it open, scanning his way through a series of complaints, threats and colorful swearwords.

He responded, telling her he'd be back to the ranch tomorrow morning with a box full of auto parts and a fat, bonus check. He didn't let on that Travis had told him the whole story. He might as well let Danielle keep some of her dignity.

He dealt with the most pressing issues on his phone, then switched to the sports magazine, finding an article on his favorite basketball team. He read it and then checked the NASCAR stats. A crack of thunder rumbled in the distance, and the wind picked up outside. Sudden waves of rain battered the windowpanes, while the lights flickered, putting the room in darkness for a split second.

A few power flickers later, Caleb felt himself dozing off, and he set the magazine aside.

The next thing he knew, he was jolted awake by a deafening crash. The room was in pitch darkness, and the storm howled on outside. He rocketed out of bed, rushing to the window, guessing at the direction of the sound.

A flash of lightning revealed the Escalade was intact. But a large tree had fallen across the dirt road, crushing the low fence in front of the cottage, its topmost branches resting against the front wall. Perfect. They were going to need a chain saw before they could go anywhere in the morning.

He let the curtain drop, and as he did, a loud, long crack reverberated through the building. Before he could react, a roar shattered the air and the building jolted, wood groaning and splintering in the night.

Caleb was out the door in a shot, taking the stairs three at a time, terrified that the tree had come through the roof and Mandy had been hurt. He flung open her door. It was either unlocked or he'd broken it down. He wasn't sure which. But his entire body shuddered in relief at the sight of her standing next to the sofa, peering out the glass doors, lightning illuminating the room like a strobe light.

"It was a tree," she told him, turning in her bra and panties. "Sheared the balcony railing right off."

He strode across the room. "Are you okay?"

She nodded. "I'm fine. Wow. That's some storm going on out there." Lightning strikes were coming one after the other, thunder following almost instantaneously.

"I don't think you're safe up here." He found himself putting a protective arm around her shoulders. His gaze went reflexively to her sky-blue bra and silky underwear. It was completely inappropriate to stare, but he couldn't help himself.

"I'm fine," she argued. "How many trees can possibly—"

Another tree cracked and crashed in the woods nearby.

She blinked at him. "This must be the storm of the century."

"Put your clothes on," he told her. There was no way he was leaving her up here.

She glanced down at her body, seeming to suddenly remember what she was wearing. She quickly folded her arms across her breasts.

"I'm not looking," he lied. "Now, let's get downstairs." He wanted a sturdy story between them and any falling debris.

Mandy crossed the room and struggled into her jeans, slipping her arms into her shirtsleeves.

Caleb tried mightily not to watch, but he couldn't stop himself from taking a few surreptitious glances.

"Should we call the office?" she asked.

"I think they've long since closed. And I'm pretty sure they know the property's getting wind damage. Nobody should go out in this."

"I guess staying here is the safest," she agreed, tucking her messy hair behind her ears as she bent to put on her boots.

She turned then, and she seemed to realize for the first time that he was nearly naked.

"I rushed up here," he defended. "I thought you might be hurt."

Her mouth tightened into a smirk. "You're a knight in shining…boxers?"

He crossed to the door and pulled it open. "You can't embarrass me."

She moved toward him. "Not modest?"

"Not at all. You can see me naked any old time you want."

"Pass," she tossed over her shoulder, striding out into the rain.

He shut the door tight, double-checking it before he followed her downstairs. Rain splattered against his hair, wind chilling his wet skin, while the lightning and thunder continued to crack through the black sky.

In his own suite, he lit a couple of the decorative candles, dried off with a towel and switched his wet boxers for his damp jeans. Going commando under his jeans wasn't the most comfortable feeling in the world, but his options were limited.

She stood in the middle of the room, hands on her hips. "I suppose you'll want the bed."

He flipped back the comforter and stretched out. The love seat would barely fit a ten-year-old. "You're welcome to share," he told her.

"I don't think that's a good idea."

"As opposed to one of us staying awake all night? It's a big bed, Mandy."

"Can I trust you?"

He rolled his eyes. "Trust me to do what? Not to attack you while you sleep?" He leaned over and pulled back the opposite edge of the covers. "Give me a break, Mandy."

The thunder rumbled as she took a single, hesitant step forward, looking decidedly uncertain. Not that he blamed her. Despite his bold words, it was going to be a challenge to keep his hands to himself.

"Can I trust *you*?" he countered, hoping to keep things light.

"Ha. I'm still mad at you."

"Doesn't mean I'm not hot," he goaded.

In response, she marched defiantly to the bed. "You're not that hot."

"I'm sorry to hear that."

She stuck her nose in the air, turned her back and plunked down on the edge of the bed, tugging off her boots and dropping them to the wooden floor. Her socks followed. Then her hand went to the snap of her jeans, and he heard the zipper pull down, and she shimmied out of them.

Okay, he was a gentleman, and he was proud of his self-control. But, good grief. Was the woman insane?

# Six

An insistent, intermittent buzzing dragged Mandy from the depths of a deep sleep. She was comfortable, toasty warm, and she sincerely hoped it wasn't time to get up yet.

As consciousness returned, she felt Caleb shift against her. She knew she should recoil in shock at having cuddled up to him while she slept. But his big body felt so good against her own, that she decided to pretend she was asleep for a few more seconds.

The buzzing stopped, and his deep, husky voice penetrated the darkness. "Yeah?"

He didn't pull away, either, and she let herself sink into the forbidden sensations. She'd kept her blouse on, while he was wearing his blue jeans, so there was no danger of intimate skin contact. Still, her belly was snuggled up to his hip, her breast against his arm and her calf against his.

"Anybody hurt?" His voice sounded stronger, and her brain engaged more thoroughly on his words. "Good. So, how bad is it?"

She heard the rustle as he swiped a hand across his fore-

head, into his hairline, and she could picture him blinking his
eyes open in the darkness.

"Tell her to call Orson Mallek. He can source the parts
worldwide." Caleb shifted, his arm grazing her nipple, and it
was all she could do not to gasp in reaction. "A week will crip-
ple us," he said. "Tell them forty-eight hours max."

Arousal invaded her system, hijacking reason. The urge to
wrap herself around Caleb and give in to her desires, to hell
with the consequences, was quickly gaining traction in her
brain.

"Colorado," he said into the phone.

She felt him shift, and knew he was squinting at her in the
dim light, probably wondering if she was awake or asleep. It
was getting to the point of unreasonable that she could have
slept through the conversation.

It was time to put up or shut up.

Grabbing a final scarp of sanity, she drew away, shifting
onto her back, putting some space between them.

"Call me when you know something. Thanks."

"Something wrong?" she asked sleepily, hoping against
hope he'd buy that she'd only just woken up.

"A breakdown in the chassis plant."

"Is it serious?"

"Depends on how long it takes to repair." He moved to his
side, propping on an elbow, facing her in the predawn glow.
"We can go a couple of days before we have to start cutting
back shifts. After a week, we're looking at temporary layoffs.
I hate to have to do that."

She found herself curious. "How many people work for your
company?"

"In that plant, a few hundred."

"Overall?"

"I don't know. Thousands, anyway."

"You have thousands of people working for you?" It defied
Mandy's imagination.

"Not directly." He chuckled.

"Nobody works for me."

"And you don't work for anyone else, either. It's a whole lot simpler that way."

"Technically, I work for my dad. Though," she allowed, "that's definitely going to change for a while."

"Who'll take over the ranch?" Caleb asked, laying his head back down on the pillow. "Is Seth the heir apparent?"

Mandy thought about it. "It's hard to say. Especially with his mayor campaign coming up. Travis's the most hands-on of us all, but he's more of a day to day, roll up his sleeves guy. Seth definitely takes the strategic view, but he's not out on the range very often these days. Abigail's the organized one. She knows pretty much everything about everything."

"And you?" Caleb asked. "What's your strength?"

"I don't know. Diplomacy, maybe."

He chuckled. "You have got to be kidding me."

"Hey," she protested. "People like me. I broker compromises all the time."

"Not for me, you didn't."

"Jury's still out on that one. I predict that someday you'll be thanking me for my role last night."

"I wouldn't hold your breath."

"My point is—" she fought the urge to engage further in a debate with him about selling the ranch "—we all have different strengths."

"What about your other sister, the little one?"

"Katrina?"

"I haven't seen her yet."

Mandy resettled herself, bending one knee, which brushed up against Caleb's thigh. She let it rest there, pretending she didn't realize she was touching him. "That's right. You left before it happened."

"What happened?" There was concern in his voice.

"Nothing bad," Mandy hastily put in. "Katrina attended a fine arts boarding school in New York City. She's still in New York. A principle dancer with Liberty Ballet Company."

"Seriously?"

"I'm serious. She loves it. Then again, she always did hate the ranch."

His tone turned contemplative. "So, Lyndon Valley produced more than one city dweller."

"You two would probably have a lot in common." Mandy kept her voice flip, careful not to betray her disquiet at the thought of Caleb and Katrina. She wasn't jealous of her baby sister. She'd never cared about being glamorous before, and she wasn't about to start now.

"What about you?" Caleb asked. "Do you like the ranch, living and working so closely with your family?"

"Absolutely." Mandy couldn't imagine any other life. She loved the quiet, the simplicity, the slower pace and the wide-open spaces.

"What about when you get married?"

"Nobody's asked me yet."

"You plan to raise your children on the ranch?"

"I do." She nodded with conviction. "Kids need fresh air, hard work, a sense of responsibility and purpose."

Caleb was silent for a long moment.

"What about you?" Mandy asked. "You plan to raise your children in a high-rise apartment?"

He stretched onto his back, lacing his fingers behind his head. "That's a very long way off."

"But you do plan to have children one day."

"I don't know." He sighed. "I didn't have much of a role model for a father."

"You're nothing like he was."

"I'm nothing like your father, either." He turned to look at her. "He's a fantastic family man. I'm better at business, focused, driven and narcissistic."

"You cared that you might have to lay people off just now," she pointed out. "That isn't narcissistic behavior. It is empathetic, compassionate behavior."

He turned toward her again, his thigh coming fully up

against hers, his midnight-blue gaze capturing hers in the gathering dawn. "You comfortable behind those rose-colored glasses?"

"You cared, Caleb."

"I'm not the devil incarnate. But that doesn't mean I should be raising children."

"What *do* you want to do? With your future?"

"I've been thinking in two- or three-month increments for an awful long time now."

"Okay," she allowed. "Where do you want to be in three months?"

His gaze softened on hers, and he reached out to smooth back a lock of her hair. "I can tell you where I want to be in five minutes."

Her chest hitched, and her lungs tightened around an indrawn breath. His finger traced down the curve of her cheek, along her neck, to trace the vee of her blouse. Her pulse jumped and prickly heat formed on her skin.

"You took off your jeans," he told her in a husky voice. "Why did you take off your jeans?"

"They're uncomfortable to sleep in."

"I thought it was to make me crazy."

She shook her head. "You kept your pants on, I figured we were safe enough."

His mouth curved in a small smile. "Since you cuddle in your sleep?"

"I never knew I did that." She felt as though she could fall forever into the depths of his sexy eyes. "I've never slept with a man before."

"No way."

"I was in a girls dorm in college."

His hand dropped away, and his expression turned guarded. "You're not…"

"A virgin?" She couldn't help but laugh at the guilt on his face. "Didn't I just tell you I went to college?"

"You scare me, Mandy."

She sobered, unfamiliar feelings bubbling to life inside her. She might not be a virgin, but her experience was with swaggering eighteen- and nineteen-year-olds. They were about as different from Caleb as a person could get.

"You scare me, too," she told him on a whisper.

"Scaring you is the last thing I want to do."

She nodded, and he slowly leaned in to kiss her.

His lips were firm but soft, confident as they slanted across hers. They parted, hot and delicious. And he pressed her back into the pillow, one arm snaking around the small of her back, pulling her up against him.

A surge of desire swelled inside her. Her back instinctively arched, and she parted her own lips, opening to his tongue, savoring the intense flavor of his passion. Her arms went around his neck, anchoring her, while her breasts rubbed against his chest. Her nipples went hard, tight, intensely sensitive.

He groaned, sliding his hand down her hip, over her silky panties, down her bare thigh. His kisses wandered along the crook of her neck, circling her ear, separating her blouse to kiss his way to the tip of her shoulder.

She pressed her lips against his neck, drawing his skin into the heat of her mouth, tasting salt and dried rainwater. His hand convulsed on her bottom, voice going hoarse. "You're killing me, Mandy."

"Is that good?" It felt good from her side. Very, very good.

He kissed her shoulder, kissed her neck, kissed her mouth, dragging her pelvis tight against his. "You need to tell me yes or no."

She opened her mouth to say yes.

But he pulled back, and his sober expression stopped her.

"I..." She suddenly hesitated. This wasn't college. This was far more complicated than college.

"We step over this cliff," he warned her in an undertone, "we can't come back again."

She struggled to interpret his words. "Are you saying no?" she asked in a small voice.

When he didn't answer, her stomach clenched tight. Was she being swept along on this tidal wave alone? How humiliating. She stiffened.

When he finally answered, his voice was controlled and compassionate. "I'm saying you're not the kind of woman I usually date. You need to think about this."

She pulled back farther, feeling as if she'd been doused in cold water. She hardened her tone. "Excellent suggestion."

Without giving him a chance to say anything more, she flounced out of the bed and snagged her jeans from the floor. "In fact, now that you mention it, breakfast is probably a much better idea."

She strode her way toward the bathroom, hoping against hope the light was too dim for him to get a good view of her scantily clad rear end.

Feet apart, wearing the brand-new pair of steel-toed boots he'd purchased at the Lyndon shopping mall, Caleb chainsawed his way through the third fallen tree on Bainbridge Avenue. The physical work felt good, and tearing trees apart gave him an outlet for his sexual frustration.

Lyndon was a mess this morning. Mandy hadn't been far off when she'd guessed last night was the storm of the century. The wind, rain—and even hail in some places—had taken down trees, damaged buildings and sent several people to the hospital. Fortunately, no one had serious injuries.

Mandy was on the clearing crew a few hundred yards down the road. Hands protected by leather gloves, with about a dozen other people, she was hauling branches and sections of tree trunk to waiting pickup trucks. Though Caleb's gaze strayed to her over and over again, he told himself that this morning had been for the best. If she wasn't ready, she wasn't ready. And he wasn't going to push her into something she'd regret.

In other parts of town, Caleb knew many other crews were working, while construction experts, carpenters and engineers assessed the damage to buildings and other town infrastructure.

His phone buzzed in his breast pocket, and he shut down the chain saw, setting it on the ground by his feet. He stripped off his leather gloves, releasing the pocket button and fumbling his way into the deep pocket to address the persistent buzzing.

"Terrell here," he barked shortly.

"Caleb? It's Seth."

"Oh, hey, Seth." Caleb swiped back his sweaty hair. "Everything all right with your dad?"

"Better and better. They're going to start some physical and speech therapies in a few days."

"That's great news."

"Agreed. Listen, have you seen any of the storm coverage? It's all about how bad Lyndon got hit last night."

"We're in the thick of it," Caleb replied, glancing around once more at the destruction. "Mandy and I are still in town."

Seth's tone turned worried. "Is she okay?"

"She's a hundred percent. We're helping out with the cleanup."

"Good. That's a relief. Listen, the cleanup is what I wanted to talk to you about. As the president of Active Equipment, is there a possibility of you making a donation to the town? Maybe a couple of loaders."

"Absolutely," Caleb responded, wondering why he hadn't thought of it himself. "Let me see which dealers are closest, and how quickly they can respond."

"That would be terrific."

"Hey, no problem. They can use all the help they can get here."

"And…uh…Caleb?"

"Yeah?"

"Would you be comfortable with me making the public announcement? I don't want to steal your PR or anything."

Caleb got it. "But it wouldn't hurt your mayoralty campaign any to be the front man on this?"

"Exactly."

"Hey, go for it," said Caleb. "It was your idea. You deserve the credit."

"Thanks." Seth's tone was heartfelt.

"Happy to help out. Are you coming into town?"

"I'm going to try. But it may take a while. The airport's closed."

"Wow." Caleb was surprised to learn about the airport. "I'm working on Bainbridge. This thing must have hit the entire town."

"Get to a television when you can. They've got aerials."

"I'm on the business end of a chain saw for the moment. And I think power's out all over the place."

"Mandy's okay?" Seth confirmed.

"She's a trouper," said Caleb, his gaze going to where she struggled with a section of tree trunk that had to be thirty-six inches across. To his astonishment, she smiled while she worked, obviously making a joke to the man beside her.

"That, she is," Seth agreed. "I'll be there as soon as I can."

"Roger, that." Caleb signed off.

After making a few calls to Active Equipment headquarters and giving them Seth's contact information, Caleb resettled his gloves and yanked on the pull cord for the chain saw. The action restarted the engine, and he braced his foot on the big log in front of him, ripping his way through the next section of the downed cedar tree.

Working methodically, he made it to the end of the tree, sheering off branches and bucking the trunk into manageable sections. Then he glanced up to see Travis approaching, thirty feet away.

Caleb shut it down again, wiping his forehead. "Where'd you come from?"

Travis glanced around. "Whoa. This is unbelievable."

"Tell me about it. You should have heard them coming down last night. You here to help?"

"I am now." He tugged a pair of work gloves out of the back pocket of his jeans. "My original plan was to bring Danielle in to the airport."

Caleb glanced around but didn't see Danielle among the workers. "Airport's closed."

"We know that now. But she was getting pretty antsy this morning."

"Where is she?"

"I dropped her off at the coffee bar. She wasn't exactly dressed for brush clearing."

Caleb cracked a smile. "I think it would be dangerous to let her loose out here."

"She might break a nail?"

"She might get somebody killed."

Travis raked a hand through his short hair. "Yeah, she's definitely better with a computer than with power tools. She's making calls to see what her options are for getting back to Chicago."

"She can take my jet," Caleb offered, seeing an opportunity to make amends for some of the unfortunate complications of her trip to Colorado.

Caleb retrieved his phone and dialed Danielle's cell. He made the offer of the jet and asked her to touch base with Seth to make sure the heavy-equipment donation went quickly and smoothly. Then he signed off.

"That'll give her something productive to do," he told Travis.

Travis glanced around. "Where do you need me?"

"See the tall kid in the blue T-shirt?"

"At the black pickup?"

"He's keeping the chain saws fueled and sharp. Grab one, and you can start at the other end of that tree." Caleb pointed as he moved on. "If we can open up this next hundred yards, we'll have a corridor to the highway."

"Will do," said Travis. "By the way, it was nice of you to let Seth organize that equipment donation."

"His idea," said Caleb, flipping the switch and setting up to restart the chain saw. "Besides, Lyndon will be lucky to have him as mayor."

Mandy hopped up onto the tailgate of a pickup truck to take a break from the heavy hauling work. She was tired and sweating, and her shoulders were getting sore.

Somebody put a cup of coffee in her hand. She offered her thanks and took a grateful sip. She normally took cream and sugar, but she wasn't about to complain. It was nearly two in the afternoon, and she'd been hauling brush steadily since breakfast.

Her animosity toward Caleb had been forgotten when the sun came up and they saw what the storm had done. In fact, it seemed frivolous now to have even been thinking about love-making this morning.

"You eaten anything?" Danielle's voice startled Mandy, and she glanced up to see the perfectly pressed woman picking her way across the debris-strewn road to the pickup truck.

"What are you doing here?" Mandy couldn't help exclaiming.

Danielle was wearing slacks today, but they looked like expensive, dove-gray linen, and they were topped with a jewel-encrusted mauve sweater and paired with pewter-colored calfskin boots. Her makeup was perfect, and not a single hair was out of place.

"Travis brought me into town."

"Travis's here?" Mandy glanced around, but didn't catch a glimpse of her brother.

"I was hoping to catch a flight to Chicago. But the airport's closed."

As Danielle arrived at the truck, Mandy looked for a blanket or a stray piece of clothing to throw on the tailgate to protect the woman's expensive slacks. She spotted a quilted shirt, grabbed it and shook it out, laying it inside up on the tailgate and motioning to it.

"Thank you," said Danielle, awkwardly hopping up and settling herself. She snapped open her designer handbag and extracted a deli sandwich, handing it to Mandy.

"You're a saint." Mandy sighed, accepting the offer.

"You're amazing," Danielle returned. "How on earth can you work this hard?"

"Practice." Mandy took a big bite of the thick sandwich.

"Well." Danielle smoothed her slacks, setting her handbag down in her lap. She gave a delicate, self-deprecating laugh. "I've been dialing my fingers to the bone."

Mandy smiled at the joke. "Nobody expects you to do manual labor. Anymore than they'd expect me to compose a legal brief."

"That's very kind of you to say."

"Don't even worry about it. Thanks for the sandwich."

They sat in silence for a moment, the sound of chain saws, truck engines and shouts surrounding them. Bainbridge Street was a hive of activity.

"I've been working with your brother Seth."

Mandy swallowed. "On what?"

"Caleb's having him coordinate a donation from Active Equipment to the town of Lyndon, loaders, backhoes, etc. He'll be on Channel Ten to make the announcement in a few minutes."

Mandy's tone went thoughtful. "Really?" Her gaze went to where Caleb was bucking up trees. "I assume it's a political stunt?"

"Move," said Danielle. "A political move. And a smart one. Everybody wins."

"I suppose they do." Though it seemed a little slick to Mandy, she couldn't say she saw any serious flaws.

"Speaking of everybody wins…" Danielle looked straight at Mandy. "I have an idea."

"For Seth's campaign?" Mandy hoped it didn't involve her. She was planning to stay firmly on the ranch and out of sight throughout the mayor race.

"For finding Reed."

Mandy swallowed, her attention perking up. "I'm listening."

"I don't know how long it normally takes to sell a thirty-million-dollar ranch. But, I'm assuming it's a while." She brushed some imaginary lint from the front of her slacks. "So, I've been thinking, and I've come to the conclusion that my best interests may be the same as your best interests."

Her gaze drifted to Caleb. "He's having a little too much fun out here. I need him back on the job, and the shortest route to that end would appear to be finding Reed."

"You think he's having fun?" Mandy couldn't help interjecting. "He hates it here. He can't wait to leave."

"So he says."

"He doesn't want to be in Colorado," Mandy insisted. And he sure didn't want to be in the Lyndon Valley, on his own ranch, surrounded by painful memories.

Danielle smiled patiently, and a wealth of wisdom seemed to simmer in her dark brown eyes. "I'm not going to take that chance." Then she became all business. "Here's what we're going to do. You're going to give me your cell phone, and I'm going to dial a number, and you're going to talk to a man named Enrico. Tell him everything you know about Reed's disappearance."

Mandy hesitated. She couldn't help remembering Danielle's suggestion that they track Reed's credit-card use. She wanted to find him, but this felt a little too off the beaten path for her. "Is Enrico a code name?"

Danielle's laughter tinkled. "His name is Enrico Rossi. He's a private investigator."

"Would I be breaking the law?"

"You? No?"

Mandy felt her eyes go wide, and her blood pressure slipped up a notch. "But Enrico will?"

Danielle cocked her head. "I haven't the first clue what Enrico might or might not do. But he will find Reed."

Mandy was tempted. Frightened, but tempted. "Will I go to jail for this?"

"None of his clients have so far."

Mandy tried to figure out if Danielle was joking. "You're scary, you know that?"

"I'm practical." Danielle waved a dismissive hand. "There's an off chance he'll hack a password or two, but he's not going to steal anything, and he's certainly not going to harm anyone. And, since you won't be paying him, there's absolutely no legal trail that leads back to you."

"I won't be paying him?" This was sounding stranger and stranger all the time.

"He owes me a favor."

Mandy felt her shoulder slump. "Good grief."

"It's nothing clandestine or mysterious. I was his defense attorney. Pro bono. When I was first out of law school."

"So, he's a criminal." A criminal who could find Reed and stop Caleb from making a colossal mistake that would reverberate for generations. Where was the moral balance on that?

"He had a misspent youth."

"What did he do?" Mandy was absolutely not getting caught up with thieves and murderers, not even to find Reed.

"He was a big bad street kid, who got into a fight with another big bad street kid, who it turned out, was trying to recruit Enrico's little brother into a gang. Enrico won. He was charged with assault. I got him off."

That didn't sound so bad. In fact, it sounded kind of noble. "What happened to his brother?"

"He just won a scholarship to UIC. He wants to go into law."

"So, Enrico's a good guy?"

"Enrico's a great guy. Eat your sandwich, and we'll make the call."

It turned out that Enrico didn't sound remotely like a tough, streetwise criminal. He was articulate and seemed intelligent, and he said he was confident he would find Reed. When

Mandy saw Caleb and Travis approaching the pickup truck, she quickly finished the call and disconnected.

"Thanks," she whispered to Danielle as the two men approached.

"You look unexpectedly cheerful," Travis said to Danielle. While Caleb focused on Mandy. "You holding up okay?"

"I'm feeling optimistic," Danielle responded, sending a brief glance to Mandy.

"I'm just fine," Mandy answered Caleb. She drew a breath, both nervous and excited after her call with Enrico.

"Pretty hard work," Caleb observed.

"Piece of cake," Mandy responded with a shrug. She was tired, and she'd definitely be sore in the morning, but she still had a good few hours left in her.

Danielle retrieved two more sandwiches from her purse and passed them to the men. Both smiled and voiced their thanks, digging right in.

"Any news from the outside world?" Caleb asked Danielle between bites.

"Seth should have made the announcement on air by now. Equipment will be on a flatbed truck coming out of Northridge this afternoon. They're hoping to have the airport up and running by tomorrow. And I was able to book a couple of rooms at the Sunburst Hotel." She looked to Travis. "I guessed you might want to stay over?"

"You guessed right," he responded, glancing around at the destruction. "They'll need me another day at least."

"Mandy and I can keep our cottages at the Rose," Caleb put in. "Apparently, they're structurally sound. Though they can't guarantee we'll have electricity. But they did offer us a discount."

"I'll take the cottage at the Rose," Travis put in. "Mandy can stay at the Sunburst with Danielle. She'll be more comfortable there."

Caleb's jaw tightened, and his eyes narrowed in what was obvious annoyance at Travis's unilateral decree.

"Sure," Mandy quickly agreed. She didn't care where she slept. It wasn't as if she and Caleb had plans for a clandestine meeting.

She might have been swept off her feet in his bed this morning. But she'd had plenty of time to reframe her mind-set. Caleb had been right to suggest some sober second thought on the matter. Making love with him would have been a colossal mistake. One she had no intention of making.

# Seven

All the way back from Lyndon, Caleb told himself he had done the right thing by giving Mandy the option to change her mind. It was the honorable thing to do, and he didn't regret it for one minute. Though he'd desired her beyond reason, he couldn't ignore the fact that she wasn't worldly, she was a family friend, and compared to the women he normally dated, she was quite innocent—in a fresh, compelling way that even now had him wishing he could have thrown caution to the wind.

Damn it.

He had to get her out of his head.

He pushed the door to the Terrell ranch house open, forcing himself to walk into the quiet gloom. Without Mandy or Danielle here, the place seemed to echo around him. He dropped the small duffel bag he'd bought in Lyndon onto the floor of the hall, flipped on a light and made his way into the living room.

Ghosts of his memories hovered in every room, in every knickknack, in every piece of furniture. He'd liked it in Lyndon. It had been a long time since he'd worked that hard physically, longer still since he'd had that sense of community and accomplishment.

He wondered what was going on at the Jacobses' place. He pictured Mandy, imagined her voice, her laughter, her jokes and the convoluted rationale for her contrary opinions. He missed her arguments most of all.

The vision disappeared, and the silence of the house closed in around him. A small, family portrait propped up on the mantel, seemed to mock his presence.

He moved closer, squinting at it.

The picture had been taken when Caleb and Reed were about fifteen. His father had dressed them up, gathered them together in the living room and insisted on wide, happy-looking smiles. Seeing it now, all Caleb could remember was that his father had screamed at Reed earlier that day, pushing him to the ground and demanding he resand an entire section of fence because of some perceived flaw.

He lifted the photo. If he looked closely, he could see that Reed's hands had been bleeding. Closer, still, and he could see his and Reed's brittle eyes. His mother had the haunted look that Caleb remembered so vividly. Though he'd pushed the memories away after he'd left, the fear that he hadn't known the half of his mother's anguish rushed back now.

If he'd known back then what he knew now, he'd might have taken a shotgun to his father. He should have taken a shotgun to his father. He'd have spent the rest of his life in jail, but his mother would have lived, and his brother would have been spared ten years of hell.

He glared at his father's expression, the false smile, the ham fists, the mouth that had spewed abuse, sending fear into the hearts of everyone around him.

Caleb's hand tightened on the frame.

Before the impulse turned into a conscious thought, he reflexively smashed the picture into the stone hearth. Glass shattered in all directions, the wooden frame splintered into three pieces, mangling the photo. He gripped the mantel with both hands, closing his eyes, concentrating on obliterating the memories.

"And you really think selling the place will bring you closure?" Mandy's voice was soft but implacable from the entryway.

Caleb straightened and squared his shoulders. "I didn't hear you come in."

"No kidding."

"I need a shower." He turned on his heel, heading for the staircase, stripping off his shirt as he crossed the room. He wasn't fit company right now. And he wasn't going to let himself take his temper out on Mandy. What he needed was to scald some of his anger away.

Hopefully, when he finished, she'd have the sense to be gone.

He hit the top of the stairs, and pivoted around the corner, tossing his shirt to the ground and reaching for the snap of his jeans. He passed his brother's room; a shiver ran up his spine. His feet came to a halt, and he stood still for a long moment, gritting his teeth, his fists clenched, a sharp pain pounding through the center of his forehead. He swallowed hard, then kept walking, slamming the bathroom door behind him.

He twisted the taps full on and finished stripping off his grimy clothes. Then he wrestled the shower curtain out of the way and stepped into the deep tub. Under the pulsing spray, he scrubbed his body, shampooed his hair, then he stood there, staring at the familiar tile pattern until the water finally turned cold.

He turned the taps to Off, and the nozzle dripped to a stop while he valiantly tried to stuff his memories back into their box. He was beginning to realize he never should have come here.

There was a tentative rap on the bathroom door. "Caleb? You okay?"

He flung the curtain aside in frustration. "Go home, Mandy."

There was silence on the other side.

"I mean it," he shouted. The gentleman in him was exhausted, and he didn't have the fight left to keep his hands off her. She needed to get far away.

"Right," came a short, angry response. It was followed by a few footfalls and then silence.

Thank goodness.

He methodically toweled off, then rubbed a circle in the steam of the mirror. Once again, he borrowed his brother's shaving gear, telling himself that getting cleaned up, eating a decent meal and getting a good night's sleep would give him some perspective. The memories were from ten years ago, not from yesterday. It would be easier to get rid of them this time.

Finished shaving, he wiped his face and tossed the towel into the hamper in the corner of the bathroom. Naked, he turned and opened the door, and found Mandy sitting cross-legged on the floor across the hall.

He barked out a pithy swearword, while she quickly turned her head, squeezing her eyes shut.

"What the hell are you doing?" he demanded.

"I didn't want to leave," she squeaked, coming to her feet, face turned to the side, eyes still squeezed shut. "You seemed really upset downstairs."

"And you couldn't have foreseen *this?*" He wrapped a towel tightly around his waist, stuffing in the loose end.

"At our house, we don't... I mean, there are six of us living there."

"Well, there's nobody else living here." There was no need for him to cover up to cross the hall.

"Sorry."

Her contrite voice took the fight right out of him. It wasn't her fault. What the hell was the matter with him, anyway?

"Don't worry about it." Truth be told, he was more sorry about giving her an eyeful than he was about being seen naked. He couldn't care less about that.

"I'm the one who's sorry," he offered.

She opened one eye and cautiously peeked back at him.

He propped his bare shoulder against the doorjamb and folded his arms over his chest. "What are you doing here, Mandy?"

"We haven't had a chance to talk. You know, alone. Since…"

"Since you turned me down that morning in Lyndon?" It had been the topmost thing on his mind, too.

Her brows went up. "You mean, since *you* turned *me* down."

That sure as hell wasn't the way he remembered it. "You were the one who said you preferred breakfast."

"You were the one who said I should think about it."

"So?"

Her voice rose. "So, who tells a girl who's kissing him back to *think about it?*"

"Someone who's a gentleman and not a frat boy."

"I thought you'd changed your mind."

"I thought you'd changed yours."

She took a step toward him. "So, what you meant was…"

He straightened away from the doorjamb and met her in the middle of the hall, letting his desire for her pulse free once more. "What I meant was that you needed to be sure."

"I'm definitely not sure," she admitted.

"That's what I thought." He swallowed his disappointment, and he told himself he had no right to be annoyed.

In the silence that followed, she lifted her index finger and pushed it tentatively toward his bare chest. Before she could touch him, he snagged her wrist and held it fast. His gaze bore into hers. "I'm not going to let you do this to me again." He was a man, not a saint. And she'd have to practice her little seduction games somewhere else.

She took a step in, brushing up against him, her eyes going smoky, her lips slightly parted in an invitation that was clear as day. "So, your answer is no?"

He gave his head a little shake. "Maybe you'd better make sure I understand the question."

She tossed her thick, chestnut-colored hair, tipping her chin to gaze up at him, pressing closer still, and he braced himself to hold them both steady.

"The question, Caleb Terrell, is do you want to make love with me?"

Before he could form a conscious thought, his lips swooped down on hers, kissing her deeply, drinking in her sweet, fresh taste. He bracketed her face with his hands, backing her against the hallway wall, letting his fingertips explore the satin of her skin, the softness of her hair. He kissed her a second time, and a third and a fourth, desperately wishing the moment could last forever.

When he finally forced himself to stop, all but shaking with the effort, he breathed deeply and drew back a few inches, gazing into her eyes. With the pad of his thumb, he smoothed her flushed cheek, drinking in her extraordinary beauty. When he spoke, his voice had dropped to a husky whisper. "The answer, Mandy Jacobs, is yes."

She smiled. "I couldn't stop thinking about you." Her arms twined around his neck. He hugged her close, lifting her from the floor, kissing her deeply, crossing the short distance to his bedroom.

Moonlight filtered through the window, while a glow of light cascaded in from the hallway. Caleb set her gently on her feet. She was wearing a plain, hunter-green T-shirt and soft, faded jeans. She'd discarded her boots, and her sock feet made her seem shorter than normal.

He pulled up from the hem of her T-shirt, slowly peeling it away from her body, popping it over her head to reveal a lacy, mauve bra.

"I love your underwear," he breathed.

She smiled, and her eyes glowed moss-green in the soft light.

He flicked open the snap of her jeans. "I want to see more of it." He slipped his hand beneath her waistband, leaning in for a gentle kiss, stroking his thumbs along the smooth softness of her skin. Her abdomen was flat, waist indented, hips gently rounded.

One palm strayed to the mound of her breast, cupping it through her bra, feeling the distinctive pebble beneath the wispy fabric.

She gasped in response, thrusting forward, and he circled the sensitive spot with his fingertip.

He tasted her neck, kissed his way along her shoulder, sliding her bra strap out of the way.

Her palms pressed against his bare chest, smoothing their way down to his belly, as he used his free hand to push down her zipper.

"You're overdressed." He tugged down her jeans, slipping them off along with her socks, tossing them all to the floor. Then he stared at her for a long minute, unable to drag his gaze from her perfection.

"You're making me self-conscious," she complained.

He reached out, grazing his knuckles over her navel. "Do you have any idea how gorgeous you are?"

"I'm a sturdy, little workhorse."

He grinned. "Not hardly." He slipped his hand beneath the low waist of her panties. "You're a sexy, sculpted fantasy come to life."

She met his gaze, and he could see her skepticism.

"That's not a line, Mandy." He toyed with the other bra strap, pushing it off her shoulder, staring at the picture she made, not quite believing it could be real.

With anticipation killing him, he drew her back into his arms, kissing her hot mouth, probing with his tongue, bending her backward. He tugged off the towel, then moved his hands to her bottom, pressing her close, feeling the silk of her panties against his bare skin.

Her hands went to his hairline at the back of his neck, her fingers burrowing their way upward. She kissed him back, deeply and thoroughly, small purrs forming deep in her throat.

He flicked the clasp of her bra, discarding it with the rest of her clothes, covering her bare breast with his palm, groaning at the intense sensation of her spiked nipple and the softness that molded to his fingertip.

"Tell me you have condoms," she breathed.

"Oh, yeah." There was no way he was stopping this time.

Her small fingers stroked the length of his chest, over his belly, across his thighs, closer and closer, until he hissed in a breath. "You are definitely killing me now."

He hooked his thumb in her panties, stripping them down, getting them off at least one ankle before he reveled in her nakedness pressed against his. His mouth zeroed in on her breasts, feasting on one and then the other.

She whispered his name, her hands convulsing against his hair. He lifted her, pressed her back onto the bed and stretched out beside her. He kissed and caressed the length of her body. She dampened his neck, his shoulder, his chest, kissing her way down his abdomen, until he stopped her, pressing her onto her back, moving over her, letting his weight move between her spread legs.

He took a second with the condom.

Their gazes locked, hers a clouded jade, his barely able to focus.

He brushed his thumb across her lower lip, dipping it inside the hot cavern of her mouth. She suckled, swirling her tongue across the sensitive pad.

He kissed her hard, and she arched her back, twisting her hands into the quilt.

"I'm sure," she gasped, and he arched forward.

The second he was inside her, a roaring need took over his brain. Desire pulsed to every point of his body. His hands roamed her breasts, his lips moved from her mouth, to her shoulder, tasting everything in between.

She was all motion beneath him, her breaths coming in small gasps, her body arching to meet his rhythm, her arms rigid, head tipped back and her eyes closed shut.

He lost track of time, sensation after sensation building

within him. He held on as long as he could. But when she cried out his name, and her small body convulsed, he followed her over the edge, oblivion washing over him in waves.

The roaring in his ears slowly subsided. Though his muscles were spent, he braced his elbows, worried that his weight might crush her. But he didn't want to move, didn't want to withdraw, didn't want real life crowding in on paradise.

When worry for her comfort trumped his longing, he moved off. But he bent one knee, laying his leg across her thighs, and he wrapped his arms around her, pulling her into the cradle of his body, resting a palm across her warm, smooth belly to keep the connection intact. "You're amazing," he whispered huskily in her ear.

"You're not so bad yourself."

"Glad to hear it." He kissed her lobe, thinking he could happily start all over again.

They breathed in sync for a few minutes, and even as reality returned, a strange sense of calm stole over him.

It was odd. This was still his childhood bedroom, still the family ranch. Three oil paintings of quarter horses hung on his wall. The scents of the fields wafted in the window. And the sounds of the animals punctuated the night.

But for some reason it felt softer, the edges didn't seem so sharp.

"What?" she asked, twisting her head to look at him in the half light.

"I didn't say anything."

"You sighed like the world was coming to an end."

"It's not."

"Are you upset?"

"No."

She moved to a sitting position, her expression pensive. "Regrets?"

"No." He vigorously shook his head, pulling her back down, wrapping an arm tightly around her. "Absolutely none."

She seemed to relax, and her fingertips brushed across his

chest, while her warm breath puffed on his neck. He burrowed against her thick hair and inhaled the clean, citrus scent.

"It's funny," he ventured. For some reason, he wanted to put the feeling into words. Unusual for him, but he plunged on. "This is the closest I've ever come to being content in this room."

"That's good." She twisted her neck to look up at him. "Do you think maybe we banished some demons?"

"Maybe," he allowed.

"I feel very powerful," she joked.

"Then again—" he kept it light "—it could be that you are the most fun I've had in this house since my mom made chocolate mint fudge on our eighth birthday."

She grinned. Then she sobered and drew back, eyeing him quizzically. "Wait a minute. Did I beat the fudge, or was it the other way around?"

"Not a fair comparison. Apples to oranges."

She socked him in the shoulder. "Man, did you ever miss that opportunity."

"Ouch. Sorry."

"You better be. Chocolate mint fudge. Like it could hold a candle to me."

"It could when I was eight."

"You're not making this better, Caleb."

He chuckled low.

"You know," she began, coming up on her knees. "We may be on to something here."

He reached for her, not wanting this space between them. "Oh, I think we are. And I think we should do it again."

She batted at his hand. "I meant, changing your perception of the ranch. Not just your bedroom. And not just with sex. But the whole thing."

Something cold settled into Caleb's stomach. Was she really going to turn this into a sell-the-ranch, don't-sell-the-ranch thing?

"I know exactly how we could do it," she rattled on, voice decisive.

"Mandy, don't—"

"You need to talk to Reed, *really* talk to Reed."

"How the hell did Reed get into this conversation?" Annoyance put an edge to Caleb's voice.

She stopped. She blinked.

He tried but didn't quite keep the edge out of his tone. "Last time I checked, it was just you and me in this bed."

"But… He's your brother."

"That means something completely different to you than it does to me."

Caleb knew his anger stemmed from disappointment. But what had he expected? He and Mandy were still the same people. They still had divergent goals. Nothing had fundamentally changed because they'd sweated naked in each other's arms.

She shook her head in response to his statement, her rich hair flowing with the motion. "No, it doesn't. This land, your family, Reed. They're all part of your history and your heritage. You couldn't erase them by running away when you were seventeen, and you can't erase them by selling out now."

His annoyance was growing to full-out anger. "I did *not* run away."

"Semantics." She waved a dismissive hand. "Why did you smash the picture?"

Caleb set his jaw but didn't answer. He'd smashed the picture because he couldn't stand to see his father's smug face staring out at him one minute longer.

"Why did you smash the picture?" she repeated.

"Drop it, Mandy."

Her tone turned softer. "If you didn't care anymore, you wouldn't have smashed the picture." She gave a heartfelt sigh. "Staying away for ten years didn't fix it, did it?"

"This is none of your business," he told her firmly. It was temporary, a blip on his radar. A few days—a few weeks, max—and he'd be back to his regular life in Chicago. The ranch would cease to exist for him. And that's the way he wanted it.

"Do you think you've been repressing your true feelings?"

Suddenly, Caleb simply felt tired. He didn't want to fight with her. Mandy was sole bright spot in all this madness.

He reached for her, urging her back down into his arms, genuinely trying to see things from her perspective.

"If it makes you happy," he told her. "Yes, I've been repressing my feelings. My childhood sucked. Reed made a stupid choice from which our relationship will probably never recover. And, I'm sorry to have to be so blunt. But there's nothing you can do to help. I know you disagree, but I'm making the right choice."

"It's—"

He pressed his index finger across her warm, swollen mouth. "For me, Mandy. It's the right choice for me."

Her green eyes turned soft and sympathetic.

He forced out a smile. "But you've made it better for right now." He couldn't resist, so he kissed her mouth one more time. "You've made things much better for right now."

Desire surging, he wrapped an arm around her waist and pulled her close. She was instantly kissing him back, her soft, sinuous body wrapping itself around him one more time.

He made love to her slowly, gently, savoring every second of the peace she offered.

Afterward, they lay still and silent for a long time.

It was Mandy who finally broke it.

"I need to go home," she whispered.

His eyes came open. "Why?" He didn't want her to leave. He didn't want her to move an inch, at least until morning.

But she twisted her neck to look at him. "It's coming up on eleven."

"You have a curfew?"

"Travis looked pretty suspicious when I left."

"So?"

Travis's interference was definitely not welcome in this. Whatever was between Caleb and Mandy was none of her brother's business.

"So, if I come home after midnight, he's going to put two and two together."

"And?"

"And, he'll be upset."

Caleb propped himself on one elbow. "Are you telling me this was a clandestine fling?" Even as he said the words, he asked himself to come up with an alternative. What were they going to do? Date until he left for Chicago? Own up to her brothers that they'd slept together?

"I think that's the best way to handle it, don't you?"

"You're an adult," he reasoned out loud. "Your private life is none of your brother's business."

Mandy laughed. "You going to tell him that?"

Caleb was willing, if that's what Mandy wanted him to do.

"I could tell him," she mused with a nod. "But then there'd be a fight."

"I'm not afraid of Travis." Caleb had no intention of lying about his relationship with Mandy.

"I meant with me, not you. And, with everything else going on, I really don't have the energy to fight Travis."

"I don't like this," said Caleb. He wanted her to stay right where she was. He wanted to hold her in his arms all night long, maybe even beyond that.

She cocked her head, defying his mood by giving him a saucy grin. "A few minutes ago, you seemed to like it just fine."

"I don't want to go sneaking around behind your family's back."

She patted his chest. "For now, let's just keep it quiet. Who knows what happens next between us. Maybe nothing."

Caleb was hoping for a lot more than nothing.

"If you go ahead with your plan to sell, you know you could be gone in a matter of days," she reasoned. There was no inflection to her tone, impossible to tell if she'd miss Caleb or not.

Then she gave a wry half smile. "You want to start world war three over something this insignificant?"

*Insignificant?*

"Because, believe me, Caleb, Travis is as overprotective as they come." She glanced at her watch. "I go home now, he can wonder, but he won't know. And if he doesn't know, he can't go off the deep end."

Caleb ran his fingers through her messy hair. "This is a stupid plan."

"But it's my plan." This time, there was a distinct edge to her voice. "Some decisions you get to make, Caleb. This one is mine."

He stared at the determination in her green eyes.

"Okay," he finally agreed. He'd keep the secret. Lady's choice. And he didn't kiss and tell.


The lights were on, and Travis was still up when Mandy came through the front door of the Jacobses' ranch house. He appeared in the kitchen doorway, a screwdriver in one hand, a rag in the other.

He stared at her for a long, silent minute as she tugged off her boots and tucked her loose hair behind her ears.

He took two steps forward. "Tell me you didn't."

"Didn't what?" She steeled herself for a moment then met his gaze full-on.

"Mandy." He smacked the screwdriver and rag on top of the dining-room table. "He'll break your heart."

"I have no idea what you're talking about." She had her suspicions, but she didn't know for sure, so it wasn't a lie.

"What do I always tell you?" He came forward at an angle, giving her the impression he was circling in.

"You're going to have to be a little more specific."

"We're not like you, Mandy. We're guys. We'll say anything, do anything—"

"Caleb's not like that."

Travis scoffed out a cold laugh. "What did he tell you?"

"He didn't tell me anything. And I don't know what you're talking about." She stomped to the sofa and flopped down, picking up this month's *Equestrian* magazine and opening it in front of her. "And I really don't want to have this conversation with you."

Travis moved to the armchair across from her. "He's from Chicago, Mandy. He's not staying."

"Don't you think I know that?" Mandy didn't expect Caleb to stay. Her wildest wish was that he'd hang around long enough to meet up with Reed. Beyond that, she had absolutely no illusions.

"The women he goes out with," Travis continued. "They know the score. They expect the lies. They know they're lies."

"Caleb has not lied to me."

"Then how'd he get you into bed."

Mandy determinedly flipped her way through the pages of the magazine. "None of this is any of your damn business."

"I love you, Mandy."

"Shut up."

"He doesn't."

She glanced over the top of the magazine. "What a ridiculous thing to say. Of course he doesn't love me. Why would he love me?"

"Then why won't you believe I have your best interest at heart?"

"I'm not a child, Travis. I like Caleb. Caleb likes me. Despite your cynicism, that's all there is to it. I'm not about to get hurt. And that's all you need to know."

"Then, why were you up there tonight?"

"He needs help," Mandy answered honestly.

"And you're going to be his Florence Nightingale?"

"He needs to see Reed. The two of them need to talk, really talk. You don't know what they went through as children." She breathed deeply, absolutely sincere in her argument.

Travis sat back, his posture relaxing. "I have a pretty good idea what they went through. I knew them both quite well."

Mandy dropped the magazine and sat forward. "Then help me find Reed. Caleb is determined to sell the ranch out from under him. He almost did it while we were in Lyndon. If I hadn't spoken up about the water rights, we might already have new neighbors. Reed needs the ranch, and Caleb needs Reed."

"You spoke up about the water rights review?"

"Yes."

"To Caleb's potential buyer?"

She paused. "It came up in conversation."

"And you think Caleb still likes you?" Reed asked on a note of astonishment.

"He understood."

"Mandy, the world isn't the happy fun place you seem to picture. People aren't sweet and kind and friendly, looking to do each other favors 24/7."

"Will you stop?"

"Reed and Caleb are grown men," Travis warned her darkly. "Neither of them is going to thank you for interfering."

Well, at least Danielle was on her side. She'd definitely thank Mandy for interfering.

"What if it was you?" Mandy asked. "What if you and Seth were estranged? Would you not want someone to facilitate your reunion? If you were about to lose the ranch, would you not want someone to help you out?"

Travis moved from the armchair and angled himself next to Mandy on the sofa. "Those two men have a very dark past. They're not going to recognize what you're doing as helpful. They're going to hate you for interfering."

"Reed would never hate me." And she had to believe Caleb wouldn't, either. Oh, she was under no illusion that he was falling for her in a romantic sense. But he had been a gentleman, more than a gentleman.

"Reed's been hurt pretty bad."

"Yes, he has," Mandy agreed. She paused, looking directly

at the brother she'd loved all her life. "And he's our friend. Do you really want me to turn my back on him?"

Travis mouthed a swearword, rocking back on the sofa. "You shouldn't be sleeping with Caleb, Mandy."

"I am not going to—"

"Stop talking right now," Travis barked. "Before you have to lie to me. If you fall for him, it's going to be a disaster." He paused, his mouth turning into a thin line. "Then again, if you're sleeping with him, it's already too late."

Mandy felt her throat close up with emotion. She couldn't think about her feelings for Caleb, not right now, not when so much was at stake. "I have to find Reed."

Travis hesitated, then he reached out and rubbed her shoulder. "Okay, little sister. Okay. I'll help you find Reed."

"You will?" she managed.

"I will."

"Good." She nodded, feeling stronger already. "Great. Danielle gave me a name—"

Travis recoiled. "Danielle?"

"Yes. She wants Reed to come back, so that Caleb will go back to Chicago. There's some Brazilian deal with a ticking clock." Mandy waved a dismissive hand. "Anyway. She put me in touch with a private investigator. And he's going to find Reed for us. All we have to do is keep Caleb from selling the ranch until then."

# Eight

Caleb gazed up and down the wide hallway of the main Terrell barn, overwhelmed by the magnitude of the job in front of him. He'd had his secretary calling moving and storage companies this morning, but they all said they needed an estimate of the volume to be moved and stored. So Caleb had to figure out what to keep and store, and what to sell with the ranch.

He couldn't see the point of keeping the saddles and tack. Those things they'd sell as is. They'd also sell the horses and livestock. Same with the equipment and the vehicles. Whoever bought the ranch would likely have a use for much of the equipment, and Caleb was inclined to give them a good deal if it meant streamlining the sale.

The office—now, that was a different story. His boots thumped against the wooden floor as he crossed the aisle to stare in the open door of the office. It held two desks, five file cabinets and a credenza that stretched under the window. Some of the paperwork would stay, but a lot of it would be personal and business records that would have to be kept for the family. Well, for Reed. And that meant sorting through everything.

Caleb let his shoulders slump, turning his back on that particular job and making his way farther into the barn. About twenty horses were stabled inside. He made a mental note to make sure the hands were exercising each of them every day. He'd spoken briefly to their half dozen full-time hands, the cook and with the two men who were up from the Jacobses' place.

Everything was at least under temporary control.

A horse whinnied in one of the stalls, drawing Caleb's attention. He took a step closer, squinting into the dim stall.

"Neesha?" he asked, recognizing the Appaloosa mare. "Is that really you?"

She bobbed her head, seeming to answer his question.

A beauty, she was chestnut in the front, with just a hint of a white blaze. Her hindquarters were mottled white above a long, sleek tail.

She lifted her head over the stall, and he scratched her nose, rubbing her ears. She'd been a two-year-old when he left, one of the prettiest foals ever born on the ranch. He glanced into tack room, realizing her saddle and bridle would be easy to find using his father's ultra-organized system. He also realized he'd love to take her out for a ride.

Someone entered through the main door, heavy steps, long strides, booted feet, likely one of the hands.

"Caleb?" came Travis's flat voice.

Caleb's hands dropped to the top rail, fingers tensing around the rough board. He was under no illusion that Mandy could keep up a lie to her brother. So, if Travis had pressed her last night, he was likely here looking to take Caleb out behind the barn.

Caleb braced himself and turned.

Travis came to a halt, but when he spoke, there was no malice in his voice. "I guess it's been a while since you saw Neesha."

"It's been a while," Caleb agreed, watching Travis carefully. A sucker punch was no less than he deserved.

"You up to something?" asked Travis.

Caleb had no idea how to answer that question.

"Hear from any new buyers?" Travis tried again.

"Nothing so far." Caleb allowed himself to relax ever so slightly. Perhaps Mandy was more devious than he'd given her credit for.

"I'm trying to get an estimate for moving and storage." His gaze was drawn past the big double door, toward the ranch house. He couldn't begin to imagine how big a job it would be sorting through the possessions in the house. In addition to the rooms, there was the attic, the basement. He'd like to think he was emotionally ready to tackle it, but a thread of uncertainty had lodged itself in his brain.

Travis nodded. "A lot of years' worth of stuff in there."

"It's a bitch of a situation," said Caleb.

"That it is," Travis agreed. "We've got to ride the north meadow fence today. You up for it?"

"With you?"

"With me."

For a brief second, Caleb wondered if Travis was luring him away from the homestead in order to do him harm. But he quickly dismissed the suspicion. If Travis wanted to take his head off, he'd have tried by now. From everything Caleb knew and had learned, the man was tough as nails, but he wasn't devious.

"Sure," Caleb agreed. The house could wait. It wasn't as though it was going anywhere.

"I'll take Rambler," said Travis.

The two men tacked up the horses and exited into the cool morning sunshine. The meadow grass was lush green, yellow-and-purple wildflowers poking up between leaves and blades, insects buzzing from plant to plant, while several of the horses in the paddock whinnied their displeasure at being left behind.

They went north along the river trail, bringing back Caleb's memories of his childhood, and especially his teenage years. He, Reed and Travis had spent hours and hours on horseback out in the pastures and rangeland. They'd had a special clearing by the river, where they'd hung a rope swing. There, they'd swam in the frigid water, drank beer they'd bribed the hands to bootleg for them, bragged about making out with the girls at school and contemplated their futures. Funny, that none of them ever planned to leave the valley.

"I did a search on Active Equipment," Travis offered, bringing Rambler to walk alongside Neesha. "You've been busy."

"Had nothing better to do," Caleb responded levelly, though he was proud of his business achievements.

Travis chuckled. "I bet you fly around the world in that jet, going to parties with continental beauties, while your minions bring in the millions."

"That's pretty much all there is to it." Caleb pulled his hat down and bent his head as they passed beneath some low-hanging branches. He was surprise by how natural it felt to be in the saddle.

"Gotta get me a job like that."

Caleb turned to look at Travis. "Are you thinking of leaving Lyndon Valley?"

"Nah, not really. Though I wouldn't mind tagging along on one of your trips sometime, maybe Paris or Rome. I hear the women are gorgeous."

"Open invitation. Though, I have to warn you, it's mostly boardrooms and old men who like to pontificate about their social connections and their financial coups."

"You're bursting my bubble."

"Sorry."

They were silent while the horses made their way down a steep drop to a widening in the river. There, they waded hock-deep to pick up the trail at the other side, where they climbed to the flat.

"You remember the swing?" asked Travis.

"I remember," Caleb acknowledged. If they turned north and followed the opposite riverbank, instead of veering across the meadow, they'd be there in about ten minutes.

"You remember when Reed dislocated his shoulder?"

Caleb found himself smiling. It was the year they were fifteen. Reed's arm had snagged on the rope, yanking his shoulder out of his socket as he plummeted toward the deep spot in the river. He'd shrieked in pain as he splashed in, but he'd been able to swim one-armed through the frigid water back to shore.

Fresh off a first-aid course in high school, Caleb and Travis managed to pop the shoulder back into place.

"He never did tell my dad," Caleb put in.

Caleb had helped his brother out with his chores as best he could for the next few weeks, but Reed had pretty much gritted his teeth and gutted it out.

"I thought it was funny at the time," said Travis. "But five years ago, I dislocated my own shoulder. Codeine was my best friend for about three days. Your brother is one tough bugger."

Caleb knew Reed was tough. Reed had been taller and stronger than Caleb for most of their lives. He'd uncomplainingly taken on the hardest jobs. When Caleb had become exhausted and wanted to quit, risking their father's anger, Reed was the one who'd urged him on, one more hay bale, one more board, one more wheelbarrow load. He would not quit until he'd finished an entire job.

"And he never backed down from a fight," said Travis.

Caleb stilled. He let his mind explore some more of the past, remembering the day he'd walked away from the ranch. For the first time, it occurred to him that Reed probably saw leaving as backing down, and staying behind as a way of holding his ground against their father. He'd wanted Caleb to stay, begged him to stay, asked Caleb to stand toe to toe with him when it came to Wilton.

"And he hasn't changed," Travis continued. "It's a little harder to make him mad now, but once you do, stand back."

Caleb knew he'd made Reed angry. Back then he'd done it by walking away. Now he'd done it all over again by inheriting the ranch. It didn't matter that he was right. It didn't matter that Reed was misguided. The damage was done.

An image of his brother's mulish, teenage expression flashed into Caleb's brain. His throat suddenly felt raw. He knew a line had been drawn in the dust. He also knew he was never going to see his brother again.

He pressed his heels into the mare and leaned forward in the saddle, urging her from a walk to a trot to a gallop. He heard Travis's shout of surprise, and then Rambler's hooves pounded behind them.

The world flashed past, Neesha's long strides eating up the ground, her body strong beneath him, her lungs expanding, breaths blowing out. He settled into the rhythm, breathing deep, fighting to clear his mind of memories.

But the memories wouldn't stop. He saw Reed when they were seven, wrestling on their beds when they were supposed to be asleep, their father's shouts from the living room, the two of them diving under their covers, and lying stock-still while they waited to hear Wilton's footsteps on the stairs.

He saw them chasing down an injured calf when they were thirteen, waving their arms, yelling until they were hoarse, corralling it where they could look at the gash on its shoulder. Reed had held it still, while Caleb applied antibiotic ointment and crudely stitched the wound.

Unfortunately, their efforts had only served to make their father angry. He told them they'd wasted far too much time and effort on a single calf and made them work an extra two hours before allowing them to come in for a cold dinner.

But there were also good times, when Wilton had been out on the range, sometimes for days at a time. When their mother would relax and smile, and they'd play board games, watch silly sitcoms and eat hamburgers on the living-room sofa. Reed had been there for the good times and the bad. They'd struggled through homework together, commiserated with each other over unfair punishments, drank illicit beer, raced horses and teased each other mercilessly at every opportunity.

Travis shouted from behind him, and Caleb saw they were coming up on the fence-line. He pulled back on the reins, slowing the mare to a walk, forcing deep breaths into his tight lungs.

"You going for a record?" Travis laughed as he caught up. Both horses were breathing hard, sweat foaming out on their haunches.

"Haven't done that in years," Caleb managed without looking in Travis's direction.

"It's like riding a bike."

"Tell that to my ass." Caleb adjusted his position.

Travis laughed at him. "And we're going all the way around Miles Butte."

"That'll take all day." And half the night. "We'll be lucky to get home by midnight."

"You got something you have to do?" Travis watched Caleb a little too carefully, waiting for his answer.

Yes, Caleb had something he wanted to do. He wanted to see Mandy again.

But, apparently, Travis wasn't about to let that happen.

Mandy hadn't seen Caleb in two days. She'd read in one of Abigail's women's magazines that if a man wasn't into you, there was little you could do to attract him. But if a man *was* into you, he was like a heat-seeking missile, and nothing would slow him down.

Caleb definitely wasn't a heat-seeking missile. And it had occurred to her more than once over the past two days that he might have got what he wanted from her and now moved on. Maybe Travis was right, and that was the way they did it in Chicago.

Even this morning, they were taking two vehicles from the ranch to Lyndon for the first water rights review meeting. Seth, Abby and Mandy ended up in the SUV, while Travis and Caleb drove the pickup truck. It wasn't clear who had orchestrated the seating arrangements, but surely any self-respecting heat-seeking missile could have managed to get into a vehicle with her.

Mandy tried not to focus on Caleb as they turned off the highway onto Bainbridge. There was plenty to be optimistic about between her father's continuing progress at the rehab clinic in Denver and Seth getting more and more excited about the upcoming campaign. He and Abigail had been discussing and debating political issues all the way from the ranch to Lyndon. And, with Seth and their father pretty much out of the picture, Travis seemed to be relishing his new role as de facto ranch manager.

Not that Mandy was jealous.

Though, now that she thought about it, everyone in her family seemed to be moving into some kind of new phase in their lives. Except for her. Other than supporting Travis at home, finding Reed and getting the Terrell family back on track, what was next for her?

"Mandy?" Abby interrupted her thoughts from the front passenger seat.

"Hmm?"

"Can you check my briefcase back there? I want to make sure I brought all five copies of the information package."

Mandy reached for the briefcase where it was sitting on the SUV floor, pulling it by the handle to lay it flat on the seat beside her. She snapped the clasps and pulled it open.

"The green books?" she asked, thumbing her way through the rather professional-looking coil-bound, plastic-covered volumes."

"Those are the ones."

Mandy counted through the stack to five. "They're all here."

"Thanks," Abby sang. Then she turned her attention to Seth. "I've got us all at the Sunburst. You're sharing with Travis, and I'm with Mandy. I put Caleb on his own. I figured, you know, the big, bad, Chicago executive might not be used to sharing a bathroom."

Seth laughed, but Mandy couldn't help remembering that

Caleb had shared a bathroom with her at the Rose Inn. He'd seemed perfectly fine with that. Then again, they'd been trapped in a storm. It could be considered an emergency situation. But he'd worked like a dog for the next three days. And he hadn't complained in the slightest about the accommodation, the food or the hard work. He didn't strike her as somebody who required creature comforts.

She opened her mouth to defend him, but then changed her mind. She really shouldn't be thinking so much about Caleb. She should be thinking about Reed, and how to find him, and how soon she could reasonably touch base with Enrico Rossi and check the status of his investigation. Or maybe she could call Danielle directly. Perhaps she'd heard something from Enrico.

Seth pulled into the parking lot at the side of the Sunburst Hotel. Travis's pickup truck was already parked, and he and Caleb were getting out. Mandy watched Caleb's rolling, economical movements as he pulled a small duffel bag from the box of the pickup truck. His gaze zeroed in on the SUV, finding hers as he strode across the parking lot toward them.

She quickly looked away and concentrated on climbing out the back door. He swung open the back hatch and began loading his arms with their luggage. Travis followed suit. Seth grabbed the last bag, and beeped the SUV lock button. Mandy was left with nothing but her shoulder bag to carry into the lobby.

Caleb fell into step beside her.

"How're you doing?" he rumbled.

"Just fine," she told him primly, concentrating her focus on the short set of concrete steps that led into the glass entrance.

A set of double glass doors slid silently open in front of them, welcoming them into the gleaming high-ceilinged, marble-floored, floral-decorated lobby. Pillars formed a big circle around a patterned tile floor, while the service desks formed an outer ring in front of the walls.

"I've got a copy of the confirmation," Abby announced, slipping a sheaf of papers from a side pocket in her bag.

"Let me get the check-in." Seth strode up to a uniformed woman at the registration desk.

Caleb lengthened his strides after Seth, leaving Mandy behind. He caught up and put his credit card on the counter. Seth immediately shoved the card back toward Caleb. The two men had a brief debate, and it looked like Seth was the one to back off.

Mandy positioned herself beside a pillar, out of the route of direct walking traffic, next to Abigail and the luggage.

A few minutes later, Caleb returned to them.

"Ladies." He nodded. "I assume these are your bags?" He scooped up their suitcases.

"Those are ours," Abigail confirmed.

"Then, right this way. You're on the tenth floor. As am I, and Caleb and Seth are on seven."

"One second," said Abigail, finding a glass-topped table to set down her briefcase.

She opened it, pulled out two of the green packages and took a few steps across the lobby to hand them to Travis. "Lunch is at the Red Lion next door. The meeting starts at one o'clock. We have dinner reservations at the Riverfront Grill. And then I thought we'd go to the Weasel." She did a little shimmy as she mentioned the name of the most popular dancing bar in Lyndon. "It's Friday night, so they'll have a band."

Travis took the books from her hands, giving her a mock salute. "Works for me. See you guys in a few."

Caleb headed for the elevator, and Mandy fell into step behind him.

On the tenth floor, they exited, finding their room five doors down. Abby inserted the key card, holding the door open for Caleb with the bags. Mandy brought up the rear.

"This looks nice," Caleb noted politely, setting the bags on the padded benches at the foot of each of the queen-size beds. The room had a small sitting area near a bay window with a view of the town. The two beds looked thick and comfortable, and the bathroom appeared clean, modern and spacious.

"I'll see you both at lunch," he finished, heading for the door.

He opened it, got halfway out and then stopped, turning back. "Mandy? You have a minute? I've got something I want to ask you about, but it's buried in the bottom of my bag." He gestured into the hallway. "You mind?"

Surprised and confused, and worried it might have something to do with the sale of the ranch, Mandy nodded. "Uh, sure. No problem." She moved after him, telling herself it couldn't be a sale. Not this fast. Not without any warning.

"Great." He flashed a smile at Abigail. "Thanks."

Outside in the hallway, they moved three doors farther down. Caleb inserted his own key card, opening the door to a larger room with a king-size bed and a massive lounge area beside a pretty bay window.

They entered the room. He dropped his bag on the floor. The spring-loaded door swung shut and, before she knew what was happening, Mandy was up against the back of the closed door. Caleb's hands had her pinned by her wrists, and he was kissing her hard and deep.

She was too stunned to move. "What the—"

"I've been going crazy," he groaned between avid kisses. "You're making me crazy. I thought we'd never get here. I thought we'd never get checked in. I thought we'd never get a second alone."

Mandy recovered her wits enough to kiss him back. So, not the sale of the ranch. And okay, this was definitely a heat-seeking missile.

She relaxed into the passion of his kisses.

His lips moved to her neck, pulling aside her shirt. A rush of desire tightened her stomach, tingling her skin. Her eyes fluttered closed and her head tipped back, coming to rest against the hard plane of the door as her toes curled inside her boots.

"I don't understand," she managed to mutter, clinging to

his arms to balance herself. "You've ignored me for two days. I didn't hear a word."

"That was Travis. He used every trick in the book to keep me away from you." Caleb pulled back. "What did you tell him, by the way?"

"I didn't... Well, I mean, I didn't *tell* him. But he knows."

"Yeah, he knows," Caleb agreed. "But can we talk about your brother later? I figured we've got about three minutes before they come looking for us."

She blinked at him in astonishment. "You don't mean?"

"Oh, man. I *wish*. But, no. I was only planning to kiss you some more."

The regional water rights review meeting was shorter than Mandy had anticipated. The state representative introduced the process and told participants how they could provide written comments in advance of the next meeting. Having five people attend from the Jacobs and Terrell families, along with dozens of other ranchers from the Lyndon Valley area served its purpose in showing the organizers the level of interest from the valley and from the ranching community.

There were also a number of people representing nonranching interests. That had been one of Seth and Abigail's concerns, that ranchers might be pushed out as the area tried to attract newer industries.

Caleb asked questions, and Mandy was impressed with both his understanding of the process and his ability to zero in on the significant details. If she found Reed, and if he returned to the ranch, she hoped Caleb would stay involved until the end of the review. Even if he had to do it from Chicago.

As the meeting broke up, and the group made their way toward the doors of the town hall, Abigail linked an arm with Mandy. "Did you bring along a dress for tonight?"

"A what?"

"A dress. You know, that thing that replaces pants on formal occasions."

Mandy gave her sister a look of incredulity. "No, I didn't bring a dress." Why on earth would she bring a dress? This was a community meeting. In Lyndon.

"Well, we've got a couple of hours before dinner. Let's go to the mall and be girls for a while."

Mandy glanced over her shoulder at Caleb. She'd been hoping to steal a few more minutes alone with him before they all convened for dinner. "I'm not sure—"

"Come on. It'll be fun." Abigail raised her voice. "Wouldn't you guys like to escort two gorgeous women out on the town tonight?"

Travis stepped up. "Why? You know some?"

She elbowed him. "Mandy and I are going for a makeover."

"Great idea," said Travis, voice hearty. "You two ladies take your time. Have fun."

Mandy shot Caleb a helpless look.

He came back with a shrug that clearly stated "see what I mean?"

"Fine," Mandy capitulated, mustering up some enthusiasm, even as she wondered whether Travis had co-opted her sister to the cause of keeping her and Caleb apart.

"I haven't been in Blooms for ages," said Abigail, towing Mandy toward the SUV. She called back over her shoulder. "You guys okay to walk back to the hotel?"

Seth waved them off. "We'll see you at the restaurant."

Abigail hit the unlock button for the vehicle, and its lights flashed twice. "They can go find a cigar bar or something."

"Did Travis put you up to this?" Mandy asked across the roof of the vehicle.

Abigail gave her a blank look. "What do you mean? Why would Travis care what we do?"

Mandy peered closely at her sister. Abigail wasn't the greatest liar in the world. And she always had been much more interested in hair, makeup and fashion than Mandy. Maybe this was some kind of a bizarre coincidence.

"So, you just want to go shopping?"

"No," said Abigail. "I want to go shopping, hit the hair salon and get our makeup and nails done. I'd also suggest a facial, but I don't think we have that kind of time."

"Fine." Mandy threw up her hands in defeat. "Let's go be girls."

Abigail grinned and hopped into the driver's seat.

They drove the five miles to Springroad Mall, parked next to the main entrance, stopped to make sure the salon could fit them in later in the afternoon, then made their way through the main atrium to Blooms, the town's biggest high-end ladies' wear store. It occurred to Mandy that the last thing she'd purchased here was a prom dress.

"Something with a kick," said Abby, leading the way past office wear and lingerie. "I want a little lift in my skirt when I'm dancing."

"What happened to you in Denver?" Mandy couldn't help asking.

"I realized life was short," Abigail responded without hesitation. "I should be out there having fun and meeting people. So should you." She stopped in front of a rack of dresses.

"I'm really interested in the campaign," Abigail continued. "But I'll admit, at first, I wasn't crazy about the idea of spending so much time in Lyndon and Denver. But now I'm really looking forward to it. I'm going to stretch my wings."

Suddenly, Mandy become worried. "You're not planning to leave the ranch, are you?" They'd already lost one sister to the bright lights of a big city.

"Of course not. Not permanently, anyway. But I do want to test other waters. And this seems like a good time to do it." She held up an emerald-green dress. "What do you think? Does the color go with my hair?"

Abigail's hair was shoulder length and auburn. Colors could be challenging for her, but the green was perfect.

"Absolutely," Mandy replied.

A salesclerk arrived, offering to start a dressing room for

each of them. She took Abigail's choice of the green dress, and they moved on to the next rack.

Abigail quickly selected another. "You should go for red," she exclaimed, holding up a short, V-necked, cinnamon-red dress. It had black accents and a multilayered skirt that would swirl when she danced.

"Oh, sure," Mandy drawled sarcastically. "That looks just like me."

"That's the point. 'You' are blue jeans and torn T-shirts. We need to find something that is completely not you."

"My T-shirts aren't torn," Mandy protested. Okay, maybe one or two of them were, but she wore those only when she was mucking out stalls or painting a fence.

Abigail waved the dress at the salesclerk, who promptly took it from her arms and whisked it off to the dressing room.

Abigail's next choice was basic black. She considered one with a sequined bodice, but discarded it. Mandy had to agree. They were going to the Weasel. It was a perfectly respectable cowboy bar, but it wasn't a nightclub.

They ended up with four dresses each. Mandy considered they were all too formal, but her sister seemed to be having such a good time, she didn't want to be the wet blanket.

In her dressing room, she put off the red dress to the very last. She tried a strapless, straight-skirted design in royal blue, but they all agreed the neckline didn't work. Then a basic black cocktail dress, which was too close to one of the few she already owned. Then she tried a patterned, empire-waist, knee-length concoction, with cap sleeves and a hemline ruffle. It made her look about twelve. Abigail actually laughed when she walked out to model it.

Abigail had already decided to go with the green, so she was waiting in her regular clothes when Mandy exited the dressing room in the red dress.

Her grin was a mile wide. "It's stunning," she pronounced.

The salesclerk nodded her agreement. "I wish I had legs

like that," she commented, looking Mandy up and down. "It fits you perfectly."

Mandy glanced to her legs. She didn't see anything particularly interesting about them. They held her up, helped her balance on a horse and could walk or jog for miles when necessary. That's all that counted.

"You probably want to shave them before we go out."

"Thanks tons, sis."

"But I've never seen you look so beautiful," Abigail declared. "You absolutely *have* to get it."

"I don't know when I'll ever wear it again," Mandy glanced at the price tag. It was about three times as much as she'd ever spent on a dress before.

"Well, you'll wear it tonight," said Abigail.

"And after that?"

"After that, who knows. You're about to become the sister of the Mayor of Lyndon."

The salesclerk gave Abigail a curious look.

"Our brother Seth Jacobs is running for mayor this fall," Abigail put in smoothly. "Make sure you vote."

"There'll be the swearing-in dance," the clerk offered to Mandy. "And that's always formal."

"We're only going to the Weasel tonight," Mandy noted, considering different angles in the mirror.

Okay, so the dress did look pretty darn good. It accentuated her waist. It would twirl enticingly while she danced. And it showed just enough cleavage to be exotic without being tacky. She wouldn't mind Caleb seeing her in this.

Behind her, in the mirror, the salesclerk waved a dismissive hand. "You can wear anything to the Weasel. Lots of the younger girls dress up to go there, especially on a Friday night."

"There you go," said Abigail. She glanced at her watch.

"You'd better made a decision quick because we have to get to the Cut and Curl."

Mandy drew a breath. Okay. The red dress it was. Her lips curled into an involuntary smile. "You talked me into it."

# Nine

If Mandy was trying to drive Caleb stark raving mad, she was certainly going about it the right way. Her hair was up. Her heels were high. And the professionally applied makeup had turned her face from beautiful to stunning.

Her sassy red dress was enough to give a man a coronary.

When they walked into the Weasel, he hadn't even bothered asking her to dance, simply swirled her out onto the crowded dance floor and wrapped her tightly in his arms, before anybody else could get their hands on her. Since then, he'd been shooting warning glares at any guy who dared look twice.

Abigail was also quick to attract her share of partners. Caleb and Seth parked it at the bar, ordering up a round of beers.

Once he recovered the power of speech, Caleb put his lips close to Mandy's ear, keeping the volume of his voice just above the music of the country band. "You look gorgeous."

"You like?" she asked.

"I love."

She grinned at him, showing straight, white teeth, while her eyes flashed emerald. "Abby made me buy it."

"Abigail's my new favorite person."

"She'll be thrilled to hear it."

He spun Mandy around, then smoothly pulled her back against his body. "You should do this more often."

"Dance with you?"

"Well, yeah. That, too. But I meant dress up."

She arched a brow. "Something wrong with my blue jeans?"

"Don't be so sensitive. I prefer silk to denim on my dates. Deal with it."

"Well, I prefer blue jeans to suit jackets."

Caleb frowned at her. Then he made a show of glancing around the crowd. "Any casually dressed guy in particular catch your eye? I could dance you over and let him cut in."

"Sure," she teased right back. "What about the guy in the yellow hat?"

Caleb shook his head. "Looks a little too old for the likes of you."

"The one with the red boots?"

"Too short."

"Well…" She continued to scan the room before returning her attention to him. "Okay, what about you?"

"I'm wearing a suit. And I'm already dancing with you."

"A girl, Caleb. Pick out a girl. Who looks good to you?"

He kept his eyes fixed firmly on her. "I'm dancing with her."

"That's a cop-out."

"It's the truth. If there are any other girls in this room, I didn't notice."

"Smooth talker," she told him, but their gazes locked and held.

"What are you doing later?" he rumbled.

"I'm rooming with my sister."

"This is ridiculous," he griped, frustrated by the barriers that kept flying up in their way. "I feel like we're in high school."

"You think if it wasn't for Abigail, I'd be jumping into bed with you?"

Her question surprised and embarrassed him. Was he being presumptuous? Had he been that far wrong in reading her signals? Had he imagined her response to his lovemaking?

Sure, they'd argued afterward, but then they'd made love again. And she'd been all he could think of ever since, despite the fact Travis had kept him away from the ranch and out of cell range for two long days.

Did Mandy feel differently?

"I'm sorry," he began, feeling like a heel. "I didn't mean—"

"That's the problem, Caleb." Her look was frank. "I don't know what you mean. I just spent two days wondering what you mean."

"What I mean is that I like you, Mandy," he answered her as honestly as he could. "I like you a lot. I think you're beautiful and exciting and real. And I can't seem to get enough of you. I want to spend every minute in your company." His voice rose in frustration. "And I want to ditch all of your siblings so they'll stop getting in my way."

She broke into a smile. "That was a good answer."

"Thank you," he grumbled.

"But it's okay if you just think I'm sexy."

"I think you're that, too."

Her expression sobered. "When I didn't hear from you, I thought maybe once was enough."

"Twice," he corrected.

"Twice is enough?"

"No! I meant we did it twice already." He gathered her closer, adding some intimacy to the conversation by putting his mouth closer to her ear. "Twice is definitely not enough."

"You want to pick a number?" There was a thread of laughter in her tone. "That'll keep me from guessing where this is going and when it's going to end."

"Fifty," he told her.

"Ambitious."

"Always."

The band ended the song with a pounding drum solo, and the lead singer announced they were taking a break.

Abigail appeared next to them, commandeering Mandy for the ladies' room, and Caleb wound his way toward the bar.

He ordered a beer.

Travis stepped up. "Make it two."

"Find someone to dance with?" asked Caleb.

"Not a problem. I went to high school with half the people here."

"I recognize a few faces." Caleb glanced around the room, seeing at least a dozen people he'd known as a teenager.

The bartender set two bottles of beer on the bar, and Caleb handed him a twenty. He and Travis turned to face the crowd, Caleb scanning for Mandy.

"I see the way you're looking at my sister." Travis took a long swig of his beer.

*Again?* Caleb *really* didn't want to have this conversation. "Every man in the room is looking at your sister."

"Every man in the room isn't dancing with her."

"Only because I won't let them."

Travis opened his mouth to respond.

But Caleb interrupted him, squaring his shoulders as he angled to face Travis. He was getting this over with here and now. "You've got to back off, man. She's a grown woman."

The piped in music throbbed through the speakers, and a few dancers took the floor again.

"You don't have a sister."

Caleb crossed his arms over his chest. "I don't. But that doesn't change anything."

"It would change your attitude."

"Let's assume my attitude is not going to change in the next five minutes."

Travis took another pull on his bottled beer. "Yeah, I know."

"She's a smart woman, Travis. She's realistic and self-confident, and I'm not pressuring her to do anything."

"I'm backing off," said Travis.

The statement surprised Caleb, leaving him at a loss for words. Thanking Travis didn't seem remotely appropriate. So, he took a drink instead.

Seth appeared from the crowd. "What's going on?"

Caleb shot Travis a sidelong glance, wondering what he was going to say to his brother.

"Not much," Travis responded with a shrug.

Seth signaled for a beer and parked himself next to Caleb, facing the room along with them. "I think we're going to have to keep an eye on our sisters tonight."

Travis coughed out a laugh. "You think?"

"I never think of them as particularly beautiful," Seth continued. "But they clean up pretty good."

It was Caleb's turn to laugh. "Your sisters are drop-dead gorgeous, Seth."

"I know," said Seth in some amazement. He scooped a handful of peanuts from the bowl on the bar. "I'm picturing them on the campaign trail."

"What trail?" Travis challenged. "You're running for mayor, not governor."

"There'll still be photo ops. What do you think? One on each arm?"

"You'll look like Hugh Hefner."

"Hmm," Seth mused. "Guess I'd better rethink that."

At the far side of the room, Mandy reappeared with Abigail.

Men immediately took notice, sending interested gazes and shifting themselves in the women's direction, some of them obviously setting up to make a move. Caleb abandoned his beer and pushed away from the bar, setting a direct course for Mandy. Seth and Travis could look out for Abigail. But Caleb wasn't letting Mandy out of his sight.

Back in the hotel room, Mandy stripped off her high shoes. Abigail followed suit, stretching her bare feet out on an ottoman in their compact sitting area.

"My feet are definitely not in shape for strappy sandals," Abigail complained.

"I hear you." Mandy flopped down on the opposite armchair, stretching out her own sore feet, sharing the ottoman. She liked to think she was pretty tough, but she'd definitely been defeated by a dance floor. By midnight, even a few more minutes in Caleb's arms hadn't been enough of an incentive to add an extra blister.

"Felt a little like Cinderella, though, didn't it?" asked Abigail.

"Tomorrow, we go back to cleaning the fireplace."

"Well, horse stalls," said Abigail. "At least, that's your fate. I've been getting away with a lot of office work lately."

"I hate the office work."

"Lucky for me."

Mandy plucked at the silky layers of her dress. "Do you think the campaign is going to keep you in Lyndon a lot?"

Abigail shrugged. "More than usual, for sure. Why?"

"It's been awfully quiet at home."

Abigail grinned at her. "You missed me?"

"I did," Mandy admitted. "With Mom and Dad staying at the rehab center, and you and Seth in Denver and Lyndon, and Travis always out on the range, it'll just be me at lunch and probably just me at dinner."

"I think Travis likes his new role," said Abby. "With no Dad and no Seth, he's going to have a lot more responsibility."

Mandy had to agree. Travis seemed very happy. Once again, she got the feeling she was the only one left behind.

"Are you suffering from empty-nest syndrome?" Abigail asked, compassion in her dark, hazel eyes.

"Maybe I am," Mandy realized. "Weird. I never thought about how much my life depended on the rest of the family being there. It's like nobody needs me anymore."

"The ranch can't run without you and Travis."

"Without Travis, maybe. But you're the one who does the paperwork. The foreman knows what to do day to day. The hands know what to do. I'm… Okay, this is depressing. I think the Terrells need me more than my own family."

Abigail's eyes narrowed. "The Terrells?"

"Getting Reed back." Mandy was surprised Abigail didn't immediately understand. "Caleb's off on this crazy 'sell the ranch' tangent, and Reed's lying low. And somebody has to knock some sense into the both of them."

Abby moved her feet to the floor and sat forward in her chair. "They're grown men, Mandy."

"That doesn't mean they have a brain between them."

"That doesn't make it your responsibility."

Mandy shook her head. Her sister wasn't getting this. How had nobody else noticed? "The universe is out of balance, Abby. It has been for ten years. I love Reed."

"We all love Reed."

"There you go. I can't abandon him at a time like this, can I? He's my third brother."

Abby's face winkled in consternation. "Do you think there's any chance." She paused, watching Mandy carefully. "Any chance at all that—I mean, right now—you're somehow substituting Reed for your own family."

"I'm not—"

Abigail held up a hand. "Hear me out. We're all busy. And you're feeling adrift. And along comes this very juicy family problem that you think you might be able to solve."

"A *juicy problem?* You think I'm getting some kind of emotional satisfaction out of Caleb Terrell threatening to sell his family's ranch?"

"I think you're like a moth to a flame. Someone's hurt? There's Mandy. Someone's upset? There's Mandy. Two people in a dispute? There's Mandy."

"You say that like it's a bad thing."

"It's not a bad thing. It's a great thing. And it's an important role, *in your own family*. But when you start franchising out, it's a problem."

"This is Reed Terrell, not some stranger I picked up on the street."

Abigail chuckled at that. "All I'm saying is don't get too invested in Reed and Caleb Terrell. This may not be a problem you can solve."

Mandy's hand clamped down on the padded arms of the chair. In her mind, failure was not an option. "I have to solve it."

"And, if you can't?"

Mandy wasn't going to think about that right now. Reed gone from the Valley forever? Someone other than the Terrells living down the road? And Caleb gone, with no reason to ever return.

She hated to admit it, even to herself, but she'd started hoping he'd reconnect with Lyndon Valley, maybe come back once in a while. He did have his own jet. And then, they could…could…

Okay. Shelving that thought for now.

Abigail was watching her expectantly. "And if you can't?" she repeated.

"If I can't get them to reconcile," Mandy responded breezily. "Then, that's that. Reed will move and life will go on."

There was a long pause. "Why don't I believe you?"

"Because you're naturally suspicious. You have that in common with Travis."

"Ha. I'm naturally fun and exciting." Abigail was obviously willing to let the argument go. "Did you see all the guys who asked me to dance down there?"

Mandy smiled at her sister's exuberance, forcing herself to relax again. "Green is definitely your color."

"I'm wearing it more often. Five of them asked for my number."

"Did you give it out?"

"Nah. I'm not particularly interested in cowboys. What about you?"

"Nobody asked for my number."

Abigail's dark eyes glowed with interest. "I think Caleb's already got your number."

Mandy felt her cheeks heat.

Abigail sat up straight, staring intently. "So, I'm not crazy. You are into him."

"He's a good guy," Mandy offered carefully.

"You just told me that he's trying to sell the ranch, and you're trying to stop him. That doesn't sound like a good guy."

Mandy's cheeks grew hotter still. "Okay," she allowed. "Aside from that particular character flaw, he's a good guy."

Caleb was misguided, that was all. She was confident he'd eventually see the light. Assuming she could keep him from selling the ranch between now and then.

"He's definitely hunky," said Abigail.

Mandy nodded. There was no point in pretending she was blind. "Sexy as they come."

"So?" Abigail waggled her brows. "Did he kiss you?"

Mandy hesitated, wondering how much, if anything, she dared share with her sister.

"He *did*," Abigail cried in triumph. "When? Where? I want the details."

A few beats went by in silence.

"Are you *sure* you want the details?" Mandy asked, a warning tone in her voice.

"Yeah."

Mandy screwed up her courage. "Everywhere."

Abigail blinked in confusion. "What do you mean?"

"I mean, he kissed me *everywhere*."

Abigail's eyes went round. "We're not talking geography, are we?"

Mandy shook her head, a secretive grin growing on her face. *"When?"*

"Two days ago."

"At the ranch?"

"His ranch."

"You didn't?"

"We did."

Abby plunked back in her chair, her expression a study in shock.

"Then I didn't hear from him afterward." Mandy found the words rushing out of her. "And I thought, okay, that's it, he's from the big city, and it was a one-night stand, and I can handle it. But then we got here—"

"And he made that stupid excuse to take you down to his room."

"Yes."

"And?"

"And it was like no time had gone by. He grabbed me, kissed me, talked about going crazy for not seeing me." For Mandy, it had been both gratifying and confusing. Her emotions had done a complete one-eighty in the space of about ten seconds.

"So, why didn't he call you?"

"Out on the range. Out of cell service. Apparently Travis was keeping him busy, and he didn't have a chance to see me. He said he tried."

"And while you were dancing tonight?" asked Abigail. "Did he proposition you again?"

Mandy nodded. That appeared to be the thing about a heat-seeking missile. They didn't leave you guessing.

Abigail's brows went up. "And you're sitting here with me, because…?"

The answer to that was pretty obvious. "Because two of my brothers and my sister are in the same hotel, and I don't want to upset anyone."

"You think *I'll* be upset because you spend the night with Caleb?"

"I think you'll be… I don't know." Mandy tried to put it into words. "Disappointed?"

"You're twenty-three years old. Besides, you already did it once. You think my delicate sensibilities can't stand being five rooms away while you have a sex life?"

"And there's Travis."

"What's Travis got to do with this?"

"He warned Caleb to keep his hands off me."

Abigail sputtered out a laugh. "Grow up, Travis. It's none of his damn business."

"I know that. And you know that. And believe me, that's Caleb's opinion. But I don't want to upset Travis."

Abigail sat forward again. "Mandy, honey, this family's emotional health is not your responsibility. I'm not suggesting you sleep with Caleb or you don't sleep with Caleb. What I am suggesting, is that you make up your own mind. You're allowed to do that."

It wasn't as simple as Abigail made it out to be. In families, people had a responsibility to the group, they couldn't just selfishly think of themselves alone.

"You think that when I date a guy, I'm worrying about your opinion?" Abigail asked.

"Well, I'd never—"

"I don't. And neither does Travis when he's dating a woman. And you shouldn't, either. Now." Abigail brought her palms firmly down on her lap. "If the rest of us weren't here, what would *you* do?"

Mandy pondered her sister's question. If she had it to decide all on her own, remembering their lovemaking from last time, thinking about his words and her feelings on the dance floor, taking into account that Caleb was here only temporarily?

Mandy bit down on her lower lip.

Abigail waited.

"I'd already be down the hall in his room," she admitted. "I'd be with Caleb."

Abigail's grin was a mile wide.

Three minutes later, standing barefoot outside Caleb's hotel-room door, Mandy was forced to tamp down a swell of butterflies battering her stomach. She was pretty sure he'd be glad to see her, but there was no way to be positive. Other than to knock on his door.

Right.

She brushed her palms against the skirt of her red dress, took a deep breath, glanced both ways down the corridor and knocked.

After only a few seconds, Caleb opened the door. His expression registering surprise, but the surprise was followed quickly by a broad smile that lit the depths of his blue eyes.

He reached for her hand, tugging her quickly inside the room.

"Hey, Mandy," he whispered gruffly.

As the door swung shut behind her, his lips came down on hers in a long, tender kiss.

He pulled back, grin still firmly in place as he smoothed back her hair. "You're here."

She couldn't hold back her answering smile. "I am."

"Can you stay?"

She nodded, and he drew her into a warm, enveloping hug, wrapping his body possessively around her.

For some reason, she suddenly felt trapped. "Uh, Caleb?"

"Hmm?" he asked between kisses.

"I know you probably want to jump straight into bed."

He immediately pulled back again, his hands gently, loosely cupping her bare shoulders. "Hey, no."

There was genuine regret in his eyes. "I'm sorry about what I said earlier. That was presumptuous and disrespectful. You being here, in my room, doesn't mean anything you don't want it to mean." His words sped up. "Seriously, Mandy. No pressure."

Her heart squeezed with tenderness. "I'm not saying we shouldn't go to bed at all. I just thought, maybe first—"

"You want a glass of wine?" He took her hand and led her to the big sitting area at the far end of the huge, rectangular room. A big, bay window overlooked the river and the moon hung high above the mountains. It was a clear night, with layers of stars twinkling deep into space.

"Wine sounds good." She perched on one end of the couch.

"We can talk," he said as he moved to the wet bar, stopping to turn on some soft music, before returning with two glasses of red wine. "Merlot okay? I can order something else if you'd like."

She accepted the glass. "This'll be fine."

He sat down at the opposite end of the couch, leaving a wide space between them.

She leaned back, and their gazes locked for a long, breath-robbing minute. The air seemed to sizzle, and her skin broke out in goose bumps while her heart sped up, throbbing deep in her chest.

"Tell me about Chicago," she managed, hoping to keep from throwing herself at him for at least five minutes.

"What do you want to know?"

"Where do you live?" She took a sip of the robust, deep-flavored wine. It danced on her tongue, then warmed her extremities as she swallowed. Or maybe it was Caleb's presence that warmed her extremities. It was impossible to tell for sure.

"I have an apartment. It's downtown. On top of a thirty-five-story building."

"So, it's a penthouse?" That shouldn't have surprised her. But she found it was hard for her to get used to Caleb's level of wealth. Though the fact that he owned a jet plane should have made it clear.

"I guess you could call it that," he answered easily. "I bought it because it's close to our head office. The plants are all in industrial parks in the outskirts of the city, but it makes sense to have the head office downtown."

"You don't have to apologize to me for having a downtown office."

He chuckled. "When I'm talking to you, it feels a little extravagant. Truth is, most of our international clients stay downtown, so it's for convenience as much as anything else. I'm not trying to impress anyone."

"I wouldn't think you'd have to try." She imagined people

would be impressed without Caleb having to lift a finger in that direction.

He gave a mock salute with his wine glass. "Was that sarcasm?"

"Truthfully, it wasn't. Though I am struggling to picture you with a list of international clients."

"That's why I'm forced to wear a suit. It helps them take me more seriously."

She smiled at his joke and drank some more wine, feeling much more relaxed than when she first walked in.

"We've had inroads into Canada and Mexico for quite some time," Caleb elaborated. "Our first expansion of a plant outside of the Chicago area was Seattle. With the port there, we had access to the Pacific Rim. It turned out to be a really good move. So, now, we have buyers from Japan, Korea, Hong Kong, as far away as Australia. That's when we bought the jet. We started doing trade shows over there. In many Asian cultures, status is very important. So that meant I had to go, as president of the company. Otherwise, we couldn't get the right people in the room for meetings." He paused. "Do you have any idea how long it takes to fly from Chicago to Hong Kong?"

"I haven't a clue."

"Long time."

"Is that why there's a bathroom in the jet."

"And why the seats turn into flat beds."

"Not to brag," she put in saucily. "But I went as far as Denver this year."

"You're lucky. If I could do all my work in Chicago, I'd never travel at all."

Mandy didn't like the idea of Caleb not traveling. The only way she'd ever see him in the future is if he traveled to Colorado. "The jet seemed pretty comfortable," she noted.

"So, you see my point."

"Your point being, why fly commercial when you can take your own Gulf Stream?"

"Okay, now that was definitely sarcastic."

"It was," she admitted with a grin.

He sobered. "It's funny. What looks like luxury and unbelievable convenience that ninety-nine percent of the population can't access, is really just me trying to survive." He set down his wineglass and shifted closer to her. "I don't know if I'm saying this right. But money and success aren't what you expect. The responsibility never goes away. You worry everyday. Literally thousands of people depend on your decisions, and you never know who's your friend, who's using you and who's out to get you. The risks are high. The stakes are high. And you go weeks on end without an opportunity to catch your breath, never mind relax."

Mandy thought she did understand. "Are you relaxed now?" she asked.

He nodded. "Amazingly, at this moment, yes."

"That's good."

"It's you."

It was her turn to toast him, keeping it light. "Happy to help out."

He tapped his fingers against his knee. "You know, I believe you're serious about that. It's one of the things I like best about you."

"I'm relaxing?" She wasn't sure whether to take that as a compliment or not. Relaxing could also be boring. And she couldn't possibly be anywhere near as exciting as the women he usually dated.

Dated. She paused. Was this a date?

"You're not thinking about what I can do for you," said Caleb. "You're sitting over there, looking off-the-charts gorgeous, enjoying a rather pedestrian wine, without a single complaint."

She glanced at her glass. "Should I be complaining? Do I have poor taste in wine?"

"I'm definitely not saying this right. You care about how I feel, about what you can do for me. Do you know how rare that is?"

"Do I really have bad taste in wine?"

Caleb laughed, picked up his glass, toasted her and drank the remainder. "It tastes perfectly fine to me." He stared softly at her for a long moment. "But I know you know what I mean."

She fought an impish grin, going with the impulse to keep joking. "I figure it's a toss up between you saying I'm boring and you saying I'm unsophisticated."

He deliberately set down his empty glass. Moved so he was right next to her and lifted her glass from her fingers. "You, Mandy, are anything but boring."

"But I am unsophisticated."

He opened his mouth, but she kept talking before he could say something that was complimentary but patently untrue. "I'm a ranch girl, Caleb. I've barely left the state. I haven't even seen my own sister at Liberty in New York."

Caleb blinked in obvious surprise. "You haven't seen Katrina dance?"

"Oh, I've seen her dance a few times, during the last years she was at college." Mandy thought back to the experiences. "She is incredible. But I haven't been to New York since she joined Liberty. I haven't seen her perform at the Emperor's Theatre as a principle dancer."

"You need to do that," he said decisively.

"I do. And maybe I should take in a wine-tasting class while I'm in the city. Clearly, my palate needs some work."

"Your palate is perfect." He kissed her. "Better than perfect." He kissed her again.

She responded immediately, arms going around his neck, hugging him close, returning the kiss with fervor, reveling in the feel of his strong body pressing itself up against hers.

"I'm taking you to New York," he whispered against her lips.

"Now?"

"Not now." His warm hand covered her knee, sliding up her bare thigh, beneath the red dress. "Right now, I'm hoping to take you someplace else entirely."

She smiled against his mouth. "I can hardly wait."

He drew back to look at her. "But after this, Mandy. Whatever happens with…" He seemed to search for words. "Whatever happens with all the stuff that's around us… Afterwards, I am taking you to New York. We're going to watch your sister perform, drink ridiculously expensive wine and stay in a hotel suite overlooking Central Park."

"Is that before or after you take me to Rio for a manicure?"

"Your choice."

His fingertips found the silk of her panties, and she groaned his name.

"Oh, Mandy," he breathed, kissing her deeply, lifting her into his arms.

He stood, striding toward the king-size bed, flicking the lights off as he passed each switch.

He set her on her feet next to the bed, threw back the covers, then gently urged her down, following her, stretching out, his gaze holding hers the entire time.

He gently stroked her cheek with the backs of his fingers, smoothed her hair, ran his fingertips along her collarbone, pushing down the straps of her dress. "I am so very glad you're here."

She kissed his mouth, ran her tongue over the seam of his lips, then opened wide and kissed him deeply and endlessly. "There's nowhere else I want to be."

He took it slow, gently and tenderly lingering over every inch of her skin with his kisses and caresses. Mandy had never felt so cherished. And when they were naked, and fused together, she curled her body around him, holding him tight, gasping as his slow deliberate strokes took her higher and higher.

Reality disappeared, and she clung almost desperately to lovemaking that went on and on. When she finally cried his name, they collapsed into each others arms. She was certain she'd ended up in Heaven.

Her heartbeat was deep and heavy. Her lungs worked overtime. And she inhaled Caleb's musky scent, clinging tightly to him, fighting sleep and willing the rest of the world away for just as long as possible.

# Ten

The next day, Caleb couldn't seem to bring himself to let go of Mandy. He held her hand, occasionally pulled her sideways against him. She'd put up with it for a short time, but then she kept freeing herself, obviously not comfortable with the intimacy around her family. Caleb didn't care who saw them, as they wandered through the grounds of the Lyndon Regional Rodeo. It was opening day, and everyone agreed it was worth staying to watch.

The rodeo had always been a fun, lighthearted, family affair, and Caleb was astonished to see how much it had grown since he'd last attended. He'd rode bucking broncs that year. He was seventeen and too young to realize he was mortal.

He hadn't finished in the money. But Reed had won the trophy for steer wrestling. Cocky, reckless and in high spirits, they'd spent his five-hundred-dollar prize on beer and flashy new boots for both of them. Now, Caleb found himself wondering if those boots, barely worn, were still stored in his bedroom closet, and what Reed had done with his pair.

He and Mandy made their way through the midway, toward

the main arena. The announcer was pumping up the crowd for the first event. Children ran from ride to ride, shrieking with excitement, sticky cotton candy in their hands and balloon hats on their heads.

One young boy cried as his helium balloon floated away. Seth was quick to snag a wandering vendor and replace the balloon. They boy's mother was grateful, and Seth was sure to introduce himself by his full name.

"Hopefully, another vote," Abigail said to Mandy and Caleb in an undertone.

"He's very good at schmoozing," Caleb agreed. He had to admit, he admired Seth's easy manner with the crowds. He seemed to know everybody, and they seemed to respect him. Those he didn't know, he quickly met.

"Are we here for the rodeo or a campaign stop?" Mandy asked her sister. Abigail just laughed in response.

Caleb was dressed in blue jeans, boots and a white Western-style dress shirt. But it was all new, and he felt like a dandy, more than a little out of place among the working cowboys. He wondered how may people assumed he was a tourist. Certainly, all the competitors would peg him right off. He wished there was time to scuff up the boots and fade his jeans.

"Hey, Mandy," a woman called from behind them.

Mandy turned and so did Caleb, and her hand came loose from his.

The woman looked to be about thirty years old. She wore a pair of tight jeans, a battered Stetson hat and a wide, tooled leather belt. She was a bit thick around the middle, her hair was nondescript brown, and her red checked shirt was open to reveal a navy T-shirt beneath. She clearly belonged here at the rodeo.

"You riding today?" she asked Mandy.

Caleb looked at Mandy with curiosity. She competed in rodeo events?

"Not today," Mandy answered. "We just happened to be in town and thought we'd take it in."

"Heard about your dad," the woman continued, her expression switching to one of sympathy. "I was real sorry about that."

"Thank you," Mandy acknowledged. "We appreciate it. But he's doing very well, making more progress every day."

"Good to hear. Good to hear." Then the woman stuck out her hand to Caleb. "Lori Richland."

"Used to be Lori Parker," Mandy put in.

Caleb recognized the name. Lori had been a year behind him in high school. He didn't remember very much about her.

He accepted her hand. "Caleb Terrell."

"Woo hoo," she sang. "Wait till I tell Harvey I got a look at you." She gave Caleb's hand a playful tug, looking him up and down. "We heard you were back in town. Sorry to hear about your dad, too."

"Thank you," Caleb said simply.

Lori turned her attention to Mandy. "I've got Star Dock over at the stables if you want to enter the barrels."

"I hadn't planned—"

"Go for it," Lori insisted. "He loves competing." She looked back at Caleb. "The crowds and the applause does something for that horse."

"Hey, Abby," Lori called over Mandy's shoulder. "Steer undecorating?"

Abby approached them. "Yeah? If you've got a horse here, I'm game."

"Pincher's been doing really well lately. And tell your brothers to check with Clancy over at the pens. We need some good local competitors in team, steer roping."

Caleb had a sudden flashback to him and Reed practicing roping out on the range. They'd had plans to someday compete together, but Reed's big body made him a natural for steer wrestling, while Caleb had liked the adrenalin rush of the bucking horses.

Lori looked directly at Caleb. "What about you? What are you going to enter?"

Caleb held up his palms in mock surrender. "Not today."

He was not getting anywhere near anything that bucked. And he was completely out of practice for all of the events.

Mandy leaned over to Lori and spoke in a mock whisper. "He's been away in the big city. Riding a desk for a few years."

Lori checked him out up and down. "Doesn't look too soft."

"Why does everybody keep being surprised about that?" Caleb asked Mandy.

"Because it's true." She patted his shoulder consolingly. "You don't look too bad for a city slicker."

"You're too kind," he drawled.

"You should take it as a compliment," said Mandy.

"Maybe we'll throw you in the greased pig chase," Lori teased Caleb.

"Pass," said Caleb. "But you go right ahead and have a good time with that."

Lori tipped her head back and gave a throaty laugh.

"Barrels start in about an hour," she said to Mandy. "Better check the schedule for the rest." With a wave, she strode away into the crowd.

"You're going to compete?" Caleb asked.

"Sure," said Mandy. "I could win a thousand dollars."

"Don't want to pass up a chance like that." He found his gaze drifting to Travis and Seth. Abigail had obviously given them the news about the chance to enter the rodeo, and they now had their heads together talking strategy.

For a sharp second, Caleb missed Reed so badly, it brought a pain to the centre of his chest.

Then Mandy slipped her hand into his. She leaned in, and her tone went sultry. "You want to be my stable hand?"

He tugged her tight against his side. "I'll be anything you want me to be."

She grinned. "I'm holding you to that."

He kept her hand in his as they headed for the horse pens in the competitors area around back of the arena.

There, she quickly got down to business, signing up, paying

the entry fee and checking out the horse and tack Lori had offered her.

When she was ready to go, Caleb crossed to the competitors grandstand, where he could get a better view. He caught
sight of the other Jacobs siblings in the distance, getting ready
for their own events, and he had to struggle not to feel like the
odd man out.

But once the barrel-racing event started, he got caught up
with the cheering, coming to his feet when Mandy galloped
into the arena. She made a very respectable run. Halfway
through the competition, and she was in second place.

She joined him sitting in the stands for the last few competitors, leaning up against him as they laughed and cheered.
She managed to hang on to third place until the last competi-
tor knocked her to fourth, just out of the money.

Caleb gave her a conciliatory hug, telling her he was sorry.

But she shrugged philosophically. "Easy come, easy go."

"I'll spring for a corn dog if it'll make you feel better," he
offered.

She turned up her nose. "What corn dog? I'm holding out
for Rio."

He pretended to ponder for a moment. "I suppose I could
do both."

"Truly?" She blinked ingenuously up at him.

"Yes," he told her sincerely. He realized in that moment he'd
give her anything she wanted.

"You're a gentleman, Caleb Terrell," she cooed, threading
her arm through his.

"And, dust notwithstanding—" he pretended to wipe a
smudge off her cheek "—you, Mandy Jacobs, are a lady."

Her face was scrubbed clean of makeup today, and her hair
was pulled back in a simple ponytail, but in the sunshine she
looked just as beautiful as she had last night. He had trouble
tearing his gaze away from her.

Her attention went to the ring. She cheered and gave a shrill whistle as the barrel-race winners received their awards in the middle of the arena.

"You just whistled." He laughed.

"Bet the girls back in Chicago don't do that."

"They don't eat corn dogs, either."

"Poor things. They don't know what they're missing."

The team roping had started. Caleb couldn't help but admire the talent of the cowboys and the rapt attention of well-bred horses. A few of the steers escaped, but most were swiftly roped and released by the cowboys.

"Here we go." Mandy leaned forward as her brothers lined up in the box. The steer was released, and the men sprang to action, horses hooves thundering, ropes spinning around their heads. Travis took the head, turned the spotted steer, and Seth quickly followed-up with the heels.

The horses stilled, and the flag waved. Their time was five point three seconds, causing Mandy to shout and punch a fist in the air. The time had put them in first place. They released their ropes and tipped their hats to the crowd, acknowledging the cheers.

They shook hands as they rode out of the arena, and Seth playfully knocked off Travis's hat. One of the clowns retrieved it for him, and the two disappeared from sight around the end of the fence.

Caleb felt another hitch in his chest. His reaction was silly. Even if he did meet his brother after all these years, it wasn't as if they'd be doing any team roping. Caleb was way too far out of practice. Besides, he was too old to come off a horse.

"Are you hungry?" Mandy asked.

"You don't seriously want a corn dog."

"I was thinking a funnel cake. Sprinkled with sugar, please."

"How on earth do you stay so slim?" Most of the women he knew in Chicago survived on leaf lettuce and bok choy.

"Exercise and clean living," she answered.

"So, you're serious?"

"I never joke about funnel cake."

Caleb shook his head in amazement, coming to his feet. "One funnel cake, coming up. You going to eat the whole thing, or will you share?"

"With you, I guess I could share."

He gave her a wink and made his way down the worn wooden benches, meeting Travis and Seth at the bottom.

"Nice." He nodded, shaking each of their hands in congratulations. He checked the board to find them still on top with six competitors left. "Looks like you might finish in the money."

"Seven-hundred and fifty bucks," Travis confirmed with a sharp nod. "That'll pay for the trip."

"I'm going on a funnel-cake run. Anyone interested?"

"Gads, no," said Seth. "I don't know how Mandy eats those things."

"She's got a sweet tooth," said Travis. His level gaze stayed on Caleb for a couple of beats.

Caleb raised his brows. If Travis had something to say, he might as well spit it out.

Seth glanced between the two men.

"You heard anything from Reed?" Travis asked, surprising Caleb.

The question triggered emotions that were close to the surface today, and it took him a second to recover. He shook his head. "Not a word."

"He still takes first in the steer wrestling every year," said Travis.

Caleb nodded his acknowledgment but didn't answer.

But Travis wasn't finished yet. "Mandy thinks you should talk to him before you sell the ranch."

The announcer's voice became more animated over the loudspeaker as the next team of ropers left the box, stirring up a cloud of dust.

"Mandy thinks a lot of things," said Caleb.

"I'm not sure she's wrong on this."

"Well, I can't talk to him if he's not here." Caleb made to leave.

"You can hold off on the sale," said Travis.

"You're selling?" asked Seth, an obvious note of incredulity in his voice. "Why on earth would you do that?"

"Yes," Caleb answered shortly, pivoting in the dust and starting to walk away.

"Whoa," Seth caught up to him, but Travis, at least, had the good grace to stay behind. "What gives?"

"What gives is that I'm not explaining myself to you and Travis in the middle of a rodeo crowd."

"Fair enough." Seth nodded easily, keeping pace. "But what about Reed? He get a say in this?"

"Reed left town, no forwarding address, no phone number."

"But how can you sell it without him?" Seth paused. "You know, I honestly thought he'd inherit the whole thing."

Caleb altered his course to angle toward the concession stands. "Well, he didn't. I did."

"Not the whole thing."

"Yes, the whole thing."

"But—"

"Haven't a clue," Caleb preempted the obvious question.

Seth's tone turned thoughtful. "And that's why Reed disappeared."

"I would think so." They came to the lineup and joined the end.

"Are you getting a funnel cake?" Caleb asked Seth.

"Just keeping you company."

"Not necessary."

But Seth didn't leave. After a few minutes of silence, he spoke up again. "Do you need the money?"

Caleb laughed darkly at that suggestion. "The money's Reed's. It's going to sit in a bank account until he shows his face."

"And the rush is?"

"Has it occurred to you that this is none of your business?"

"Absolutely."

"Then, go away."

"Has it occurred to you that I'm your friend?"

Caleb couldn't form an answer to that one. He liked and respected Seth, but he was beginning to feel as if he was surrounded by kind, well-meaning, meddlers, pushing him in a direction he didn't want to go.

"Seriously, Caleb. This is a huge decision."

"It's already listed."

"Unlist it."

"I don't want it," Caleb barked. "I don't need it. And Reed's better off without it." He glared at Seth, while the festival swirled around them, midway rides jangling, children shrieking and the rodeo announcements blaring in the distance.

After a long minute, Seth gave a curt nod of acquiescence. And Caleb turned to the teenager in the paper hat and placed his order.

# Eleven

The trip to Lyndon and the rodeo day over and done with, Mandy and the local vet were working their way through a list of minor injuries and ailments in the ranch's horses. Mid-afternoon, were inside the barn looking at a quarter-horse colt who'd been limping on and off for about a week. The colt's left fetlock felt warm, and Mandy was worried about infection.

"Mandy?" a whispered voice questioned from behind them, the person obviously being careful not to spook the colt.

Mandy smoothly rose from the colt's leg and turned to find Robby, one of the young hands, waiting.

"There's someone on the office phone for you," he told her quietly. "Danielle something? She's pretty insistent."

"I'll take it," Mandy agreed, optimism rising within her. "Can you give Dr. Peters a hand while I'm gone, Robby?" She dusted her hands off on her jeans and moved from the stall to the main barn aisle.

The young man set aside his manure fork and took Mandy's place in the stall.

Anticipation tightened Mandy's stomach as she paced her

way quickly to the small office that sat just inside the main door of the barn.

She closed the door behind her for privacy and picked up the phone. "Danielle?"

"Mandy?"

"It's me." Mandy forced herself to sit down on the leather chair with wheels, telling herself to stay calm. "You have news?"

"I do. Enrico found Reed."

Mandy's spirit soured. "Yes!" They'd found him. They'd finally found him. "Thank you."

"Right now, he's staying at a hotel in Helena."

"Really?" That information surprised Mandy. "Reed is in Montana?" She'd assumed he was at least still in Colorado.

"The Bearberry Inn. He's been there a couple of days, but there's no way of knowing how long he'll stay."

"Don't worry. I'm leaving right away." Mandy hopped up from the chair, cataloging exactly what she'd have to do to get to the airport, get to Helena and find Reed. When she did, she was cornering him and demanding to know what the heck he thought he was doing.

Okay, maybe she wouldn't demand. Maybe she'd just ask him. But, first, maybe she'd just hug him. After the past few weeks like he'd had, the man was going to need a hug.

"Call me when you get there," said Danielle. "And please, please convince him to come home. Whatever it takes."

"I will," Mandy promised.

"If we can wrap this up by Wednesday, my life gets a whole lot easier."

"Uh, okay." Two days. "I'll do my best." Mandy signed off.

As she headed across the yard, toward the house, she remembered the Brazilian deadline was looming. That was obviously the rush. Danielle was going to do everything in her power to get Caleb to Sao Paulo in time to deal with the banking regulators.

That meant there was every chance he'd be gone before

Mandy got back. As soon as Reed agreed to return, she'd have to call Danielle. Danielle would obviously call Caleb, and Caleb would have no reason to stay in Colorado, especially if his business depended on him getting to Brazil.

That meant the two brothers might not even see each other. They might not get a chance to talk. And once the crisis was over, things could easily go back to the status quo, Reed here, Caleb there, still estranged from each other.

Mandy trotted up the stairs, across the porch and into the ranch house foyer. Maybe keeping Danielle's search a secret from Caleb had been the wrong idea. Taking Caleb with her to Helena made much more sense. If he'd come, he'd have to talk to Reed. That would break the ice. And he'd still have time to make it to Brazil. And, afterward, maybe he'd come back.

She pulled off her boots in the front foyer and headed for the second floor, intending to have a quick shower and pack an overnight case.

She warmed to her modified plan. Reed was sure to be happy with Caleb's honor and generosity. The two brothers could talk in Helena, resolve things and then… Well, the plan got a little fuzzy after that, but at least it was a start.

She stripped of her shirt, peeled off her jeans, discarded her underwear and stepped into a hot shower.

She hadn't talked to Caleb since they'd returned from Lyndon last night after the rodeo. Seth and Travis had finished in second place, and after a celebratory beer and a round of burgers, she and Caleb had driven back together.

He'd been unusually quiet on the drive, but had kissed her good-night, and he'd told her he was going to miss her overnight. Nothing wrong with that. Everything was fine between them. She could safely broach the subject of Reed.

Perhaps she could do it between kisses. That would be manipulating the situation. But it was for a good cause.

Then again, that was probably a bad idea. She'd go with a straight-up outline of the facts. Caleb liked facts, and the facts were on her side in this.

She dressed, blow-dried her hair, put on a touch of makeup, a pair of clean jeans, a striped T-shirt and a navy blazer. Then she tossed a few clothes into the overnight bag, left a note to her brothers, saying she'd call them when she got to Helena, and jumped into a pickup truck.

The ride to the Terrell ranch took its usual twenty minutes, but it felt much longer. She pulled up to the house, took a very deep, bracing breath and set out to reason with Caleb.

When she knocked, he called out a huffed "come in."

"Caleb?" she called back as the door opened. She could hear scraping sounds coming from the living room.

She followed the noise, rounding the corner from the foyer to find him surrounded by cardboard packing boxes, a tape dispenser in his hand, as he sealed one of them up.

"What are you doing?" Her tone came out sharper than she'd intended.

"Packing." He voiced the obvious.

"But, why?" What had happened? Had she missed something? Had he already sold the ranch?

"Mostly, because it's not going to pack itself," he answered.

"But I thought—"

"Can you hand me another box?"

Mandy was too stunned to move. She felt sick to her stomach.

"Did you sell?" she managed on a harsh whisper.

"Not yet."

She put out a hand to brace herself against the back of the sofa, all but staggering in relief. There was still time.

"A box?" he asked again.

"Sure." She picked up a flattened box from a pile beside her feet and handed it over. She met his gaze. "And, if we find Reed?"

His jaw tensed. "Seriously, Mandy. I'm not having that conversation all over again."

She swallowed against her dry throat. "But, if we did find him. Like, right away. Would you be willing—"

He smacked the box on the coffee table in the middle of the room, startling her. The thread of anger in his voice was crystal clear. "What is *with* you people? This isn't a Jacobs family decision. It's my decision."

His tone set her back. "But—"

"No." He jabbed his finger in her direction. "No, Mandy. I am packing. I am selling. I am going to Brazil and then back to Chicago. And I'm not changing my mind. You won't change it. Seth won't change it. And neither will Travis."

So much for gentle. So much for reasonable. "You're a stubborn fool."

"You're not the first one to notice."

She came around the end of the pile of boxes, staring straight into his eyes, lowering her voice. "You step over this cliff, Caleb, and we can't come back."

He went still for a very long moment, staring levelly back. "We, as in you and me?"

"As in your brother, your family, your heritage."

"I can live with that." It was obvious he was serious, completely serious. There was no way she'd get him to Helena.

Though she told herself it was a much less significant matter, she couldn't seem to stop herself from asking. "What about me and you?"

His expression didn't change. He leaned in and gave her a fleeting kiss. It wasn't exactly a cold kiss, but it didn't invite anything further. "Me and you are still going to Rio."

She tried not to let his words hurt her, but they did. So her voice was laced with sarcasm when she answered. "Is that an 'I'll call you sometime, babe'?"

"That's not what I said."

She bit her tongue. He was right. He'd been up front and honest all along the way. All he'd ever offered was Rio and New York City. If it wasn't enough for her, she should have spoken up a long time ago.

She knew she couldn't change Caleb. But she could still help Reed. Pretending everything was fine, she stretched up and kissed Caleb on the cheek. "Rio sounds good. I gotta go. The vet's working with the horses today, and he's, well, they'll need me down there."

"Sure," Caleb agreed, flipping the box over to reinforce the bottom with a strip of tape. "See you later."

"Later," she echoed, turning to leave.

Caleb worked for about an hour, reassuring himself he was doing exactly the right thing. He couldn't stay here. He growing frighteningly attached to Mandy, and it got worse every day.

But every time he turned around in this house, there was another picture, another memento, another annoying memory trigger, like the woodsy scent of the throw blanket his mother had knit for the back of the sofa.

It had taken a long time for Chicago to feel like home, and he wasn't about to lose that. Not for the sake of his family's land, and not to be near Mandy for a few more days.

Mandy. He blew out a breath. He hadn't wanted to fight with her. But she had to understand. There was no hope that he'd erase his childhood, nor would he ever come to terms with it. The best he could hope for was to leave it far, far behind. So he didn't have to think about it every day of his life.

Still, he shouldn't have taken it out on her.

She was entitled to her opinion. And she held that particular opinion only because she was a compassionate, generous, caring person. She couldn't stand to see anyone hurt or upset, and that included Reed. And what did she get from Caleb for her trouble? Anger and the cold shoulder.

He needed to apologize.

Silently acknowledging he'd been a jerk, he deserted the packing job and headed for his SUV. He rammed it into Drive and peeled out.

Down the ranch roadway, he took the corners fast, his back tires breaking loose on the gravel ranch road. Then he sped along the main valley road to the arched gateway to the Jacobses' ranch. It was five minutes up the driveway, and then he was pulling up front of the house.

He knocked once, then let himself in to find Travis and Seth at the table, digging into steaks.

He glanced around. "Is Mandy upstairs?"

Seth shook his head. "You didn't talk to her before she left?"

"Left?"

Mandy sure hadn't said anything to Caleb about leaving.

"For Helena," said Travis. "I thought you must have gone with her, taken your jet."

Caleb walked farther into the room, his hands going to his hips. "She didn't say anything to me."

Seth glanced at his watch. "She said she'd call us when she landed at the airport. You hungry?"

No, Caleb wasn't hungry.

Mandy was gone. She'd left after their fight. What did that mean? Was she going to pull the same stunt as Reed and disappear when things didn't go her way?

What the hell was the matter with her?

He struggled to keep the anger from his voice. "Did she say where she was going in Helena?"

"Nope," said Travis, obviously unconcerned. Sure, *now* he didn't worry about his sister.

"Do you have any business interests there, suppliers?" Caleb pressed.

"Nothing," said Seth.

"She did have a college friend who was from there," Travis offered. "I don't know her name or anything."

"But it was a woman?"

Seth gave him a confused look.

Travis scoffed out an amused laugh.

Caleb headed for the door. "If you hear anything, send me a text."

"Will do," said Travis.

"Where you going?" Seth called out behind him.

"Helena," Caleb answered. "Let me know if you hear from Mandy."

"What on earth is going—" Seth's voice abruptly disappeared as Caleb shut the front door.

Caleb stomped his way back to the SUV. It seemed impossible that Mandy had a sudden desire to visit an old friend. Unless the old friend was in trouble. But, if that was the case, she should have told him. He could have lent her his jet to get to Helena.

Unless it was Mandy going to see her old friend for solace. Could she be that angry with him? She'd said yes to Rio. That was a good sign, right?

He started the vehicle and pulled it into gear, wheeling through the roundabout and back out the driveway. He reached for his phone and dialed her cell with his thumb.

He got voice mail, and didn't really care to leave a message.

By the time he hit the main road, his confusion had turned to anger. No matter what her reason for leaving, the least she could have done was call him, or send him a text if she was too mad for a civil conversation. She'd let her brothers know where she was headed. Well, at least the rudimentary details. A motel name would have been nice.

Coming up on the highway, he dialed the pilot. It would be late before he got to Lyndon, but the airport was equipped for after-dark takeoffs, and they could land in Helena on instruments.

Having managed to get a flight from Lyndon to Denver last night, then a flight into Helena this morning, Mandy had camped out in the restaurant of the Bearberry Inn for over two hours. It was three in the afternoon, but there was still no sign of Reed.

The front desk had refused to give out his room number, and she didn't want to call him, for fear he'd refuse to see her. She'd chosen a table in a back corner where she could watch both the restaurant and the front desk across the lobby without being easily seen.

She figured her last hope was to get him to come back to Lyndon Valley right away. If she did it quickly, there was a chance Caleb would still be there. If not, she was certain he'd finish packing and leave for Sao Paulo, sale or no sale. But if she could make it in time, Caleb, the stubborn fool, would be forced to have a conversation with his brother.

Just as Mandy was ordering her third cup of coffee, her patience was rewarded. She caught a glimpse of Reed's profile, his tall, sturdy frame, striding across the lobby toward the bank of elevators. Quickly canceling her order, she tossed some money on the table and jumped up, grabbing her shoulder bag and slinging it over her blazer.

She trotted out of the restaurant, determined to catch him. A few feet away, she called out his name.

He turned and stared at her in obvious shock.

"Mandy?" He glanced around the expansive lobby. "What on earth are you doing here?"

"I'm looking for you." She immediately hugged him, and he hugged her back. But her joy at finding him turned almost instantly to frustration. Drawing back, she socked him in the shoulder. "What is the matter with you?"

"Me? I'm not the one who appeared out of nowhere."

"Do you have any idea how worried I've been?"

A couple of guests gave them curious glances as they walked past, causing Reed to take Mandy's arm and lead her toward a glass door that led to the hotel courtyard.

"Why would you worry?" he asked. "What are you doing in Helena? How on earth did you know I was here?"

They made it outside to the relative privacy of an interior courtyard with a table-dotted patio, a manicured, green lawn, towering trees and colorful, raised brick gardens.

"I didn't know if you'd been kidnapped, shanghaied, injured, arrested or mugged."

"Kidnapped? You've got to be kidding me. Like somebody's going to hold me for ransom."

"You know what I mean."

"I'm fine. Nobody's going to mug me, Mandy. At night, on the darkened streets? *I'm* the guy people are afraid of."

"I can't believe you didn't call me."

"I can't believe you were worried."

"Why didn't you at least send me a text?"

"Because I didn't want anyone to know where I was."

She jabbed her thumb against her chest, voice going up. "*I'm* not anyone."

"You'd have told your brothers."

"I would not."

He gave her a look of disbelief.

Okay, maybe she would have, if they'd asked. She wasn't the world's best liar.

He glanced around the courtyard. "Do you want to sit down?"

"Sure," she agreed, taking a deep breath. She'd found him. Whatever else happened, at least she'd found him.

He guided her to one of the small tables, pulling out her chair before taking the seat across from her. "You shouldn't have come."

Okay. Now was the time to tread carefully. She had to make Reed want to come back to the ranch and be willing to speak to Caleb. Otherwise, she'd never get him to budge.

She struggled with where to start.

"Mandy?" he prompted.

"Why Helena?" she asked, giving him a smile, intending to ease her way in, telling herself to relax and act as though everything was normal.

"Besides the fishing? It's good ranch country, Mandy. I've had a job offer here."

"Of course you've had a job offer. You could probably have a thousand job offers if you wanted them."

He allowed himself a smile. "You're such an optimist."

"I am," she agreed. "And I have faith in you. You're an amazing person, Reed, a phenomenal person—"

"You know, don't you?"

She played dumb. "Know what?"

"About the will." He waited.

"Fine," she conceded. "I know about the will."

"How?"

She straightened in her chair, leaning over the round metal-framed, glass-topped table. "Can I start by saying I understand that you're upset."

"You can if you want. But that doesn't tell me anything. And it only puts off whatever it is you're dancing around here."

"It was a mistake to leave, Reed."

He scoffed out a laugh.

"You don't understand what's going—"

"How do you know about the will?"

"I want you to come back."

"You do, do you?"

"I do."

"You don't know what you're asking."

She reached across the table for his big hand. "I know exactly what I'm asking. If you'll just—"

"How did you find out about the will, Mandy?"

She closed her eyes for a brief second. "Fine. Caleb told me."

Reed gave a snort of derision, pulling his hand back. "Didn't take him long."

"Didn't take me long at all," came another deep, masculine voice.

Mandy's heart all but stopped.

She turned her head. "Caleb," she breathed.

"Was this stunt part of some grand plan?" he asked her, not even acknowledging his brother.

Reed came to his feet.

"I found Reed," she stated the unnecessary. "That's what I wanted to tell you—"

"You hoped I'd follow you?" Caleb demanded.

She was confused by his statement. "Follow—"

He gave a cold laugh. "Of course you knew I'd follow you. How could I not follow you?"

"What?" she couldn't help asking, giving a small shake of her head. If she'd wanted him to follow her, she'd have told him where she was going.

"That's what this was all about, all along." His blue gaze crackled into hers. "You realized you couldn't get me to talk to him by being honest."

What? No. Wait a minute.

Reed stepped forward. "Nobody invited you to join us."

Mandy whirled her gaze. "Reed, no. Let him explain."

Caleb sized up his brother. "What the hell is the matter with you?"

Reed's voice was stone cold. "Somebody stole my ranch."

"You didn't stay to defend it."

"Right. Like I'm going to hang around under those circumstances."

"You hung in there with Wilton."

Reed clenched his jaw down tight, and the edges of his mouth turned white. "Shut up."

"I don't think I will."

Mandy was starting to panic. She stepped between the two angry men. "Reed. Listen to me. He's giving it back. Caleb's giving you back the ranch."

"I'm selling the ranch," Caleb countered.

She ignored him and continued talking to Reed, her words spilling out fast. "That's how I found out about the will. Caleb came to Colorado to give it back to you."

"It doesn't matter," said Reed.

"How can it not matter?" she practically wailed.

"I don't want it," he spat.

"That's ridiculous," said Mandy. Her gaze took in both of them. "Come on, you two, quit being such—"

"You heard him," said Caleb.

She rounded on Caleb. "Of *course* he wants it back."

"Are you reading his mind?"

"I'm using logic and reason." Her expression of frustration took in both of them. "Something that seems to be in ridiculously short supply in this conversation."

Caleb angled his body toward Mandy, arms still by his sides, hands curled into fists. "You heard him. He said no."

"He'll change his mind."

"No, he won't." Caleb's gaze flicked to Reed. "He's as stubborn as a mule."

"At least I don't cut and run," Reed returned.

Caleb glared at his brother. "Back off."

"That's your specialty," said Reed. "And it's exactly what you're doing right now."

"I'm getting rid of an albatross that's been around our necks our entire lives."

"Around your neck?" Reed countered, squaring his shoulders, voice getting louder. "*Your* neck."

Caleb ignored the outburst. "I'll send you a check."

"Don't bother."

Mandy's stomach had turned to churning concrete. "Please, don't fight."

"Quit it," Caleb told her.

"Don't you yell at Mandy." Reed inched closer to his brother, shoulders squared, eyes hard as flints.

For a horrible moment, she thought they might come to blows.

"I'm not yelling at Mandy." When Caleb glanced back down at her, his expression had softened. "I'm not angry with you, Mandy. I swear I'm not. But you have your answer. He doesn't want the ranch."

"He does," she put in weakly.

"Are you ready to go home now?" Caleb asked.

Mandy shook her head. "I'm not going home. I just got here. Reed and I haven't even had a chance to—"

Caleb's voice went dark again, suspicion clouding his eyes. "To what?"

For a second, she thought she must have misunderstood. But his expression was transparent as usual. He actually thought there was something between her and Reed.

Mandy threw up her hands. "You can't possibly think that."

After all they'd been through? Could Caleb honestly think that? He'd asked her three times, and she'd told him over and over that they were just friends.

"So, you're staying here with him?" Caleb pressed.

She mustered her courage. Fine. If he wanted to think that, let him think that. "Yes, I am. I'm staying here with Reed."

Caleb's voice went quiet. "Is that what this was all about?"

She didn't understand the question.

"All along? Your plan was to make me like you, worm your way in until I can't—"

"Are you *kidding me?*" she all but shouted.

Did he seriously think she'd sleep with him to get him to stay? To not sell the ranch? Had he gone stark, raving mad?

He stared at her for a long minute. "Then, prove it. Prove you were being honest about your feelings all along."

What was he asking?

"Him or me, Mandy. What's it going to be?"

She froze.

Caleb couldn't ask this of her. She wasn't leaving Reed. If she did, Reed would disappear, and this time they wouldn't find him.

"So, it's him." Caleb's voice was completely devoid of emotion.

She hated his expression, hated his tone, hated that he was putting her in this impossible position. Under these circumstances, there was only one answer.

"Yes," she ground out. "It's him."

Caleb was silent, the breeze wafting, birds chirping in the trees, faint traffic noise from the other side of the building.

Finally, he gave her a curt nod, turned abruptly and stomped back into the hotel lobby.

She and Reed said nothing, simply staring at each other.

"I didn't mean for it to go this way," Mandy offered in a small voice, trying desperately not to picture Caleb getting in a cab or maybe a rental car in front of the hotel, making his way back to the airport, flying to Lyndon, packing up the ranch, maybe meeting with another buyer and never seeing her again.

Reed sat back down at the table, his expression implacable. "Did you honestly think putting yourself in the middle would help?"

Her chest tightened, and her throat started to close. "I…" She was at a loss for words. She'd thought it would help. She'd hoped it would help.

"Mandy, all you did was give us something more to fight about." Reed's words pierced her heart.

"I didn't mean…" She'd thought it would work. She'd honestly thought once they saw each other, they'd realize they were still brothers, that they still loved each other, and they'd reconcile.

But now she was in the middle, and Caleb was furious with her. He thought there was actually a chance that she was romantically interested in Reed. And he was gone. Likely gone for good.

Her voice began to shake. "I was only trying to help."

Reed nodded, and his fingers drummed on the glass top of the table. "I know. You can't help being you."

She drew back in confusion.

His expression eased. "We should get you a cape and a mask, Mandy. Swooping in, solving the problems of the world."

"I'm not…" But then Abigail's words came back to haunt her. Was this what she'd tried to warn Mandy about? *Was* Mandy substituting Reed for her own family? *Had* she become way too invested in Reed and Caleb's relationship?

Had she made a colossal mistake that was going to hurt them all?

Reed's dark eyes watched her closely while she struggled to bring her emotions back under control.

"Mandy?" he asked softly, a sad, ghost of a smile growing on his face. "How long have you been in love with Caleb?"

Mandy's stomach dove into a freefall. *"What?"* she rasped. "I didn't… I'm not… It isn't…" She could feel her face heat to flaming.

Reed cocked his head and waited.

She couldn't explain.

She wouldn't explain.

She didn't have to explain.

"I only slept with him," she blurted out.

Reed's lips formed a silent whistle. "And you just forced him to walk away and leave you with me? Oh, Mandy."

"I'm not in love with him," she managed. Falling in love with Caleb would be the most foolish move in the world. "It was a fling, a lark. It was nothing."

Reed reached across the table and took her hand in his. It was big, strong, callused. "You shouldn't have come here."

"I know that now," she admitted. She should have listened to her big sister. She should have minded her own business. Maybe if she had, Reed and Caleb would have found their way back without her.

"Go to the airport," Reed advised. "Go to Caleb right now."

But Mandy vigorously shook her head.

It was far too late for her to go to Caleb. And it wasn't what Reed thought. Caleb never offered her anything more than a plan for a fling in Rio. And even that was over now. She was pushing Caleb right out of her heart. Forever.

# Twelve

Caleb's jet took off from the Sao Paulo airport, heading north-west into clear skies. The past two days had been an exercise in frustration, but with Danielle's help, he'd defeated the Brazilian banking system's red tape, and they were ready to start shipping raw materials next week.

They had a plant manager in place who spoke very good English. Their accounting and computer systems were set up, and they'd approved the hiring of three foremen who were now looking for local skilled trade workers.

"I'm going to set up a meeting with Sales and Accounting for Friday," said Danielle, punching a message into her PDA. "We have to watch the gross sales ceiling for the first six months, and I want everybody to understand the parameters."

"I'm not sure about Friday," said Caleb. He had to give final instructions to the moving company. The sooner the better as far as he was concerned.

"Why not?"

"I need to go to Colorado."

She whirled her head in his direction. "Wait a minute. *What?*"

"The outstanding water rights issue is playing havoc with property values, but I told the broker to take any deal. I want this done."

"But, your brother."

"What about my brother?"

"We found him. He's back. Sign the damn thing over to him and forget about it."

Caleb wasn't sure he'd heard right. "What do you mean *we* found him?"

Danielle straightened, her tone completely unapologetic. "Mandy wasn't going to get anywhere on her own, so I had Enrico make a few calls."

"Enrico found Reed?"

"Yes."

"And you didn't think you should run this by me?"

"I didn't charge you anything. Besides, you were off in la la land, reconnecting with your roots and ignoring your own best interests."

Caleb coughed and shifted in his airplane seat. "Okay, setting aside for a second that you went behind my back, Reed doesn't want the ranch. He turned it down."

"So? Put it in his name, anyway. I can have something drafted by the time we land in Chicago."

"I'm selling it," Caleb stated flatly, his frustration growing by the second.

"That's a ridiculous waste of your time. We need you in your office, with your head in the game, not out on the range, chasing—"

"Since when is my life managed by consensus?"

"Since you stopped managing it for yourself."

"I take a couple of weeks, a couple of weeks to visit my hometown."

"Since when could you care less about your hometown?"

Caleb didn't care about his hometown. Okay, maybe he did.

A little. It was fun hanging out with Travis again. And Seth was a great guy. And Mandy. He sucked in a breath. Mandy was going to be impossible to forget.

He'd tried to tell himself she'd lied about her feelings for him. But then he'd been forced to admit, she was. He'd been an absolute ass to accuse her of sleeping with him to get him to give Reed back the ranch. She'd never do that.

He'd even tossed the idea of seeing her again back and forth in his brain about a thousand times. Assuming that she'd be willing.

"Is it Mandy?" Danielle asked, startling him from his thoughts.

"Mandy what?"

"Are you going back to see Mandy?"

Caleb pressed his head hard against the high-backed seat. He had no idea how to answer that question. Mandy and the ranch were two completely different issues, but somehow they'd gotten all tangled up into one.

"If you've got a thing for her, you might as well go get it over with."

Caleb didn't have a thing for Mandy. Okay, well, he definitely had a thing for her. But the way Danielle put it, it sounded so crass. "How is this any of your business?"

"It's not. But we have this lawyer-client confidentiality thing going on, so I feel like I can be honest."

"Go be honest with someone else."

"Caleb." Her voice took on a tone of exaggerated patience, and she folded her hands in her lap. "We agreed that the solution was to give your brother back the ranch. I've handed it to you on a silver platter. You need to take it."

"I'm selling it," he repeated. He held the trump card, because there was nothing she could do to change his mind.

"Why?"

"Because he doesn't want it, and he's better off without it."

"So, you're doing this for him."

"Right."

"Yet, you haven't spoken to him in ten years."

"I spoke to him the other day." And it had been a surreal experience.

The person he'd fought with in Helena had been Reed, only not Reed. The new Reed was a twenty-seven-year-old man, broader and stronger than he'd been as a teenager, self-confident, self-assured. Part of Caleb had wanted to sit down and talk things over with him. And part of Caleb had wanted to throw Mandy over his shoulder and carry her away.

Mandy had said they were just friends. Yet, she stayed behind with Reed.

No, Caleb wasn't going to go there. Mandy told him she wasn't romantically involved with Reed, and he was going to believe her. The remaining question was whether she was interested in being romantically involved with Caleb.

Three days ago, he might have said maybe. Today, he'd definitely say no. But what if he went back? What if he treated her properly this time? Was there a chance of something between them?

He'd regretted walking away from her the second his feet hit the pavement in Helena. And he'd regretted it every minute since.

"I'm going to Colorado," he told Danielle with determination.

She shook her head and leaned back in her seat. "I can't save you from yourself, Caleb."

Sitting at his office desk, hitting send on a final email before he headed to the Chicago airport, Caleb heard someone enter through the open door.

He didn't look up. "Tell the driver I'll be ten more minutes."

"You have a driver?" came a deep, male voice.

Caleb turned sharply, swiveling his high-backed, leather chair to face the doorway.

Reed's large frame nearly filled the entrance. His boots added an inch to his six-foot-three-inch frame, and his midnight-black, Western-cut shirt stretched across his broad shoulders. In the office, he looked even more imposing than he had outside the hotel.

Caleb instantly came to his feet.

Reed didn't look angry, exactly. But he didn't look happy, either.

"What are you doing in Chicago?" was the only thing Caleb could think to say. He couldn't help but wonder if Mandy was with him.

"Wanted to talk to you," said Reed, taking a few paces into the office.

"Okay," Caleb offered warily. He'd been feeling off-kilter since he last saw Mandy, and his emotions continued to do crazy things to his logic. He really wasn't in the mood for a fight.

Reed stepped up to the desk. "Don't sell the ranch."

Caleb's jaw went lax.

"It's mine," said Reed.

Caleb didn't disagree with that. Morally and ethically, the ranch belonged to Reed.

"And I want it," Reed finished.

"You want it?" Something akin to joy came to life inside Caleb. Which was silly. The ranch wasn't good for Reed.

"Yes."

"Just like that." Caleb snapped his fingers.

Reed's dark eyes went hard. "No. Not just like that. Just like ten years of sweat and blood and hell."

"I was going to give you the money."

"I don't want the money. I want the land. My land. Our mother's land."

Caleb's heart gave an involuntary squeeze inside his chest.

"Did you forget her great-grandmother was born at Rock Creek?" asked Reed, voice crackling hard. "In that tiny falling-down house next to the waterfall?"

Of course Caleb hadn't forgotten. His mother had told them that story a hundred times.

"And her grandfather, her father. They're all buried on the hill, Caleb. You going to sell off our ancestors' bones?"

"You going to live with the memory of *him?*" Caleb blurted out.

"You going to let him defeat us?" Reed squared his shoulders. "He was who he was, Caleb."

"He killed her."

"I know. Do you think I don't know? And I can't bring her back." Reed's voice was shaking with emotion. "But do you know what I can do? What I'm going to do?"

Caleb was too stunned by the stark pain on his brother's face to even attempt an answer.

"I'm going to have her grandchildren. I'm going to find a nice girl, who loves Lyndon Valley, and I'm going to give her babies, and my first daughter will be named Sasha, and she will be loved, and she will be happy, and I will never, ever, *ever* let anyone hurt her."

Caleb's chest nearly caved in, while his heart stood still.

"Are you going to stand in my way?" Reed demanded, bringing his fist down on the desktop.

"No," Caleb managed through a dry throat.

"Good." Reed abruptly sat down and leaned back, crossing one boot over the opposite knee.

Caleb slumped in his chair. "Why didn't you say all that in the first place?"

"I've said it now."

"You're going to find a nice girl?" Caleb couldn't help but ask.

Reed nodded. "I am. A ranch girl. Someone like Mandy."

Caleb's spine went stiff, and his hands curled into fists.

Reed chuckled, obviously observing the involuntary reaction. "But not Mandy. Mandy's yours."

"No, she's not."

"Yeah. She is." Reed's tone was gruff, his eyes watchful. "Unless you're going to cut and run on her, too."

"I've never—"

"She's in love with you, Caleb. Not that you deserve her."

Reed had it all wrong.

"No, she's not. She's…" Caleb wasn't sure how to describe it. "Well, ticked off at me for one thing."

"Because you were such a jerk in Helena?"

"So were you."

Reed shrugged. "She'll forgive me in the blink of an eye, once I tell her I'm moving back."

"I'll sign it over to you today," Caleb offered. Now that the decision was made, he felt as if a weight had been lifted from his shoulders.

"What about Mandy?"

"That's between me and Mandy."

Caleb's brain was going off in about a million directions. Was it possible that she loved him? Had she told Reed she loved him? What business did she have loving him? She was a Lyndon Valley woman, and he was a Chicago man. How was that going to work?

"You slept with her, right?"

"None of your damn business."

"Do you think a woman like Mandy would sleep with just anyone?"

Of course Caleb didn't think she'd do that. And he couldn't help remembering how it felt to have her sleeping in his arms, the taste of her lips, the satin of her skin. And he wanted to feel it all again, so very, very badly.

"I thought you were going to take my head off in Helena." Reed chuckled low. "She had no idea what she did, by the way, telling you she was staying with me."

Caleb remembered that moment, when she had a choice and she hadn't picked him. He never wanted to feel that gut-wrenching anguish again. Mandy belonged with him. Not with Reed and not with any other man. Him, and him alone.

"You should go talk to her," Reed suggested.

"I *was* going to talk to her. Good grief, can I make at least one decision on my own?"

"Apparently not a good one. When were you going?"

Caleb pasted Reed with a mulish glare. "The jet's warming up on the tarmac."

"You have a jet?"

"Yes."

"Bring a ring."

Caleb drew back. "Excuse me?"

"You better bring a ring. You've been a jerk, and you need to apologize so she'll forgive you. And that whole thing's going to go a whole lot smoother with you on one knee."

"You haven't spoken to me in ten years, and you come back and the first thing you do is tell me who I should marry?"

"Second thing, technically," said Reed.

"Where do you get your nerve?"

"I'm bigger than you. I'm stronger than you. And it's not me who wants you to propose."

Caleb scoffed out a laugh at that. "It's not?"

"No. It's you."

Caleb stared at Reed, suddenly seeing past everything to the brother that he'd loved, still loved. Because, despite everything that had happened between them, it was still the same Reed. And he was still smart and, in this case, he was also right.

Caleb grinned. "You want to catch a ride back to Lyndon?"

Mandy had sworn to herself she wouldn't wallow in self-pity. She wouldn't pine away for Caleb, and she wouldn't let herself get involved any further in the brothers' conflict. She was going cold turkey.

Abigail was right. It was none of Mandy's business. They were grown men, and she had to let it go and let them work it out for themselves. Or not.

When it came down to it, Travis was right, too. Getting involved with Caleb had brought her nothing but heartache. What had she been thinking? That she could spend days and nights with a smart, compelling, exciting, successful man, and her heart wouldn't become involved.

She ran a curry comb over Ryder's haunch, dragging the dust out of the gelding's coat.

It was ironic, really. She'd spent the better part of her life giving advice out to people. She could be quite obnoxiously meddlesome at times. But she was always so certain she was right. She harped on people to take her advice, since she usually had some distance from the problem and a better perspective than the person who was in the thick of it. Yet, when people who loved her gave her perfectly reasonable, logical, realistic advice, she blew them off and did it her own way.

It served her right.

And she was now exactly where she deserved to be, losing Reed as her dear friend and neighbor and desperately missing Caleb. Reed had been right. She loved Caleb. She was madly, desperately in love with a man who'd never again give her the time of day.

If she closed her eyes, she could still feel his arms around her.

"Mandy?" his voice was so real, it startled her.

Her eyes flew open, and she blinked in complete astonishment. "Caleb?"

How could he be standing in her barn?

But he was.

She blinked again.

He *was*.

"Hello, Mandy." His tone was gentle. He was wearing a pair of worn blue jeans and a soft flannel shirt, looking completely at home as he slowly walked toward her.

She gripped the top rail of the stall with her leather-gloved hand. "What are you doing here?" she managed.

A slow smile grew on his face as he drew closer under the bright, hanging fluorescent lights. "You want to go to Rio?"

She watched his expression closely. "Is that a joke?"

"I'm completely serious."

"No. I am not going to Rio with you." She meant what she said. She was completely done with the Terrells.

He came to a halt a few feet away from her. "You said you would."

"That was before."

"Before what?"

Before her plan to fix everything had crashed and burned around her ears. Before she'd learned the truth about herself. Before she'd fallen in love with him and opened herself up to a world of hurt.

"Before we fought," she said instead.

"We didn't fight."

She shot him with a look of disbelief.

"Okay," he agreed. "We fought. And I'm sorry. I know you were just trying to help."

She shook her head, rubbing her palms across her cheeks and into her hair, trying to erase the memories. "I meddle. I know I meddle. And *I'm* the one who's sorry."

"I forgive you. Now, come to Rio."

"No."

"Come to Rio and marry me."

"N— *What?*"

"I thought…" He moved slowly closer, carefully, as if he was afraid to spook her. "I thought we could fly to Rio, get a manicure, have a blender drink and you could marry me."

There was a roaring inside her brain while she tried to make sense of his words. "Caleb, what are you trying to—"

He reached out and took her hands. "I'm trying to say that I love you, Mandy. And I like it when you meddle. I especially like it when you meddle with me."

Her heart paused, then thudded forcefully back to life, singing through her chest.

He loved her? He *loved* her?

Exhilaration burst through her.

She let out an involuntary squeal and launched herself into his arms. He hugged her tight, lifting her off the ground and spinning her around.

"Why? How?" she couldn't help but ask, voice muffled in the crook of his neck. She didn't expect this, didn't deserve this.

"I don't know why, but how? Mostly I just think about how beautiful you are, how sexy you are, how smart and caring and funny." He drew back and kissed her mouth. His lips were warm, soft, delicious and tender.

When he finally drew back and lowered her to her feet, she gazed up into his eyes. "I love you, too, Caleb. So very much."

"So, you'll come to Rio?"

"You know my family won't let you marry me in Rio."

"They can come along. I have a pretty big plane."

"We have to wait until my dad gets better."

"Of course we do," he agreed, kissing her all over again.

He captured both of her hands in his. His blue eyes danced under the lights. "You by any chance interested in a ring?" he asked.

She swallowed, unable to find her voice.

He tapped his shirt pocket, and she made out a telltale square bulge.

Joy flooded her. "You brought a ring to this engagement?"

"I did. A diamond."

Her lips broke into a grin. "Let's see it."

He reached into his pocket and extracted a small, white leather box. "It was Reed's idea."

"You talked to Reed?"

"He's inside with your brothers."

"Reed is *here?*" She couldn't believe it.

"Any chance we can focus on the ring right now?" Caleb popped open the spring-loaded top.

A beautiful, square-cut diamond solitaire in yellow gold was nestled against deep purple velvet. The sight took her breath away.

He leaned in and spoke in a husky whisper. "Do I know how to do a proposal or what?"

"That's one gorgeous ring."

"You like it?"

"I love it."

"Because we can exchange it if you want."

"Are you kidding? What else could I possibly want in a ring?"

Using his blunt fingers, he extracted it from the box.

She held out her left hand, and he smoothly pushed it onto her ring finger. It fit. She held her hand at arms length, flexing her wrist and watching the sparkle.

"This should shut Travis up," she mused.

"Yes." Caleb kissed her finger with the ring. "Because that was my secret plan. I figured, you know, if you'd marry me, it would be a bonus. But what I was really looking to do was get your brother off my back."

"We're really going to do this? You and me? Us?" Both her brain and her emotions were operating on overload. Caleb had come back to Lyndon Valley. He loved her. They were staying together. It defied imagination.

"Just as soon as you'll let me."

Uncertainty suddenly overtook her. "But, what then? Where do we go? Where do we live? My family's here. You're there."

"Well, Reed will be back living at his ranch."

She froze. "Seriously?"

Caleb nodded.

"He's coming home?"

"He's already home."

She hugged Caleb tight, and his arms went fully around her. "Part time here," he said. "Part time in Chicago. We made it work for two weeks. I'm sure we can make it work for the rest of our lives."

Mandy sighed and burrowed herself in his chest. "For the rest of our lives."

Once again, Caleb couldn't seem to bring himself to let go of Mandy.

Back inside the ranch house, her brothers, Abigail and Reed all gathered around them, admiring her ring, hugging and kiss-

ing and laughing their congratulations. When they eventually
gave way, Abigail went to the kitchen to find a bottle of champagne.

Caleb lowered himself into a leather armchair, and drew
Mandy down into his lap, settling her against his shoulder,
holding her hand and toying with the engagement ring on her
finger.

His brother shot him a knowing grin, and Caleb smiled
back, marveling at how the years had melted away. On the
airplane and later in the car, he and Reed had talked. They'd
talked about their years as children and teenagers, what had
happened to each of them after Caleb had left for Chicago and
Reed's plans for the future.

Seth retrieved six champagne glasses from the china cabinet, setting them out on the dining-room table. "So, Caleb. Are
you moving back here, or are you taking our sister away?"

"Both," said Caleb, casting a long glance at Mandy's profile.
"We'll have to play it by ear to start. I'm hoping Reed won't
mind if we stay at his place while we're in the valley."

"Welcome anytime," said Reed.

"Seriously?" Mandy asked in obvious surprise. "You're
going to stay at your ranch?"

"Seriously," Caleb told her. "A very wise woman once told
me I needed to change my perception of it."

He leaned in close to her ear. "I figure we'll need to make
love in every room in the house."

She whispered back. "Not when Reed's around."

"What are you two whispering about?" asked Abigail as she
appeared with a bottle of champagne.

"I'm sure you don't want to know," Travis sang, lifting the
bottle from his sister's hands and peeling off the foil.

"I've been thinking," Caleb said to Reed, framing up an
idea in his mind. "It's not really fair for Mandy and I to set up
a permanent place in your house."

Reed frowned at him. "Why not?"

"I think we should be partners."

His brother shrugged. "Keep half of it if you want. But you're on the hook for the years we have a loss."

Caleb shook his head. "The ranch is yours. Danielle's already drafted up the papers. But I'll buy half of it back from you."

Reed scoffed out a laugh. "Right."

The champagne cork popped, and Abby laughed as the foam poured over Travis's hand.

"It's been recently appraised," Caleb noted. "So there'll be no trouble establishing a price."

Reed stared levelly across at him. "You think you're going to give me fifteen million dollars?"

"Fourteen five, actually. I hear the water rights are screwing with land values."

Abigail and Travis began handing around the full glasses.

"I'd take the offer," Seth told Reed.

"Don't be ridiculous," Reed countered.

"I'd play hardball if I was you," said Abigail. "Where's he going to find another ranch with such terrific neighbors?"

"Play hardball," Mandy agreed with her sister. She bopped the side of her head against Caleb's chest. "Give him the fifteen."

Then she sat up straighter and accepted a glass of champagne from her sister.

Travis handed one to Reed.

Reed brandished his own glass like a weapon. "I'm not taking any money for the ranch. And that's final."

"Mandy," Caleb intoned.

"Yes?" she answered, twisting her head to look at him.

"Please meddle."

She grinned, leaned in and gave him a very satisfying kiss on the lips. "Whatever you say, darling."

Caleb crooked his head to one side to paste Reed with a challenging look. "She's my secret weapon."

Seth raised his glass. "Congratulations, Caleb. You are the luckiest man in the world."

"Agreed," Caleb breathed.

Reed spoke up. "To the Jacobs and the Terrells. A new family."

"Here, here," everyone agreed, clinking glasses all around, then taking a drink.

"To my beautiful bride," Caleb whispered, gently touching his glass to Mandy's.

Her green eyes glowed with obvious joy. "Do you really want me to convince Reed to take the money?"

"Absolutely. Go get him, tiger."

\* \* \* \* \*

## COLORADO CATTLE BARONS:
**From the mountains to the boardroom, these men have everything under control—except their hearts.**

# "I'm not living under a rock, Katrina."

"I never thought you were."

He swung his leg over the wide seat of the ATV. He wasn't insulted. He couldn't care less what she thought of his simple habits.

Truth was, he didn't know why she'd struck a nerve. Maybe it was because she pointed out the vast differences between them, and how far she was out of his league. Not that it mattered, he ruthlessly reminded himself.

No matter how sexy Miss Katrina Jacobs might appear, he was keeping his hands and his thoughts to himself. His life was complicated enough.

Dear Reader,

Welcome to the second book of the COLORADO CATTLE BARONS series from Desire. With a burly, tough cowboy and an elegant ballerina, shuttling from Colorado cattle country all the way to downtown Manhattan, this story explores the themes of "opposites attract" and "a fish out of water."

In book two of the series, cattleman Reed Terrell experiences a financial windfall following the death of his abusive father. He's reunited with his beautiful, refined former neighbor Katrina Jacobs, who's battling underhanded elements in the New York City dance world. When Reed's defensive instincts kick in, he finds himself falling in love.

I hope you enjoy *A Cowboy in Manhattan*. And I hope you'll look for Katrina's sister Abigail, along with some of the other residents of Lyndon Valley, Colorado, in future books featuring the Colorado Cattle Barons. I'd love to hear from you, so please feel free to drop me a line through my website, barbaradunlop.com.

*Barbara Dunlop*

# A COWBOY
# IN MANHATTAN

BY
BARBARA DUNLOP

MILLS & BOON

Published in Great Britain 2012
by Mills & Boon, an imprint of Harlequin (UK) Limited,
Eton House, 18-24 Paradise Road, Richmond, Surrey TW9 1SR

© Barbara Dunlop 2012

ISBN: 978 0 263 89186 7
ebook ISBN: 978 1 408 97771 2

51-0612

Harlequin (UK) policy is to use papers that are natural, renewable and recyclable products and made from wood grown in sustainable forests. The logging and manufacturing processes conform to the legal environmental regulations of the country of origin.

Printed and bound in Spain
by Blackprint CPI, Barcelona

**Barbara Dunlop** writes romantic stories while curled up in a log cabin in Canada's far north, where bears outnumber people and it snows six months of the year. Fortunately she has a brawny husband and two teenage children to haul firewood and clear the driveway while she sips cocoa and muses about her upcoming chapters. Barbara loves to hear from readers. You can contact her through her website, www.barbaradunlop.com.

For my husband

# One

As the pickup truck rocked to a halt in front of her family's Colorado cattle-ranch house, Katrina Jacobs started a mental countdown for her return to New York City. In the driver's seat, her brother Travis set the park brake and killed the engine. Katrina pulled up on the silver door handle, releasing the latch and watching the heavy passenger door yawn wide-open. Then she slid gingerly down onto the gravel driveway, catching most of her weight on her right foot to protect her injured left ankle.

A week, she calculated. Two weeks, max. By then she would have done her duty as a daughter and a sibling. Her ankle would be in shape. And she could get back to her ballet company in Manhattan.

Katrina hated Colorado.

Travis retrieved her small suitcase from the truck box. From experience, she knew it would be covered in stubborn grit, just like everything else in Lyndon Valley. She could vacuum it as much as she liked, but the dust would remain.

She wrenched the stiff door shut and started to pick her way across the uneven ground. She'd worn a pair of navy suede Gallean ankle boots, with narrow toes, low heels and kicky little copper chains at the ankles. They topped a pair of skinny black slacks and a shiny silver blouse.

She probably should have gone with sneakers, blue jeans and a cotton shirt, but she couldn't bring herself to traverse both JFK and Denver International looking like a hick. She wasn't often recognized in public, but when she was, people inevitably snapped a picture. Between cell phones and digital cameras, everyone in the world was potential paparazzi.

In his faded blue jeans, soft flannel shirt and scuffed cowboy boots, Travis fell into step beside her. "You want to take Mom and Dad's room?"

"No," she responded a little too quickly. "I'll bunk with Mandy."

Katrina hadn't lived at home full-time since she was ten years old. That summer, with the support of her rather eccentric aunt, she'd enrolled in New York's Upper Cavendar Dramatic Arts Academy, a performing-arts boarding school for girls. Maybe it was because she'd left home so young, but to this day, she was intimidated by her stern, forceful father. His booming voice made her stomach jump, and she was constantly on edge whenever he was around, worried that he'd ask an embarrassing question, mock her career or make note of the fact that she was an all-around inadequate ranch hand.

Her father was away from the ranch right now, having just moved to a rehab center in Houston with a leading-edge stroke recovery program. There he was impressing the staff with his rapid improvement from his recent stroke. Still, the last thing Katrina needed was to be surrounded by his possessions.

"He loves you," said Travis, his voice gentle but his confusion evident. "We all love you."

"And I love you back," she returned breezily, as she took the stairs to the front porch, passing through the door into the cool, dim interior of her childhood home. It was large by ranch house standards, with a big, rather utilitarian entryway. It opened up into a large living room, with banks of bright windows overlooking the river, a redbrick fireplace and enough comfy furniture to hold the family of five children and often guests. The kitchen was spacious and modern, with a giant pantry and a big deck that led down to a rolling lawn. And upstairs, there were six bedrooms, though one had been converted into an office after Katrina had left for good.

She knew love was compulsory. But the truth was, she had nothing in common with the rest of her family. They saw her as some spoiled, fragile princess who couldn't even ride a horse, never mind toss a hay bale or swing an ax straight.

For all that she was a principal dancer in a ballet company that regularly sold out New York City's Emperor's Theater, and that she'd made the cover of *Dance America* and the *Paris Arts Review*, in Colorado she'd never be anything but the girl who couldn't make it as a ranch hand.

"Hey there, Kitty-Kat."

Before she could respond to his greeting, her oldest brother, Seth, swooped her up in his strong arms.

"Hi, Seth." Her hug was slightly less enthusiastic. She was embarrassed by the childhood nickname her two brothers had bestowed upon her.

He let her go, and she stepped aside with a determined smile on her face. The smile faltered when she caught sight of a third man behind him. A taller, broader man, with penetrating gray eyes, a grim mouth and what she knew would be callused hands that could probably lift a taxi cab right off the asphalt. Though it had been a few years since she'd seen him, there was no mistaking their neighbor Reed Terrell.

He gave her the slightest of nods. "Katrina."

"Reed," she nodded in return, a fuzzy hitch coursing through her chest. It was trepidation, she told herself, a visceral reaction based mostly on his size and strength and overall rugged appearance.

Just then her sister Mandy burst down the stairs. "Katrina!" she cried, elbowing Seth out of the way and pulling Katrina into her arms.

Katrina hugged her sister tight in return. The next youngest after Katrina, Mandy was the one who had always tried to understand Katrina's passion for dance.

Mandy released her, scanning Katrina from head to toe. "You look *gorgeous.*"

Katrina knew it was a compliment. But when her family called her *pretty,* she couldn't seem to help hearing *useless. Pretty* didn't get you anywhere in Lyndon Valley.

"Thank you," she told her sister, self-consciously smoothing back the wisps of blond hair that had escaped from the twisted knot at the back of her head. Maybe she should have gone with sneakers and blue jeans after all, or perhaps skipped her makeup this morning. She could feel her family sizing her up and finding her frivolous.

"You remember Reed?" Mandy gestured to the big man standing silently in the background.

"Certainly," said Katrina.

Her gaze involuntarily met his again, and a shiver ran through her body, momentarily making her knees go weak. For a woman with a dancer's balance, it was a ridiculous reaction. What was the matter with her?

She tried to drag her gaze from his, but for some reason, it stuck like glue.

"I can't wait for you to meet Caleb again," Mandy rattled on in an excited voice. "You probably don't remember much about him, since he left Lyndon ten years ago."

"I know he's Reed's twin brother," said Katrina.

Reed's nostrils seemed to flare when she uttered his name. The men were fraternal twins, not identical. She remembered Caleb as a smaller, less intimidating version of his brother.

Good thing.

For Mandy's sake.

Katrina caught her sister's expression, and saw that her eyes were sparkling with unadulterated joy.

"Congratulations," she put in belatedly, giving Mandy another tight hug.

"We're thinking of a late-fall wedding. You know, after Dad is up and around again. You'll be a bridesmaid, of course."

"Of course," Katrina forced out a laugh. She wasn't wild about family togetherness. But Mandy loved it, and Katrina wouldn't do anything to mar her sister's big day.

"You'll look so beautiful in a bridesmaid dress."

"It's what I do best," Katrina joked, keeping the smile pasted on her face. For some reason, she darted a look at Reed and saw his eye-roll.

He obviously thought she was being conceited. Fine. Easy for him to judge. She was willing to bet not a single person in his entire life had ever called him useless. Around here, he'd be revered for his strength and his hard work. He didn't have to live with being pretty.

Not that he wasn't attractive. In fact, there was an appealing dignity to his craggy features. His chin might be overly square, and his nose slightly crooked, but his eyes were an intriguing, silver-flecked gray, and his full lips were—

Wait a minute. She gave herself an abrupt mental shake. What on earth was the matter with her? Reed was a tough, hulking, strong-willed cowboy. He could out-macho anyone in Lyndon Valley, and there was nothing even remotely appealing about that.

Since Reed Terrell was alive, conscious and male all at the same time, he had the hots for Mandy's sister Katrina. It didn't mean he had to act on it, and it sure didn't mean he'd succeed even if he tried. Everything about the woman said she was out of his league, from the wispy updo of her wheat-blond hair to her sexy boots, the clingy slacks and shimmering blouse in between.

When he'd met her earlier at the Jacobs ranch, her earrings had been dangling strands of gold, silver and diamonds, while a matching necklace glimmered against her dainty cleavage. She should have looked comically out of place on the ranch, but she didn't. She looked like a princess inspecting the commoners, someone to be revered and admired, then left untouched. Which was exactly what Reed intended to do.

Now he entered the foyer of his own family's ranch house,

shutting the door against the gathering dusk, another long day of work behind him. For years, Reed had lived in the spacious, two-story house with his exacting father. Though his father was dead, out of habit, Reed placed his hat on the third hook from the left and straightened the mat beneath his feet. There was a place for everything, and everything was always in its place in the Terrell household. His father had prized practicality, but also quality, so the hardwood floors were clear maple, the furniture was custom-made and the kitchen appliances were top-of-the-line, replaced every ten years.

The outbuildings that housed the cowboys and staff necessary to run the big ranch were also kept in tip-top shape, from the cookhouse to the bunkhouses to the barns and sheds. The line shacks were all getting older, but they were still kept clean and in good repair.

"Danielle wants to talk to you," his brother Caleb announced as he walked down the hallway from the kitchen at the back of the house, phone in hand.

"I don't have anything more to add."

Caleb frowned. "You can't let fifteen million dollars just sit in a bank account."

"You can always take it back," Reed responded, squaring his shoulders. He still thought it was ridiculous that his brother had paid him for half the family's ranch.

"Would you let me hand you half of Active Equipment for free?" Caleb referred to the company he'd spent the past ten years building in the Chicago area.

"Don't be ridiculous."

"Same difference." Caleb held out the phone. "Talk to her. She has some ideas."

Danielle Marin was Caleb's lawyer. Following the debacle of their late father's will, she'd drafted the papers that switched ownership of the Terrell ranch from Caleb to Reed. Then she'd worked out the financial transaction where Caleb bought half of it back.

Reed wasn't exactly grateful to her for helping to put him in his current financial position, but he had to admit, the woman seemed to know what she was doing.

He took the phone. "Hello?"

As usual, Danielle's tone was crisp, no-nonsense. "Hi, Reed. I was wondering if you'd had a chance to look over the package I emailed to you yesterday?" Then her voice became muffled as she obviously spoke to someone at her end of the line in Chicago.

"Not yet," he answered. He only opened his email about once a week. He didn't have a lot of technically inclined friends. Most of the people he knew still called on a landline or simply stopped by the ranch when they had something to say.

She sighed into the receiver. "You're losing both income and investment potential every day you wait."

"You've pointed that out."

"Can you give me some general parameters? Do you want to keep your investments in the country? Go international? Blue chips? Emerging markets?"

"I was thinking about buying a sports car," he drawled, impatient with having to worry about the damn money. There were real problems requiring real solutions right here on the ranch.

Her voice instantly perked up. "So, you're saying I should keep some ready cash for luxury purchases?"

"I was joking, Danielle. We don't have paved roads in Lyndon Valley."

"You could always drive it on the highway. What appeals to you? Lamborghini? Ferrari?"

"It was a *joke*."

"Stop joking."

It was Reed's turn to sigh. "Fine. Keep the money in the country." He at least knew he wanted that much.

"Right. So, maybe some blue chips? Or do you want to look at a percentage of a start-up? I can make some recommendations on sectors and states."

Reed didn't want to think about this right now. Quite frankly, all he wanted to do was to strip off his dusty clothes, take a hot shower, grill up a steak, and then picture Katrina's deep blue eyes for a while before he drifted off to sleep.

"I'll let you know," he told Danielle.

"Soon?"

"Yeah. Sure. Soon. See you." He handed the phone back to his brother.

"You're a pain in the ass, you know that?" Caleb pointed out as he put the phone back to his ear. Then his expression faltered. "No, not you, Danielle."

Reed chuckled at his brother's embarrassment, feeling better already.

He crossed through the living room, took the staircase to the second floor, took off his clothes and tossed them into the hamper before stepping into a steaming shower. As he rubbed in the spice-scented shampoo, he realized his hair was getting too long. He supposed he could find a few more reasons to make the drive into Lyndon and get it cut while he was there, or he could buzz it short with his razor again. Though the last time he'd done that, Mandy had laughed at him for days.

Thoughts of Mandy took him to thoughts of Katrina. He switched the water to cold, finishing off with a brisk rinse before stepping out of the deep tub.

He changed into clean jeans and pulled a worn gray T-shirt over his head, running his fingers through his damp hair. He left his feet bare, padding down to the kitchen. The barbecue was out back on the deck, overlooking a bend in the Lyndon River. But it was a warm May day, and shoes were definitely not necessary.

He smelled steaks grilling and knew his brother had a head start on dinner. He'd learned that steaks were the only thing Caleb knew how to cook. Thinking about his brother's ineptitude in the kitchen made something warm settle deep into Reed's chest.

It had only been a few weeks since he'd reconciled with his fraternal twin brother. They'd been estranged and angry with each other since their mother had passed away ten years ago. They'd both blamed their cruel, domineering father for her death from untreated pneumonia. But their reactions had been poles apart. Caleb had left home in anger. Reed had stayed behind to protect his mother's ranch heritage.

Reed heard a female voice through the screen door.

Mandy, obviously.

When Caleb had come home to settle problems with the will, the two had reconnected and fallen deeply in love. Reed smiled. He'd always thought of Mandy as a sister. It would be nice to have her officially become part of the family.

He grabbed himself a cold bottle of beer from the fridge, flipped the cap into the trash can and headed outside. There, he stopped short, seeing Katrina sitting at the table. Hearing his footsteps, she turned toward him.

A glass of red wine dangled between delicate fingers tipped with sculpted nails. And she was laughing at something Mandy had said. Her jewel-blue eyes were alight in the evening sunshine. The slanting rays glinted off her shimmering blouse where it clung to softly rounded breasts. As a professional dancer, her body had a perfect shape and symmetry that kick-started his libido.

As she took in his expression, her smile faltered, and the glow left her blue eyes. "Hello, Reed." She paused. "Something wrong?"

He realized he was scowling. She was Mandy's sister. He shouldn't be secretly fantasizing about her. She might not spend much time in Lyndon Valley, but he was going to have to make this work.

"Nothing's wrong," he insisted, striding forward. "I'm hungry." He forced himself to focus on Caleb who was wielding a spatula over the grill.

"About ten minutes," Caleb offered.

Since dishes, salads and bread were already set out on the rectangular table, Reed chose one of the low-slung wooden Adirondack chairs, parked his body and took a swig of his beer.

Mandy moved to the barbecue beside Caleb, placing her hand lightly on his shoulder, their backs to Reed and Katrina.

"Did you have a nice flight in?" Reed asked Katrina, keeping his tone polite and even.

"It was good." She nodded, her tone even in return. "Very comfortable." She swiveled to perch herself backward on the bench seat at the table, fully facing him.

In his peripheral vision, he saw Mandy playfully kiss his brother's cheek and whisper something in his ear.

"First class?" he asked Katrina.

"Why?"

He caught the narrowing of her eyes. "No reason."

"You think I'm a princess?"

"I'll take that as a yes." Truth was, he was thinking that nobody had a "very comfortable" flight in coach. He was also thinking that first-class seating was a waste on somebody as petite as her.

Their gazes clashed for several seconds.

"Staying long?" he tried, wondering if she'd turn that into an insult, as well.

But her expression faltered, and she didn't answer for a moment. "A week. Maybe two."

"Still dancing?" He didn't know anything about her life in New York City, except that she was some kind of important ballerina, and Mandy was anxious to go see her perform.

"Still dancing," she confirmed, with a quirk of a smile. "You're still ranching?"

"Still ranching." He nodded. "You must be here on vacation?"

"Yes," she replied, the barest hint of sarcasm in her tone.

"What?" he probed.

"What?" she responded, concentrating on taking a sip of her wine.

"It's not a vacation?" he guessed.

She glanced sideways at her sister for a split second. Then she shrugged. "No pool deck or palm trees. But I guess you could call it a vacation."

"Princess," he muttered through a smile.

"A girl's got to keep up her tan."

He gave a pointed glance to his deeply browned forearms. "Not a problem around these parts."

"I bet you've got those farmer-tan lines at the short-sleeve mark."

He couldn't seem to stop his smirk. "I bet you've got those princess tan lines at the bikini mark."

She didn't miss a beat. "Much more attractive."

To that, he gave her a mock toast. "No argument from me."

Then, to his surprise, she leaned forward and lowered her voice. "Truth is, I twisted my ankle."

He leaned forward to meet her, lowering his own voice to match. "Is that a secret?"

She shook her head. Then she shrugged her slim shoulders. "Not exactly, I just…" Her red lips pursed together, and he couldn't help thinking about kissing her.

Her cheeks flushed a light rose.

Was she thinking about kissing him back?

As quickly as it formed, he banished the thought. It was a ridiculous assumption.

"Are you embarrassed about hurting yourself?" He settled on a much more likely explanation.

"It was a silly accident," she confessed. "I'm usually really careful about my shoes, but—"

"Rare, medium or well?" Mandy called to them.

Reed didn't take his gaze off Katrina. "Rare."

"Medium," she put in. "And nothing too big, please."

Reed felt a smile grow. "You're not up for a cowboy twelve-ouncer?"

Her hand moved to rest on her flat stomach. "My dance partner has to be able to lift me."

"Maybe you need a stronger partner."

"What I need is to lose two pounds."

"You look perfect to me." The soft words were out before he could censor them.

A slow blink camouflaged her reaction. Then she brought her teeth down on her bottom lip and determinedly turned her attention to Caleb, who was carrying the platter of steaks to the table.

Reed had said something wrong. He wasn't sure what it was, but she'd abruptly shut him out.

Katrina didn't know why she'd told Reed about her ankle last night. It was a foolish slip of her tongue. It compromised her ongoing efforts to keep her two worlds apart, and this morning she vowed to do better.

In the years since her father's sister, her generous Aunt Coco, had taken her under her wing and convinced her parents to let her move to New York City with her, she'd been living two separate lives. In New York, enrolled in the ballet program at the Academy, she felt vibrant and alive. She was a part of the cultural mosaic Auntie Coco, a renowned contemporary painter, had been so careful to expose her to while she was growing up. She fitted in. She was normal, accepted, even respected. In Colorado, she was out of step. An anomaly who could never show weakness.

She often wondered why her aunt had decided to rescue her from the ranching world, what it was she'd recognized as a kindred spirit in a ten-year-old child. She'd always meant to ask. But Coco had died of a sudden aneurism two years ago before Katrina had had the chance.

Now, she came to the bottom of the stairs of the Jacobs' house and took a bracing breath. Her two brothers and two sisters were already dressed for the day's work, sitting at the breakfast table eating pancakes, bacon and scrambled eggs. It never ceased to amaze her that Mandy and Abigail could consume so many calories and keep such trim figures.

As she pivoted around the end of the staircase, she was careful not to limp. Then again, Reed would probably tell Caleb, and Caleb would tell Mandy, and once again she'd be the pathetic, weak branch on the robust Jacobs family tree.

She approached the breakfast table to a chorus of good mornings, taking the empty place next to Mandy, searching the table for fruit, or maybe a whole-grain muffin. But a platter of fluffy pancakes was handed her way, followed by maple syrup and a mounded serving tray of eggs.

"Thanks." She nodded to Abigail, setting the heavy platter down in an empty spot in front of her plate. "Is there maybe an apple or something in the fridge?"

Everything seemed to still for a moment as four sets of eyes turned her way.

"I'm not a huge breakfast eater," she explained, ignoring the tantalizing scents of melting butter and warming syrup.

Abigail started to stand.

"No, no." Katrina quickly waved her off, coming to her feet. Pain tripped in her ankle from the sudden movement, but she schooled her features. "I'll get it." She quickly headed for the kitchen.

"Abigail and I can stay on the ranch for a few more days," Seth said, his conversational voice coming through the big, open pass-through between the kitchen and dining room. "But then they'll need us in Lyndon to help with my campaign."

Katrina spotted the family cook, Henrietta, in the pantry off the kitchen, restocking the shelves from a cardboard box. She smiled a greeting to the familiar woman as she pulled open one side of the big stainless-steel refrigerator.

In the pocket of her slacks, her cell phone vibrated. She retrieved it to see an unfamiliar New York City number.

"Hello?" she inquired, moving to a far corner of the kitchen, where a solid wall blocked the noise from her siblings' conversation.

"Hello, Katrina."

Her teeth clenched at the sound of Quentin Foster's voice. A member of the Liberty Ballet Board of Directors, the last time they'd spoken, he'd been hitting on her.

"I wanted to see how you were feeling," he continued, tone solicitous.

"Fine," she told him evenly, wondering how she could diplomatically end the call. He was an important man in the organization, but his flirtatious manner had gotten entirely out of hand.

"We're all very worried about you."

"I'm fine. I'll be back soon."

"Back?" His tone slipped. "Have you left the city?"

"I'm visiting family. I really need to go. Thanks for calling."

"Katrina, wait."

She braced herself. "Yes?"

"Have you had another chance to think about what I said?"

About becoming his lover? "I haven't changed my mind."

In her peripheral vision, she caught her brother Seth's curious gaze on her. "I do have to go. Thank you for your concern." She quickly hit the off button then shut down her phone, turning her attention back to her family.

"Mandy's riding up to take a look at the Blue Lake herd today," said Travis. "And I'll check to see how many have moved through the canyon."

Katrina knew there was a science to herd distribution across their vast rangelands, taking in the seasons, weather reports and rainfall, but she had no idea how it worked. More than once, she'd privately mused that if she'd lived in the 1800s, she'd probably have died young of stupidity or been killed off by her outraged community because of her ineptitude.

"What time is the vet due in?" asked Abigail, refilling her coffee cup.

"He said around eleven," Mandy offered. "But you know how those things go."

"I have to touch base with the campaign office before I do anything else," said Abigail, reminding Katrina of her oldest brother's upcoming campaign for the mayor's seat in Lyndon.

Katrina selected a smooth, deep-green Granny Smith apple from the crisper drawer, rinsing it under the tap before returning to the table.

"What about you?" Travis asked her as she sat back down.

"Me?" she responded, confused by his question. Were they still talking about the mayoralty campaign?

"You want to ride up to the lake with me today?" asked Mandy.

Katrina hesitated, glancing at the expressions around the

table. She couldn't believe they'd forgotten. She'd never mastered riding a horse. The animals still frightened her. The thought of sitting on top of one for six hours made her cringe.

"I have a pretty rigorous rehearsal and training routine," she told everyone.

Seth waved a dismissive hand. "Take a day off."

"I—"

"The fresh air will be good for you," Travis declared.

Only Mandy was looking at her curiously.

"I wish I could," Katrina lied with a shake of her head. "But I need to stay in shape."

"Horseback-riding is good exercise," said Travis.

"Is there a bicycle anywhere around here?" She tried to change the subject. Jogging would be the simplest exercise, since she didn't have access to a gym. But the jarring would be too hard on her healing ankle, especially over uneven ground.

Her siblings glanced at each other.

"A bicycle?" Seth repeated the question.

"I like to bike," said Katrina. "It's good for my quads."

Travis snorted. "A little productive work would be good for your quads too."

"Travis," Abigail warned.

"There might be an old bike in the blue shed," said Mandy. "We can look after breakfast." She glanced at the apple in Katrina's hand. "You sure you don't want something hot?"

Katrina shook her head. "I'm good." She took a big bite of the apple, mumbling her appreciation of the tart flavor.

After a drawn-out moment, everyone's attention went back to their own meals.

After a few minutes, Mandy rose to take her dishes into the kitchen then returned to the dining room and slid back into her chair. "We'll go whenever you're ready," she said to Katrina.

"I'm ready now." Katrina rose. She'd rather eat her apple on the run than sit here on edge, waiting for more uncomfortable questions and opinions.

She'd worn blue jeans and a simple white blouse this morning, and she popped her feet into a pair of sneakers.

Mandy stuck a battered Stetson onto her head. Her boot heels clunked on the wooden porch, while Katrina followed silently on rubber soles. She wished she'd thought to bring along a hat. She had a white baseball cap from the Met that she could easily have tucked into her suitcase.

It took about five minutes to walk the path to the blue shed, called that because of its blue door. There was also the green shed, the yellow shed and the view shed, which had a red door. Katrina had never figured out why her family wasn't consistent with the names. But she'd stopped asking questions like that a long time ago.

Mandy pushed open the door and made her way into the crowded storage building. "You haven't told me what you thought of Caleb."

"He seems like a nice guy," Katrina answered honestly as she followed inside. Caleb had been friendly, polite and funny last night.

Mandy turned to stare, her tone turning incredulous. "'A nice guy'? That's all you've got for my fiancé? He's an *amazing* guy."

"I only just met him again."

Caleb was six years older than Katrina, and she barely remembered him from when she was a child.

"Well, sure. But it's pretty obvious, don't you think?"

Katrina couldn't help but grin at her sister's mock outrage. "I'm sure he's amazing. And it's pretty obvious he's got it bad for you."

"Yes, he does," Mandy answered with conviction, wrinkling her nose and sticking it primly in the air. She turned sideways to slip between a set of shelves and an ATV.

Katrina followed, tone playfully placating. "And who could blame him? You're a great catch."

Even in the dim light, Mandy's eyes sparkled as she moved some plastic bins out of the way. "What about you?"

"I'm not a particularly good catch." What could Katrina bring to a relationship? An extensive designer wardrobe? An ability to make small talk at cocktail parties? A demanding and precarious career?

"I meant are you seeing anyone?"

"Oh."

Mandy moved a tarp as she made her way farther into the shed. "But of course you're a great catch. You're like some kind of dream trophy wife."

Katrina didn't want to be a trophy wife. "I'm not seeing anyone."

"Really? What about all those debonair rich guys who go to the same parties as you?"

"None of them have asked me out."

"They have so," Mandy contradicted.

"Okay, some of them have. But nobody lately." Unless you counted Quentin Foster. Katrina shuddered at the mere thought of the offensive man. He hadn't asked her for a date. His had been a bald proposition, followed by an unsettling threat.

"New York men don't know a good woman when they see one," Mandy put in staunchly. "Aha. Here we go."

Katrina banished thoughts of Quentin, coming up on her toes to peer over a wooden crate. Sure enough, there was a sturdy-looking mountain bike propped up against a workbench. She normally rode a stationary one at the gym a few blocks from her apartment, but she was willing to adapt.

"Will we be able to get it out of there?" she asked Mandy.

"Easy." Mandy hoisted it in the air, over the clutter and outside. There she pumped up the flat tires at the compressor.

Katrina was more than a bit in awe of her older sister. "I can't believe you did all that."

"All what?"

"Pumped up the tires. You actually know how to run a compressor."

"You actually know how to stand up in toe shoes. So, what's the plan? How far do you want to ride?"

Katrina shrugged. "Fifteen, twenty miles." Then she'd limber up, work on her arms a bit, and see how her ankle was holding up.

"I'm going up to Caleb's later," said Mandy.

"That's nice."

Mandy glanced at her watch. "If you wait until afternoon to leave and take the river trail, I can meet you at the Terrells' and drive you home after dinner."

Katrina hesitated. She wasn't wild about spending more time with Reed. The man made her jumpy and self-conscious. But Mandy was the closest thing she had to a buffer against her other siblings. If Mandy wasn't around, she feared her brothers would try to railroad her into something uncomfortable, like riding a horse.

"Sure," she found herself saying. "I'll meet you up at Terrells'."

# Two

Reed couldn't seem to get his father's voice out of his head. As he had when Wilton Terrell was alive, he got up every morning focused on an ambitious list of jobs around the ranch. Then he worked as hard as he could until the end of the day. And if something went wrong, if he made a mistake, did less than one hundred percent, he'd reflexively brace himself for Wilton's anger.

Obviously he knew he'd never have to deal with his father's anger again, but his emotions were taking a while to catch up. He couldn't say he was sorry the obstinate old man had died, though he was beginning to recognize what a powerful impact Wilton had had on his life.

His brother Caleb told him it was crazy to keep up the breakneck pace. Caleb was searching for a full-time ranch manager to add to the foreman and ranch hands that helped with the day-to-day work. But Reed couldn't switch gears that easily.

Now, he returned the cleaning supplies to the tack room, hung up his saddle and emptied the combs and brushes he'd used on his horse, replacing them in their respective drawers and closing the cabinet before shutting off the light and exiting the room.

The sun was hitting the horizon in an orange ball, decorated by pink clouds above the snowy peaks of the distant Rockies. He crossed the wide driveway turnaround, heading for the house. A truck pulled up, and he caught sight of the Jacobs' ranch logo on the door. Before he could stop it, a hitch of excitement shot through him. But then he saw that only Mandy was inside the cab. No Katrina.

He lengthened his stride, coming up to the driver's door and pulling it open for her. "Hey, Mandy."

She smiled a greeting as she slid out of the cab, reaching back inside for a baking tin sitting in the center of the bench seat.

"Brownies," she offered, waving it in front of his nose.

"Sounds great. Caleb's probably inside."

"With Katrina?"

Reed felt another small shot of adrenaline. "Katrina's here?"

"I sure hope so. Mom left her a box of things to sort through in the attic, then she was coming up here."

"I've been in the barn for a while." He might have missed Katrina's arrival. Then again, he didn't see another Jacobs' pickup anywhere, so perhaps Mandy was mistaken.

"Hmm." Mandy's gaze searched the yard.

"What?"

"She rode up here on a bike."

"You mean a horse?"

Mandy gave an eye-roll as she started for the front door. "Yeah, because I usually mix those two things up."

Reed automatically fell into step and lifted the tin from her hands. "Katrina rides a motorcycle?" He simply couldn't picture it.

"A bicycle. She wanted to get some exercise."

Okay. Weird, but okay. They mounted the stairs, and Reed pushed the door open, waiting for Mandy to go inside.

"I don't see how they could possibly make it any more complicated," Caleb was saying into the phone as he paced from the living room into the entry hall. He lifted his chin in a greeting to them both. "I don't think Danielle wants to fly all the way down to Brazil." He paused. "In person? Really?" He braced his hand against the end of the archway and gave a disgusted shake of his head.

Mandy moved down the hall to the kitchen, glanced inside, then came back.

"Katrina here?" she stage-whispered to Caleb.

He narrowed his eyes in confusion.

"Is Katrina here?" she repeated.

He gave her a shrug of incomprehension. "Tell her to take the jet," he said into the phone. "We're going to have to give that woman a huge bonus."

Mandy turned to Reed, her forehead wrinkling in worry. "She was going to ride up the river trail. She should have been here by now."

"On it," said Reed, moving immediately back to the door and heading outside.

Katrina was probably stuck somewhere along the trail. Or maybe she'd grown tired and was resting. There was a slim chance she gotten herself into real trouble. But the river trail was well-marked and relatively smooth and safe. The odds were definitely on the side of a delay rather than a catastrophe.

He strode back across the driveway, hopping onto an ATV that was parked next to the barn. He turned the key and the machine roared to life beneath him. He glanced at the sky, judging he had at least an hour before dark. It should be plenty of time, but he wasn't going to waste any of it.

He drove about four miles down the trail before he spotted her. The bike was tipped at the edge of the trail, and Katrina was crouched over it, looking small and forlorn in the midst of an aspen grove. She stood as he approached, and her shoulders relaxed as she obviously recognized that it was him. He saw the chain was off the bike, and her small hands were black with oil.

He'd give her an A for effort, but a failing grade for actual accomplishment. He knew six-year-olds who could reattach a bicycle chain. He brought the ATV to a stop and killed the engine as he dismounted.

"Looks like you've got a problem," he opened, struggling not to smile at her rather adorable helplessness.

She gestured to the bike. "I came around the corner, hit a bump, and the chain fell off."

His smile broke through as he checked out her blackened hands. "Any luck putting it back on?"

"Are you mocking me?"

He moved on to inspect the broken-down bicycle. "I'm making small talk, Katrina. Quit being so sensitive."

"I'm not being—"

"You've got a chip a mile wide on those skinny little shoulders."

"I'm not an auto mechanic," she harrumphed.

"And I'm not a ballerina."

She didn't seem to have a response to that.

"There's no point in getting my hands dirty fixing it here," he noted, lifting the bike by the frame and carrying it to the ATV. "Unless you're set on riding it the rest of the way."

"In the dark?"

"I wouldn't recommend it." He balanced the bike on the wide front rack, uncoiling a bungee cord to fasten it down. "But it's up to you."

"No," she responded tartly. "I don't want to ride a bike the rest of the way."

"You okay?" he asked belatedly, wrapping the cord around the bike frame and hooking the end to the rack. She didn't appear hurt, but he supposed that should have been the first question out of his mouth. That was a miss.

"I'm fine," she huffed.

He glanced up, taking a more detailed look at her. "You didn't fall or anything?"

She shook her head. "The chain came off." She held up her hands. "I stopped and I tried to put it back on."

"I can see that."

"I didn't just sit down and wait for a knight in shining armor."

"That's a relief. Because you got me instead."

She blinked sheepishly, seeming to remember her own manners. "Thank you," she offered.

He couldn't help but grin at her discomfort. "That wasn't what I was fishing for. But you're welcome." The sight of her looking so vulnerable in the vastness of the landscape tightened his chest. "Anytime."

"I guess these things come in threes."

"Threes?" He glanced around, wondering if he'd missed something.

"I had that ballet shoe come apart on me," she offered ruefully, glancing at her ankle. "And I almost took a tumble over some cables near the stage because they were partially hidden by a curtain."

He sure didn't like that mental picture. But he kept his tone easy. "You do seem to be accident-prone."

"Ironic." She sighed. "Because this time I was purposely attempting to stay *out* of trouble."

"Admirable," he acknowledged.

"Mandy wanted me to go horseback riding," she continued. "And my brothers wouldn't let me say no, and I knew I'd just slow the whole process down. And I thought…" She gestured to the disabled bike. "Bike-riding is one of my favorite exercises."

Surely she didn't ride a bike in the bumper-to-bumper traffic of New York City. "Through Central Park?" he hoped.

"In my gym," she admitted. "A stationary bike."

He wanted to tease her about that. But the truth was, he was glad to hear it. Better to be inside a building than fighting for road space with delivery vans, buses and taxis.

"I can set this one up as a stationary for you," he found himself offering. "In the barn. On a stand. It wouldn't be high-tech, but I can add a little resistance, and you'll stay safe and sound." Even as the words poured out of this mouth, he asked himself what the hell he thought he was doing? He had a million more pressing jobs that needed his attention.

She moved toward the ATV. "Wouldn't my brothers have a laugh at that."

He watched her grow close, transfixed by her beautiful face, the depths of her eyes, the motion of her deep pink mouth.

"We can keep it our secret," he offered.

She hesitated, watching him closely. "I'd jog, but I can't because of my ankle. And I have to do something." She drew a deep sigh. "I spent all day yesterday sitting on airplanes. I was going to warm up on this ride, and then get in some stretching. But now, my muscles are cold."

"You're cold?"

"Too cold to stretch."

He quickly unbuttoned his shirt.

"What are you—"

He stepped in and draped it over her shoulders. "Put it on," he said gruffly. It was going to get even colder once they got up to speed on the trail and the wind hit them.

"I don't need—" Her gaze caught and held on his bare chest. She blinked twice, then looked away, wordlessly slipping her arms into the sleeves. They hung about six inches past her fingertips, so she rolled them up to a thick band around her forearms.

She fastened the shirt buttons, and her cute black tights and pink T-shirt disappeared beneath the voluminous cotton.

She glanced down at herself. "Lovely."

He cocked his head to one side. "I think it's the spring tent collection from Dior."

"You know Dior?"

"How do you mean?"

"It's a fashion-design house."

"No kidding," he drawled.

"It's just—"

"We do have satellite television out here."

"And you use it to watch fashion shows?"

"Hardly," he scoffed. "But they make the occasional pop-culture reference during professional bull-riding."

"Did I insult you?" she asked, looking genuinely regretful.

"I'm not living under a rock, Katrina."

"I never thought you were."

He swung his leg over the wide seat of the ATV. He wasn't insulted. He couldn't care less what she thought of his television-watching habits.

Truth was, he didn't know why she'd struck a nerve. Maybe it was because she pointed out the vast differences between them, and how far she was out of his league. Not that it mattered, he ruthlessly reminded himself. No matter how sexy Miss Katrina Jacobs might appear, he was keeping his hands and his thoughts to himself. His life was complicated enough.

"Hop on," he told her gruffly, sliding forward to give her room on the seat behind.

She approached the ATV with caution, obviously sizing it up.

"You need some help?"

"No," she flashed.

"Hand on my shoulder," he instructed.

After a long hesitation, she touched him tentatively.

"Other hand."

"Sorry."

"Left foot on that peg."

"Okay."

He captured her forearm to steady her. "Step up and swing your leg over the seat. Grab my other shoulder if you need to."

She did. Her slight weight rocked the ATV, and her butt came down on the seat, her breasts brushing his back and her thighs coming up against his.

She sucked in a breath.

"You're going to have to hang on to me," he warned.

"I know."

He turned the key, and the ATV rumbled to life.

"Katrina?" he intoned, waiting for her to follow his instructions.

"My hands are filthy."

"I can take it." He reached back and grasped each of her wrists, wrapping her slim arms around his waist and anchoring her hands to his bare stomach.

Her breasts pressed tighter against his back, her cheek rested between his shoulder blades, while her inner thighs cradled his hips. Raw, painful desire rocketed through him, and he wondered how long he could reasonably take to drive back to the house. He wanted her to stay wrapped around his body for hours and hours.

In the shower on the second floor of the Terrells' house, Katrina's skin still tingled where she'd been pressed up against Reed's body—which was pretty much everywhere, from the inside of her knees to the hairline above her temple. The ATV had rumbled between her legs, while the heat from Reed's bare back had seeped its way through his shirt, her T-shirt and right through her bra.

Mandy had brought along a change of clothes for Katrina. In fact, she'd brought along Katrina's entire suitcase. She'd drawn Katrina aside and confessed she was plotting to have them spend the night at the Terrells', so she could be with Caleb. Katrina had easily agreed to stay. Away from her family's ranch was good for her state of mind. And it was less emotionally draining to be here with Mandy than interacting with all of her siblings. Caleb had been warmly receptive to the plan. Reed was best described as neutral.

Now, Katrina pulled back the blue-and-green-striped shower curtain and carefully climbed out of the deep tub. The bathroom was neat but compact, with little counter room around the sink and only a couple of spots for hanging clothes and towels on the back of the door. While she dried off and wrapped a white towel around her wet hair, she realized the error in her planning.

Her sweaty clothes were in a heap on top of the hamper, while her fresh clothes were still folded in her suitcase in the guest room. She was going to have to cross the hallway wrapped in nothing but a towel. There wasn't even a robe she could borrow hanging anywhere in the bathroom.

Resigned, she wrapped the biggest towel firmly around her body, tucking in the ends between her breasts. She rubbed a spot in the steamed mirror, turning and coming up on her toes to make sure the towel covered the necessities, just in case she met someone on the way. Then she gathered her wrinkled exercise outfit and her underwear, rolling them into a neat ball before cracking the bathroom door to make sure the hallway was all clear.

She listened carefully but couldn't hear a sound. The guest-room door was about ten feet down the hallway in the opposite direction of the stairs. It was open, and it would only take her about five seconds to make it there.

She took a breath, opened the bathroom door wide, listened one last time, then scampered across the hardwood floor, scooting safely into the guest room, quickly closing the door behind her. She closed her eyes with a heartfelt sigh, and leaned solidly up against the door.

"Katrina?" Reed's voice made her eyes fly open.

She gave a little shriek. The towel slipped, revealing her breasts for a brief moment until she grasped the corners, struggling to form a coherent word. "Wha—"

"Sorry." He quickly averted his gaze. "Mandy asked me to bring you some fresh sheets."

"I…" She could feel her face flush hot. The rest of her body flushed, too. Desire zipped from one extremity to the other, settling in a slow burn at the base of her abdomen.

She swallowed. She had to say something. But she couldn't for the life of her figure out what that might be.

Reed moved toward her, keeping his gaze studiously on the floor in front of him. "I'll get out of your way."

She told herself to move, unblock the door so the man could leave already. But her feet were glued to the floor, her heart pumping deep and slow inside her chest.

He came closer and closer, and all she could do was stare.

A knock on the door behind her nearly made her jump out of her skin.

"Katrina?" Mandy called. "You in there?"

The absurdity of the situation suddenly hit her. And Katrina recovered her sense of humor. What was she expecting Reed to do here? Make a move with Mandy and Caleb downstairs? Ridiculous. She quickly found her voice.

"I'm naked in here," she called out to Mandy. "And Reed's remaking the bed."

There was a stunned silence on the other side of the door.

"You shouldn't have done that," Reed intoned. "Get out of the way."

Mandy stammered from outside. "I'm… Uh…"

Reed snagged Katrina's bare shoulder, moving her off to one side. His warm, callused palm left a distinct tingle in its wake. He quickly swung the door open.

"Mix-up," he told Mandy. "Your sister thinks she's funny."

"He was lying in wait for me," Katrina countered, still feeling breathless.

"I thought you'd take longer in the shower," Reed protested.

"Why? Because I'm from New York City?"

"Because you're a girl."

"I'm a woman."

Mandy's attention was flying back and forth between the two.

Reed's nostrils flared as he sucked in a deep breath. "And now you have fresh sheets."

"Thank you," Katrina returned breezily.

She was scrambling to tamp down her powerful sexual reaction to him. It was strange and more than a little unsettling to have her hormones run amok like this.

Maybe it was brought on by the stress of the afternoon. He had rescued her, after all. He'd lent her his shirt and brought her back here to where she was safe and warm. Had his white-knight behavior tripped some anthropological hormonal switch, making him seem like mate material? She sure hoped it was temporary.

"Caleb's pouring the wine," Mandy offered, watching her closely.

"Then I'll get dressed," said Katrina, pasting on an unconcerned smile.

These things were obviously mind over matter, and she was a very disciplined person. Reed was just a man. And a stubborn cowboy at that. She preferred her men more urbane and refined, a guy who could pull off a tux and discuss literature, fine cuisine and world events.

Mandy stepped backward into the hall, obviously intending to wait there until Reed joined her.

"It was an *accident,*" Reed told Mandy with firm conviction.

"I know." She nodded. "Could have happened to anyone."

Reed set his jaw in annoyance and moved through the doorway.

Once in the hall, he turned back to glare his annoyance at Katrina.

"You're not funny," he admonished. But a split second later, his frank, heated gaze slid from her towel-covered hair to her bare feet and back again.

Her toes curled into the soft carpet, and her stomach rolled anxiously. Hoo boy.

Katrina woke up in the Terrells' guest room in the early, dark hours of the morning and couldn't seem to get back to sleep. Bothered by the time-zone change, her nagging ankle, and the fact that Reed was sleeping on the other side of the thin bedroom wall, her brain couldn't seem to relax.

Since Mandy had brought all of Katrina's sister's clothes to the Terrells' house, she had options. She changed into a simple black-and-white leotard, then searched her way through the house for a suitable space to exercise. She found a big rec room in the basement that was perfect. It had a smooth Berber carpet, a big open space in the middle and a ledge that ran the length of the room at a height where she could brace her hand for balance.

She plugged in her earbuds, turned on her player and made her way through a low-impact aerobic workout, getting the blood flowing and warming up her muscles. Then she ran through a familiar stretching routine, easing down into the splits, bending sideways first, then forward at the waist, stretching out her arms.

After a few minutes, she paused, sensing someone watching.

She turned toward the door to find Reed leaning laconically against the doorjamb.

"I saw the lights." He straightened and ambled into the room, dressed in jeans and a white T-shirt, hair tousled, muscles bulging everywhere.

She pulled her legs beneath her and rolled to her feet. "I couldn't sleep. Time-zone change."

"Yeah, me, too. Not the time-zone thing. But I couldn't sleep." He pointed above his head. "I'm cooking sausage and eggs. You hungry?"

She shook her head. "I'm not much of a breakfast eater."

Reluctant to stop while her muscles were warmed up, she crossed to the edge of the room, bracing her hand on the ledge. Facing Reed, she raised one leg behind her, gently gripped her toes and stretched out her quad.

"You don't seem to be much of an eater at all," he observed.

"Weight's an issue in my profession." Not only was a sleek form vital to her look on stage, but she had her partners to think about.

"How much do you weigh?"

She shot him a look of disbelief. "Do you really expect me to answer that?"

He shrugged and moved farther into the room. "Why not? I must weigh two, three times what you do."

"Reed, you don't ask a lady her weight."

"Say that again."

"You don't ask a lady her weight?"

"No, the Reed part."

She gave him a frown. What was that? Was he flirting? Why would he flirt?

He stared back in silence for a long moment. Then he said, "I made you something."

Though the words took her by surprise, she rolled with it, telling herself it was better to move on. If Reed started flirting with her, she'd have to decide how to react. She knew how she was supposed to react, but it was completely different from the way she wanted to react.

She pulled her feet together and bent forward, putting her hands flat on the floor. "What did you make me?"

"It's a surprise."

"You want me to guess?" She stood again and raised her leg to the ledge, stretching her body along its length.

"No, I…" He paused. "How do you *do* that?"

"Do what?"

"Go all pretzel-like."

"Practice." She'd started when she was ten years old, when everything about her body had been extraordinarily flexible. "Is it something to eat?" she asked him. "If it is, you should know I like fruit and whole grains."

"Is that why you skipped the brownies last night?"

"I noticed you ate mine."

"Always happy to help a lady in distress."

She couldn't help laughing at that. "Ever the gentleman."

"Yes, I am."

She straightened. "Okay, I'll admit, you've got me curious."

His eyes warmed. "You want to come and see?"

"Depends. Where are we going?"

"The barn." His gaze scanned her body. "You'll have to put on something warmer than that. And remember, the hands are working out there."

She glanced down at her simple leotard set. "You know I go up on stage in less than this."

"Not in Colorado, you don't."

"Fine." She started for the door, passing by him and calling over her shoulder. "You got any more of those cotton shirts? That'll cover up everything that counts."

"What's mine is yours." He started in behind her. "In fact, I've got a nice set of pajamas you might like. Red-and-gray plaid, very boxy. You take the tops."

And he'd take the bottoms.

Oh, he was definitely flirting. She stopped abruptly in the doorway and he almost barreled into her.

He raised a hand and braced himself on the doorjamb. "What?"

She turned. "You shouldn't do that."

"Do what?"

"Talk about sharing pajamas."

His lips curled up in the barest of smirks. "Is that what you thought I meant?"

"You know you did."

There was a silent pause.

"Okay," he admitted.

He stared down at her, and a pulse pounded in her temple, while heat coiled in the center of her body.

He leaned almost imperceptibly in, and his voice went husky. "You should get dressed."

"I know."

He blinked. "Now," he muttered.

He was absolutely right. They'd taken this as far as they dared. She quickly turned and mounted the staircase.

She felt him behind her as far as the main floor. Then, she noted thankfully, he broke off to return to the kitchen.

Back in the guest room, she forced the sexy exchange from her mind, firmly telling herself to get it under control. She changed to some casual clothes and went back downstairs.

Together, they crossed to the main barn, traversing its length to a quiet corner behind a half wall. There she stared in astonishment at the contraption he'd made out of the bicycle.

"How did you do this?" she asked him. "*When* did you do this?"

The mountain bike was propped up on a rack, with the front wheel removed and rollers pressing against the back wheel. The rollers were attached to a long bolt with a butterfly screw that could be used to change the tension.

"This morning," he answered. "I told you, I couldn't sleep."

"I didn't think you were serious."

"About not sleeping?"

"About—" She gestured. "About disabling my bike."

"It's what you wanted."

"It's not what I wanted. It's what you offered." She didn't know why she was annoyed. Maybe because he hadn't given her a choice. Maybe she was touchy today when it came to men telling her what to do. Or maybe anger was just the easiest emotion for her to deal with right now when it came to Reed.

"It's too dangerous for you to be cycling around the ranch," he informed her.

"In your opinion."

"In everybody's opinion."

"So you decided to stop me?"

He nodded sharply. "I did."

"Don't you think that might be a little high-handed?"

"What? Keeping you safe?"

"I'm a grown woman, Reed."

"And?"

"And it's not up to you to decide how to keep me safe."

He gave a grunt of disbelief. "I'm the one who has to come rescue you."

"Nobody asked you to rescue me."

"Mandy did."

"Well, I didn't."

"So, I should have left you there?"

"You should have asked me before disabling my bicycle."

She wasn't sure why she was drawing this out. Truth was, it was going to be a whole lot easier to bike in here where it was smoother on her ankle and she didn't have to watch for obstacles and worry about breakdowns.

"Do you want me to take it apart?"

She caught a glimpse of hurt in his tightening expression and instantly regretted her reaction. "No. No, I don't."

"Good enough, then." His tone was sharp. He turned on his heel, leaving Katrina alone.

# Three

No good deed ever went unpunished. Reed banged a frying pan against the stovetop, wondering if he was just too stupid to remember that fact.

He was up to *here* with being criticized and having his efforts go unappreciated. It was one of his father's favorite head games, pretending to want one thing, then changing the rules at the last minute and acting as though Reed had misunderstood the instructions.

He turned the sausages in the big skillet and cracked a couple of more eggs into a glass bowl.

"Smells good," came Caleb's voice as he entered the room, making a show of sniffing the air. "I can't believe you're such a good cook."

"I can't believe you're such a hopeless cook," Reed returned.

His brother had spent the past ten years building up his business, Active Equipment, while living in downtown Chicago. If it weren't for restaurants and take-out food Caleb would have starved to death years ago.

"I thought you'd be out working by now." Caleb crossed to

the coffeemaker, snagged a cup from the lowest shelf and poured himself some coffee.

"Guess I'm just lazy."

"Whoa," Caleb drew back at the tone of Reed's voice. "What's up?"

"Nothin'." Reed took a fork and beat the dozen eggs into a scramble, adding onions, peppers and a dollop of milk.

Caleb settled back against the countertop. "It's just you and me here, bro. He's gone."

Reed drew a breath and forced his features to neutral. "I know he's gone. Corby says the parts are in for the irrigation system on the oat field. Thought I'd start up there."

"Get one of the hands to do it."

"No need." Reed wasn't about to become an armchair rancher. The irrigation system needed fixing, and he knew how to fix it.

Caleb took a long sip of the black coffee. "Did you get a chance to look at the ranch manager résumés?"

"Not yet."

"Are you ever going to look at the ranch manager résumés?"

"Said I would." Reed dumped the egg mixture into a sizzling pan. Caleb was the one who wanted to hire a full-time manager. Reed didn't have a problem running the ranch himself.

"Who put the burr under your butt this morning?"

"Morning, Caleb," came Katrina's voice. Her soft footsteps sounded in the pass-through as she entered the kitchen from the living room.

Reed reached for a spatula, stirring the eggs without turning around. He could feel his brother's gaze linger on him a moment longer.

"Morning, Katrina," Caleb offered cheerfully. "Sleep well?"

"I did. Thank you." Her voice was sweet, melodious, without a trace of upset. Obviously, she'd moved on. Well, he would, too.

He turned to face her. "Eggs?"

Puzzlement flicked through her blue eyes. "No, thank you."

He knew he'd asked her that once already this morning. But what did she expect? That he'd own up to having spent the past hour with her? That he'd give Caleb the details of their argument?

Offering her some eggs was a perfectly ordinary thing to do in this circumstance.

"Fruit?" he continued, not quite masking the edge to his tone.

"Love some," she responded, lips compressing ever so slightly.

"There are oranges on the table, grapes and plums in the fridge. Help yourself."

Caleb moved into action. "Let me—"

"I'm sure she's capable of opening a refrigerator door," Reed told his brother.

"What is your *problem?*" Caleb demanded.

"It's fine," Katrina cut in, heading for the fridge. "He's worried that I'm nothing but decorative."

"She's our guest," Caleb exclaimed.

"Who's a guest?" asked Mandy, breezing into the kitchen. "Me?" She beelined for Caleb, planting a kiss on his cheek. Her hair was damp, her face free of makeup, and she wore a cotton shirt with the sleeves rolled up to midforearm, a faded pair of jeans and no-nonsense boots. She was the kind of woman to whom Reed ought to be attracted.

"Me," corrected Katrina, from behind the open fridge door. By contrast, she now wore a clingy pair of hunter-green slacks with rhinestones decorating the pockets and the hems. Her butter-yellow tank top was cropped, showing off smooth arms, a strip of skin above her waistband, her navel winking sexily every time she moved. Her earrings sparkled with tiny green stones while a silver medallion dangled above the scooped neckline of her top.

She was on a cattle ranch for goodness' sake, not at a nightclub.

"Okay..." Mandy drawled, obviously waiting to be brought up to speed on the discussion.

Katrina straightened, a deep purple plum in her hand. "I was about to offer to do the dishes." She pasted Reed with a challenging expression, then took a slurping bite of the plum.

He nearly dropped the spatula.

"Don't be ridiculous," Mandy quickly put in.

It took Reed's lungs a moment to start functioning again. "If you gals need to head home right away…"

Caleb's arm snaked out around Mandy. "I'm not letting this one go yet."

"I have work to do at home," Mandy admonished.

"Hire another hand. I'll pay for it. You're my fiancée, and I have dibs."

Katrina's gaze rested on Reed, making him feel guilty for his snarky attitude. But he'd done her a favor this morning, and she'd treated him like something nasty on the bottom of her shoe. She might get away with that back in New York City, but it wasn't cutting it out here.

"Exactly how long do you expect me to stay?" Mandy teased Caleb.

His voice went deep, communicating more emotion than a single word. "Forever."

Realizing he'd nearly burned the eggs, Reed twisted the burner control to the off position and moved them to one side.

"Cute." Mandy patted Caleb's cheek, seeming completely unaffected by his staunch declaration.

"Well, *I* should get back," said Katrina.

"Oh, no." Mandy walked forward toward Katrina before coming up against the tether of Caleb's hand in hers. "Stay."

Katrina turned to her sister. "Why would I stay?"

*Stay and ride your bicycle,* Reed found himself fuming. The least she could do was give it a try.

"You might as well be here as down there," said Mandy. "We haven't had a chance to talk." She tugged playfully at Caleb's hand, while he held her fast. "And I don't think this one's going to let me leave."

Out of the corner of his eye, Reed saw Katrina glance his way.

"Reed's not going to care," said Mandy.

"I don't want to get in the way."

Reed turned to face her full-on. "This isn't a country club."

Her head jerked back, eyes going wide, as if he'd wounded her, and he immediately felt like a heel.

"Reed!" Caleb admonished. "What the hell?"

"It's okay," said Katrina, setting down the half-eaten plum. "Obviously, I should—"

"No, you *shouldn't*." Mandy shot Reed an annoyed glare. "He's in a bad mood, that's all. Terrell men get that way."

"Excuse me?" Caleb was obviously affronted at being lumped in unfavorably with his brother.

Katrina seemed to be at a loss. She suddenly struck Reed as a fragile, frightened bird. And he had to struggle against an overpowering urge to reach out and reassure her. He wanted to draw her into his arms and apologize for anything he'd ever done, thought of doing or might do in the future to hurt her.

But the rational side of him knew that would be ridiculous. She'd trounced all over his best intentions this morning, and now she was using those big, gorgeous blue eyes to bring the world onto her side.

Well, he wasn't falling for it.

"You're more than welcome to stay," Caleb told her staunchly.

Katrina looked to Reed, and he felt his defenses melting like spring snow. He fought against it, but stubborn as he was, she won the battle without lifting a finger.

"You're welcome to stay," he echoed his brother's invitation.

Then he determinedly turned his attention back to breakfast. The sausages were overdone, as were the eggs. He'd forgotten to push down the toast, and he couldn't seem to remember what the hell he'd done with the strawberry jam.

Katrina felt as though she was ten years old again, trailing along behind Mandy through the Terrell barn, feeling out of place, her nose wrinkling at the smell, making sure she steered clear of anything with hooves and teeth.

"There's a gorgeous meadow up by Flash Lake," Mandy was saying. She stopped beside a stall to scratch the nose of a chestnut mare. "It's really not that far to ride. The fireweed's up, and the lilies and columbine. You should see something more than the ranch yard while you're here."

"You don't remember, do you?" Katrina asked.

"Remember what?"

"That I don't know how to ride."

Mandy turned. "That's ridiculous."

"No, it's not."

"Of course you know how to ride."

Katrina shook her head, then tucked her loose hair behind her ears. "You guys used to put me up on a horse a lot. But I could barely hold on. I sure couldn't control it." If her horses hadn't willingly followed her sisters' and brothers' animals back home, she'd have been permanently lost in the wilderness.

"I can teach you," Mandy broke in.

Katrina laughed at that, deciding it was time to come clean. It had to be better than riding. "I'm afraid of horses, Mandy."

Her sister's forehead wrinkled. "What are you talking about?"

"They scare me half to death."

"Why?"

"Because they're big. They're strong. They're unpredictable, and one of them bit me once."

Mandy shook her head. "You can't put up with that. You have to show them who's boss."

"Does that sound like me?"

Mandy crossed her arms over her chest, leaning back against a stall fence and lifting one heel to brace it on the bottom rail, while the mare nudged at her ear. "I guess not," Mandy allowed, firmly pushing the horse's head away.

Katrina gave a self-deprecating grimace. "I can't even boss around five-foot-two male ballet dancers."

Mandy laughed at that. "I really could teach you."

"To boss my ballet partners around?"

"To ride horses."

Katrina took an involuntary step backward. "I don't think so."

"It's easy."

"Maybe so, but I don't want to learn how."

"But—"

"I'm only going to be here for a week, and there aren't a lot of horses in New York City."

Mandy's eyes narrowed. "But you'll come back, though, especially once Dad's home."

Katrina felt a familiar knot form in her stomach. Maybe it was because she'd left home so young and she didn't really know her father. Or maybe it was because she'd always sensed his disappointment in her. But the thought of being in the same room, of coming under his scrutiny, of dealing with the walking-on-eggshells feeling she got whenever he looked her way, made her want to turn and run.

"Katrina?" Mandy prompted.

"My schedule's pretty busy."

"But you do get time off."

"I do. But there are rehearsals. I'm doing a little teaching now." Katrina turned and started walking, not wanting to face her sister while she stretched the truth.

Mandy followed her lead. "You really do hate it here, don't you?"

"It's…" Katrina struggled for the right words. "Intimidating."

"I don't see why." Mandy urged Katrina down a side aisle.

"Of course you don't. You're like Ms. Super-Rancher."

Mandy laughed while she pushed open a door, and the sunlight flooded through. "You make a bigger deal about everything than it has to be. You always have."

"I do not." Katrina stopped short, unease shooting through her.

They'd walked outside into a large, green field, fences in the far distance. It was dotted with horses, in ones and twos, heads down, grazing.

"I won't let them get you," Mandy assured her.

"I'm not in the mood for an intervention." At her mother's insistence, Katrina was here to touch base with her family. But she wasn't here to conquer her fears and become a better human being.

"We're just walking. It's nicer out here than it is in the barn."

"In the barn, they're all behind fences."

"If they attack, I'll throw myself in front of you."

"Funny." Mandy might be taller and heavier than Katrina, but it was still a hundred-odd pounds against two-thousand. If a horse went rogue, Mandy wouldn't be able to save her.

Mandy turned so they were headed along the fence line, and Katrina felt a little better. At least there was a handy escape route if they needed one.

"So, what's the deal with you and Reed?"

Katrina stumbled on a clump of grass. "Huh?"

"Everything was fine last night."

"Everything was fine this morning, too."

Mandy crammed her hands into the front pockets of her jeans. "I know Reed very well. We were like brother and sister for the ten years Caleb was away. He's mad at you, and I'd like to know why."

Katrina shrugged. "You'll have to ask him."

"He won't answer."

"Then I guess we'll never know."

Mandy shook her head. "What makes you think you can start lying to me now?"

"Practice."

"Katrina. Seriously. Sometimes I feel like I don't even know you."

Katrina counted to ten inside her head. She knew she should say something innocuous and noncommittal, brushing off the comment and moving on. But some obstinate corner of her brain compelled her to speak up. "Maybe it's because you don't."

Mandy stopped dead. "What?"

Katrina knew it was past time to shut up. Unfortunately, her mouth didn't seem to get the message. "Travis says you all love me."

"We do."

"You don't even know me. You don't know I'm afraid of horses. You don't know I'm afraid of chickens. You don't know I'm afraid of Dad."

Mandy drew back in obvious shock. "Dad?"

Katrina's mouth seemed to be on autopilot. "And you have absolutely no idea that I'm afraid my ankle won't heal properly and that my dancing career will be over."

Mandy immediately reached for Katrina's hands, drawing her close, searching her expression. "Sweetheart, what's going on? What's wrong with your ankle?"

"It's nothing," said Katrina.

"What is it?" Mandy insisted.

Katrina waved a dismissive hand. "I had one of my pointe shoes give out, and I twisted my ankle."

"Are you okay?"

"I'm fine. I'd rather you didn't tell anyone."

"They'll want to know you're hurt," Mandy insisted. "They'll want to help."

"There's nothing they can do. I just need some rest, to let it heal."

"It was your shoe? Does this kind of thing happen often?"

"Hardly ever. Thank goodness." Katrina was having an unlucky streak, and she was going to get past it. Her ankle would heal. She should never have admitted out loud that she was worried. She wasn't. Not really.

She drew a bracing breath. "Mandy, I'm sorry. I didn't mean to say anything. I don't know what I was thinking—"

"I'm not the least bit sorry." Mandy tugged firmly on her sister's hands. "I want to know you, Katrina. No matter what's going on inside that crazy head of yours, we all *do* love you."

"I'm not crazy." Just because she didn't like ranching, didn't make her insane.

"Bad choice of words."

Suddenly, Katrina felt dead-tired. She didn't want to have this debate. It was bad enough that Quentin was out to get her and that her career might be hanging in the balance; she didn't need to add her childhood baggage to the mix.

"Do you think someone could drive me back to our place?" She'd make an excuse to catch a flight in the morning.

Mandy gave her head a vigorous shake. "Not a chance. Now

that we've broken the ice, we are going to talk, young lady."
She tucked Katrina's hand into the crook of her arm and began
walking again.

Katrina scoffed out an exclamation of disbelief. "I don't think
so." It was a momentary lapse, not the breaking of an emotional
dam ten years in the making.

"So, what happened with Reed?" Mandy repeated.

"Nothing."

"I think he likes you."

"I think he hates me."

"Yeah? Well, you're afraid of chickens, so I'm not much for
trusting your judgment."

"I really want to go home." Katrina sighed.

"If by home, you mean Caleb and Reed's house for margaritas, then that's exactly where we're going."

"I can't drink margaritas. I'll get fat."

"Oh, yes, you can. We'll burn off the calories somehow. But
you, my darling, are in serious need of a stiff drink and a big
sister."

"Your sister claims I've upset you." Reed's voice interrupted
Katrina in what she guessed was her thirteenth mile on the
makeshift stationary bike, burning off the four giant golden
margaritas from this afternoon. She and Mandy hadn't exactly
had a full-on heart-to-heart, but they'd definitely broken the ice.

The sun was going down now, but Katrina was still feeling a
little tipsy. The barn had grown quiet while she rode, with only
the occasional whinny punctuating the steady whirr of her bike
wheel.

"I'm not upset." She reached for the plastic water bottle in
the wire holder on the bike frame, popping the top and squirt-
ing some of the tepid liquid into her mouth.

"Good to know." He crossed his arms over his broad chest,
leaning sideways against a rough wood post.

Katrina snapped the cap back into place and slid the bottle
back into its holder. She braced her hands on the handlebars
and upped her speed.

A few moments went by in silence. Lights flicked off in the far reaches of the barn, and doors banged shut behind ranch hands packing it in for the night.

"Gone far?" asked Reed.

"Fourteen miles or so, I think." She swiped the back of her hand across her damp forehead. She was dressed in lightweight black tights and a baggy white tank top, but the air in the barn was still warm and close around her.

He went silent again, gazing dispassionately at her while she rode.

After about five minutes she cracked, straightening on the bike seat to look at him. "What are you doing?"

"Waiting."

"For what?"

"Mandy says you're worried about your ankle."

"Mandy needs to stop discussing my private business with everybody in the valley."

"I already knew about your ankle."

"She didn't know that."

"She does now."

Katrina stopped riding and huffed her frustration. "Are you going to get to your point?"

"I already did. Your ankle."

"What about it?"

He shifted away from the post, moving closer to her. "Will you let me look at it?"

Though she'd stopped riding, she was still growing hotter. "Are you a doctor?"

"No."

"A physiotherapist?"

"Nope."

"Guy with an ankle fetish?"

Reed cracked a grin. "No. But I've worked on a lot of horses with strained tendons."

She coughed out a laugh. "Good for you."

He braced a hand between hers on the handlebars. "I know how to make a herbal wrap that will increase circulation."

She crooked her head to look up at him. "Is this a joke? Did Mandy put you up to this?"

"I'm completely serious."

"I'm not a horse."

His gaze flicked down for a split second. "In fact, you are not. But the principle's the same." He motioned for her to lift her foot.

She ignored the gesture. "I thought you were mad at me."

"I am."

"So, why do you want to help?"

"Because you need it."

"And because Mandy asked you?"

"Mmm-hmm."

Katrina considered his expression seriously. "Were you ever in love with my sister?"

"No." He reached down and lifted her ankle, crouching and resting her leg across his denim-covered knee.

She didn't fight him. "Are you lying to me?"

"No."

"So, there's nothing between you and Mandy?"

"She's marrying my brother. That's what's between us." He tugged at the bow and loosened the laces of Katrina's sneaker.

"I don't even know how to interpret that." Did he mean Caleb had come between him and Mandy?

Reed gently removed Katrina's shoe and set it on the worn, dusty floor. "There's nothing to interpret."

"You're being deliberately oblique."

Reed shook his head, slipping off her sock. "What makes you think I had a thing for Mandy?"

"Because you're doing her a favor. By helping me. What other reason would there—"

His large warm hands wrapped around her ankle, and she jumped at the electric sensation.

"It's not Mandy." He rotated her ankle. "Does this hurt?"

Katrina sucked in a breath and tried to tug her foot out of his grasp.

"Hold still."

"It hurts."

"Sorry." His thumb pressed on the inside of her foot below her ankle bone. "This?"

"Yes," she hissed.

He tried the opposite side of her foot and glanced up.

She shook her head in an answer.

"Point your toe?"

She did.

"Other way."

She flexed. "Ouch."

"Yeah," he commiserated, moving back toward the sorest spot. He made small circles with the pad of his thumb, massaging in a way that hurt, but the pain wasn't too sharp.

She steeled herself to keep still.

"Relax," he instructed. His attention moved farther up her calf.

Okay, that didn't hurt at all. In fact, it felt very nice. Very, very nice. She closed her eyes.

His deep voice was low and soothing as it rumbled in the cavernous space. "I'm going to move you."

"Hmm?"

"You lean over any farther and you're going to fall off the bike seat." His hands left her leg, and suddenly he was scooping her from the bicycle, lifting her, carrying her.

"What—"

"Over here." He nodded to a small stack of hay bales against a half wall.

He set her down, and the stalks of hay prickled through her tights.

She shifted. "Ouch."

"Ouch?"

"It prickles."

Reed shook his head in disgust, coming to his feet, striding away, his boot heels clomping on the floor.

Katrina straightened. But just as she was debating whether to hop her way back to her discarded sock and sneaker or get her bare foot dirty, Reed returned with a dark green horse blanket over one arm.

He spread it across the hay bales, then unceremoniously lifted her to place her on the thick blanket.

"Better?" he asked, tone flat.

"I only have thin tights on," she protested, gesturing to the contrast of his sturdy jeans. "The hay pokes right through them."

"Did I say anything?"

"You think I'm a princess," she huffed.

"You are a princess." He crouched down in front of her, lifting her foot to his knee again.

"I have delicate skin and thin clothing."

His strong thumb began to massage again, working its way in circles up the tight muscles of her calf. "Am I hurting you now?"

"No."

"Good. Lean back. Try to relax. We'll talk about your clothes later."

She leaned back against the hay. "They're nice clothes."

"For Manhattan."

"For anywhere."

"Shut up," he said gently.

She did. Not because he'd told her to, but because his hands were doing incredible things to her calf. She found herself marveling that such an intense, powerful, no-nonsense man could have such a sensitive touch.

He took his time, releasing the tension from her muscles, gently working his way toward the injured tendon. By the time he got there, the surrounding muscles were so relaxed that it felt merely sore, not the burning pain she'd been experiencing for the past two weeks.

He moved away from her ankle, back up her calf, leaving bliss in his wake. Then, to her surprise, he started on the sole of her foot. She wanted to protest, but it felt too good as his fingers dug into the ball of her foot and the base of her heel. And when he switched to the other foot, she was beyond speech. Her sympathetic nervous system fully engaged, and her brain went to autopilot.

"Katrina?" Reed's deep voice was suddenly next to her ear.

She blinked against the fuzziness inside her brain, realizing that he'd leaned down on the hay bales beside her. Her eyelids felt heavy, and her mouth couldn't seem to form any words.

"Do I have to kiss the princess to wake her up?" he joked.

"Am I sleeping?"

"I hope so. You were snoring."

"I was not." She brought him into focus and saw that he was grinning. She couldn't believe she'd fallen asleep during a foot massage. "Do you have magic hands?"

"I do," he intoned.

The barn was quiet, the light dim all around them. They were alone and his eyes were pewter-dark, molten, watchful. His face was hard-wrought, all planes and angles, beard-shadowed, with that little bump on his nose that seemed to telegraph danger.

She had a sudden urge to smooth away that imperfection, to run her fingertips across his whisker-roughened chin and feel the heat of his skin. He'd said something about kissing her. Was he thinking about it now? Would he do it?

Her gaze shifted to his full lips, imagining their softness against her own.

"Katrina." His voice was strained.

She wanted him to kiss her, desperately wanted to feel those hot lips come down on hers, his hard body press her back into the hay, his magic hands wrap around her waist, along her back, over her buttocks, down her thighs. She just knew he would take her to paradise.

"The herbal wrap," he said.

She blinked. "Huh?"

He eased away from her. "I should put it on your ankle now, while your muscles are warmed up."

"But…" No. That wasn't how this was supposed to end.

"It'll help," he assured her.

"Reed?"

He straightened, no longer looking at her, his voice growing more distant. "I know you're not a horse. But trust me. The principle really is the same."

She didn't doubt it was. But that wasn't her problem. Her problem was that she was powerfully, ridiculously, sexually attracted to Reed Terrell, and it didn't look like it was going away anytime soon.

# Four

Reed swung the eight-pound sledgehammer over his head, bringing it down on the wooden stake with a satisfying thump. He drove it halfway into the meadow grass, then hit it once more, anchoring it firmly into the ground. He took a step back and set down the hammer. Then he consulted his house plans, lined up the electronic transit to position the next stake before repeating the process.

An hour later, as the sun climbed across the morning sky, he stripped down to his T-shirt, tossed it aside and shaded his eyes to gaze across the flat meadow that overlooked Flash Lake into the foothills and far across to the Rockies.

He'd known for years that this would be the perfect spot. Milestone Brook babbled fifty feet from where he'd build his deck. He already knew he'd put in a footbridge, teach his sons to fish for rainbow trout and build a picnic table on the opposite side of the bridge so his family could spend Saturday afternoons eating hamburgers, playing horseshoes or badminton.

He could picture the living room. He could picture the view. He could picture six kids racing around in the yard. He could even picture his future wife chasing down a toddler. She'd be beautiful in blue jeans and boots, a cotton shirt and a Stetson.

In his mind's eye, she turned and smiled. And he realized it was Katrina.

Reed felt as if he'd been sucker-punched.

He shook his head to clear it. That wasn't right. It wasn't right at all. He'd come up here today to get away from Katrina. His burgeoning attraction to her reminded him that it was past time to get going on the rest of his life. And the rest of his life sure didn't include a tiny, blond-haired, blue-eyed ballerina.

"Reed?" Her voice startled him, and he spun around to see her crossing the meadow toward him.

She moved steadily closer. Her hair was pulled up in a ponytail. She wore tiny diamond earrings that sparkled in the sunshine. Designer jeans clung to her hips, while a deep purple cap-sleeved T-shirt molded to her breasts, nipping in at her waist, ending just above her low waistband. Even without makeup, her lashes were thick and dark, her lips deep red, and her cheeks soft pink.

"What are you doing?" she asked him, glancing around at his work.

"What are *you* doing?"

"Walking." She came to a halt a few feet away. "It's a low-impact exercise."

"I thought you were biking for that."

"Variety," she answered, tipping her head to one side.

He fought an urge to take a single step forward, cup her face, and drink in a deep kiss. But somehow, it seemed sacrilegious, as if he was cheating on his future wife.

She peered pointedly around. "A building site?"

"I'm staking out the foundation," he admitted. "For my house."

"Seriously?" She shaded her eyes to scan his work. "You're building a house up here?"

"No. I'm building a secret military installation, with a formal dining room and a view of the lake."

She gave an eye-roll and paced her way toward the pattern of stakes. "It's big."

He found himself following behind. "Four bedrooms."

"Where's the front door?"

"You're standing on the porch."

She pointed. "So, here?"

"Go on in."

She glanced back at him to grin. "Thank you."

"Dining room on the right," he told her, oddly pleased to share his plans with someone. He'd designed them himself, keeping them secret from his father and everyone else. "Straight ahead takes you into the great room and the kitchen."

"On the left?"

"Media room, then utility room. You can cut through there to the garage."

She walked straight through the future great room toward the back of the house.

"That'll be a breakfast nook," he described. "There'll be French doors here that go out onto the deck."

"Great view," she put in.

"Isn't it? Master suite will have the same view."

She gazed out at the river. "But I don't understand."

He stopped next to her in the position he planned for the deck railing, resting his hands in his front pockets. "I like a nice view of the lake."

"I don't understand the new house. What's wrong with the old one?"

He'd made plans to build the new one before his father had died. But he saw no reason to change the plans now. "Caleb and Mandy can live there."

"But they're only going to be here part-time, right?"

"Probably. But they'll want their own space. And I'll want mine. So will my wife."

She turned to stare at him, and her eyes went round, her tone became incredulous. "You're getting married?"

"Yes, I am."

"Do you have a secret fiancée?"

"Not yet."

"Who?" she asked.

"I told you, not yet."

"But who is she?"

"I don't know."

Katrina canted a hip to one side, while her face screwed up in puzzlement. "You're building a house for a fiancée you haven't yet met?"

"You got a problem with that?"

She paused. "Truthfully, I think it's kind of sweet."

"I was going for practical."

"Well, you got sweet."

He scoffed out a laugh. "I'm not sweet."

She lifted her left ankle and twisted it in the air. "Your wrap helped."

"Yeah?"

"I'm positive it did," she confirmed, while his mind wandered back to their near kiss last night in the barn.

A rumble sounded in the distance, and Katrina braced her feet to the ground, turning sharply toward it.

"What's that?" she asked.

"Horses." He listened for a moment. "Small herd."

"Where?" She took a sideways step in his direction, her gaze darting around.

"Over the rise. Coming this way."

They were definitely at a gallop, and Reed wondered what might have startled them. Could have been anything.

"But there's a fence, right?" Katrina asked.

"What do you mean?"

"Between us and them?"

"Nope."

She paled. "Nope?"

He shook his head to confirm, and she moved so close she was touching him.

The sound grew louder.

"They're headed for the lake," Reed reassured her.

"Are we going to be trampled?" She turned her face into his chest.

He struggled not to laugh, placing a reassuring arm around her shoulders. "No, we're not going to be trampled. They'll head straight downhill."

"You can't know that."

"Even if they don't, they'll see us. They'll go around us."

"Are you lying? Are we about to die?"

He grasped her upper arms, putting her away from him, staring down into her eyes. "Seriously, Katrina. Calm down."

Her eyes were wide, ice-blue with fear. "What if they're angry?"

"They're thirsty," he assured her.

The herd appeared on the rise, their hooves thundering, the ground shaking. Katrina squealed and threw herself against his chest.

"See? They're turning," he told her.

Exactly as he'd expected, they curved around the knoll, taking the downhill route toward the lake. The dozen sleek brown, black and white bodies moved off into the distance. The sound diminished, and the ground vibrations disappeared.

Reed noticed Katrina was shaking.

"Hey." He smoothed back her hair. "Big-city princess, there's nothing to worry about."

"I'm sorry," she mumbled.

"Nothing to be sorry about."

"Then I'm embarrassed."

"Okay, that's a valid emotion."

She socked him in the bicep with the flat of her fist. "I'm not used to horses."

"No kidding."

Now that she'd calmed down, he allowed himself to focus on the feel of her in his arms. She was softly curved, perfectly proportioned. The top of her head only came to his chin, but she was looking up, and if he dipped his head, tipped it on an angle, his lips would be on hers.

His hand convulsed against the small of her back. Her hips

pressed against the V of his thighs. Her hands were warm where they rested against his back. And a surge of desire crested in his veins.

His gaze met hers, opaque and darkened to midnight-blue. The world stilled and paused for breath around them, the birds going silent, the wind going still; even the sound of the brook was muffled in the thickening air. His free hand rose to cup her cheek, sliding into her hairline as he dipped his head. Her sweet breath mingled with his.

"Tell me no," he rasped. Nothing short of her genuine protest would stop him this time.

But she stayed silent, stayed pressed against him, her lips slightly parted.

He cursed under his breath and crossed those final inches that brought his lips flush against hers. The burst of passion was instantaneous, igniting every fiber of his body to a roaring need. Her lips were full, tender and hot, and they tasted like summer nectar.

He urged them apart, delving deep with his tongue, his fingers tangling in her hair, his other arm wrapping fully around her waist, pressing her tight against his intense desire.

His kiss was too hard. His hold was too tight. He lifted her easily off the ground, even as a small speck of sanity that was struggling deep inside his brain ordered him to slow it down, to let her go, to back off.

But she moaned against his mouth, the vibration setting off another chain reaction of passion. Her hands fisted into his sweat-dampened shirt, while the softness of her breasts burned an imprint into his chest.

A horse whinnied in the distance, and the sound of the brook flowed into his ears. Birds came back to life, while the breeze picked up, cooling his overheated skin.

With steely determination, he forced himself to break the kiss. "I'm sorry," he breathed, still drinking in the feel of her soft curves.

"I'm not," she gasped.

His body convulsed. "Don't say that."

"Okay." A pause. "I won't."

He sucked in a couple of deep, deep breaths, forcing his hand to fall away from her cheek. Then he regretfully touched his forehead to hers. "I was out of line."

"Why are you blaming yourself?" Her breathing was as deep as his. "There are two of us here."

"I'm trying to be a gentleman."

She drew slowly back. Wisps of blond hair had worked free from her ponytail. Her lips were swollen red, cheeks flushed, eyes bedroom-soft with a sensual message. "In some circumstances, being a gentlemen is overrated."

Reed groaned his frustration. "You're killing me, Katrina."

"Not exactly what I was going for."

"You want me to kiss you again?" he demanded, knowing he couldn't take much more of her flirtatious teasing.

"You want to kiss me again, cowboy?"

"More than I've ever wanted anything in my life."

They stared at each other in charged silence.

"But I won't," he determined, gritting his teeth.

He wouldn't, because if he kissed her again, he knew he wouldn't stop. It wouldn't matter that the bedroom of his future house was nothing but a few stakes in the ground—he'd make passionate love to her, right here in the thick grass of the meadow. And then he'd have to build a different house, in a different location, because she'd be all he ever remembered here.

Katrina wasn't completely without experience when it came to men.

Okay, so she was mostly without experience when it came to men. But it wasn't her fault. She'd gone to an all-girls school until she was eighteen, graduating straight into the Liberty Ballet company. Until graduation, she'd been surrounded by girls and the few male dancers who'd participated in performances. The male dancers were nice guys, many of them fun and funny, but none of them interested her romantically.

She'd dated a little in the past year, mostly men she'd met

at fundraisers or parties connected to the dance company, but nothing had ever turned into a relationship.

And then there was Quentin. But she sure wasn't counting that. Reed's kiss, on the other hand, she would definitely count. Quentin was a member of Liberty Ballet's board of directors. Close to twenty years older than Katrina, he'd been dogging her since she'd become a principal dancer. Frustrated by her lack of uptake on his intense flirting, he'd finally cornered her in his office two weeks ago, forced a slobbery kiss on her mouth and baldly propositioned her. When she'd broken away, firmly telling him she wasn't interested, he'd grown angry and threatened to destroy her career.

She didn't know how or if he'd be able to make good on that threat. But he certainly knew the movers and shakers of the ballet world.

She ran a brush through her wet hair, gazing into the dresser mirror in the Terrells' guest room. Odd, the differences between Quentin and Reed. Quentin was urbane, educated, fastidious and debonair. Reed was raw, passionate, assertive and unruly. But there was no contest over who she'd trust.

Her fingertips went reflexively to her lips. She could swear they were still tingling from Reed's kiss this afternoon. He'd been the one to call a halt. He'd broken away and given them both a moment of sanity. If he hadn't done that, she was sure she would have lost her virginity to a rugged cowboy right there in the middle of a Lyndon Valley meadow.

She shook her head, even as her smile and the warm glow remained. Like any woman, she'd fantasized about her first time making love. It had always involved a posh hotel suite, and a man who'd laid his bow tie and tux over a French provincial armchair before joining her in a lacy, canopied bed. Lyndon Valley, blue jeans, an imperfect nose and a beard-rough chin weren't even on her radar.

"Katrina?" Mandy rapped lightly on the door.

"Come in," Katrina called, determinedly banishing thoughts of Reed and tightening the sash of her satin robe.

The door opened. Like Katrina, Mandy had showered recently. Her damp chestnut hair was combed back in a ponytail, and she'd pulled on a hunter-green T-shirt over a pair of beige cargo pants.

"How're you doing?" Mandy opened, letting the door swing closed behind her, getting comfortable on the corner of the bed and curling her bare feet beneath her. "Ankle holding up?"

"I'm fine," Katrina answered. "It's doing okay."

She really was fine, she realized. Quentin was far away and suddenly easy to push from her thoughts. He'd been obliterated by Reed. She felt buoyant and upbeat from all that fresh air. Her ankle had survived the walk with surprising strength. It felt a whole lot better than it had yesterday.

"Seth called," said Mandy.

"Is he ordering us back home?" Katrina crossed to her suitcase, open on a low table in the corner of the room. She'd been wondering how long her other three siblings would let her and Mandy hide out at the Terrell ranch.

"Sort of. He wants us to go to Lyndon with him tomorrow. The Lyndon Hospital is hosting a charity ball, and he thinks it'll be good for the campaign to have a strong Jacobs contingent by his side."

Katrina glanced over her shoulder. "He wants us to campaign for him?"

"Nah. All we have to do is show up, dance and smile for the cameras. Cakewalk for you."

Katrina retrieved a simple black knit skirt and a filmy copper cap-sleeved blouse. "Are we talking ballgowns and the whole nine yards?"

Mandy nodded. "It'll be formal."

"Then I'll have to go shopping." Which was a waste, since Katrina had a dozen perfectly appropriate ballgowns hanging in her closet in New York City. "And maybe do something with my hair. And I don't know what I've got for shoes."

If she could be positive any photos taken at the event would only be used locally for Seth's campaign, she wouldn't worry. But she and her fellow dancers at Liberty Ballet were under strict orders from the publicity department that every single public appearance, every picture, every interview, had to comply with company policy.

From the top of her head to the tips of her toes, she had to be esthetically perfect.

"Lyndon does have stores," said Mandy.

"And I'm going to need them," Katrina joked, stepping into the skirt.

"You'll probably have a lot more fun this trip. You're dressing up and dancing instead of slogging through the barns and worrying about horses."

Katrina paused, sensing a conspiracy. "You didn't tell Seth what I said?"

"No, no." Mandy determinedly shook her head. "It's a coincidence, I promise." She paused. "But there are some nice things about Colorado, you know."

Katrina fastened the skirt at her waist. "There are some nice things about New York City, too."

"You mean like traffic and muggings?"

"I mean like Central Park and the Met."

"Lyndon has an arts center, an orchestra and a museum."

Katrina slipped off the robe and put on the blouse over her lacy bra, fastening the tiny buttons up the front. "You really love it here, don't you?" She padded across the bedroom and joined her sister on the opposite corner of the bed.

"I really do," Mandy agreed.

"Won't you and Caleb mostly live in Chicago after the wedding?"

"We think it'll be about fifty-fifty. I'll put up with Chicago for him, and he'll put up with Lyndon Valley for me."

"So, one of you will always be unhappy?" Katrina didn't want to question the wisdom of her sister's marriage plans, but theirs didn't sound like a particularly smart arrangement.

Mandy's voice went soft. "Caleb hated his father. He didn't hate Lyndon Valley. And now that Wilton is gone, he'll remember all the things he loved about the ranch."

"You sure?"

"I'm positive."

Katrina plucked at the quilt. "Well, I'll never leave New York City."

"Not even for the right man?"

"The right man is already there."

Mandy straightened, her expression perking up. "I thought you said you didn't have a boyfriend."

"No boyfriend." Katrina was taking a page from Reed's logic. "I haven't met him yet. But I know he's out there, picking out an impressionist painting for his penthouse, balancing his stock portfolio and dry-cleaning his tux."

Mandy laughed, even as Katrina's thoughts flicked back to Reed.

"Did you know Reed was building a house?" she found herself asking her sister.

"What do you mean?"

"He showed me the building site today. Up in one of the top meadows beside Flash Lake. He's got it all staked out. I didn't see the drawings, but he talked like it was all planned. He says he's going to find himself a wife and start a family. You and Caleb get to keep this house."

"Really?" Mandy drew the word out in obvious contemplation.

"So this is something new?" Katrina confirmed.

"He told Caleb he was planning to raise a family here on the ranch. But, as far as I know, he didn't say anything about building a new house." Mandy shifted on the mattress. "I take it you're not fighting anymore?"

Katrina felt her cheeks heat and struggled to control the reaction. "We were never fighting." She glanced away. "It was… He just… He's helping me with my ankle."

Good grief. Why was she having trouble with such a simple explanation? It wasn't as though she was lying. Everything she was saying was true.

Mandy blinked. "Katrina?"

"Hmm?"

"What's going on?"

"What do you mean?"

"Are you attracted to Reed?"

Katrina formulated an answer. "Reed is Colorado."

If ever there was a man who was a perfect metaphor for a place, he was it.

"And you hate Colorado."

"I'm intimidated by it."

Mandy's gaze was probing. "So you're intimidated by Reed?"

"Why does this conversation feel like a chess game?"

"Because you're being evasive."

"I like my men in tuxedos," Katrina answered honestly.

Mandy grinned and chuckled. "Then tomorrow night at the ball ought to be very interesting."

"Why?"

"Because Reed will be in a tux."

"Not a problem," Katrina answered with conviction. It was one thing to dress a man up, but the grit of Colorado tended to stick.

The elevator door opened into the lobby of the Sunburst Hotel in downtown Lyndon, and Katrina nearly stumbled on her high-heeled silver sandals. Reed didn't look remotely gritty. Quite the contrary, he looked fantastic in a tuxedo.

Next to a marble pillar and an oversize leather furniture grouping, he was joking with Caleb, Travis and Seth. He was the tallest of the three, broad-shouldered, clean-shaven, with his hair freshly trimmed and his dark eyes zeroing in on her.

"Wow." The word whooshed out beneath her breath. She had to remind herself to keep walking between Mandy and Abigail.

"You mean Caleb?" Mandy asked, a thread of amusement in her tone.

"Right," Katrina returned without missing a beat. "Caleb." Her gaze stayed glued to Reed.

"Seth's tie is crooked," Abigail put in, quickening her pace, clearly hoping to get to Seth and correct the problem before anyone else noticed.

"Liar," Mandy muttered to Katrina.

"Who? Abigail?"

"Admit it, you're attracted to Reed."

"Not at all," Katrina lied.

"You haven't taken your eyes off him."

"I was thinking he's too tall." Among other things. He was also too strong, too determined, too attractive and far too good a kisser for a Colorado cowboy.

"He looks great in a tux," Mandy singsonged.

"All men look great in a tux." Though few men looked *that* great in a tux.

As they drew closer, Caleb gave a low whistle of appreciation, his gaze warm on Mandy in an off-the-shoulder, full-skirted, full-length gown in shimmering silver.

"I love it when you dress up like a girl," he told her, putting an arm around her bare shoulders, placing a gentle kiss on her temple.

Abigail finished with Seth's tie, chatting to him about the attendees at the ball, enumerating those he should seek out. Travis joined in their conversation, joking about who could make the biggest financial contribution to Seth's campaign, as the three started toward the hotel exit. Mandy took Caleb's arm and they fell into step behind, leaving Katrina and Reed to bring up the rear.

"You look very nice," Reed offered to Katrina, taking in her slim-fitting, butter-yellow satin gown. The V-necked bodice was crisscrossed with tiny strands of crystals that also ran the length of the spaghetti straps accenting her bare shoulders. The back dipped low, while the hem flared out. The skirt was snug at her hips, but loose enough along the length of her legs to allow for dancing.

She'd bought some inexpensive but fun dangling crystal earrings that now hung below her simple updo. She'd paired them with an elaborate necklace of crystals interspersed with yellow topaz snug against her throat. Her makeup was to Liberty Ballet standards, a little heavier than Katrina preferred, but nobody in the ballet company would have a complaint if her photo ended up in a national magazine.

"Thank you," she answered Reed, still drinking in his appearance.

He'd skipped the bow tie, going instead for a classic Windsor knot of taupe silk with a matching pocket square in the black coat, all over a crisp white shirt. The tux fitted him extremely well, and she wondered if it was possible that he owned it.

His strong, weathered hands and his slightly imperfect nose were the only things that stopped him from being equally urbane as any man she'd met in New York City. The realization was both disconcerting and exhilarating.

He held out his arm. She automatically slipped her hand into the crook of his elbow, the strength of his ropy muscles evident through the supple fabric.

"You look very nice, too," she returned the compliment.

"I feel like a penguin," he grumbled. "Do you have any idea how hard it is to move in one of these things?"

Katrina gestured to her slim-fitting dress. "As opposed to moving in this?"

"Nobody expects you to hop out of the car and change a tire."

"You're planning to change a tire tonight?"

"You never know what might happen."

She couldn't help but laugh at that.

He took her hand and pressed it to his jacket pocket.

She felt a hard, rectangular lump against his hip. "What on earth?"

"Multitool," he told her. "Knife, screwdriver, file, pliers."

"You're armed with a tool set?"

"Yes, ma'am."

"We'll be in a ballroom," she pointed out. "I expect there's a maintenance crew. And the worst thing likely to happen tonight is a broken shoe buckle."

They passed through the hotel exit to the sidewalk, where a lineup of shiny black SUVs waited for guests. She glanced around but didn't spot her sisters and brothers.

"I can fix a broken shoe buckle," said Reed. "I can also repair a harness, remove a splinter, whittle some kindling and fix an outboard motor."

"I can't do any of those things, with or without a multitool. Well, maybe remove a splinter," she allowed. Then she glanced ruefully at the tiny clutch purse that contained nothing but the bare necessities. "But not with anything I brought along to-night."

Reed opened the back door to one of the vehicles. "That's the beauty of the system," he told her, cupping his palm over her elbow to help her into the seat.

She glanced up questioningly.

He gave her a grin and a waggle of his brows. "You brought me. You don't need anything else."

"You're a living, breathing multitool?" she guessed.

His eyes darkened ever so slightly, and his tone went low. "That I am."

Had he just turned shoe-buckle repairs into a flirtation?

Before she could decide, he gently shut the door behind her, rounding the back of the vehicle to climb in the other side.

"To the Hospital Ball?" the driver asked Reed.

"Yes, please," he answered, stretching his arm across the back of the seat.

The driver nodded and pulled the vehicle into traffic.

Reed angled his body so that he was gazing at Katrina. He didn't say anything, just watched her while they made their way along Seventh Street toward Main.

She gazed back, meeting his eyes, strangely not feeling the need to break the silence. The moment stretched on, and she found herself remembering their kiss, his touch, his taste, the sound of his voice rumbling next to her ear and the woodsy scent of his skin.

"You going to be able to dance?" he asked gruffly, with a nod toward her left ankle.

"I think I can make it through a waltz or two," she answered.

Progress was slow on her ankle. Then again, at least she was making progress. For the few days before she'd come back to Colorado, the healing had seemed to stall. She'd been terrified it would never get better, or it would take so long to get better that she'd lose her position with the ballet company.

A shiver ran through her at the unsettling thought.

"Save a dance for me?" Reed asked quietly, his eyes glinting silver.

"I will." Katrina realized once again how safe she felt with Reed. There was nothing to worry about right now. Nothing was going to cause her any trouble tonight. Not even a flat tire.

As Reed would have expected, Katrina was the belle of the ball. Dinner had ended, but the dancing was not yet underway. So far, it had taken her nearly twenty minutes to make it halfway across the ballroom toward the ladies' room. Men stopped her, clustered around her, asking questions, obviously offering compliments, lingering when they shook her hand, making excuses to touch her.

Reed downed a swallow of champagne, wishing he had something stronger to quench his thirst.

Travis Jacobs took the chair next to him, nudged his elbow, and offered him a single malt, neat, in a heavy crystal glass.

Reed gratefully accepted. "Thanks."

Travis slouched back, propping his elbow on the opposite chair, his voice a drawl. "I see the way you're looking at my sister."

Reed took a swallow of the Scotch. "Same way every other guy in the room is looking at your sister. You don't like it? Don't let her dress like that."

"You Terrells need to keep your hands off the Jacobs women."

Reed gave a snort of derision. "Caleb's marrying one of them, and I haven't touched any of them."

Kissing Katrina didn't count. It was a well-accepted fact that *touching* in this context meant something considerably more than kissing.

Just then the orchestra came up and the lights went down. Reed and Travis both watched as yet another man approached Katrina. His gaze scanned her thoroughly from head to toe, then he stood far too close, his expression animated, his hand too familiar on her arm. Katrina took a step back, but the guy didn't let her go.

Reed firmly set down his Scotch glass and came to his feet. "I assume dancing is acceptable," he said to Travis, even as he moved away from the table.

"If it gets her out of that jerk's clutches, go for it."

Reed nodded in response, already pacing his way toward Katrina.

Once there, he snaked a proprietary arm around her slim waist. "Sweetheart," he drawled, his hard glare causing the jerk to pull back as if he'd been scalded.

"Are you ready for that dance?" he continued, turning his attention fully onto Katrina, dismissing the other man with a cold shoulder.

The man withdrew, muttering something unintelligible.

A beat went past.

"Did you just rescue me?" Katrina asked in obvious amusement.

"Story of my life."

"I was fine."

"You didn't look fine." Reed knew he should remove his hand from her waist, but he left it there anyway.

"He was a little too friendly," she admitted. "But I could have handled it."

"You didn't need to handle it. That's why you brought me along, remember?"

She pivoted to look at him. "I thought you were only planning to fix shoe buckles and remove splinters."

He couldn't help but smile at her joke. "I also dance."

"The two-step?"

"If that's what you want."

She cocked her head. "This is a waltz."

Reed removed his arm from her waist, tucking her hand into the crook of his arm. "Then let's waltz."

He steered her toward the dance floor where the ensemble was playing a classic ballad. There, he drew her into his arms, and his entire body seemed to sigh in satisfaction as she settled against him.

She was fluid and graceful, light on her feet, sensitive to his slightest nuance. He tucked her more closely to his body, his hand coming in contact with the bare skin revealed by the plunging V at the back of her dress. Her soft skin was so distracting that he struggled for something coherent to say.

"You're a very good dancer," he opened.

There was a smile in her voice when she answered. "Thank you. I've had a few lessons."

He gave a sheepish grin in return. "I guess you have."

"But it was nice of you to notice," she continued with what sounded like sincerity. "And you're not so bad yourself."

"High-school gym class," he admitted. It wasn't something he'd done frequently since then, but when he did, he always enjoyed it.

The lights dimmed further, and the band switched songs to another famous fifties cover tune. Reed saw no reason to let her go, so he let one song blend into the next, keeping her snugly in his arms.

They silently wound their way toward a set of doors that were open to a wide veranda. It was darker at this end of the ballroom, the music was lower and a cool breeze wafted in from the riverbank. She molded closer against him.

"Cold?" he whispered, gathering her tight, even as he turned so that his body was blocking the breeze.

"I'm fine," she answered into his chest.

Reed was fine, too. In fact, he was a whole lot better than fine. He wished that time would stop, that the world would fall away and leave him here alone with Katrina.

But then he caught sight of Travis far across the room, closely watching their every move. And he knew the world wasn't going anywhere anytime soon. Not that Reed blamed Katrina's brother for worrying. Reed definitely shouldn't be trusted with her.

"You go to things like this in New York City?" he found himself asking, curious and wondering how safe she'd be with neither of her brothers around to run interference.

Did she dress this provocatively for functions in New York? It was obvious she wasn't wearing a bra, and he couldn't help but wonder what exactly she had on underneath the clingy satin dress.

"Things like what?" she asked, voice slightly dreamy.

"Dances, charity functions."

"Yes." She nodded. "We're contractually obligated to make public appearances. It's good for contributions to have recognizable performers attend Liberty Ballet fundraisers."

Reed didn't like the sound of that. "It's compulsory? What if you don't want to go?"

She tipped her chin to look up at him. "It's my job."

Reed's spine stiffened. "It's your job to dance with random men?"

"Random men with a lot of money to contribute."

"I don't like it."

"Really?" she drawled. "And your opinion counts why?"

Reed didn't have a good answer for that. "What about your brothers?"

"What about them?"

Reed's glance darted to Travis again, finding him absorbed in a conversation with two other men. "Do they know?"

"You mean, do they know..." she made a show of glancing surreptitiously around the dance floor then lowered her voice to a stage whisper "...about my wicked little ballroom-dancing secret?"

A surge of jealousy hit Reed at the thought of her other dance partners. Giving into impulse, he stepped through the patio door, spinning her outside, away from the crowd.

"Hey," she protested.

But instead of stopping, he let their momentum carry them along the fieldstone wall. He came to a halt beside a square stone pillar, his forearm tightening across the small of her back, the darkness closing around them to give privacy.

She gasped in a breath, lips parting, eyes wide.

He gave her half a second to say no, then swooped in for a kiss. He came down harder than he'd intended, openmouthed, tongue invading, greedily savoring the sweet, moist heat of her mouth.

After a startled second, she tipped her head back, welcoming him, her tongue tangling with his. Her spine arched, and her hips pressed against the steel of his thighs. Her arms twined around his neck, and his free hand closed over her rear, the thin fabric of her dress all but disappearing in his imagination.

"Are you naked under this?" he rasped, kissing her neck, her shoulder, brushing a spaghetti strap out of the way to taste her tender skin.

"Are you naked under that?" she asked in return, tone teasing, her hands slipping beneath his jacket to wrap around him, branding him through the cotton of his shirt.

"Yes," he hissed, then resumed the kiss that went on and on, pushing want and need into every fiber of his body. His world contracted to Katrina, her taste, her feel, her scent. His hands roamed, while his lips savored, and her lithe body imprinted itself on his skin.

A woman's laughter penetrated his consciousness, as a group of people wandered onto the deck.

Reed forced himself to let go, fisted his hands and gritted his teeth, struggling hard to bring himself back under control.

When he found his voice, it was a mere rasp. "What are we doing?" What was *he* doing? What on earth had gotten into him?

Her hands were still braced on his chest, and her lips curved into a secret smile. "I believe it's called kissing."

It was so tempting to fall back into the moment. But he couldn't allow it. This chemistry between them flew out of control the instant he let his guard down.

"What is the *matter* with *me?*" he ground out.

Why couldn't he leave her alone? She was a family friend and a neighbor, soon to be an in-law. She wasn't some temporary pickup in a honky-tonk.

She eased away, straightening the strap of her dress. "Are you saying 'not here'?"

He wished it were that simple. "I'm saying not ever."

Her smile faltered, and he immediately felt like a cad. Bad

enough he'd accosted her. Now he'd insulted her. He hadn't meant it the way it sounded. He raked a hand through his short hair, putting more space between them. "I'm sorry."

She pressed her lips together. "No problem." She made to move around him.

He reached out. "Katrina."

But she brushed his hand away. "No need for an explanation."

He snagged her wrist, stopping her. "It's not that I don't want—"

"You're embarrassing me, Reed." Her tone was brittle; her crackling blue gaze staring straight ahead.

He leaned down, lips close to her ear, attempting to make it better. "Listen to me."

"No." She tried to free her wrist.

"I want you, Katrina," he confessed. "I want you very, very badly."

"I can tell."

He mustered his strength. "Give me a break. Your sister is marrying my brother."

She pinned him with a glare. "Is this some archaic chivalry thing?"

"Yes." For want of a better term, it was.

She leaned into him, the tip of her breast brushing his arm. "Well, you might want to get over that."

"Katrina," he warned on a growl.

"Because I want you, too, Reed. Very, very badly."

His hand went lax at her frank admission. It gave her a moment to escape, and she took it.

# Five

Katrina couldn't believe the way she'd taunted Reed. She'd never said anything remotely that bold to a man.

She made beeline back to the Jacobs' table, her emotions vacillating between rattled, embarrassed and just plain annoyed.

She was a grown woman. Where did he get off protecting her from herself? As though she wasn't capable of making up her own mind? She knew her sister was marrying his brother. So what? She and Reed were adults.

From the empty round table she caught a glimpse of him far across the ballroom. His gaze scanned the cavernous room, stopped on her and he immediately headed her way. She took a bracing sip of her champagne.

Annoyed. She was definitely going with annoyed.

Her brother Travis dropped down in the chair beside her. "What's this I hear about you being afraid of horses?" he asked.

"What's this I hear about you riding bulls again?"

"Who told you that?"

"Mandy said you did the rodeo down in Pine Lake."

"At least I'm not afraid of them."

"You ought to be. You're not eighteen anymore."

"Nice deflection," Mandy put in as she took the chair on the opposite side of Katrina. Caleb pulled out the one next to her.

"Music's nice," Katrina observed, turning her attention to Mandy.

"I could teach you to ride in under a week," said Travis.

"A nice eclectic mix of songs," Katrina noted to no one in particular. "That's my preference for an evening like this."

"Excuse me?" an unfamiliar male voice sounded just behind her.

Katrina turned to see a rather handsome man in his mid-thirties, his hand held out to her, palm up.

"Would you care to—" The man's gaze abruptly flicked upward. "Never mind," he muttered, dropping his hand. "I'm sorry." Then he turned away.

Katrina watched his retreat in puzzlement. Not that she wanted to dance. Her ankle was starting to ache. But it was very strange behavior.

"Thing is," Travis carried on in a firm voice. "There's absolutely no reason for you to be afraid of them."

Katrina turned back, knowing she wasn't going to be able to avoid the topic forever. But as she turned, she met Reed's hard gaze. He'd planted himself on the chair directly across from her, his face twisted into a tight frown. She guessed that explained the would-be dance partner's abrupt departure.

"You're in pretty good shape," Travis continued talking to Katrina. "And you must have decent balance."

"Decent," Katrina agreed, still watching Reed. The meddler.

"You might want to tackle that chicken fear, too," said Mandy, a gentle teasing note in her tone.

Katrina took a long swallow of her champagne. It was her third glass tonight, and she noted the alcohol was putting a pleasant lethargy in her limbs. Reed's expression began to look faintly amusing, and the company of her siblings didn't seem quite as intimidating as usual.

Abigail arrived and took the chair next to Reed. "What are we talking about?" She glanced to the faces around the table.

Travis spoke up. "Katrina's irrational fear of Colorado."

"It's not a fear," she defended. "More…" She paused to find the right word. "A distaste."

"That's silly," said Abigail. "What's not to love around here? The mountains, the trees, the clear air, the clean water."

"The dust," said Katrina, polishing off her champagne. She glanced around for a waiter. Hang the calories. She wanted to maintain this buzz.

"You get used to the dust," said Mandy.

"You're missing my point." Katrina's tone was sharp enough that her siblings sat back in surprise. A little voice inside her told her to shut up, but just then a waiter came by, offering her a fresh glass of champagne, and she knew this was the day to go for it.

She accepted a fourth glass.

"Then what is your point?" Travis demanded.

In her peripheral vision, she saw Reed direct his frown at her brother.

"I don't want to change for Colorado," she carried blithely on. "I want Colorado to change for me."

"Now *that's* what I call a diva," said Travis.

"Travis," Mandy objected.

"Is that what you all think of me?" Katrina knew they did, but this was the first time she'd brought it out into the open.

Travis opened his mouth to speak, but Caleb intoned in a low warning. "Travis."

Katrina's champagne glass was suddenly removed from her hand. Startled, she glanced down and realized Reed had leaned across the table to take it from her. He set it down out of her reach.

"Hey," she protested.

"Excuse me while I put on the kid gloves," Travis drawled.

"She's your sister," said Caleb.

"And that means I get to have an honest conversation with her."

"Not tonight, it doesn't," said Reed. Somehow, he had appeared by her side.

Katrina glared at Travis. "I am not a diva." She knew divas, and Travis had obviously never met one. "Just because I don't happen to like horses or Holsteins or cowboys."

"Your family is full of cowboys," Travis pointed out.

"But you all clean up nice," chirped Mandy in an obvious attempt to lighten the mood.

Caleb backed up her effort, making a show of raising his glass. "Let's hear it for clean cowboys."

Abigail and Mandy immediately played along. "Clean cowboys."

Travis grimaced, but Caleb stared him down until he gave in and raised his glass.

Katrina quickly stretched out to snag her own. "Too bad they don't stay that way long."

Everyone groaned, but it quickly turned to good-natured laughter.

She took a big swallow.

Reed muttered darkly in her ear. "You about done?"

"Done what?" she asked tartly, reminding herself that she was angry with him. It hadn't been very gentlemanly of him to break off their kisses. Then again, he'd kind of stood up for her against Travis just now.

"Abigail," said Reed. "I think Katrina's ready for bed."

A saucy comeback was on the tip of Katrina's tongue. But when she swiveled to deliver it, she caught Reed's thunderous expression. And she wasn't quite brave enough to embarrass him.

"Are you going to wrap my ankle?" she asked him instead.

"No."

"But it's sore."

"You've had too much champagne."

"It's still sore."

She wanted to get him up to the hotel room, alone, where she would… Okay, she wasn't exactly sure what she'd do, but at least they could talk. This idea that they were going to nobly fight their attraction to each other because of Mandy and Caleb was ludicrous.

"Wrap her ankle?" Abigail asked.

"She strained her tendon dancing," said Reed. "I've been using my herb wrap."

"Crackerjack cure," said Caleb.

"You hurt your ankle?" asked Abigail.

"It's getting better," said Katrina, somewhat surprised that Mandy hadn't already shared the information with their sister.

Mandy reached out and took Katrina's hand. "Maybe you should head back to the hotel. You've probably had enough dancing."

"Sure," Katrina agreed, playing the dutiful baby sister. Then she glanced innocently up at Reed. "You'll take me back?"

His jaw tightened. "Abigail? Are you ready to go?"

"Absolutely," said Abigail, and Katrina heard her rise from her chair. "I'm exhausted."

Since Katrina and Abigail were sharing a room, there'd be no private conversation with Reed tonight. But Katrina wasn't giving up. Tomorrow, they'd all troop back to the ranches. Eventually, she and Reed would find themselves alone.

Katrina soon discovered that things Reed didn't want to happen, didn't happen. After the charity ball in Lyndon, she and Mandy had spent a couple of days at their own ranch. But her sister soon found a reason to return to Terrells', and Katrina found an excuse to go with her.

There, Reed was polite but resolute. He spent his days in the far reaches of the ranch, and his evenings in the company of Caleb and Mandy. If Katrina asked him a direct question, he answered. And he continued to wrap her ankle each evening, but he was careful never to get caught alone with her.

So she was surprised on a midday to hear his voice on the porch of the ranch house. She'd run through a workout and a few dance routines in the basement rec room this morning and was now looking for Mandy.

"It'll only take me a few hours," Reed was saying.

"That's not the point," Caleb returned. "We have hands for those kinds of jobs."

"I have no intention of spending my entire afternoon in the office."

"Once we get things set up with a manager, you'll be able to do or not do any old job you want around here."

"Good." Reed's tone was implacable. "Today I want to fix the well pump at Brome Ridge."

"You're impossible."

"Deal with it. I'll probably be late getting back tonight." His boot heels clunked on the porch, and Katrina took her chance.

She burst through the front door. "Did you say Brome Ridge?" she asked Reed.

He stopped dead, as if frozen to the floor.

"I've been wanting to get up there before I leave," she rattled on. "I've only got a couple of days left. Would you mind?" she smiled brightly.

"Forget it," said Reed.

"Take her along," said Caleb.

Reed shot his brother a glare. "It's a working trip, not a picnic."

"I won't get in the way," Katrina promised. Trapped in a pickup, Reed would have to talk to her. She'd be heading back to New York City very soon, and she wasn't ready to pretend their attraction had never happened.

"You always get in the way." Reed's glare turned on her, his gray eyes hard as slate.

"Quit being such a jerk," Caleb put in. "Go ahead, Katrina."

"Back off, Caleb."

"Which truck?" asked Katrina.

Caleb nodded. "Parts are in the back of the green one."

"She's not going," Reed ground out.

But Katrina was already on her way down the stairs, heading across the wide driveway turnaround to the green pickup truck.

She hopped in the passenger side, slammed the door shut, and watched Reed argue with Caleb a few minutes longer. Finally, he turned, stalking across the driveway toward the pickup.

He yanked open the passenger door. "Get out."

"No."

"Yes."

She nodded to where Caleb was staring at them from the top of the stairs. "Your brother thinks you've gone insane."

"You are not going to do this to me," he vowed.

"Do what?" She mustered up an expression of calm innocence. "What is it you think I'm doing here, Reed?"

He blinked, a split second of uncertainty crossing his face.

"All I want to do is talk," she pressed. "I'm going to be gone in a couple days. It may be years before I'm back. You're a nice guy. You helped me with my ankle. You built me a stationary bike. You don't want a chance to say goodbye?"

He stared at her in silence, and she could read his hesitation. He was wondering if he'd imagined her intense attraction to him, their near-combustible chemistry, the fact that they shouldn't be allowed to be alone together if they didn't want it to race out of control.

He wasn't imagining a thing. But she didn't have to tell him that.

"Do you think I can't keep my hands off you?" She kept her tone light and teasing, even though nervous energy was churning its way through her stomach. "Is your ego really that big?"

His jaw snapped tight, and he stepped back, abruptly slamming the car door.

Katrina let out a breath of relief.

He yanked open the driver's door, dropped into the seat, started the engine and peeled out of the driveway, leaving a rooster tail of dust and small stones.

Katrina rocked against the passenger door, then flew upright. She grappled with her seat belt, fastening it tight and low across her hips.

Neither of them spoke for a good half hour as they wound their way along the rutted dirt-and-grass road up through the trees to where the pastures fanned out on the higher rangelands. Reed shifted the truck into four-wheel drive, and Katrina hung on as they traversed a shallow creek.

"Is this going to be a long, silent ride?" she finally asked.

"This was always going to be a long silent ride. I expected to be alone."

"Well, good news," she announced brightly. "I can make small talk and entertain you."

He shifted to a lower gear, pointing the truck up a steep, muddy rise. "I guess the cocktail-party circuit had to come in handy at some point."

"That's where you want to go? Insulting me?"

"I don't want to *go* anywhere. And it was an observation, not an insult."

"You're lying."

"Okay," he allowed. "It was a joke."

"It wasn't funny."

He quirked a half smile. "I thought it was."

"You're not a very nice man, Reed Terrell."

He looked her way for a long moment.

She glanced to the rutted road, to Reed, and back again. There was a curve coming up. She waited for him to turn his attention to driving. "Uh, Reed."

"I'm not a nice man," he confirmed softly. "And you should remember that." Then he glanced out the windshield and made an abrupt left turn.

Katrina was forced to hold on tight again. "I'm not afraid of you, Reed."

"That's okay. I'm scared enough for the both of us."

Katrina didn't know how to respond to that. The idea of Reed being afraid of anything was patently absurd.

A long time later, the truck rocked to a halt on the dirt road, an aspen grove fanning out on the downhill side, and a steeper hill running up the other.

Reed shut off the engine. "We'll have to walk it from here."

"Walk?"

He pushed the driver's door open. "Unless you want to wait here. I shouldn't be more than a few hours."

"No, no." She reached for her own door handle. "Walking is fine." Luckily, she'd worn comfortable runners. Her midcalf, low-rise tights weren't perfect for bushwhacking, neither was her tank top, but she gamely hopped from the seat.

Reed retrieved a worn leather tool belt from the box of the truck, strapping it around his waist, stuffing a hammer, tape measure, screwdrivers, wrenches and pliers into the loops and pockets. Then he tucked some lengths of rod and pipe beneath his arm, hoisted out a battered red toolbox and turned for a trail that wound up the side of the hill.

Katrina quickly fell into step with him. "You want me to carry anything?"

He snorted. "Yeah, right."

"I was just trying to be helpful."

His long strides were incredibly efficient, and she had to work to keep up.

He glanced over his shoulder. "Let's not pretend you're going to be any use as a pack animal."

"Let's not pretend you're going to give me a break."

"You should have stayed back at the ranch house."

The trail grew steeper, and, as they neared the crest, she was forced to grasp at the branches of trees to pull herself forward. "And miss all this?"

Reed stood tall on the top of the ridge, a sloping meadow splayed out before them, falling away to a deep valley before rising to the next hilltop.

Katrina sucked in a few breaths. "There's a well up here?"

Reed pointed north along the ridgeline. "It pumps into a pond around the bend. The cattle like it up here in late summer. This meadow catches the prevailing wind and that keeps the bugs down. But if there's no water source, they have to trek all the way back to the river."

"See that, you are a nice guy."

"I'm a practical guy." His gazed scanned her. "You doing okay?"

"Perfectly fine."

"Your ankle?"

"Almost better."

"Okay." He started along the uneven ridge, quickly outpacing her and drawing away.

If she'd hoped to engage him in a conversation, it wasn't going to work out. Reed was obviously determined to keep her at a distance. Not that she knew what to say. Just getting him alone had proven so difficult she hadn't formulated much of a plan beyond that.

After hiking for nearly an hour, they came to a muddy-bottomed pond beneath a twenty-foot windmill tower. The wind had picked up, and the whirring, clunking noise of the windmill made conversation difficult.

Reed set down the toolbox and began inspecting the arms that connected the pump to the windmill. A complex series of tubes and connections ran between the two. After a few moments, he selected a wrench and pulled hard on what seemed to be a stubborn bolt. It broke free, and he disconnected the mechanism.

Now that Katrina was standing still, she began to cool off. It didn't help that the sun had disappeared behind a thick layer of cloud; they were completely exposed to the wind here on the ridge. She had to fight off the odd mosquito, but she didn't dare complain. Instead, she gritted her teeth while Reed worked his way through whatever problem he'd discovered.

When the rain started, Reed swore.

He turned to look at Katrina, then he did a double take. "Are you cold?"

"I'm fine," she responded, but her teeth were chattering.

Reed dropped a big wrench, swore again, and stalked toward her. As he'd done when he found her on the trail with her broken bicycle, he stripped off his shirt.

"I don't need—"

"Shut up."

"I'm sorry," she found herself saying, even as the warmth of his cotton shirt wrapped around her. She tugged the ends together and crossed her arms over her chest.

"Sit down," he told her. "It'll be less windy if you're low to the ground." Then he glanced up at the sky and heaved a frustrated sigh. "You shouldn't have come up here."

"I'm fine," she repeated, perching herself on a clump of meadow grass. He was right, sitting down did help to keep her out of the wind. Now, if only the rain would stop.

But the rain didn't stop, and the more it rained, the more frustrated Reed became, and the more colorful the language coming out of his mouth. As the rain turned to a downpour, the wrenches kept slipping from his hands. He was obviously having trouble seeing clearly, and he dropped something. He peered into the mud, feeling his way around the tufts of grass.

After a long search, he tossed the wrench to the ground. "Damn it! Katrina, I can't let go of this. You're going to have to help."

She came to her feet, his wet shirt hanging loosely to midthigh. "What should I do?"

He took what seemed to be a calming breath. "Look in the toolbox. Lift out the top tray and see if you can find a nut-and-bolt set. It's better if it has some washers."

"Washers?"

"Wide, round disks of metal."

"Right." Trying not to shiver from the wet and wind, she opened the lid to the toolbox. The stormy day was complicated by the fact that the sun was now sinking behind the hills.

"Can you see anything?" he asked.

"Not really." She reached in to feel her way around instead.

"Don't!" Reed shouted, and she immediately stilled.

His voice moderated. "Some of the things in there are sharp. You could cut yourself."

"I can't see," she apologized.

"It's okay. Close the lid." He waited while she closed it and flipped the catches. "Now, can you pick up the box and move it over here?"

Katrina stood, bent down and gripped the handle of the metal toolbox with both hands. Then she pulled up with all her might. Nothing happened. She screwed up her determination and tried again.

It lifted a couple of inches off the ground, and she moved it forward before dropping it down.

"Don't hurt yourself," Reed warned.

"I'm good," she gasped. She lifted again, swinging it closer. Then again. And again.

"You're doing fine," he told her.

"This is pathetic."

"For a cowboy, yeah," he agreed. "For a ballerina, we make allowances."

"Thank goodness I'm going back to New York City."

There was a breath of silence before he spoke. "Thank goodness."

"I'm almost—" Her feet slipped out from under her, and she landed in an undignified heap on the muddy ground, brown water spraying around her. "There," she finished, seriously regretting her decision to come along on this trip. Exactly *why* did she think she needed to be alone with Reed?

"You okay?" he asked.

"Define *okay*."

"Are you injured?"

"No. Bruised, yes."

Reed stretched out his arm, his fingertips almost made it to the handle of the toolbox. Katrina gave it a hard shove, sliding the box, and he grasped the handle in his fist, lifting it and moving it to where he could search for a bolt.

"I can't believe you carried that thing all the way up the hill," she told him.

"I have size, muscle mass and testosterone on my side."

"You're incredibly useful."

"And you're incredibly pretty." He glanced at her. "Well, not right now."

She clenched her jaw. "I hate being pretty."

"What's to hate? You bat those beautiful blue eyes and the world falls at your feet."

"Is that how you see it?"

"That's not how I see it. That's the way it is."

"You think the world gives me a free ride."

His opinion didn't surprise her. She'd known all along that was how he felt, that she was some decorative plaything. He was as bad as Quentin. Though she supposed she should credit Reed with trying to keep his distance. At least he didn't think it was his right to sleep with her.

"I think your world is a completely different place than mine," he said.

"Do you think yours is better?" She honestly wanted to know.

"I think it's harder," he admitted, still searching through the toolbox. "I don't think everyone can make it out here, and I think—"

"You think it's *easy* becoming a professional dancer?"

"I didn't say that."

"You thought it."

"I was about to say, I think people stay cleaner in your world." He seemed to find what he was looking for, pulling an object out of the box and squinting at it in the dusk.

"I work hard," she told him defensively.

"You should work at getting rid of that chip on your shoulder." He returned to the repair.

"I do not have—"

"Admit it, Katrina. You think you're better than the rest of us."

"I—"

"You live in the bright lights of a big city. You dress in designer clothes. You hobnob with the rich and famous. You eat in the best restaurants. And every few years, you come back to Colorado to go slumming." He reefed hard on the wrench.

"That's not *fair.*"

"And for some reason, this time, you've decided I should be part of your down-home experience."

Katrina's jaw dropped open. Reed thought she was slumming it by kissing him? Was he crazy?

"Thanks, but no thanks, Katrina." He rose, collecting some of the scattered tools. "I'll keep my self-respect, and you can run back to those champagne-swilling dandies at your snooty cocktail parties."

Katrina lurched to her feet. "Wow," was all she managed. She stared at his slick, half-naked body, powerful and magnificent in the waning light. "Did you ever get that wrong."

He bent to fiddle with something on the pump contraption, and the piston came to life with a rhythmic, sloshing sound.

Apparently satisfied, he closed a sheet-metal cover and fastened it. He gathered up the remaining tools, shoving some of them back into his tool belt, putting others in the box and securing the lid.

He stood and looked around at the dark surroundings. "We have to get back."

He waited for her to stand and start moving, then he took the lead, making his way along the ridge, heading toward the steep trail that led to where they'd parked the truck. Thankfully, he took it slower this time, and Katrina didn't have to struggle quite so hard to keep up.

But when they came to the top of the trail, Reed stopped abruptly. The top of the bank had sloughed away, and the trail had turned to a rivulet of mud and water, coursing down in the direction of the road.

"I don't think so," said Reed, holding out his arm as a block between her and the edge of the bluff.

"What do we do now?" she asked, peering into the gloom of the aspen grove, listening to the whoosh of the water below them.

He set the toolbox down, well back from the edge, and he stripped off the leather tool belt, plunking it on top. "I'm not dragging you through the bush in the dark, that's for sure."

"I'll be fine," she assured him, wondering if it was a lie. Just how difficult would it be to make their way back through the thick woods?

"There's a line shack about a mile that way." He gestured with his head in the opposite direction of the well. "We'll wait it out there."

That seemed like an only slightly more palatable option.

"It'll be pitch-dark by the time we get there." She was already having a hard time picking her way across the uneven meadow. And she was cold and wet and miserable.

"Yes, it will. So, up you go." He scooped her into his arms.

"Hey!"

"You'd rather walk?"

"Yes!"

"No, you wouldn't. I've got leather boots and long pants, and I've been hiking these hills my entire life." He adjusted her in his arms.

"You can't carry me a whole mile."

"I could carry you twenty miles without breaking a sweat. And even if I couldn't, I'm not letting you risk your ankle."

"This is ridiculous," she huffed.

"Welcome to my world, Katrina. It can be cold, wet, dirty and unforgiving."

She wrapped her arms around his neck in surrender. "This is exactly why I went off to boarding school."

"You were right to do that." His tone was gruff. "And you're right to stay away. Colorado's a bad place for you."

Katrina didn't disagree. But for the first time in her life, it didn't feel like an insult.

# Six

Inside the line shack, Reed set Katrina on her feet, instructing her to hold still while he located a box of matches to light the two oil lamps that would be sitting on the small kitchen table. He knew where everything was in the compact, single-room shack, and he didn't want her walking into the furniture.

"Will somebody come looking for us?" her voice wafted across the cool room to him.

"What do you mean?"

"When we don't come back, will they come looking?"

Reed couldn't help but smile to himself. He struck a match, lifted the glass chamber and lit the lamp's wick. The idea that Caleb would mount a rescue operation because Reed was a few hours late was laughable.

"I'm old enough to stay out after dark," he told Katrina. He quickly moved the match to the second lamp and lit it, as well. Warm yellow light filled the small room, highlighting a compact kitchen, two worn armchairs, a bed in one corner, along with the scarred wooden table and four battered kitchen chairs.

"Won't they worry?" she pressed.

"Not for a day or so."

"But we could be hurt."

"We're not hurt."

"They don't know that."

He took in her bedraggled appearance and tried not to feel guilty, reminding himself that she was the one who'd insisted on coming along. "They'll know that odds are we're stuck."

"But—"

"This kind of thing happens all the time." Next, Reed went to the small woodstove between the armchairs. There was a cardboard box nearby with old newspapers, dry kindling and split firewood. He opened the glass-fronted stove door.

"Not to me, it doesn't," Katrina huffed to his back.

He heard her make her way farther into the shack. "We'll be fine."

"I know."

He crumpled the paper. "So stop worrying."

"I'm not worried."

He laid down a few pieces of kindling. "I can tell."

"I'm not worried. Cold, maybe."

"It'll warm up soon."

"And hungry."

"You? Hungry? Who'd have guessed."

"I eat," she protested.

"About enough to keep a bird alive." Not that she was skinny. She had a killer compact figure, smooth curves, tight muscle tone. He set a few pieces of firewood on top of the kindling.

"I guess I'm an easy keeper."

He grinned at her horse reference, striking a match then tossing it into the stove, watching the paper catch and light before closing the door. "Well, I'm definitely not. I'll see what I can find us to eat."

"There's food here?"

"I hope so." It was going to be a long night if he couldn't find a can of stew or a jar of peanut butter.

"What can I do?"

It was on the tip of Reed's tongue to make a joke about how

little she could do out here, but before he could speak, he caught a glimpse of her delicate features. Her soaking, stringy hair, those wet, bedraggled clothes, and he didn't have the heart to tease her.

"Check the bureau beside the bed. Sometimes the cowboys leave dry clothes in it."

In reaction to his words, she shook water droplets from her fingertips, and took a long look down at her soaking clothes.

Reed could stand to stay wet if he had to, but he'd much rather dry off and warm up.

She headed for the far corner of the shack while he moved one of the lamps to the small countertop and checked the kitchen cupboard. He found a box of pancake mix and a bottle of maple syrup. Not exactly gourmet, but it would keep them from going hungry.

"Not much here," Katrina called to report.

He turned, squinting into the darkened end of the room.

She came toward him, into the lamplight, holding something in each hand. "Tops or bottoms?" She unfurled a pair of gray sweatpants and a large, white T-shirt.

He couldn't help being reminded of his offer to share his pajamas. He nodded to the sweatpants. "Looks like those might be a bit large for you."

"Unless I want a blanket." She tossed them his way, and he snagged them out of midair.

She shook out the T-shirt. "Can I trust you to turn your back while I change?"

"Absolutely," he vowed. "My mama raised me to be a gentleman."

"My auntie raised me to be a bohemian artist."

"I don't even know what that means."

Her blue eyes danced as she obviously fought a smile. "It means I probably won't turn my back while *you* change."

Reed fought the temptation to tease her in return. But that was a dangerous road to go down. Instead, he forced himself to turn away, concentrating on finding a bowl in the sparsely equipped cupboard. It was already going to be a very long night. "Change your clothes, Katrina."

While he whipped up the batter and heated a pan on the two-burner propane stove, she rustled her way into the dry T-shirt.

"Your turn," she told him, moving up beside him at the counter. "That smells good."

He handed her the spatula. "You know how to cook pancakes?"

She took it. "Haven't a clue."

He glanced down at her, his chest contracting at the sight. Her hair was raked smoothly back. Her face was shiny clean. And the boxy T-shirt accentuated her slim frame, showing off her shapely legs.

It took him a second to find his voice. "When those bubbles burst, flip it over."

"I can do that." She determinedly took up a position in front of the mini stove.

She'd laid out her wet tank top and slacks, along with Reed's soaking shirt, on a kitchen chair near the woodstove to dry. Reed stripped his way out of his own jeans, stepped out of his boxers and pulled on the soft sweatpants. Katrina kept her back turned. He'd known she was bluffing.

She gave a little whoop when she successfully flipped the pancake.

"Now what?" she called over her shoulder.

He draped his clothes on another kitchen chair and moved up behind her. "Give it a minute, then we'll start another."

"I'm pretty good at this," she bragged.

"Outstanding," he agreed. He retrieved a dinner plate so they could stack the pancakes.

She dumped the pancake from the pan onto the plate and placed the pan back on the stove.

"First you spoon in the batter," he demonstrated. Then he tipped the pan so that the batter spread thin.

"You're very domesticated," she noted.

"Survival instinct."

"Your mom teach you to do that?"

Reed nodded through the familiar hitch in his chest. Even after all these years, he couldn't help but react whenever he talked about his mother. Which wasn't often. "She did."

Katrina's voice lowered. "How old were you when it happened?"

He pretended to misunderstand the question. "When she taught me to cook pancakes?"

"When she died," Katrina clarified.

He kept his voice even. "Seventeen."

There was a silent pause.

"I remember she was beautiful," said Katrina.

"She was," he agreed. And she'd been kind and gentle, and far too delicate to be toiling in the wilds of Colorado ranch country. Not unlike Katrina.

"You mind talking about her?"

Reed bought himself a moment by flipping the pancake. "I don't mind," he lied.

"It must have been hard."

"It was."

"And then Caleb left."

"What are you trying to ask me?" Reed would rather get to the point and get out of this conversation.

She shrugged. "I'm not sure. How it impacted you, losing such a big part of your family all at once. If you were lonely."

"Were you lonely?" he asked her, instead of answering.

"Huh?"

"You left your family."

She nodded but didn't elaborate. A few seconds later, she wrapped both hands around the handle of the frying pan and dumped the next pancake onto the plate.

"You want to try?" he offered, relieved to move on to something more mundane.

"Sure." She accepted the spoon, doled out the batter and tipped the pan.

"Well done." He smiled.

"I was lonely," she admitted, setting the pan back down on the heat.

He clenched his jaw. So much for letting the maudlin stuff go.

"I was only ten years old," Katrina continued, eyes taking on a faraway expression. "For a while there, I really wanted to come home. But Auntie Coco talked me out of it. She was a pistol. No matter how much the other kids teased me, no matter how hard the studies or the dancing, no matter how much I missed my mom, she'd tell me to keep my chin up, my head clear and try just a little bit harder."

Reed found himself engaging. "What was the most difficult part?"

Katrina turned to face him, and it hit him just how close together they were standing. "What was the most difficult part for you?"

He gazed into her eyes, debating whether to lie. For so many years now, whenever he was asked about his father, he'd glossed over Wilton's cruelty. It was an ingrained reflex. But he found he didn't want to lie to Katrina.

"That my father was junkyard-dog mean."

Her delicate brows went up.

"He was dictatorial, demanding and ruthless. He yelled at me every day of my life, hit me and nearly worked me to death for ten long years." Reed reached around her and flipped the next pancake.

"Are you serious?" Katrina's voice was a horrified whisper.

"I am."

"But why didn't you leave? Caleb left. Couldn't you have—"

"And let Wilton win?"

Katrina paused. "So, you were taking a stand?"

"I was."

She seemed to ponder his words.

"You think I was nuts." He'd sure heard enough of that reaction from Caleb.

But Katrina gave her head a slow shake. "I'm envious." Moving in what seemed like slow motion, she reached up to brush her fingertips along his bicep.

His muscle contracted under her touch, and it was all he could do to hold himself still.

She tipped her chin and met his gaze. "I admire you. There are days when I wish I could tell the world to go to hell and back it up with brute strength."

The urge to haul her into his arms was so powerful, that he had either to move away or give in. He used retrieving the next pancake as an excuse. "Hungry?"

Her hesitation lasted only a split second. "Starving."

"Bring the plates," he instructed. "And some forks." He transferred the pancakes and the bottle of maple syrup to the small table near the center of the room. He moved the oil lamp to make room for the dishes, and its light bounced off the scars that had been gouged into the wooden tabletop over many long years of use.

She joined him, taking one of the two chairs that weren't being used as clothing racks.

He sat down and pulled in his chair. "It's not exactly the Ritz."

She gave an exaggerated pout. "You mean no caviar and champagne?"

Using his fork, he transferred two of the pancakes to her plate, then he pushed the bottle of syrup her way. "And the wine pairings leave something to be desired."

She blinked at him over the soft yellow lamplight. "You surprise me when you do that."

"Do what?" Deciding it didn't make sense to use up another plate, he moved his clean one back to the counter and shifted the serving platter with the remaining two pancakes in front of him.

She watched his movements until he sat down. "When you talk about wine pairings and Dior."

"You are such a snob."

"I'm not," she protested, hand resting on her fork, showing no signs of getting started on the meal.

Since she wasn't using the syrup, he poured some of it on his own pancakes then pushed it back to her.

"You've spent your entire life on a ranch in Colorado," she elaborated.

He cut into the tender pancake. "Do you honestly think you're making it better?"

"Okay. How do you know about wine pairings?"

He reached across the table and drizzled the syrup on her pancakes. No sense in letting the things get cold. "How do *you* know about wine pairings?"

"Fine restaurants, parties, I read a little."

He gave a chuckle. "Me, too."

"But—"

"I've been to Denver and Seattle, even as far as L.A. I once toured a vineyard in the Napa Valley. Get over it and eat your pancakes."

She ignored his instruction. "Really? You toured a vineyard?"

"Surprised they let me in?" He took a bite. He wasn't about to sit here and starve waiting for her.

"You're twisting my words."

"I don't need to twist them to make you sound like a snob, princess. You're doing that all by yourself."

"You surprised me." To her credit, she did sound contrite.

"Apparently," he allowed.

She glanced down at her plate then inhaled deeply. "These really do smell great."

"Taste them. They're pretty good."

She cut tentatively into one with her fork. "It's been years since I've had maple syrup."

"Welcome to the wild side."

"I probably don't need two."

"You probably do."

She lifted her fork to her mouth. "Here we go."

He couldn't believe she was making such a production out of it. But finally, she took a bite, chewed and swallowed.

"Oh, my," she breathed. Her eyes sparkled and her red lips turned up in a beautiful smile.

Reed instantly lost his appetite for anything but her.

"Good?" he managed in a slightly strangled voice.

"Ambrosia." She consumed another bite. "Who needs wine pairings anyway."

"You like it on the wild side?" He didn't intend it, but his tone turned the question into a double entendre.

She glanced up. Her expression stilled. Her gaze darkened. "Yes."

Reed's fork slipped from his fingertips, and his hands clenched into fists. Though his brain screamed no, his desire shouted it down. He gave in to his desire.

"Come here," he commanded.

Her expression turned serious. She rose on her bare feet, moving toward him, draped in that boxy, oversize T-shirt. Her hair was stringy and wet, makeup smudged around her eyes, yet she still managed to be the most beautiful woman he'd ever seen.

He snagged her hand, eased his chair back, pulled her into his lap and captured her lips in one smooth motion. He wrapped one arm around her gorgeous body, cradling her face with his free hand as his lips and tongue plundered her mouth. He'd missed her taste so much. How on earth had he managed to stay away?

Her body curled against his bare chest, delicate hands wrapping around his back, their warmth all but burning his skin. She returned his kisses with passion and enthusiasm.

His fingertips found her bare thigh, trailing slowly beneath the hem of her shirt. It took him mere seconds to realize she was naked beneath, and he swore under his breath.

"What?" she breathed, her rear end pressing tightly against his growing arousal.

"I'm not stopping this time." He kissed her again.

"I sure hope not." She kissed him back.

"But this is a bad idea." His mouth opened wide, and he all but devoured her.

When the kiss finally ended, she surprised him by turning in his lap, straddling him, her arms snaking around his neck, even as the tips of her breasts brushed against his chest. "I promise you," she whispered huskily, her maple-sweet breath puffing against him. "The world will still be turning tomorrow morning."

Reed didn't doubt that was true. But he feared his own world might tip on its axis and never go back to right.

Then she kissed him again, and all reason left his brain.

He acted on instinct, moving his hands beneath her shirt, sliding along her sides, pushing the soft fabric higher and higher. They didn't stop until he'd peeled it over her head, tossing it aside, gazing at her perfection for long, satisfying seconds before he wrapped her naked body in his arms.

"You are so incredibly gorgeous." He kissed the tip of her shoulder, then the tender hollow of her neck.

"Does it matter?" she asked.

"That you're gorgeous?" He brushed the pad of his thumb across her nipple.

She gasped. "Yes."

He did it again.

"I meant—"

Again.

She groaned and arched her back, and he leaned down to kiss one hard pink nipple, drawing it into his mouth, swirling his tongue, finding immense satisfaction in the way her fingertips dug into his biceps.

But he forced himself to withdraw. If he wasn't careful, they'd be making love right here on a kitchen chair. There was a bed in the shack. It wasn't much of a bed, but he was determined to use it.

He took up her mouth with his, came carefully to his feet, holding her tight, her legs still wrapped around his waist. He was never more grateful for the habitual condom tucked into his wallet.

They crossed to the bed, and he dragged back the covers, easing down until he was sitting, lying back, drawing her full length on top of him before turning enough to strip off his sweats and pull her naked body against his own.

He ordered himself to slow down their kisses, curb his wayward hands that seemed determined to experience every inch of her soft skin. Her legs were toned and perfectly shaped. Her stomach was flat, creamy skin, with a sexy sweet navel. Her breasts were exactly the right size, fitting the palms of his hands, nipples dark pink, beaded under his touch.

Her shoulders were smooth, neck long and sexy, and her blond hair splayed messily out across the pillow, beckoning his hands. He burrowed his face into it and inhaled.

"I could breathe you in all day," he whispered.

Her hands trailed across the flat of his chest. "And I could touch you forever." She turned and met his gaze. "Or kiss you," she offered, moving in on his lips, voice going lower. "I could kiss you forever."

Her words nearly caved his chest in with emotion. He cradled her face, holding her steady while he kissed her long and deeply.

She wrapped a leg over his body and his hips reflexively arched toward her. His hand slid over her breast, down her stomach, gently easing between her legs.

She flinched, and he froze, pulling back. "Something wrong?"

She shook her head.

"Katrina?"

She kissed him deeply, but something had changed. There was a tension in her body that hadn't been there before.

"You change your mind?" It might kill him, but she was entitled.

"No," she insisted, kissing him again.

"Stop," he ordered.

"You change your mind?" she asked.

"Of course not. Are you kidding me?" He drew away so that he could look her in the eyes. "Tell me."

She clamped her jaw.

He knew he should leave the bed, but he couldn't help hoping there was a simple explanation. Something other than the fact she had cold feet. Which he'd have to respect. A pithy swear word formed on his lips. But he kept it there. "You can say no, Katrina. I'll be—"

"I'm a virgin," she blurted out.

He reared back. *"What?"*

"I haven't changed my mind. I'm just a little nervous."

*"What?"* he repeated, unable to articulate anything more coherent.

She didn't answer, just stared at him with those gorgeous blue eyes, looking more desirable, more forbidden, sexier than he could possibly be expected to stand.

"I want it to be you, Reed," she whispered.

He tried to shake his head, but he couldn't seem to make the simple motion. A better man would walk away. A better man would have *stayed* away in the first place. Up to this moment, he'd have claimed he was a better man.

Then she reached up to touch his cheek, her fingertips trembling ever so slightly. "I *so* want it to be you."

Reed catapulted over the edge. He swooped in to kiss her, telling himself to be gentle, but losing the battle with instinct. His hands roamed the satin of her skin, lips trailing behind, kissing her everywhere, swearing to himself he was going to make it good for her, but unable to slow the pace of his desire.

He touched her again, fingers easing inside her hot, snug body, jolts of unadulterated lust ricocheting through every fiber of his being.

"I don't want to hurt you," he rasped. He couldn't stand the thought.

"You won't," she told him.

But he knew she was wrong. "I will."

"Then just get it over with."

"I don't think so." He brushed and stroked, until she relaxed, then squirmed beneath his hand. Her skin was flushed, and her breath was coming in quick pants.

Then he moved over her, didn't give her a chance to tense and swiftly pushed in solid.

She gasped and reflexively jerked away from the invasion.

But he held her fast, gritting his teeth, forcing himself to still. "Sorry."

"It's—" She sucked in a couple of breaths. "Ouch."

"Yeah." He kissed her gently, slowly, savoring the taste of her lips, holding his lust in check while he let her body get used to him.

Then she kissed him back. Her arms went around him. And her hips gently flexed.

He stroked her thighs, positioning her legs, moving slowly at first. Then, encouraged by her reaction, he increased the pace. She was hot and slick and gorgeous in his arms. Her scent surrounded him, while her breathing seemed to echo in his soul. He couldn't stop tasting her, couldn't stop touching her, as his primal brain kicked his body into an accelerating rhythm.

Heat flashed in front of his eyes, popping like colored fireworks. He braced an arm in the small of her back, tilting her toward him, as he kissed her deeply, thrusting his tongue in and out of her mouth. A roar in his ears rose like a freight train, obliterating everything else.

He barely heard her cry out his name. But her body shuddered, convulsing around him, and he surrendered to paradise.

The world came slowly back into focus, and he realized he had to be crushing her.

"I'm sorry," he shifted.

"No!" She tightened her hold. "Don't move."

"You okay?" He pushed his weight onto his elbows, freeing a hand to brush her damp, messy hair back from her face.

"I'm not sure."

"Did I hurt you?"

"Little bit."

"Little bit?" he pressed. "But not a big bit?"

She mustered a smile, and he couldn't resist kissing it. Then he braced her body against his.

"Hold still for a minute," he instructed. "Let me do the work." He gently rolled onto his back, bringing her with him until she was on top, and there was no danger of him squishing her. Her slight weight felt good against him.

"You can stay there just as long as you like," he told her.

"Really?" She pulled back far enough to look him in the eyes. Her gaze was soft on his, voice barely above a whisper. "Because that might be a very, very long time."

"No problem." He brushed the pad of his thumb across her

swollen lips. "It'll be two, maybe three days before they come looking."

He'd happily keep her in his bed that long and longer. He didn't know what had happened, or more accurately, what had *not* happened in her past: why she'd waited, or why she'd picked him. But right now nothing mattered except that she had.

"I went to an all-girls school," Katrina found herself explaining, still draped across Reed's naked body. She'd hate him to think there was something wrong with her. "From when I was ten all the way to college. I mean, we saw the boys from the affiliated school occasionally. But it wasn't as if we had time to get to know them."

"Are you saying you didn't date in high school?"

"I didn't date in high school," she confirmed.

She slowly slid from his body to his side and let her cheek rest on his shoulder.

He settled a wool blanket over them.

"And then I went to the college affiliated with Liberty Ballet," she continued. "I've been really busy with my dancing career. So, you know, even though I live in New York City, and my social life is quite active with all the events and parties—"

"Katrina?"

"What?"

"Are you apologizing for being a virgin?"

"Yes. I mean, no. I'm not apologizing." Exactly. "I'm telling you it wasn't my fault."

His body rumbled with laughter, and his lips brushed the top of her head. "You don't understand men at all."

"That's what I'm trying to tell you." The man was exasperating.

"Yeah?" His tone turned serious. "Well, listen up, Katrina. Because I understand men perfectly."

"Bully for you."

"You've got it all wrong."

"I've got what all wrong?"

"How I'm feeling. What I'm thinking."

"Okay, what are you feeling and thinking?"

He seemed to choose his words, his tone deep near her ear. "I'm feeling privileged and proud. I'm thinking someday, a long time from now, when I'm very old and very tired, and there's nothing left of my life, I'll be remembering this night, and you, and that I was the first."

Something flip-flopped Katrina's stomach. She drew back, tipping her chin so that she could gauge his expression. "That's a really great line, Reed."

"Thank you."

"Ever used it before?"

"Of course not. How can you ask that?"

So he was serious? He'd be thinking of her on his deathbed? She had no idea how to respond, so she laid her head back down on his shoulder and just breathed for a few minutes.

Reed spoke first. "But is there something wrong with all the men in New York City?"

"Not to my knowledge."

"Because I was with you all of five minutes before I realized I'd never be able to keep my hands off you."

"Five minutes?" She couldn't help but be pleased to hear that.

"Did they ask you on dates and you turned them down?"

"Five minutes?" she repeated.

"Focus, Katrina."

"I am focusing."

"The men? In New York City?"

She gave up. It was really just her ego that wanted him to admit it anyway. "Some asked for dates," she admitted. "Most I turned down. The others didn't really work out. And Quentin Foster, well he just skipped right to the proposition."

"Quentin Foster."

"Just a guy," said Katrina, regretting even saying the man's name out loud.

"Did you meet him at one of your fancy parties?"

She shook her head. "He's on the board of directors for Liberty. I've known him for a while. He's a big contributor, and people kowtow to him. I don't think he has much of a life outside the ballet company, because he's always hanging around. He comes to rehearsals. And he's forever closeted with the ballet company director discussing... I don't know what they discuss, funding, I guess."

Reed came up on his elbow. "And he propositioned you?"

She scrunched her face up in a grimace. "Yes."

"As in solicited sex?"

"Is there another kind of proposition?"

Reed blinked several times. "A man in a position of power over you actually asked you to sleep with him?"

She came up on her elbow, mirroring his posture. "Is there something confusing about the way I'm putting this?"

"You said no," Reed confirmed.

"Absolutely. Quentin had hinted around for months, and I tried to ignore him and avoid him. But then one day, he cornered me, and came right out with it, and I said no."

"Good for you."

"Thank you."

"What did he do then?"

She dropped her head back down on the pillow. "He was upset."

Reed waited.

Katrina didn't feel like lying, and she didn't feel like dressing it up, so she told Reed the truth. "He told me he could be a valuable friend, but I didn't want him as an enemy."

"When was this?" Reed's voice had gone cold.

"About three weeks ago. And then those strange things—" She caught herself. It was wild, paranoid speculation. It didn't even deserve to be said out loud.

"Strange things?" Reed's voice went cold. "You're talking about the cables and your ballet shoes."

"No," she lied.

"Then what?"

"I'm not going to tell you. It's too crazy. I'm too crazy. Everything's fine."

He laid his head down on the pillow, touching his forehead to hers. His voice went low again. "You have to tell me."

"Why?"

"This is pillow talk. All secrets are revealed during pillow talk."

"This isn't a secret."

"Good. Then there's no reason not to tell me."

"It's silly."

He shrugged. "Then who cares if you tell me or not?"

She heaved a heavy sigh. "Fine. But you can't laugh. And you can't call me a princess."

"I'm going to call you a princess whether you tell me what's on your mind or not." He brushed a few stray hairs from her cheek. "I like calling you princess. You should take it as a compliment."

"It's not a compliment. You're telling me that I'm spoiled."

"But in a delightful, exotic, sexy way."

"Ha!"

"Tell me the whole story, Katrina."

"Fine. He propositioned me a few times. And then he phoned me here and asked me if I'd thought about his offer. I told him I wouldn't change my mind."

"And when did your ballet shoe fail?"

"Why are you giving me the third degree?" It wasn't as if she'd done anything wrong.

"When did you hurt your ankle?"

"Can we back to kissing or something?" She really didn't want to talk about this.

"Give me the chronology."

"No."

Reed ignored her answer. "First, he propositions you. You say no. You narrowly miss some cables. He asks again. You say no. Your shoe fails and you're injured. He asks again. You say no…"

"That's the most far-fetched theory I've ever heard."

"No. That's what you're thinking yourself."

"There's absolutely no way—"

"Did someone check the shoes afterward?"

"I threw them away."

Reed raised a meaningful brow.

Katrina understood his suspicions. "I have a dozen pairs of ballet shoes. Nobody could have guessed which ones I'd use that day." But she was convincing herself as much as she was convincing Reed.

He seemed to ponder that information.

She wasn't going to buy into any kind of paranoia. "Those were accidents, coincidences."

Reed slowly smiled. "Okay," he agreed.

"Yeah?"

"Yeah."

She let her body relax, trailing her fingertips across his chest. "I shouldn't have said anything. We were having fun, and I messed it up."

Reed slipped his arms around her, drawing her close, speaking against her ear. "You were right to say something. You should always tell me when something goes wrong. Have I mentioned that I know how to fix things?"

"There's nothing to fix."

"Maybe not."

"Maybe the shoes, if I still had them."

Reed chuckled, and Katrina forced the theory from her mind. There was no connection between Quentin and the accidents. He hadn't even called again. Clearly, he'd given up. She could relax and stop worrying. When she went back to New York City, everything would be fine.

# Seven

The next day, it took them two hours to make their way back down the washed-out trail. Then it took Reed four hours to dig the truck out of the muddy road. And they had to stop every half mile or so to remove debris from the road or winch the truck across a particularly rough patch.

All in all, as a "morning after" went, it left a lot to be desired. Though Reed continually told Katrina to wait inside the cab of the truck, she donned a pair of leather work gloves and helped as best she could. Her efforts were pathetic, and she ended up with scratches on her arms and a bruised knee.

It was nearly six in the evening when they pulled the mud-caked truck up to the Terrell ranch house. To Katrina's surprise, her brother Travis was in the yard with Caleb, loading a couple of horses into a trailer. They both waved a cursory greeting and went back to their work.

As Katrina jumped from the pickup, Mandy trotted around the barn on horseback, smiling at them as she dismounted.

"You're just in time for dinner," she called, leading the dun mare toward the truck.

"Were you worried?" asked Katrina, keeping her back to the truck, well away from the big horse.

"About what?" asked Mandy, glancing at Reed as he rounded the hood.

"We were only supposed to be gone a few hours."

"Did the rain slow you down?"

"It did," Reed confirmed, halting next to Katrina.

"Did you get the pump fixed?" Mandy asked him.

"Up and running again," he confirmed.

"So, that's it?" asked Katrina. They'd been stranded out in the wilds of the ranch for twenty-four hours, and nobody so much as blinked an eye? What if they'd been hurt? What if they'd been trampled by horses or cattle?

"You had a phone call from New York City," said Mandy. "Someone named Elizabeth Jeril."

"She's the director of Liberty," said Katrina.

"She seems anxious for you to call back."

Katrina's thoughts went to her ankle. She realized she'd barely thought about it for the past two days. Through all the hiking and climbing, it hadn't hurt at all. And the dance routines she'd tried yesterday morning had gone exceedingly well.

She was ready to dance again.

"I'll call her in the morning." Katrina couldn't help a brief glance at Reed while she spoke. He was so rugged and sexy against the backdrop of the Rockies that her breath left her lungs.

"I should probably head back home," she managed, knowing that for the first time in her life she'd have a regret at leaving Colorado.

"But I'm not ready for you to go," said Mandy, stepping forward and pulling Katrina into a hug.

Katrina hugged back, keeping a wary eye on the mare. The animal moved, and Katrina jerked away, coming up against Reed.

"Chicken," Reed teased under his breath.

"She's scared of those, too," Mandy pointed out.

"I'll take my chances with the traffic and the panhandlers," Katrina retorted.

Caleb and Travis approached, stripping off their leather work gloves.

"I'm about done," said Caleb, lifting his hat and swiping the back of his hand across his hairline.

Travis nodded at the muddy truck, and Katrina remembered to step away from Reed.

"Nice," Travis noted.

"Half the hillside came down around it in the storm last night," said Reed.

"You stay at the line shack?" asked Caleb.

Katrina braced herself, unable to look at anyone. Would they guess? Would they ask? What would Reed tell them?

"We did," Reed answered easily. "The princess was forced to eat pancakes and maple syrup for dinner."

*"Hey,"* Katrina protested. She hadn't been the least bit snotty about their dinner last night. All in all, she thought she'd been a trooper.

"She nearly walked out on me when she discovered there wasn't a wine cellar," Reed added.

She shot him an angry glare.

Caleb laughed.

"That's my baby sister," Travis added.

"That's not why you're leaving, is it?" asked Mandy.

Katrina caught something in Reed's expression, and she suddenly knew what he'd done. He'd deflected any hint of suspicion that they might have done anything other than fight last night. She should be grateful to him, not angry.

She'd make sure she told him so later.

She turned back to Mandy. "That's not why I'm leaving. I have to get back to work."

"I suppose you do," Mandy allowed, her voice tinged with sadness.

Caleb pulled a cell phone out of his pocket. "I'll get Seth and Abigail up here. The least we can do is have a farewell barbecue."

* * *

On the back deck of his ranch house, Reed stood to one side, watching Katrina laugh with her two sisters. She seemed more relaxed on the ranch than she'd ever been, but, ironically, she looked even more untouchable. She'd showered, as they all had, and she'd changed into a simple, clingy, white knit dress. Her legs were bare, and she wore her navy suede ankle boots with a looping, blue-beaded choker and matching earrings.

Her hair was swept up in a wispy blond knot, and her face all but glowed with carefully crafted makeup. Her eyes shimmered a sexy deep blue in the waning light. If somebody were to snap a picture, there wasn't a doubt in his mind it would make the cover of *Elle* or *Vogue*.

Still, he couldn't help but wish she was back in that ugly old boxy T-shirt, in the line shack, in his bed.

Caleb appeared beside him, and Reed shifted his attention to the river.

"I hear you're building a house," said Caleb, handing Reed a cold bottle of beer.

Reed accepted it. "You heard right."

"Been planning it long?"

"Working on the drawings for a couple of years now."

Caleb nodded.

"Waylon Nelson," Reed told his brother into the silence.

"Come again?" asked Caleb.

"You should hire Waylon Nelson."

"Who is he and why would I hire him?"

"Ranch manager," said Reed.

Caleb straightened in obvious surprise. "You read the résumés?"

"I told you I would."

"I thought you were lying to get me off your back."

"I was. But I changed my mind."

"Good. Good. That's great. Waylon Nelson. Okay. I'll take another look at him. But if he's got your vote…"

"He does. Hire him now." Reed took a swallow of the beer. "Right now."

Caleb's eyes narrowed in obvious confusion.

Reed allowed his gaze to return to Katrina. "You're going to need the help. I'm heading to New York City."

Caleb's head snapped up, and he turned to stare at Katrina. Then, immediately, his attention went back to Reed. He stepped up close, voice lowered to a hiss. "You didn't."

Reed lifted his brow in a question.

"You slept with Katrina?" Caleb accused. "You *slept* with Mandy's sister? What is the matter with you?"

Reed stared straight into his brother's eyes. "A, I wouldn't tell you if I had. And B, that's not why I'm going to New York City."

"Then why are you going to New York City?" Caleb demanded, clearly convinced his suspicions were correct, and clearly still loaded for bear.

Reed kept his gaze steady. "I'm a young single guy with fifteen million dollars to spend. There's a long list of good reasons why I'm going to New York City."

And on the top of that list was Quentin Foster.

Caleb backed off ever so slightly. "You're looking for business investments?"

"Maybe," Reed allowed, though the possibility was exceedingly slim.

"You need Danielle to meet you there? I can call her."

"How about I call Danielle if I need her?"

"But you *will* call her."

"If I need her."

"Don't go signing anything without her," Caleb warned.

"I'll be fine." Reed could sign his fist into Quentin Foster's malicious, conniving nose without any assistance from Caleb's lawyer.

"Why don't you take the jet?" Caleb offered.

"Sure."

"You can drop Katrina off."

"No problem."

Reed supposed a better man would feel guilty about misleading his brother. But he hadn't technically lied. Whether he'd slept with Katrina was none of Caleb's business. And Reed certainly wasn't heading for New York City in the hopes of having a fling with her.

He was going along to protect her. Nothing more, nothing less. Hell, once they hit the bright lights and big city, she wasn't going to look twice at a rangy, weather-beaten cowboy like him, even if he did know something about Dior and had once taken a tour of a winery in Napa Valley.

In the taxi heading into midtown Manhattan, Katrina felt as if two worlds were about to collide. In the backseat next to her, Reed looked relaxed, slouched back, seat belt loosely around his hips.

"Have you been to New York City before?" she found herself asking. She didn't think he had, but he didn't seem at all out of place, and he wasn't gawking around like a tourist at the tall buildings.

"Nope," he answered. "Anything in particular I should see while I'm here?"

"The Liberty Ballet at the Emperor's Theater."

He smiled at her joke. "Wouldn't miss that."

"What interests you?" she asked. For that matter, what was he doing here? How long was he staying? And what were his expectations?

When he'd announced he was coming, he'd made some vague statements about seeing the City, maybe doing business even. He hadn't so much as hinted that he had any intention of continuing their physical relationship. But she couldn't help but wonder. Okay, she couldn't help but hope. No. She couldn't hope. She had to leave it alone.

"I wouldn't mind meeting some of your ballet colleagues," he mentioned evenly.

"Really?" That surprised her.

The car came to a smooth halt in front of her apartment building.

Reed gave a shrug. "If you don't think I'd embarrass you."

She took in his blue jeans, plaid shirt and the folding tool strapped to his belt in a worn leather case. "You might want to rethink the boots."

"I promise I'll clean up." He leaned slightly forward. "Can you wait a few minutes?" he asked the driver.

The man nodded as he popped the trunk.

Reed turned back to Katrina. "I'll walk you up."

So he wasn't staying. Okay. It would have been odd if he had. She only had the one bedroom. Not that she wasn't willing to share. Still, he hadn't asked about being her house guest.

"I'll be at the Royal Globe Towers," he told her with a wry half smile, making her wonder if he could read her mind.

Then he hopped out of the car, meeting her on the sidewalk with her suitcase in his hand.

The doorman nodded to her in recognition, and they moved smoothly onto the elevator, riding up ten floors to her compact apartment.

"This is nice," said Reed, taking in the French Provincial chairs and love seat, the proliferation of plants and the small dining-room table tucked against the pass-through to her tiny kitchen.

"Not much of a view," she apologized. If you craned your neck, you could just barely see past the stone building next door to the street below.

"You made it nice inside." He gestured with the suitcase toward a closed door.

"Yes, please." She quickly opened the bedroom door and flipped on the bedside lamp.

Reed set her suitcase down on the bed.

"You're rehearsing all day tomorrow?" he asked, standing close.

She nodded, holding her breath. Would he touch her? Hug her? Kiss her?

"Dinner after?" he asked.

"Sure. Yes." She quickly nodded.

"I'll call you? Seven?"

She gave another nod, and her tongue flicked involuntarily across her lower lip.

He obviously caught the movement. His gaze held for a long second on her lips.

She felt them soften, tingle, part ever so slightly.

Reed cleared his throat. "I'd better get back to the car."

Disappointment washed through her.

He took a step back. "Have a good rehearsal."

"Thank you."

He moved closer to the door. "Hope the ankle holds up."

"Me, too."

He was halfway through the door when he called back. "I'll dress differently tomorrow."

She couldn't help but smile. "Okay."

"You have a favorite place?"

"Anything will do."

"Okay. Bye." And he disappeared.

She heard the apartment door shut behind him, and she let out a heavy sigh, dropping down onto the bed.

He didn't stay. He didn't kiss her. He didn't even hug her goodbye.

How was a woman supposed to feel about that?


Caleb's assistant at Active Equipment had arranged for Reed's hotel room at the Royal Globe Towers. Entering the opulent suite last night, Reed had decided his brother was getting spoiled from being so rich. What man needed a four-poster, king-size bed, a chaise lounge and two armchairs in his bedroom? The living room had two sofas, a stone fireplace and a dining table for eight, along with two dozen candles and three bouquets of flowers and a marble bathtub in the bathroom that could hold a family of six.

It was ridiculous.

He'd have moved into something more practical, but he wasn't planning to be in New York very long. And Katrina lived in Manhattan, so he preferred to stay in this part of town.

Still, he didn't want to spend his entire fifteen million in the clothing shops on Fifth Avenue. So, this morning, he'd taken the friendly concierge woman's advice and hopped on the subway to

Brooklyn. There he found a nice shopping district that seemed to cater to ordinary people.

After wandering the streets for a couple of hours, he was enticed into a small bakery by the aromas of vanilla and cinnamon. The place had only a few small tables with ice-cream-parlor-style chairs, but a steady stream of customers came in and out for takeout. He bought himself a sugar-sprinkled, cream-filled pastry and a cup of coffee from the stern-looking, rotund, middle-aged woman at the counter and then eased himself gently into one of the small chairs.

The doors and windows were open, letting the late-morning air waft through. The staff were obviously busy in the back, smatterings of English and Italian could be heard, bakers appearing occasionally as the middle-aged woman and a younger assistant served customers.

Reed could hear a truck engine cranking through the open door to the alleyway behind the store. There was a sudden clang of metal, followed by a male voice shouting in Italian. The bakery went silent for a brief moment, then the customers laughed a little. Reed didn't understand the language, but it didn't take much to get the gist.

The older woman marched away from the counter, through the kitchen hallway, sticking her head out the open door and shouting at the man.

Reed thought he could figure that one out, too.

The man shouted back, and she gestured with her hand, scowling as she returned to the counter. The last of the current customers took their paper bags and moved out onto the sidewalk, leaving the bakery empty.

"Engine trouble?" Reed asked the woman, wiping his hands on a paper napkin as he came to his feet.

At first, he thought he was going to get an earful himself.

"The delivery truck is ancient," she offered rather grudgingly.

Reed gestured to his empty plate, giving her a friendly smile. "That was fantastic." It was easily the best pastry he'd ever tasted. Same went for the coffee—it'd been strong but flavorful.

She nodded an acknowledgment of his compliment, but still

didn't smile in return. The younger woman, however, gave him a broad, slightly flirtatious grin.

Then another bang reverberated through the alley, and both women jumped. It was followed by a deafening clatter and clang, and another string of colorful swearwords.

Reed moved swiftly and reflexively around the glass display case, down the short hallway, past the heat and bustle of the kitchen, past stacks of boxes, buckets and bins, and out the back door.

The alley was narrow and dusty. Stained, soot-covered brick walls rose up on either side. The awful noise was coming from the engine of a five-fifty panel truck, with Gianni Bakery written on the side in chipping blue paint, that blocked the alley.

A balding man sat in the driver's seat with the door propped open.

"Shut it down!" Reed called, making a slashing motion across his throat.

The man shot him a glare.

"Shut it down," Reed repeated, striding forward. "You've dropped a valve."

"Always takes her a few minutes to warm up," the man responded with confidence.

Reed reached in and turned the key to Off.

"What the—"

"It's dropped a valve," Reed repeated. "If you keep it running, you'll blow a connecting rod."

"You a mechanic?" the man asked.

"Rancher," said Reed, stepping back. "But I've worked on plenty of diesels in my time. Some older than this."

"I've been limping her along for a few months," said the man.

"Does it idle a lot?" asked Reed, knowing that was the most likely explanation.

"In the winter," the man said, reaching for the key.

"Don't do that," Reed warned. "You need to call a tow truck."

"I don't have time to call a tow truck."

"If you try to start it you'll only make it worse."

The man clamped his jaw, rocking back in the worn, vinyl driver's seat. "We've got deliveries to make."

"Do you have a backup? Another truck maybe?"

This one wasn't going anywhere anytime soon, and probably never. Even on the ranch, where they jerry-rigged pretty much anything back together, they knew when it was time to put something out to pasture. There wasn't much point in replacing the engine in a twenty-five-year-old truck.

The man shook his head. "I've been looking for another truck for six months. The used ones are as worn out as this, and the new ones cost a fortune."

"Tough break," Reed commiserated.

"Irony is, these days, I need two trucks."

"Business that good?"

The man rubbed his hands along the steering wheel. "Walk-in business is slowing."

"Doesn't seem very slow today," Reed observed.

"It's slowing," the man reiterated. "We need to strengthen distribution to other retail outlets. We also need to diversify." Then he stuck out his hand. "Nico Gianni."

Reed shook. "Reed Terrell."

"You from Brooklyn?"

"Colorado."

"On vacation?"

"More business than pleasure." Reed's interest had been piqued by Nico's words, not to mention by his own experience sampling the bakery's wares. "You're saying you've got enough orders to run two trucks?"

"If I had two trucks, I'd bring my nephew in on nights, and run the kitchen twenty-four hours. The walk-in traffic may be going down, but catering, now there's some expansion potential. Expensive parties, weddings, dances. The rich don't stop getting richer."

"True enough," Reed had to agree.

Nico seemed to have a good handle on the industry, and he seemed to have a plan for his business. Reed sized up the building. "You own this place?"

"Me and the wife."

Reed couldn't help but wonder if this was what Danielle meant by buying a percentage of a business. This wasn't exactly a start-up. Though, for Reed's money, it seemed less risky than a start-up.

"So, you're saying with a little capital for a new truck or two, your business would be in a position to expand."

"It would," Nico confirmed.

"You ever think about taking on a partner?"

Nico blinked.

"I mean a minor shareholder. A silent partner."

"I don't understand."

Reed rested his hand on the top of the open truck door, assuming a casual pose. "One of the reasons I'm in New York is possibly to invest in some business opportunities."

"You're interested in a bakery?"

"Maybe. Do you know what the real estate's worth? Have the annual gross and net handy?"

"Is this some scam?"

"No."

"You an eccentric rich guy?"

"No. I'm a rancher. But if we can make a deal, I'll kick in enough cash for a couple of new trucks. You cut me in for an appropriate percentage, and maybe we both win."

"So you're looking to diversify?" Nico nodded thoughtfully.

"I'm looking to diversify," Reed agreed. "I've got this sharp, prissy lady lawyer who wants me to sit in her office and review balance sheets all day long."

Nico grinned.

"But I don't want to invest in companies," said Reed. "I'd rather invest in people. And I'd rather invest in your pastries, Nico. They're damn fine."

"It's a secret family recipe."

"I'm not surprised."

"Come inside and take a look?" asked Rico.

"Absolutely," Reed agreed. "And, can you give me the name of a good tailor who works fast?"

Rico grinned and hopped out of the truck. "Salvatore's. Around the corner. He'll fix you up."

Salvatore turned out to be one heck of a tailor. And he had a business-expansion idea that sounded as promising as Nico's. So Reed left the store with two new suits, half a dozen dress shirts and another potential business investment.

Back at the Royal Globe Towers, he called Danielle, and her assistant put him straight through.

"Good afternoon, Reed," her crisp voice came on the line. "How can I help you?"

"I just spent half a million dollars."

"On a sports car?"

"No." Reed unzipped one of the suit covers as he talked. "A bakery and a tailor shop."

There was a long moment of silence. "Reed?"

"Yes?"

"I have a law degree from Harvard, but you've got me confused."

Reed retrieved the charcoal-gray suit. Salvatore had told him he could dress it up with a white shirt or down with steel blue and a diamond-pattern tie. "I need the money to buy a percentage of a bakery and a tailor shop in Brooklyn."

"Oh. Okay. Give me the company names. I'll start an investigation."

"I don't need some bureaucratic investigation. I just need a check."

"I don't follow."

"I met the guys today. I saw their operations. I looked into their eyes and shook their hands. The deal's done. Gianni Bakery and Imperial Tailors."

"How did you meet them?"

"I was hungry."

"You're losing me again, Reed."

"Nico sells some excellent pastries, but he needs a new delivery truck. Well, two new delivery trucks." Reed stripped off the plastic covering and stepped back. He really did like this suit.

"You ate a pastry today, and now you want to invest in his business?" Danielle confirmed.

"Pretty much."

"Reed, wandering around Brooklyn is not a reasonable investment strategy. You can't do things that way."

"It appears I can."

*"Reed."*

"Danielle, it's my money."

She gave a long-suffering sigh. "Fine. Okay. I hear you. But I'm looking at their financials before we cut the check. That's not negotiable. And if you're going to spend any more than this, you have *got to talk to me.*"

"Sure," Reed agreed easily, holding the diamond-patterned tie against the steel-blue shirt then the white one.

"You keep saying yes, and then you go ahead and do whatever you want."

"Funny how that works." Reed decided to go with the blue.

"You are impossible."

"Know any good restaurants in Manhattan?"

"Dozens. What do you have in mind? Please tell me you're not buying one."

"I'm eating at one."

"Good. Steak? Seafood? Greek? Thai?"

"What about French?" French was elegant. Then again, he was going with the blue shirt. "Greek. Make it Greek."

"What part of town?"

"Midtown."

"Try…Flavian's. It's near the Park, around Sixty-Fourth."

"I will. Thanks, Danielle."

"You're keeping me awake nights."

He chuckled and hung up the phone, then stripped off his cotton shirt and headed for the enormous shower that had two massive showerheads in the ceiling and six more jets in the walls. Ridiculous. He didn't think any man needed to be that clean.

He stripped down, adjusted the water temperature and chose a small bottle of shampoo. There were still a couple of hours before he was meeting Katrina, but his stomach hitched in anticipation. He couldn't help hoping she liked his suit.

On the other hand, he couldn't help hoping she'd restrain herself with her own wardrobe. If she looked too good, it was going to be an awfully long night keeping his hands to himself and his promise to Caleb. Though, he supposed, it was going to be an awfully long night no matter what she wore. Katrina would look sexy in a burlap sack.

Katrina was gratified by the way Reed's eyes darkened to gunmetal when he took in her red dress. She'd been hoping he'd like the short, clingy, off-the-shoulder number. It was made of lustrous silk with hundreds of black beads sewn into the low neckline and in a swirled pattern down one side. She'd paired it with spiky-heeled black shoes and a matching clutch.

Her hair was loose, flowing in waves around a pair of dangling onyx earrings, with a chunky bracelet and matching choker.

"We may have to upgrade the restaurant," he told her, his gaze sweeping from her hair to her shoes and back again.

"You clean up good, too," she teased, impressed as always by his athletic physique beneath the cut of his suit.

He was freshly shaved. His hair was neat, his shirt perfectly pressed, and his tie was in a smooth knot. He'd even forgone cowboy boots for a pair of polished loafers.

"What's your favorite restaurant?" he asked her, stepping back in the hallway to make room for her to exit her apartment.

"Did you make a reservation?" As far as she was concerned, there was no need to change his plans.

"Danielle suggested Flavian's."

"Who's Danielle?" Katrina fought a spurt of jealousy at the mention of another woman's name.

"Caleb's lawyer."

"She lives in New York?"

"Chicago."

Katrina was confused. "And you called her for a restaurant recommendation?"

"It's a long story."

Katrina waited, but he didn't elaborate.

"Flavian's is fine," she told him. "The ballet company goes there a lot. They have a nice deck."

She pushed down her curiosity and told herself to quit being jealous. Danielle was likely just a friend, a business acquaintance at that. In fact, it sounded as if she was a business acquaintance of Caleb's rather than Reed's. Which didn't explain why Reed would call all the way to Chicago for a restaurant recommendation.

"Will you be warm enough if we eat outside?" he asked, gazing critically at the little dress.

Katrina determinedly put Danielle from her mind. She reached for the black wrap she'd hung on a hook near the door and draped it over her shoulders, tucking her small clutch purse under her arm.

"They have outdoor heaters on the deck," she told him. Then she stepped into the hallway and pulled the apartment door closed behind her.

He lifted the door key from her hand and secured the dead bolt for her. "You do know there's something fundamentally wrong with the dress code."

"What dress code?" As far as she knew, Flavian's didn't have a dress code.

"New York City's dress code."

She raised her brows in a question.

He pressed the key into her palm then held out his arm. "You're going to freeze, and I'm going to swelter."

She replaced the key in her purse and tucked her hand into the crook of his elbow as they started toward the elevator. "That's so you can be a gentleman at the end of the date and let me wear your jacket."

"You think this is a date?" he asked. There was a level of unease in his voice.

"What else would you call it?"

He came to a halt at the elevator and pressed the call button.

It pinged in response, and the mechanism whirred behind the closed door.

Reed peered down at her, his gray eyes narrowing for a moment before he finally spoke. "I didn't come to New York to sleep with you, Katrina."

She held the gaze for a long moment, working up her courage. "Well, that's disappointing."

He sucked in a breath. "Don't look at me like that."

"I think of you like that," she dared.

"Katrina," he warned on a growl.

"What? It's not like you can take my virginity a second time."

"My brother is marrying your sister," he repeated for what was probably the third time. "We're going to be in each other's lives from here on in. I wouldn't feel right about having a fling."

"As opposed to having a one-night stand?"

He didn't seem to have an answer for that, and the elevator doors slid open to reveal a distinguished-looking sixtysomething couple whom Katrina vaguely recognized.

"Good evening," Reed offered smoothly, gesturing for Katrina to enter first.

"Evening." The couple nodded in response.

Katrina moved into the elevator, turned and stood next to Reed. The doors closed, and the car descended.

When the doors reopened, they crossed the compact lobby and went out through the glass exit door, where a massive, white stretch Hummer limousine waited at the curb.

There was a trace of laughter in his voice. "Your ride, princess."

She stopped short, taking in the polished luxury vehicle from hood to trunk. "That's a lot of money to shell out just to mock me."

"You think I'm mocking you?"

"Absolutely." Why else would he order such an expensive car? They were only going a few blocks, and he clearly wasn't trying to seduce her.

"I'm not mocking you," he insisted. "The owner is a friend of Salvatore's. I guess he's trying to treat me well."

"Salvatore?" Reed knew someone in New York City?

He tugged pointedly at the sleeves of his suit jacket and squared his shoulders. "A tailor I met in Brooklyn this morning." He turned slightly sideways to give her a view.

She took in the crisp outfit and straightened his already perfect tie, but it gave her an excuse to touch him. "You went all the way to Brooklyn to buy a suit?"

The uniformed driver opened the door and stood back to wait for them.

"I did," said Reed.

"You do know your hotel is mere blocks from Fifth Avenue?"

"I do know that." He gestured to the open limo door.

She didn't move. "And did you know Fifth Avenue is famous the world over for fine shopping?"

He raised a brow. "You don't like my suit?"

"I like it just fine."

"Then don't be such a snob about Brooklyn. You going to get in or what?"

"I've got nothing against Brooklyn."

"Good to know." He moved past her to stand opposite the driver.

Katrina moved forward, accepting Reed's hand and, sliding onto the limo seat, made room for him to join her.

The driver shut the door and the inside lights dimmed. Subtle violet floor lighting glowed beneath their feet while tiny white lights glowed in a scattered pattern across a black ceiling. A small wet bar was illuminated powder-blue.

"Is this how you normally travel?" Reed asked, a teasing note to his voice.

Katrina crossed her bare legs. "Beats a battered pickup truck covered in mud."

"Anything beats a battered pickup truck covered in mud."

She bumped her shoulder playfully against his arm. "Are you coming over to the dark side?"

"Maybe," he allowed.

"That was quick."

The limo pulled away from the curb, the lights of Fifty-Nine Street changing the shadows inside.

"Champagne?" He leaned forward and retrieved a tiny bottle of champagne from a recessed ice bucket.

"Yes, please." She gestured an amount with a small space between her index finger and thumb, deciding to relax and enjoy herself, even if Reed was going to keep his distance.

He pulled off the wire holder and neatly popped the cork, taking two delicate flutes from the polished wood rack above the counter.

She stopped him at an inch, wanting to save room for a glass of wine with dinner. And he poured the remainder of the bubbly, golden liquid into his own glass before discarding the bottle.

He raised his champagne in a toast. "To...?"

She let herself drink in his handsome features, her tone becoming reflexively husky. "To the finer things in life."

He touched the rim of his glass to hers, his warm gaze melding with her own. "To keeping them in context."

"What's out of context?"

"I am."

The stirrings of desire whirred through her limbs. As far as she was concerned, in this moment, he was in perfect context. "You worry too much."

"No." He shook his head slowly. "I worry exactly the right amount."

She loved the way his mind worked, the practicality, the cool logic, his straightforward confidence. He wasn't a maybe kind of guy.

"What are you worried about now?" she prompted.

"The dinner bill."

She couldn't help but grin at that. "We're not splitting it?"

"As if," he coughed out a laugh.

"So it is a date."

His mouth twitched in a moment of uncertainty, and she laughed at him.

"Got you that time." She took a sip.

"It doesn't have to be a date for me to be a gentleman."

Katrina decided to leave it alone. They both knew she'd scored a point.

"So, how do you like New York City?" she asked instead.

"I like it fine so far." He took a drink of his own champagne. "It's a lot different from Colorado."

"It's cleaner."

"Yes, it is."

"Noisier."

"True."

"Quite tasty." He took another drink.

"Don't forget shiny."

His glance went pointedly to her shimmering red dress, the glossy beads and the glimmering jewelry. "You people like to be noticed."

She frowned. "Was that an insult?"

"Are you trying to tell me you don't expect to be noticed in that dress?"

Only by him. But she couldn't very well own up to that. "It's ordinary for New York City," she lied.

The car rolled to a halt in front of the brightly lit restaurant, and a doorman paced smartly across the sidewalk toward them.

"I'm not sure there's anything ordinary about New York City," Reed mused.

"An ordinary dress, in an ordinary city, for an ordinary evening," she lied again.

The doorman opened the door of the limo.

Reed exited first and immediately turned to hold out his hand for her.

Katrina took the hand, turning in the seat, feet together, knees tight, rising gracefully, just as she'd been taught by the Liberty PR staff.

A flashbulb went off, and then another, and she glanced up to see a small crowd of people had gathered on the sidewalk. It was highly unlikely they realized who she was. The huge limo telegraphed a false sense of celebrity.

"Just an ordinary night?" Reed muttered in her ear as his arm slipped protectively around her waist.

"Smile and keep walking," she mumbled back. "It's the car, not us."

"Are you sure?"

"I'm sure." Though she'd been on a billboard or two in the past month, she wasn't particularly recognizable, certainly not by the general public who might happen to be on the sidewalk outside a midtown restaurant. It was the fancy car, that was all.

Luckily, they were only steps from the glass entry doors. A second doorman swiftly ushered them inside to a compact, octagonal, high-ceilinged foyer where a maître d' was positioned next to a set of oversize, oak interior doors.

"Reservation for Terrell," Reed informed the maître d'.

"Of course, sir." The man responded with professional deference, barely glancing at the small computer screen in front of him. "Would you care to dine inside or on the balcony tonight?"

Reed looked to Katrina. "Were you serious about the balcony?"

"Yes, please." She nodded. She loved a warm evening, watching the bustle of the street below, feeling the breeze, hearing the sounds of the city.

"You're not worried about reporters with long lenses?"

"Cute," she drawled, giving him an eye-roll.

"I can put you behind a privacy screen," the maître d' put in without missing a beat.

"Not necessary—"

"Katrina?" The voice from behind her was recognizable as Elizabeth Jeril's, the Artistic Director of Liberty Ballet Company.

Katrina turned to greet her boss, and was swept quickly into a light, expensively perfumed hug combined with two air kisses.

A former ballerina, Elizabeth was slightly taller than Katrina, dark haired with dark eyes and close to forty-five. Though she didn't dance professionally anymore, she was still trim and athletic.

"We didn't get a chance to talk after rehearsal today," Elizabeth noted, pulling back. "But you looked fantastic. Did Dr. Smith check your ankle?"

"He did. It's fine," Katrina assured her. It had been sore immediately after the dancing, but the pain was nearly gone now.

Elizabeth's gaze shifted to Reed, curiosity clear in her expression.

"Elizabeth Jeril," Katrina obliged. "This is Reed Terrell. Reed is from Colorado."

"A souvenir?" Elizabeth teased, grinning as she held out her long-fingered, red-tipped hand.

"It was either me or the tacky T-shirt," Reed played along, taking Elizabeth's hand gently in his larger one.

"I like him," Elizabeth told Katrina, eyeing Reed up and down.

There wasn't much about Reed a woman wouldn't like, Katrina silently acknowledged. "Elizabeth is Liberty's Artistic Director," she finished the introduction.

"You do choreography?" Reed asked Elizabeth.

"Planning, logistics, business management. I get to worry about the money. What little we have of it."

"I understand that's a common problem with arts organizations," Reed acknowledged.

Katrina wasn't sure what Reed knew about arts organizations, but she was quickly distracted from the question as Brandon Summerfield arrived. He stopped next to Elizabeth and tucked his phone into his suit-jacket pocket.

"There you are," Elizabeth acknowledged his presence, placing a hand on his arm. The two weren't officially a couple, but they'd been good friends and colleagues for years. There was an ongoing betting pool at Liberty over when they'd take their relationship to the next level.

"Nice to see you back, Katrina," Brandon told her. He gave her a perfunctory hug.

When they separated, Reed offered his hand. "Reed Terrell. I'm in town to visit Katrina."

Brandon shook. "Brandon Summerfield. Good to meet you."

Elizabeth continued the introduction. "Brandon is the CEO of Seaboard Management, one of our most generous donors."

"Real estate," Brandon elaborated, "mostly commercial and industrial."

"Ranching," Reed responded, "mostly barns and toolsheds."

Brandon grinned, and Katrina couldn't help but smile at Reed's easy joke.

"Will you join us for dinner?" Brandon offered, surprising Katrina. Liberty Ballet Company didn't exactly operate on the class system, but dancers didn't often mingle socially with the donors outside official functions.

She was momentarily speechless.

"Oh, please do," Elizabeth echoed.

Katrina tried to gauge the woman's expression, not sure if she should accept or decline.

Reed gave her a look that said the decision was up to her.

"Okay," Katrina decided.

Elizabeth seemed sincere. And Brandon was an important player in the Liberty organization. With Quentin out there stirring up trouble, Katrina might need all the help she could get.

# Eight

It turned out to be a wonderful dinner. Katrina was impressed with how Reed had held his own with Elizabeth and Brandon. He'd asked questions about the ballet company and had seemed genuinely interested in Brandon's business ventures. She hadn't realized he took such an interest in state politics or was so knowledgeable about international commerce and the impact of commodity and energy prices on global trade.

The more she hung around him, the more depths of his personality became apparent. For a guy who'd barely left Lyndon Valley, he seemed surprisingly worldly.

After dinner, they'd said goodbye to Elizabeth and Brandon and decided to take a walk along a pathway at the edge of the park. A canopy of trees arched over them, obscuring the street-lights and muting the sounds of traffic.

"I assume this is the part where I give you my jacket?" Reed asked, even as he shrugged his way out of it.

"This would be the time," she agreed.

He draped it over her shoulders, and the warmth from his

body seeped from the satin lining into her bare shoulders and arms.

He tugged the knot loose from his tie, popping the top button. "That was a nice restaurant."

"Danielle didn't steer you wrong."

"I guess not."

Katrina couldn't help but be curious. Though she told herself to shut up, she couldn't seem to stop the question from pouring out. "Why was it that you called her to ask about restaurants? I mean, it's not like she's a New Yorker."

"The call was on an unrelated matter." He removed the tie, turned to walk backward and looped it around her neck. "There. Now you're accessorized."

"Unrelated how?"

"As in, I didn't call her specifically for a restaurant recommendation."

He sure wasn't making this easy.

"You called her on…business? Pleasure?" Katrina pressed as they made their way along the mostly deserted swath of concrete.

"Business." He pointed through a gate to a bench overlooking the tulip gardens.

"Oh." She shouldn't feel so relieved. "Ranch business?"

"New York business."

She altered her course. "You have business in New York?"

"I own part of a tailor shop and part of a bakery." He waited for her to sit on the bench.

"Really?" Why hadn't he mentioned that before? It seemed an odd thing to leave out, given their past conversations. "So, that's why you're here? To check on your businesses?"

He sat down beside her, slow to answer. "I'm here for a lot of reasons."

The lamppost put him in light and shadow. His face was rugged, all angles and strength. His eyes were dark as they watched her.

She tried not to hope he was also here for her, but she couldn't help herself. She had it bad for Reed Terrell, and no amount of reason or logic was going to change that. "Tell me the others."

He shook his head. "I don't think so."

She shifted closer to his big body, and his arm moved to the back of the bench, creating a crook of space.

She tipped her chin to look at him. "Am I one of them?"

"Not in that way."

"What way is that?"

"The way where you blink your baby-blue eyes, and part those cherry-red lips and make me forget I'm a gentleman."

His words sent a hitch of desire through her chest.

"Am I doing that?" she asked.

"Don't play coy."

"I am coy. Or at least I was coy." She tucked her hair behind her ears, lowering her voice to a tease. "Quite innocent, really. Until a couple of days ago."

He fixed his gaze straight ahead. "Don't remind me."

"Why not?" It was only fair that he share her frustration. "I've been thinking about it constantly, reliving every minute, especially while I lay there alone, in my bed—"

Reed swore between clenched teeth.

"Tell me you miss it, too."

He swore again.

She boldly put her hand against his chest.

His arm tightened around her shoulders, tugging her close while his lips came down, covering hers possessively. Her body responded with instant desire, kissing him back, twisting and pressing against him. Her arms wound around his neck, anchoring her as she tipped her head to better accommodate his overwhelming kisses.

After long, hot, sexy minutes, he rasped, "This is crazy. You're crazy. *I'm* crazy. We're playing with fire."

"We're adults," she pointed out.

"Barely."

"I can legally vote, drink and make love in any state in the Union."

"Bully for you."

"Reed. Get real. A fling is no different than a one-night stand."

He went silent.

She took it to mean he didn't have a rebuttal.

"I've had this fantasy most of my adult life," she dared to say.

"I don't want to hear this."

She took one of his hands between hers. "It was about losing my virginity. I imagined it happening in a big bed, with fine linen, maybe flowers and candles."

Guilt seemed to tighten his features. "Instead, you got me in a broken-down old line shack."

She nodded, faintly surprised at her own willingness to play that particular card. "The *you* part was fine. But I wasn't crazy about the line shack." She screwed up her courage again. "We did it on your turf, Reed. Don't you think it's fair we do it again on mine?"

He gazed at their joined hands. "You think you can reason your way into making love again?" But his expression had softened. There was even a hint of a reluctant grin.

"Yes."

"You're impossible."

"And you're stubborn."

He came to his feet. "I'm trying to be respectful."

She stood up, rounding to face him and placing a hand on his arm. Going for broke, she lowered her voice and put every ounce of vamp she could muster into her expression and tone. "Do me a favor, Reed. Respect me all night long."

His gray eyes darkened, and the half smile disappeared. "And when I leave you in the morning?"

"I'll probably jump off the balcony in sheer anguish and despondency." She came up on her toes and kissed him. The first one was quick, but then she kissed him longer, and he responded, and once again they were wrapped in each other's arms.

This time, when he set her away from him, he grasped her hand, tugging her to his side. They began walking silently back to the sidewalk, setting a beeline for the nearby Royal Globe Towers.

They crossed the opulent lobby, entered the elevator and were whisked to the top floor. Along the way, Katrina was afraid to speak, afraid to even look Reed's way for fear of breaking the spell.

She shouldn't have worried. The minute the suite door clicked shut behind them, he swept her into his arms. Even as he kissed her, he was pushing his jacket from her shoulders, tossing it, along with her purse, onto a nearby bench. The tie followed, and his lips roamed their way across her bare shoulder.

He hugged her tight, the heat of his body penetrating her silk dress. His hand closed over her breast, and sensation zipped its way through the center of her body, bringing a gasp to her lips.

He captured the sound with his mouth.

"You're amazing," he whispered, pushing the dress farther down her shoulder. "Gorgeous." He kissed her mouth. "Delicious." He cupped her cheek, the pad of his thumb stroking as the kisses continued. "Exquisite."

A heady sense of power tripped through her. She felt for the buttons on his shirt, popping them through the smooth holes, desperate to feel his skin against hers.

She separated the halves of his dress shirt, tugging it from his slacks. Her dress slipped down to her waist, and she wrapped her arms around him, pressing her breasts against his smooth chest.

He immediately lifted her into his arms, kissing her deeply and thoroughly, as he settled her against his chest, striding through the big suite, making his way into the master bedroom. The four-poster bed was turned down and a dim lamp glowed soft yellow in a far corner.

Reed set her on her feet, smoothing back her messy hair. "You want some champagne?"

She shook her head, pushing her dress to the floor.

In response, he slipped off his shoes. "A whirlpool bath?"

"No." She stepped out of the silk in nothing but a pair of tiny, lacy, black panties, her shoes and the onyx jewelry.

His hand went to the button on his pants, flicking it open and dragging down the zipper. "Some music?"

She trailed her fingertips along the six-pack of his rock-hard abs. "What are you doing?"

"Romancing you." He kicked off his pants along with everything else. He was beyond magnificent.

"Consider me romanced." She sat down on the bed, lifting her foot, presenting him with the delicate sandal.

He slipped off one and then the other. He let her foot drop gently to the floor as he bent forward, taking her mouth with his, running his hands from her hips, to her breasts, splaying his thumbs across her peaking nipples as he gently laid her back on the bed.

He rolled onto his back then, so that she was on top. He stroked his hands down her spine, dipping below her panties, palming her bottom and rolling the delicate fabric down her legs.

She kissed his chest, tasting the salt of his skin, inhaling his smoky, masculine scent. Her hands roamed his chest, working their way down his body. She'd been nervous in the line shack, uncertain of whether to touch him or how or where. But now she was curious. She followed the contours of his body, his strong shoulders, thickly muscled arms, flat nipples, the indent of his navel and lower still.

After the briefest of moments, he sucked in a breath and captured her wrist, moving her hand from him.

"Hey," she protested.

He turned her onto her back, trapping her other arm while his free hand began its own exploration.

"Not fair," she complained on a guttural groan.

"Deal with it," he advised, kissing her swollen mouth, his tongue delving deep while his caresses left scorching heat in their wake.

He moved from her nipples to her stomach, inching ever lower, finding more sensitive places until her breath was coming in gasps and her body arched.

"Reed," she gasped. "Please."

He reached for a condom.

Then he wrapped his arms fully around her, moving between her legs, gazing deeply into her eyes and gently kissing her brows, her lids, the corner of her mouth. He flexed his hips, pushing ever so gently inside.

"I don't deserve this," he groaned.

She tried to tell him he did, but her answer was swallowed by another deep, lingering kiss.

Instinct clouded her brain, while sensations radiated out from where their bodies were joined. He started slowly, but she urged him on with growing impatience. She wasn't exactly sure how this was supposed to go, but slow definitely wasn't working for her.

She clung to him, arms wrapped around his neck, her body rising to meet his while she kissed him frantically, moving from his mouth to his chin, before burying her face in the crook of his neck, sucking the taut skin, savoring the taste of him with the tip of her tongue. His hand went to the small of her back, lifting her to him, changing their angle, sending blinding sparks shooting through her body.

She gasped his name over and over again, wrapping her body around him, feeling them meld to one.

He picked up the rhythm, and she rode the crest of his wave, rising higher and higher, until a guttural groan was torn from her throat. Reed cried out her name, and fireworks went off behind her eyes, bursting over and over in impossibly vibrant colors.

An hour later, Reed had banished his guilt and self-recrimination to a far-flung corner of his brain, allowing himself to absorb the experience. Katrina was still naked, submerged now beneath the roiling water in the cedar hot tub on the hotel suite's deck. The scattered lights of Central Park fanned out behind her, while the midtown towers rose up in the distance—a beautiful city framing a beautiful woman.

"So, what do you think of my world?" she teased, voice soft and sexy, tone melodious. A wineglass dangled from her polished fingertips. Her face was flushed and dewy, her hair mussed in a soft halo.

"It's a pretty great world," he responded, popping a rich dark truffle into his mouth.

Leafy green plants surrounded them, placed in huge, ceramic pots on the floor of the deck and in smaller containers on a variety of wooden shelves. A lattice screen delineated the hot-tub deck, offering privacy. Candles flickered on polished wood, on occasional tables and on nooks and crannies in the shelves around them.

He slid his calf along her smooth leg. He wished she'd come closer. He didn't like her sitting so far away.

"View's nice over here," he told her.

"Is that a hint?"

"Absolutely."

"Promise you won't feed me another truffle?"

He shook his head. "Nope."

"What does that mean?"

"It means, you like truffles, and I'm going to feed them to you."

She crossed her arms over her chest, mulishly screwing her face. "Then I'm not coming over there."

"Oh, yes, you are." Reed leaned forward, wrapping his hands around her rib cage, easily lifting her, pushing a wave through the tub ahead of her as he moved her to his lap.

"Hey!" She held her glass of merlot out to one side to keep it from spilling.

He settled her. "That's better."

The water sloshed back to level, and he retrieved his own glass of wine.

"You are impossible," she huffed.

"Not my fault," he defended, giving in to temptation and placing a soft kiss on her hairline. "I did try to talk you out of this."

"The hot tub?"

"All of this. Coming to my hotel room. Making love again."

"Oh, that." Her body relaxed, curling into his. "I guess that was my first mistake."

He loved it when she cuddled against him. She felt custom-made to fit his arms. Her hair held the subtle scent of wildflowers. Her skin was petal-soft. Her face was as beautiful as an angel's.

"Or maybe it was my second mistake," she mused, kissing his wet shoulder. "The first was forcing you to take me up to Brome Ridge to fix that broken pump." She rubbed the water droplets on his bicep. "Then again, I suppose I never should have looked into your eyes that first day I came home. That's where it all really started." Her tongue followed her fingertips, swirling against his heated skin.

"You were attracted?" he asked, curious.

She nodded. "I could feel the sparks from across the room."

"I was pretty much a goner then, too." He sighed. "Why did you have to turn out so beautiful?"

Though *beautiful* didn't even begin to describe her. She was smart and sassy and funny, and she messed with his hormones simply by breathing.

"It's an anthropological defense mechanism," she offered. "If I can't accomplish any hard work, I can at least be decorative."

"Stop that," he told her gruffly.

"Stop what?"

"Quit insulting yourself. You work damn hard dancing."

She gazed up at him, apparently unaffected by his angry tone. "Do you think you might be just a bit biased?"

"No."

Some of the light went out of her blue eyes. "It's not the same thing as being productive."

Wanting to be clear on this, he sat up straight, moving her to face him.

She sorted her legs out and straddled his lap.

"It's exactly the same thing. You're an incredibly accomplished woman, princess. Your family, any family anywhere, should be thrilled and proud to have you as a member."

A smile grew on her face, and she reached up to touch his cheek. Her hand was warm from the water. Her breasts rose above the frothy surface, nipples peeking in and out.

"Yet, you still call me princess."

"Do you hate it?"

She shook her head. "Not when you say it."

"Good." He liked having a special name for her. He'd once meant it as derogatory, but those days had long since passed.

She gave a poignant smile. "You're not at all what I expected."

"Neither are you." He'd thought she was spoiled, frivolous, skipping merrily through life on her looks, never giving a thought to anything beyond her own sphere of luxury. She was anything but that. She was a hard worker, a deep thinker, emotionally sensitive, easily hurt and acutely aware of the negative opinions ignorant people formed about her.

Their gazes met, and he couldn't seem to stop himself from kissing her. The kiss deepened and his arms wound around her. Her smooth body pressed intimately against his, heat building between them, tantalizing him, making him ache for her all over again.

He drew back sharply, his breath ragged, frightened by how close he was to throwing caution to the wind. "I am *not* making love to you without a condom."

She downed the rest of her merlot, setting aside both of their glasses.

To his surprise, her eyes danced with amusement. She stroked the pad of her thumb across his lips. "Reed, darling," she purred. "You have *got* to stop telling me things you won't do."

"You're like a spoiled child." But he didn't mean it. He didn't mean it at all.

Despite her rebellious words, she obviously took pity on him, turning in his lap, sitting sideways, still tempting, but not nearly as dangerous.

"We'll do it your way," she agreed, looping her arms loosely around his neck and placing a soft kiss on his cheek. "Because I know we can't make love right now. And I like it here with you." Her voice dropped to a whisper. "But I want to make love. I *really* want to."

"You're killing me, Katrina."

She sighed against him. "Get used to it."

And that was the biggest problem of all. He was already used to it. He liked it here, too. The merlot was delicious, the truffles delectable, the view memorable and, if he had his way, he'd hold Katrina naked in his arms forever.


"You said they didn't know who you were," Reed challenged from where he stood in the glassed-in atrium of the harbor-tour cruise ship.

He was staring at the small magazine rack, the Statue of Liberty visible through the glass behind him.

"They didn't," she assured him, peering at the small square photo on the bottom corner of the tabloid newspaper. It had been taken last night as they exited the limo.

"Well, not last night, anyway," she allowed "They must have looked it up later."

"Katrina Jacobs on the town," he read. "You want to buy it and read the story?"

"I don't need to read the story. I was there, remember?"

"You think they caught us kissing in the park?"

"Do you care?"

"Not at all. Well, maybe if Travis saw it. He'd sure be ticked off. But to these anonymous New Yorkers?" Reed waved a dismissive hand. "I'm the guy who kissed the prima ballerina. I can strut."

"I'm a principal dancer."

He gave a mock frown. "That doesn't sound nearly as exotic."

She wrinkled her nose. "Quit complaining. I had to kiss a cowboy."

He leaned in close and snagged her hand, voice gravelly. "You did a hell of a lot more than kiss him."

The words spurred a hot shiver of remembrance. But she couldn't act on it in public.

Then a family entered the atrium, adding to the crowd, and Reed gently urged her toward the glass door. It slid smoothly open, and they exited onto the windy deck, finding an empty place at the rail.

"You going to come and watch me dance tonight?" she opened. She wished she dared ask him how long he was planning to stay in the city. That was what she really wanted to know. But she'd promised herself she wouldn't push.

"Am I invited?" he asked in return, his gaze fixed on the Manhattan skyline, growing closer as their two-hour tour came to an end.

"Absolutely."

"Then I'll be there."

"I have to be at the theater a few hours early, but I'll leave a ticket at the box office." She tried not to let her excitement rise at the thought of Reed in the audience, but her heartbeat deepened and her chest felt fuzzy. She'd dance for him tonight. It would be all for him.

"You can come backstage afterward," she offered.

He was silent for a long moment.

"If you'd like," she added, growing uncomfortable.

"Sure." There was no inflection in his tone.

Had she made a misstep? It was impossible to tell, and the silence stretched between them.

"New York really is different from Colorado," he observed.

"Taller buildings?" she asked, not really caring. Did he want to come backstage or not? Did he want to see her after the performance? Would he invite her back to the hotel? Or was he already searching for a way to let her down easily?

"Taller buildings, more noise, more people, more...I don't know...life, I guess."

She turned to study his profile. "Is it that bad?"

He shrugged his broad shoulders. "I can't imagine what it was like for you at ten years old."

"I didn't see it all at once," she remembered. "I saw the airport, then Auntie Coco's apartment. I knew there was a lot of traffic on the streets, but I never guessed how far the city sprawled."

"Were you frightened by the crowds?"

She shook her head. "Ironically, I was lonely. But I liked the dancing, and I liked the sparkling lights." She smiled to herself.

"I particularly liked the sidewalks. I liked that you could sweep the dirt away, and they were clean and smooth."

"I like dirt," said Reed.

"Is that a joke?" She couldn't tell.

"It's life," he said. "The dirt is what starts everything. You add seeds, and they grow into plants that get eaten by animals. And at the end of a day, if you're dirty and sweaty, and you smell like the outdoors, you know you've done good. You've worked hard. Something that wasn't there that morning now exists. It could be a stack of hay bales, a fence, a working motor, some clean tack. It doesn't matter what it is. Just that you did it."

"I hate getting dirty," Katrina reaffirmed. Not that Reed would be surprised by that statement. It was the constant dust on her clothes and the grit in her hair that had made her most crazy growing up.

"You're such a girl," he teased.

"Good thing I'm pretty."

His smile disappeared. "You're more than just pretty." He looked as though he was about to say something else. But then he stopped. He drew a breath. "Ever been to the Empire State Building?"

"I have."

"You want to go again?"

"With you?" Her chest hitched.

"Tomorrow?"

She gathered her courage. "So, you're staying a little longer?"

"I was invited to a party on Saturday night."

At the restaurant last night, Elizabeth had extended an invitation to Reed for Liberty's largest annual fundraising gala.

"You were noncommittal. I thought that was your polite way of turning her down." Truth was, Katrina had also thought he was signaling to her his intention to leave before the weekend.

He chuckled. "Do you think she cares if I'm polite?"

"She liked you," Katrina told him honestly. She'd rarely seen Elizabeth warm up to someone the way she'd warmed up to Reed. It was obvious enough that Katrina had felt a little jealous at the time. Maybe that's why she'd pushed him so hard to sleep with her last night.

Oh, wow. That wasn't particularly admirable.

Then she let herself off the hook. Sleeping with Reed had nothing to do with Elizabeth. Katrina simply wasn't ready to let go of the intimacy they'd found together in the line shack.

He was a great guy and an amazing lover. And she couldn't imagine herself with anybody else. Which meant, once this was over, lovemaking was over for her for a very, very long time.

"I liked her, too," said Reed.

"So, you're coming to the party?"

"Sure." He shrugged. "I wouldn't mind meeting a few more of the Liberty Ballet notables."

"You're going to need a tux. This is a pretty high-end affair."

"No problem. I'll go see Salvatore."

"You're going back to Brooklyn for a tux?"

"I like Salvatore. Besides, I own part of his company now. He'll have to give me a good price."

"Just out of curiosity." Katrina turned and leaned her back against the rounded metal rail, asking a question that had nagged at her since last night. "How did you decide to buy into a tailor shop in Brooklyn?"

He shrugged. "Instinct more than anything. I was in Brooklyn yesterday, and Nico recommended Salvatore. We got to talking about his business. He needed some help, and it made sense to me to help him out. In the end, I looked him in the eyes. I liked him, and I liked his business."

"Who's Nico?"

"The guy who owns the bakery I'm buying into."

Katrina got a bad feeling in the pit of her stomach. "Are you saying this all happened yesterday?"

"While you were rehearsing."

She was dying to ask him how much he'd invested. She was terrified that Nico and this Salvatore character had seen Reed coming. "How do you know he didn't rip you off?"

"I'm a good judge of character."

"Maybe in Colorado. But this is New York City."

"Are you questioning my judgment?"

"Yes," she answered honestly.

The muscles in his neck went tight, and she braced herself.

But when he finally spoke, his tone was neutral. "Don't worry about it."

"How much—" She stopped herself. "Never mind. None of my business."

"That's right."

"I'm sorry."

The wind whistled past them.

"I have a plan," he said.

"Do tell."

"The baker. The tailor. And the limo guy. They all have the same problem, great little businesses, solid work ethic, and short-term cash-flow issues."

"Oh, Reed, no." Not the limo business, too.

"They're good guys, family businesses that have been around for generations. I make a few more of these small investments, and when they pay off, I reinvest the profits in the next person."

"And what if there are no profits? What if you lose? Reed, this is a very big city. Con artists are everywhere."

"In a small bake shop in Brooklyn with a broken-down delivery truck, just waiting for a guy like me to come along and bail him out?"

Okay, that did sound far-fetched for a sting operation. But it didn't mean these guys weren't opportunistic.

"I'm not going to lose, Katrina," said Reed. "I'm willing to bet people are people just about anywhere. Some good, some bad, most just trying to get by."

"I didn't know they taught philosophy at Lyndon Valley High School."

His jawline set, and his eyes turned to charcoal, and she knew she'd gone too far. Then, his voice went hard as steel "Well, I'd already guessed they taught snobbery at the Upper Cavendar Dramatic Arts Academy."

Regret shot through her. "Reed, I didn't—"

"We're docking," he pointed out, turning on his heel to head for the gangway.

Sitting in row G, center orchestra, in the opulent Emperor's Theater, Reed's anger had long since disappeared. Katrina's ballet performance had blown him away, and he felt like the biggest jerk in the world for barking at the ethereal angel who'd held the audience enthralled throughout the evening. He wondered how quickly the well-heeled crowd would turn on him if they knew how he'd behaved.

Mere minutes into the performance, he'd found himself transferring his anger to her family. Why had he never heard she was this good? Why weren't they shouting it from the rooftops and dropping everything to rush to New York City and watch her dance?

Supported by rows of other dancers, she was the center of attention, all ribbons and tulle. Her skirt was gauzy mauve, her hair neatly upswept, woven with flowers and jewels as she spun gracefully across the stage, toes pointed, arms outstretched, all but floating to her partner, who lifted her as the orchestra built the music to a final crescendo.

Reed held his breath through the leaps and turns and lifts, until they finally held their position. The orchestra cut, and the crowd burst into thunderous applause.

The company gracefully repositioned themselves on the stage, lining up for a bow. Katrina's chest was rising and falling with deep breaths as she smiled at the audience. Her bright blue gaze seemed to stop on Reed's, and emotion shot through his own chest. It was all he could do not to leap from his seat and carry her off in his arms.

But the curtain came down. The applause finally died, and the audience made their way toward the aisles on either side of him. He sat still for a long moment, wondering if he was still invited backstage. After the harbor cruise, he'd fumed in the cab all the way to the Emperor's Theater, where he'd dropped Katrina off in midafternoon.

She'd tried to apologize numerous times, but he'd cut her off. He wasn't sensitive about his education or his background. What he hated was when she reminded him of their vastly different lifestyles. Still, he sure didn't have to be such a jerk about it.

She was probably still angry with him, and rightly so. Then again, was he going to let that stop him? She'd invited him backstage. She hadn't uninvited him. He could easily play dumb and show up, and then apologize for his behavior and hope she'd forgive him.

All he had to do was figure out exactly where backstage was in this huge place.

He glanced around at the rapidly emptying theater, looking for an usher. Instead, he spotted Elizabeth Jeril down near the front, in a conversation with a man. The seats beside him were empty, so he quickly exited the row and made his way down to her.

"Reed." Elizabeth greeted him with a wide, welcoming smile.

The stranger next to her turned to give Reed a suspicious once-over.

Elizabeth showed no such hesitation. She reached out her arms and all but floated toward him in her full-length silver gown. "I hope you enjoyed the performance."

Reed gently returned the hug. "Very much," he told her honestly.

"Are you coming backstage to see Katrina?"

"I'd like to."

"Good. Reed, this is one of our major donors and a member of the board of directors, Quentin Foster."

Reed's senses went on instant alert. But he schooled his features and faced the man.

"Quentin," Elizabeth continued, oblivious. "This is Reed Terrell. Reed is a friend of Katrina's."

"A close friend," Reed added, holding out his hand to shake, meeting the muddy gaze of Quentin's light brown eyes square on.

Foster was slightly short, slightly balding, with a narrow nose and a haughty, supercilious smile. He held out his own hand, pale and thin-skinned.

"A pleasure," he told Reed in a tone that said it was anything but.

Reed squeezed a little too firmly. "Katrina's spoken of you," he told Quentin.

Quentin's nostrils flared for a split second, uncertainty crossing his expression before he quickly withdrew his hand. "Katrina's dancing is coming along nicely."

"She looked great to me," said Reed.

"You're an aficionado?" Quentin challenged.

"I know what I like," Reed returned evenly.

Quentin gave a fake laugh. "The subtleties of the ballet are usually lost on the masses."

Reed dropped the conversation and spoke to Elizabeth. "Can you point the way?"

"Absolutely." She linked her arm with Reed's and led him along the front of the stage to a small door, subtly recessed into the wall paneling.

They passed through single file to a dimly lit narrow hallway and staircase.

Reed kept his footsteps and his tone measured as he chatted inconsequentially about the weather and the sights of New York City. Inside his head, he was cataloging his instincts.

Now that he'd met Foster, every fiber of his being told him to protect Katrina. Slamming the man into the nearest wall and reading him the riot act seemed like an excellent start. But he restrained himself as they passed through another door and came out into a wide, bustling corridor.

"There she is," said Elizabeth, gesturing down the hallway.

Reed's attention immediately fixed on Katrina as she emerged from a doorway. She'd changed into a simple black sheath dress with black leggings, high-heeled shoes and a short purple open cardigan. Her hair was in a wavy ponytail, and her face was free of makeup.

"Thanks," he told Elizabeth absently, already winding his way through the performers and crew clogging the hall.

When he appeared next to her, Katrina was startled, obviously surprised to see him. But he didn't pause to talk, simply slipped an arm around her waist, and gently eased her into a walk in the direction opposite to Foster.

"You ready to go?" he asked.

"Where are we going?"

"I don't care. Is this the way out?"

She settled in to his pace. "Aren't you still mad at me?"

"I was never mad."

"Liar."

"Okay, a little bit mad. But I shouldn't have been mad. I guess I'm psychologically delicate. Are we going the right way?"

"As if," she scoffed. "Take the next right."

He steered them around a corner into an empty hallway.

The other voices disappeared behind them, and he noticed they were alone. He impulsively backed her into the wall. He searched her expression, finding her more beautiful than ever. "You were amazing out there."

A genuine smile grew on her face. "You liked the performance?"

"I can't wait to watch you dance again."

Still grinning, she scoffed, "There's no need to go overboard, Reed."

Instead of responding, he cupped her chin, stilling her motion. He leaned in. "I'm hooked," he whispered, a split second before his lips touched hers.

Their kiss was instantly passionate, and he pressed his body to hers. Her arms wound around his neck, and he pulled her into a tight full-body hug.

"Reed?" she gasped, clearly struggling for breath.

He forced himself to let her go. He hadn't meant to maul her in public. "Sorry."

"It's okay."

"Are you hungry?" he asked, dredging up some manners.

She had to have used up a lot of energy out there tonight.

"I am." She nodded.

"What do you want to eat?" He'd take her anywhere. They could do anything she wanted, as long as it was together.

She blinked once, her dark lashes covering her deep blue eyes, momentarily expanding her pupils. "Room service?"

Everything inside him stilled, then his hand sought hers, tugging her away from the wall, leading her farther down the corridor.

At first, they walked in silence.

"You really liked the performance?" Her tone was slightly hesitant. "Like, truly?"

"I truly loved it," he answered.

"As in, you'd watch another ballet?"

"If you were in it." Then he shrugged. "Or if you came to watch with me."

Though it wasn't something he'd ever given a moment's thought to, he'd honestly enjoyed the ballet. He admired the dancing, the choreography, the lighting, the costumes. He liked to think he recognized hard work when he saw it.

"What about the opera?" she asked.

"I've never been to the opera."

"Would you try one?"

"Is this some kind of a test? Are you setting me up for a joke?"

She frowned at him. "Not at all. I like opera."

"Why?"

They made their way up a back staircase, and a door came into view at the end of a short hallway.

"The music, the pageantry, the stories."

"Aren't they in Italian?"

"It doesn't matter."

"I don't speak Italian."

*"Quello è sfavorevole."*

He tugged her against his side. "You are *such* a showoff."

"Unlike you? Who turned my bike into an exercise machine and laughed at me because I was afraid of chickens?"

He paused a beat. "Being afraid of chickens is pretty comical."

She tipped her head sideways against his shoulder. "You sure you want to mock the woman who's coming back to your hotel room?"

He leaned down to whisper in her ear. "Let me tell you exactly what I want to do to the woman who's coming back to my hotel room."

# Nine

Every time Reed thought Katrina couldn't possibly get any more beautiful, she surprised him. Even tonight, at the Liberty Ballet fundraising gala, among the richly dressed, she stood out like a beacon.

Across the room, her updo was smooth, her honey-toned shoulders bare, her slender arms ringed in delicate white sapphire bangles. She wore a matching necklace, gold inset with a trail of tiny white sapphires, while small studs sparkled in her ears. Her dress was snow-white, with a tight bodice liberally trimmed in deep purple piping. It topped a generous tulle skirt adorned with purple appliqué that made her look even more like his princess, or maybe his bride.

He let that image swim around his brain. It was preposterous, of course, but he couldn't help liking it.

"Enjoying the party?" Elizabeth asked, standing by his side.

"Very much," said Reed, telling the truth. He'd met a lot of interesting people, many from New York City, but a surprising number from other parts of the country. All seemed well-traveled, and some had visited Colorado.

Reed took advantage of the opportunity. "I heard Katrina had trouble with a ballet shoe."

"Terrible luck that," said Elizabeth. "I'm glad she's healed so fast. It was a bizarre accident, but we're not taking any chances."

"How so?" Reed prompted, determined to catalog whatever information he could gather.

"We've changed the standards, shortened the wear period."

"Katrina told me she had a dozen pairs of ballet shoes." Reed would love to get his hands on the others. If Katrina was right, and there was no way to know which pair she'd choose on any given night, then Foster might have sabotaged more than one.

"We replaced them all."

Destroyed the evidence. "And whose idea was that?"

"A board recommendation. Overkill in my opinion, but I suppose it's a PR move if you need one. You don't have a drink."

"I'm pacing myself."

She linked an arm with his. "An admirable quality."

He glanced down to where her fingertips trailed flirtatiously along his bicep. "You know you don't mean that."

Her laughter tinkled. "Sorry. Ingrained habit." She disentangled her arm. "You can catch more flies with honey than with vinegar."

"You catching flies tonight?"

"Liberty Ballet doesn't survive without donations. No offense to your gender, Reed. But men are more likely to pull out their checkbook for a vivacious woman."

"Do you ever get tired of doing that?"

"Of course not."

"Liar."

She shrugged. "It's my job." Then she pointed with her champagne glass. "See that man over there, white hair, glasses, laughing?"

"I see him."

"He donated a substantial sum last year. His business manager called today to say they'll have to cut that in half. My job tonight is to change his mind."

"Good luck with that," Reed offered.

"Thanks."

"I could probably intimidate him for you."

Elizabeth's laughter tinkled again. "That would certainly be a change in tactics."

"Can't flirt with him though," Reed noted.

She looked him up and down. "There is one wealthy widow here tonight, Mrs. Darwin Rosamine—"

"Not a chance," said Reed.

Elizabeth shrugged. "You look very sexy in a tux. Seems a shame to waste it."

"What about Foster?" Reed put in. He'd spotted the man a couple of times, and he was waiting for an opportunity to confront him.

"Quentin? I don't think we should send Quentin to flirt with Mrs. Rosamine."

"I meant his donation."

"He donates every year."

"A lot?"

"One of our top donors."

"Would you be willing to give me a number?"

Elizabeth drew back, her expression changing from animated to thoughtful as she considered Reed. "That would be unethical."

He returned her level gaze. "And?"

"And I could get in a lot of trouble for revealing that kind of information."

Reed waited, but she didn't cave. He had to admire that. "Hypothetically speaking, a ballpark number, what would you consider to be a top donor to Liberty Ballet?"

Elizabeth's even, white teeth came down on her bottom lip, and she smiled as she shook her head. "Hypothetically speaking, I consider a top donor to be in the range of two hundred to three hundred thousand a year."

Reed nodded. "That's a lot of money."

She took a sip of her champagne. "I can smile through almost anything for that kind of money."

"Are you saying you have problems with Quentin?"

"Nothing serious." She glanced from side to side and lowered her voice. "The biggest problem I have with him is that he's boring. He's way too fond of the sound of his own voice, and tends to corner me at parties."

"Boring how?"

"Loves to name-drop and brag about all the important events he's attended. For a skinny man, he's fairly obsessed with menus—who served which caviar, that the shrimp was overdone, that the Kobe beef wasn't, and that the pastry chef was subpar."

Reed nodded. It was annoying, but nothing compared to what Quentin had done to Katrina.

"By the way—" Reed took the opportunity "—if you ever need a good bakery, I know a great one in Brooklyn."

"I don't entertain much in Brooklyn."

"They do deliver." Reed signaled a passing waiter and chose a glass of red wine. "If I could get you a discount, would you be willing to try someone new?"

She arched a sculpted brow. "Are you serious?"

"I am. I own a small percentage of one that would like to break into the upscale catering market."

Elizabeth gave a small shrug. "Send me the information. We can talk."

"I'll have them send you some samples. Thanks."

"No problem." She nodded across the room. "I see Katrina's wearing Asper Emily tonight."

Reed watched Katrina laugh with two tuxedo-clad guests. He tried not to let jealousy creep in. "Is she securing donations?"

"One never knows who will decide to participate financially." Elizabeth paused. "You know, Katrina has a fantastic future ahead of her with Liberty." She took a sip of her champagne. "Assuming she stays in New York City."

Confused, Reed asked, "What makes you think she won't?"

Elizabeth's smile was sly. "You."

Reed laughed at that.

"I've seen the way she looks at you."

"Don't worry about it. She hates Colorado a whole lot more than she likes me."

"She must really hate Colorado then." Elizabeth wound her arm through his once more. "Walk me over to the piano. I need to speak with Samuel Wilcox, and I don't want Quentin to snag me along the way."

"Yes, ma'am."

Several people greeted Elizabeth from a distance as they walked, but none approached her directly. Reed could see Foster out of the corner of his eye, tracking their progress across the ballroom.

"Thank you," said Elizabeth as Reed handed her off to Samuel Wilcox.

Reed didn't wait for an introduction, but quickly withdrew and made his way to where Foster stood alone near one of the bars. He ditched the wineglass on the way, wanting both hands free.

"Foster." He nodded, coming to a halt.

The man's dirt-brown eyes narrowed. "Have we met?"

Reed scoffed out a laugh. "Right." If that's the way the guy wanted to play it, fine by him.

Reed put his back to the polished bar and set his tone low, though nobody was particularly close by. "My message is short. I know you propositioned Katrina. I know about the shoes. And I know where you live—"

"I haven't the faintest idea what you're talking about," Foster sputtered. But his face had flushed ruddy.

"I can also easily access your social calendar." Reed straightened, noting the bead of sweat that had formed on Foster's brow. "If you hurt Katrina, if you threaten Katrina, if you lift one finger to harm her career, I will hunt you down and wipe you off the face of this planet."

Foster pulled himself taller, his voice going shrill. "Even if I did know what you were talking about, I do *not* respond to threats."

"Yeah? Well, you might want to make an exception in this case."

"Uncivilized thug," Foster spat.

"When it comes to Katrina, absolutely. You'd be smart to remember that, too." Message delivered, Reed walked away.

Katrina was determined to avoid Quentin. The last thing she wanted was to be forced to rebuff him all over again. He'd been watching her for several minutes now, and he was headed her way. She started for the other side of the ballroom, deciding avoidance was her best strategy.

She couldn't help but wish Reed was at her side. But last time she'd seen him, he was engaged in what had looked like a serious conversation with Elizabeth. Katrina had to admit, she was rather surprised at how adroit Reed seemed to be at managing the party without much help from her. She'd never had a date give her so much space before.

She saw a chance and entered a conversation with another dancer and two of the guests, hoping it would keep Quentin at bay. Unfortunately, they were just saying good-night, and she was quickly on her own again. And her stop had given Quentin a chance to get closer.

She skirted along the edge of the ballroom toward the back, thinking Reed might have gone to one of the bars for a drink.

She didn't make it.

"Katrina?" Quentin called to her.

Caught, she heaved a sigh and pasted a polite smile on her face. "Hello, Quentin."

"You look lovely tonight." Though he uttered the words, there was a distinct insincerity to his tone.

His smile was there, if a bit fake. And there was a tenseness in his posture, a tightness at the corners of his mouth. Like he had a right to be angry with her. If anything, it ought to be the other way around.

"Thank you," she responded calmly, letting her smile fade. It was one thing to be cordial if he was trying to keep up appearances, but if he wasn't even going to make the effort, she certainly saw no reason to pretend.

His gaze moved insolently from her face, to her breasts and down the length of her body. "Putting it out for someone special tonight?"

She ignored the rude question and started to leave. "Excuse me. But I'm on my way to get a drink."

But as she began to move, he grabbed her by the arm. His grip was tight enough to be painful.

Before she could react, he stepped up close, his voice a growl. "You call him off."

"What? Let go of me." Had he lost his mind?

"That pit bull of a junkyard dog—"

Suddenly, Reed appeared. He grabbed a handful of Quentin's shirtfront and pushed him backward ten full paces, slamming him into the wall.

*"Reed,"* Katrina gasped.

"Did you think I was bluffing?" Reed demanded in a harsh voice that carried. *"Did you?"*

Quentin's mouth moved, but no sounds came out.

Katrina moved swiftly toward them, praying nobody else was paying attention. "Reed, *stop.*" She could handle this herself, discreetly and quietly. The last thing in the world Liberty Ballet needed was a sordid scene played out in full view of their donors.

But he only pushed Quentin harder against the wall. "I meant every word I said."

Quentin gasped for breath.

"Let him go," Katrina begged, glancing around.

Instead, Reed pointed a stiff finger close to Quentin's nose. "Every word."

"Security!" somebody called out from behind her.

Katrina groaned in mortification.

Quentin managed a pained but triumphant smile. "Better let me go."

"It'll take them at least five minutes to get here," Reed warned. "I can do a lot of damage in five minutes."

"You'll go to jail," Quentin wheezed.

"Do I look like I care?"

"Reed," Katrina pleaded, her panic growing.

He glanced her way. "You don't need to see this."

"*Everybody's* seeing this."

He turned back to Quentin, his enunciation slow and deliberate. "What's it going to be?"

The two men glared daggers at each other.

Finally, Quentin glanced away, giving a tight nod of acquiescence.

Reed abruptly let him go, stepping back just as the security guards came into view. Reed backed off farther, straightening his jacket. Then he turned and walked casually toward, while Katrina stared at him in abject horror.

She felt dozens of pairs of eyes come to rest on her. This story was going to race through the dance world like wildfire. Katrina would be a laughingstock. Whatever Quentin might have done to try to harm her career, Reed had outdone the effort and then some.

Reed stopped in front of her, and she felt her eyes sting with mortification. She didn't say a word, but dashed blindly for the exit. Ignoring the curious and pitying stares of the other guests, she made her long and painful way to the foyer.

Once there, she went directly to the elevators.

Reed was right behind her. "Katrina, I'm sorry you had to—"

"You're *sorry?*" She gasped for breath, barely finding her voice. She couldn't bring herself to look at him. "You think *sorry* cuts it?"

"He had it coming."

"It was a party, Reed. A civilized party."

"What does that have to do with anything?"

"At a *civilized* gathering, you can't just beat people up because they annoy you."

Reed stepped closer, his voice low but no less menacing. "He tried to hurt you. He *did* hurt you. He sabotaged your shoe."

"We've been through that. It doesn't make sense." She wasn't going to let the fear in.

"It makes perfect sense. Elizabeth said the board replaced every pair of your shoes."

"So what?"

"It was a *board* decision. Foster tampered with the others and—"

"Stop right there. He's an opportunistic jerk, but that's it. And I could have handled it myself."

"You shouldn't have to handle it."

"Why? Because you fix things?"

"Because he doesn't get to do that to you. Nobody does. I confronted him. I warned him. And he ignored me."

"Did he confess?"

"No. But I looked him in the eyes—"

"And you shook his hand? And you're such an oracle when it comes to judging people that you felt entitled to try and convict him without a shred of evidence?"

"He did it, Katrina."

She closed her eyes and counted to five. There was a broader point.

"This isn't Colorado, Reed."

He coughed out a laugh. "No kidding."

"Can you at least take this seriously?"

"I *am* taking this seriously."

She poked a finger against his chest. "This isn't the Wild West."

Reed didn't answer, simply set his jaw.

"You threatened to hurt him," she accused.

"I did not."

"You're lying."

"I'm not lying."

"I *heard* you." There was no other explanation.

A beat went past, and then another, before Reed finally spoke. "I didn't threaten to hurt him. I threatened to kill him."

Katrina staggered back.

She couldn't have heard right. Reed had seemed so urbane these past few days, so civilized. He knew how to order a good wine. He was intelligent, well-read. He could make small talk with just about anyone. But it was all a facade.

"So, that's it?" she croaked through an aching throat, more to herself than to him.

"What's it?" he asked.

"You. Underneath it all, you're still just an uncouth Colorado cowboy."

He didn't flinch. "I'll always be an uncouth Colorado cowboy."

Her stomach cramped in pain. This had all gone so horribly wrong. "I should have listened to you," she whispered.

"Yeah," he agreed. "You should have listened to me."

She felt tears build again, hot and heavy, trapped behind her eyes, making her voice quaver. "You tried to warn me."

"I never meant to hurt you, Katrina." His eyes were storm-cloud gray. "The last thing in the world I wanted to do was hurt you."

"Well, you did."

"I know."

"You have to leave." She was going to break down any second. She fought her anguish with anger. "Leave now. Leave New York City. Go back to those sawdust-covered honky-tonks where guys like you can make a point with your fists."

"I'll take you home." He reached out his hand.

"No." She determinedly shook her head, backing away. "I'm not going home. I'm going back to the party."

He jerked up his chin. "Oh, no, you aren't."

But she had no choice. "I can face them now, or I can face them tomorrow. And I want to get this over with."

"I meant you can't go back to Foster. He's still inside."

"I can deal with him."

"No, you can't."

Katrina felt a red haze form inside her brain. "This is my problem, Reed. It's my life. You need to leave now."

There was no way he was going to agree. She could see his intense frustration. She could see him considering options. She was suddenly frightened that he might haul her bodily from the hotel for her own good.

She took another step back, quickly turning away, pacing as fast as she could toward the ballroom.

Reed would leave New York City. He'd do it quickly and quietly and without bothering Katrina again. But there was one thing he had to take care of first. And Elizabeth Jeril was the person to help him.

At the Liberty Ballet administration offices, she closed her door and gestured to one of the guest chairs in front of her maple-wood desk. "My receptionist just warned me you were dangerous."

"Was she at the party?" Reed was sorry his behavior had marred the event. But he wasn't sorry he'd confronted Foster. He'd done what he had to do.

Elizabeth laughed, rounding her desk. "She heard the story this morning. Everybody in Manhattan heard the story this morning."

Reed waited for her to sit. "I have a hard time believing it was that interesting."

She plunked down on the padded burgundy leather chair, definitely seeming more amused than angry. "Most exciting fundraiser I've ever attended."

Reed took his seat. "Sorry about that."

She waved a dismissive hand. "Not to worry."

Fair enough. He'd forget the party and get straight to the point. "I need a favor, Elizabeth."

She squared her shoulders and folded her hands on the desktop. "What kind of a favor?"

"I need Quentin Foster out of Katrina's life forever."

Elizabeth's brows knitted in obvious confusion.

"And that means I need him out of Liberty Ballet forever."

She began shaking her head. "Reed, it's not going to be possible for me—"

"How much?" he asked.

"Excuse me?"

"How much will it take to get rid of Foster?"

Elizabeth blinked.

"I have a proposal for you." Reed saw no point in pussyfooting around. "I'm prepared to set up a foundation for the benefit of the Liberty Ballet Company. The endowment would provide stable funding to the organization into perpetuity."

He tightened his grip on the arms of the chair. "My only condition is that Quentin Foster is immediately kicked off the board of directors, banned from ever contributing to Liberty Ballet, and banned from ever attending any of their fundraisers. If I thought I could keep him from buying tickets, I would ask for that, too."

Elizabeth's gaze probed Reed's expression for a long minute. "What did he do?"

"Nothing that's provable."

Her eyes narrowed.

Reed didn't blame her for being confused, even suspicious. He made up his mind to put all his cards on the table. "I tell you this in confidence, and only to protect Katrina. I couldn't care less about that jackal. Foster wanted to sleep with her, and when she turned him down, he pressured her again. Then the cables appeared and her shoe malfunctioned, and he was pivotal in replacing her other shoes before anyone could look at them. I warned him off at the party Saturday, but I don't trust him. I can't trust him. I need him gone."

Elizabeth came halfway out of her chair. "Are you *kidding* me?"

"I am not."

"He used his access to the company as a board member to solicit sex with a dancer?"

"Yes," Reed answered shortly.

Elizabeth reached for her phone. "I'll turf him for that alone."

"That doesn't solve the money issue."

She paused with her hand on the receiver. "No, it doesn't solve the money issue. But I'm not throwing Katrina to the wolves for any amount of money."

"Put down the phone."

"But—"

"Elizabeth, I can solve the money issue."

She looked genuinely sympathetic. "You have no idea what you're saying."

"Why do people keep doubting me? I'm not a rocket scientist, but I do manage to clothe and feed myself on a daily basis. I'm aware of what I'm offering."

"Reed."

"Ten million dollars."

Elizabeth's jaw went lax.

"The Sasha Terrell Endowment Fund will start with ten million dollars in seed money."

"Who is Sasha Terrell?"

Reed couldn't help but grin. "*That's* your question?"

"That's my first question."

He softened his tone. "My mother."

Elizabeth nodded, then she nodded again, then she blinked rather rapidly. "That's nice. That's very nice."

"Your other questions?" he prompted.

"I can't think of any." She laughed unsteadily, covering her lips with her fingers. "Is this real?"

"It's real." Reed reached for his cell phone, dialing Danielle.

Elizabeth sat in astonished silence while Danielle's office put his call straight through.

"Reed?" came Danielle.

"It's me."

"Not another bakery?"

"Can you come to New York City?"

"When?"

"Now."

There was a long silence on Danielle's end, followed by a worried, "Why?"

"Probably better if I tell you when you get here."

"No way. I'll have a coronary en route worrying."

Reed chuckled. "I'm about to set up a ten-million-dollar endowment fund to the benefit of the Liberty Ballet Company of New York City. I want you to manage it."

To her credit, Danielle kept her cool, her tone professional. "I generally advise people to target twenty-five percent of their net worth to charitable endeavors."

"Yeah?"

"Yes."

"Have I ever taken your advice before?"

"No."

"Let's assume I won't be starting now."

"I'll be there in two hours."

"Perfect." If this was the only thing left he could do to protect Katrina, he was going to do it right.

Two days later, and Katrina still couldn't stop thinking about Reed. Riding the bike at her gym reminded her of him. Sitting in the whirlpool reminded her of him. Eating, drinking, even sleeping all brought back memories of his simmering gray eyes, his rugged face and his killer body that she could swear she felt around her every time she closed her eyes.

In her gym's locker room, she shut off the shower taps and reached for her towel. Her workout was finished, but she didn't have it in her to head home and stare at her four walls and feel lonely. So instead, she dried off and dressed, heading for the juice bar that fronted on the sidewalk on the facility's main floor.

She found a table on the deck near the rail and ordered a raspberry smoothie. At least smoothies didn't remind her of Reed. And neither did pedestrians or taxicabs. Well, as long as she stayed away from the park.

A long white Hummer limo cruised past, and her chest contracted. She blinked back tears and took a sip of the sweet, icy beverage.

"Katrina Jacobs?" a woman's voice inquired.

The last thing Katrina wanted to do was to sign an autograph or pose for a picture. But she put on a smile. "Yes?"

The tall, dark-haired woman held out her hand. "Danielle Marin. I'm a lawyer from Chicago. I work for Caleb Terrell, and I've met your sister on a number of occasions."

"Mandy?" Katrina asked in surprise, taking the hand the woman offered.

"Yes. Mandy. She's fantastic. I think we're on the way to becoming good friends."

Katrina looked Danielle up and down. She was neatly dressed, with a chic, short haircut, perfect makeup and a highly polished veneer. It was kind of hard to imagine her as good friends with Mandy.

Danielle glanced meaningfully at the empty chair on the opposite side of the small round table.

"Would you like to sit down?" Katrina felt obligated to offer.

Danielle smiled broadly and took a seat. "Thank you." She placed her small purse at the edge of the table and ordered an iced tea.

"Are you in New York on business?" Katrina opened, telling herself that at least the conversation might distract her from her depressing thoughts.

"I am," Danielle answered. "I'm also doing some work here for Reed Terrell."

Katrina couldn't tell if it was her imagination, but Danielle seemed to be watching her closely as she spoke his name.

"The bakery?" Katrina guessed, trying desperately to keep her features neutral. Then it hit her. "You're Danielle?"

"Yes."

"The restaurant reservation. Flavian's."

"That was me." Danielle smiled. "I didn't know it was you. Did you enjoy yourself?"

"Yes," Katrina managed. Then she swallowed hard. She didn't want to think about that night.

"Reed's a very nice man."

Katrina wasn't ready to speak, so she nodded instead.

"Does that mean you and he are...involved?"

"No," Katrina quickly replied. "I mean, we went out a couple of times, sure. But he was only here for a few days, and then—" She forced out a laugh. "You know what Coloradans are like. Couldn't wait to get back to the dust and sweat."

"Didn't you grow up there?"

"I haven't lived there since I was ten."

"Ah."

The waitress arrived with Danielle's iced tea.

She squeezed in a slice of lemon and concentrated on stirring. "You could always go visit him."

"I don't get to Colorado very often. It's really never been my favorite place."

"But, with Reed—"

"It's nothing like that," Katrina assured her, scrambling for a way out of the conversation. She and Reed were past tense, done, over.

"He's a very handsome man."

A thought hit Katrina. "Are you interested in Reed? I wondered when he called you for the restaurant recommendation—"

Danielle laughed lightly. "It's nothing like that for me, either. But it seems like you and he—"

"No."

"You're blushing, Katrina."

"I am? Well…"

There was a combination of pity and curiosity in Danielle's eyes. Reed had obviously shared something with her.

"You know more than you're letting on, don't you?" Katrina asked.

"I know he took you to dinner. And I can see that you're blushing. And he seems to have left town in a bit of a…hurry. That only adds up to so many things."

Katrina felt her face grow even hotter.

"And now it occurs to me that Caleb and Mandy's relationship has the ability to make things complicated for you."

"It's no problem." Though Katrina was struggling to keep her composure.

"I don't mean to pry." But Danielle's mixture of concern and curiosity somehow invited confidences.

"It never should have happened." Katrina gave up pretending.

"I hear you," Danielle agreed with what seemed like genuine sympathy.

"We're completely unsuited. Our lives are a million miles apart. And yet there was this chemical thing." Katrina stopped herself.

"I've experienced that chemical thing myself," said Danielle with a self-deprecating laugh.

"You have?" Katrina hated to admit it, but her misery felt a little better with company.

"A guy named Tr—Trevor." Danielle stabbed at her iced tea for a moment, and it looked as if she might be blushing. "He was from Texas."

"Did you sleep with him?" Katrina instantly checked herself. "I'm sorry. That was completely inappropriate."

"Not at all. I don't mind. We didn't. Oh, he tried hard enough. And he was quite a charmer. But I managed to say no."

"Reed was the opposite," Katrina confessed. "He tried to talk me out of it. But I wouldn't listen, and I— Good grief, I can't believe I'm telling you this."

Danielle reached across the table and covered Katrina's hand. "When was the last time you saw him?"

"Saturday night."

"So, the wound is fresh."

Katrina nodded miserably.

"Then you need someone to talk to." Danielle glanced around. "Do they serve martinis here?"

"You know, that actually sounds tempting."

Danielle waved to the waitress.

"I bet you're glad you said no," Katrina ventured in a low voice. If she hadn't slept with Reed, maybe she wouldn't have such a burning pain in her chest. Maybe the world wouldn't feel as if it was crushing her with its weight. Maybe she'd be able to sleep. And maybe tears wouldn't feel as if they were mere seconds away every moment of the day and night.

"Not necessarily," said Danielle, her expression going soft. "I lay awake at night wondering what it would have been like."

"Was he really great?"

"He was conceited and pig-headed and irrepressible and rash.

He was also the sexiest guy I've ever met, and I know deep down in my soul that he'd have been an extraordinary lover."

"Maybe you should go back to Texas."

The waitress arrived and Danielle ordered two vodka martinis. Katrina had never tried one, but today she was game.

"Don't think I haven't thought about it," said Danielle.

Katrina heaved an empathetic sigh. "But you'd end up with regrets either way."

"Afraid so."

"It's not fair. It's just not fair." If Katrina hadn't slept with Reed, she'd be just like Danielle, wondering what she'd missed. At least she had those few nights. At least she'd lost her virginity to a man she—

Oh, no.

The waitress set down the martinis, and Katrina grabbed one, downing a healthy swallow.

Her throat burned, and she gasped and coughed and wheezed.

"You okay?" Danielle asked, while the waitress frowned.

"Fine," Katrina managed. The warmth of the alcohol spreading though her veins felt good. "Just fine," she finished.

Danielle thanked the waitress, and the woman left.

"So, how does Reed feel about you?"

The question struck Katrina as odd. But then the entire conversation was odd. She shrugged. "Angry. Very, very angry."

For some reason, the answer seemed to surprise Danielle. "You fought?"

"And how. I told him to leave New York City, and basically never to come back again."

"Ouch."

"It's for the best." Katrina nodded, ordering herself to believe it. She took another experimental sip of the martini, and it went down better this time.

"Do you think he'll come back anyway?" Danielle asked softly.

Katrina shook her head, long and slow, lifting her glass.

"Do you think he might have fallen in love with you?"

The drink sloshed over Katrina's hand. *"What?"*

Danielle shrugged. "It's a possibility."

"It's preposterous," Katrina blurted.

"He tried to talk you out of sleeping with him."

"That's because he's a gentleman, a cowboy."

"My cowboy tried to talk me *in*to sleeping with him."

"Yours is from Texas."

A funny expression crossed Danielle's face.

"Reed knew all along it would turn out badly for us if we slept together," Katrina continued. "He's had relationships end before. He's had experience with ex-lovers."

"And you haven't?"

Katrina immediately realized what she'd given away. "Haven't what?" She played dumb.

But Danielle was too shrewd to let it go. "Had experience with ex-lovers."

Katrina didn't answer, but her face heated up again.

Danielle closed her eyes for a long second. Then she opened them. "Katrina, is there any chance you've fallen in love with Reed?"

Katrina's stomach turned to a block of lead. "No," she intoned. "Never. Not a chance." What kind of a colossal disaster would that be? She downed the rest of the martini. "But I will have another one of these."

"You should call Mandy."

"Why?"

"To talk to her about this."

Katrina dismissed the notion. "I really don't know Mandy that well."

"She's your sister."

"We're not close."

"Well, if I had a sister, and if she was as nice as Mandy, and if I was feeling the way you are, I'd be calling her in a heartbeat."

Katrina felt as if she were listening through cotton wool. "Say again?"

"Call Mandy, Katrina."

"Maybe." But what would she tell her? What could she say? That she was in way too deep with Mandy's soon-to-be brother-in-law, and that she could never come home again?

# Ten

Back home on his ranch, Reed knew he had to forget about Katrina. He had to restart his regular life and put the surreal week in New York City far behind him.

Starting right now.

But as he stared at the barbecue grill on the back deck, he couldn't seem to rouse himself to light it. Instead, while the sun descended, he lifted the half-empty bottle of beer from the table next to him and took a desultory sip of the tepid liquid.

"The door was open," came Danielle's unexpected voice from the kitchen doorway.

"Always is," Reed responded without turning.

Her high heels clicked on the deck as she made her way to him.

"I get why you did it," she told him without preamble. "What I don't get is why you did *that*."

He set down the bottle. "You want to toss a few nouns into that sentence?"

"You're obviously in love with Katrina."

Reed wasn't about to deny it. Danielle was his lawyer, after all. It wasn't like she could tell anyone.

"That's why you wanted to help her," she finished.

"Go to the head of the class."

She waited for him to elaborate. When he didn't, she stepped into the silence. "But why such a huge gesture. Ten million dollars? Were you hoping to win her back?"

"Hoping to win who back?" asked Caleb from the same spot where Danielle had just appeared.

Reed twisted his head at the unexpected sound of his brother's voice.

"Hi, Danielle," Caleb added. "What are you doing here?"

"Hey, Danielle," said Mandy as she breezed past Caleb onto the deck. Then she grinned at Reed. "You're back." She dropped a quick kiss on his cheek before plunking down in one of the four empty Adirondack chairs.

"So are you," Reed responded to Mandy, hoping against hope they hadn't overheard Danielle's revelation. "How was Chicago?"

"Noisy. How was New York?"

"Noisier."

She chuckled.

"Get who back?" Caleb repeated, glancing from Reed to Danielle.

Reed knew there were parts of the situation that shouldn't stay a secret, and parts that couldn't stay a secret. He decided now was as good a time as any to get the basics out of the way.

"Danielle helped me out with some investments while I was in New York," he opened.

Caleb's glance went to Danielle. "Yeah?"

She nodded.

"That's great." Caleb's posture relaxed. "Anybody else need a beer?"

Mandy raised her hand.

"What the heck?" said Danielle, moving to sit next to Mandy. "I'll take one."

Caleb disappeared, while Reed tried to bring some order to

the riot of emotions coursing through his body. He was normally cool under pressure, calm under stress. He could hold his own under physical danger and in the toughest of arguments. But his feelings toward Katrina took him to uncharted waters.

"How's Katrina doing?" Mandy asked. "Did you see her dance?"

"I did," Reed responded as Caleb returned, passing beers to the two women.

Then Caleb held his up in a toast to Reed. "Welcome to the world beyond Lyndon Valley."

Reed couldn't help a harsh chuckle at that. The world beyond Lyndon Valley hadn't worked out so well for him.

"So, tell me about these new investments."

Reed looked his brother square in the eye. The bakery, the tailor and the limo service were irrelevant. "I set up the Sasha Terrell Endowment Fund with ten million dollars."

Caleb blinked.

"It's for the benefit of the Liberty Ballet Company," Reed continued.

Mandy reached over and grasped his upper arm. "For Katrina?"

"For Katrina," Reed confirmed, reaching for his warm beer, swallowing it against his dry throat.

Caleb's eyes narrowed. "What did you do?"

"I just told you what I did."

"Reed, are you sure?" asked Mandy, sitting forward in her chair and leaning toward him. "I mean, it's great and all. And what a wonderful tribute to your mother. But that's a whole lot of money."

"You slept with her?" Caleb accused.

"Back off," said Reed.

Caleb paced across the deck. "What is the matter with you? I specifically—"

"It's to protect her," Reed stated.

"From you?"

"Give me a break." Reed rocked to his feet. "She doesn't need protection from me."

"Then why the ten million?"

Reed was tired of having his motives questioned. "There's a guy in New York, Quentin Foster. He's made a lot of large donations to the ballet company, and he seems to think it gives him the right to sleep with Katrina."

"What?" Caleb demanded.

*"What?"* Mandy echoed.

"That's why I went to New York," said Reed, owning up to at least part of the truth. "I told him to back off. Threatened to kill him, actually. But he wouldn't listen."

Caleb's jaw had turned to steel. "He didn't…"

"He's still breathing," said Reed. "So, no. He didn't. He asked. She turned him down, but he wouldn't take no for an answer. He's the guy who caused her ankle accident."

Mandy rose distractedly. "I have to call Katrina." But she didn't move any farther.

"The Sasha Terrell Endowment Fund will replace all of Foster's donations," said Reed, still looking directly at his brother. "And then some. He's out. We're in. And Katrina is perfectly safe."

"Now I understand," said Danielle.

Mandy's shoulders slumped in relief. Then she took the two steps that brought her to Reed and she enveloped him in a hug of gratitude.

"Thank you," she whispered, her throat obviously clogged.

Reed hugged her back. "Happy to do it."

"Why didn't you come to me?" Caleb asked.

"Didn't need to."

"She's going to be my sister-in-law. And I have a lot more money than you do."

"It's handled," said Reed, releasing Mandy. A couple of tears had leaked out of the corners of her eyes, but she was smiling.

Caleb cocked his head to one side. "But why not—"

"Leave it," said Reed, glaring at his brother.

But then comprehension dawned on Caleb's face. "I'll be damned."

"What part of 'leave it' didn't you understand?"

"What?" Mandy looked back and forth between the brothers.

Caleb shook his head in obvious bewilderment. "How long have you been in love with Katrina?"

"You don't have to answer that," said Danielle.

Caleb turned to her. "What? We're in a court of law now?"

Mandy looked to Reed, her brows knitting together. "Did I miss something?"

"She's safe, Mandy." He told her. "That's all that matters."

"But—"

He moved toward the door, wanting nothing more than to get very far away from this conversation.

"How does she feel about you?" Mandy called after him.

He paused, his respect for Mandy at war with his instinct for self-preservation. "She's in New York City. I'm here. End of story."

"Is she upset? Did you hurt her?"

Reed knew his answer was going to make Mandy angry. He regretted that. He regretted it a lot. But it was always going to end this way. He'd tried to tell that to Katrina, and he'd certainly known it himself. "She understands that our lives are completely separate."

"But you slept with her anyway," said Caleb.

"That's still none of your business." Reed started for the kitchen door.

Caleb put an arm out to stop him. Surprisingly, there was no anger in his tone. "A very wise man once told me that when a Jacobs woman sleeps with you, it means she loves you."

Reed remembered their conversation perfectly. But that was a different time, a completely different circumstance. "That doesn't bring Katrina any closer to Colorado."

"You think that's your only answer?"

Reed ignored his brother and began moving again, increasing his pace.

"That Katrina comes to Colorado?" Caleb called. "You can't go to New York City?"

Reed smacked his hand on the doorjamb as he rocked to a halt.

"There are two possible solutions," said Caleb.

Reed turned, enunciating carefully. "My world is here. I have a house to build and kids to raise and a mother to honor."

"You think Mom would want you to give up Katrina?" Caleb stepped closer.

"I think Mom would want Katrina to be happy," Reed answered with total honesty. There were more than a few parallels between the two women. And he would never, ever do to Katrina what his father had done to his mother.

"So do I," Caleb said softly, stopping directly in front of Reed. "I think Mom would want you to make Katrina happy, on Katrina's terms, in Katrina's world."

Reed opened his mouth to argue.

But Caleb wasn't finished. "I know your plan, Reed. And I understand why you're doing it. But you're wrong, dead wrong. You don't honor Mom by staying in Lyndon Valley. You honor Mom by honoring Katrina."

Reed couldn't wrap his head around it. "You're suggesting I move to New York City?" Was Caleb saying their mother would want him to move to New York City? The idea was preposterous. He was a cowboy. His life was here. He was about to dig the foundation for his house.

"Imagine," Caleb continued, voice controlled, but Reed could see the anger simmering in his eyes. "If Wilton had once, even once in his miserable, toxic life, given a damn about Mom? What she wanted, what she needed, what would make her happy instead of him?"

Reed got where his brother was going with this. "It's not just geography, Caleb."

"Then, what is it?"

Reed wished there weren't quite so many witnesses, but he supposed there was no point in backing off now. "The last thing she said to me was, no matter how I dressed up, I'd always be an uncouth Colorado cowboy."

Caleb shrugged. "So change."

Reed snapped his fingers. "Just like that?"

"Just like that."

"I'm not going to stop threatening to kill any man who hurts her."

A grin spread across Caleb's face. "Yeah? Well, maybe you could stop telling her about it."

Danielle spoke up. "But you already did that, Reed."

Reed looked at her. "Already did what?"

"You didn't kill him. You found another way." She gave a shrug. "Maybe the tux and the tie rubbed off on you. Because instead of killing Quentin Foster, you outsmarted him. That was very civilized."

It was Mandy's turn to step in, and she was fighting a smile. "Honestly, Reed, I can't see Katrina objecting if you threaten to outsmart any man who hurts her."

Danielle nodded her agreement.

"It's not quite as satisfying," Caleb allowed.

"It was pretty satisfying," Reed admitted. The only thing he'd regretted was not being able to watch Elizabeth deliver the news to Foster.

"She misses you," said Danielle, her tone softer, more thoughtful than normal. "I went to see Katrina while I was in New York City. I was trying to figure out if you'd lost your mind. You hadn't. And she misses you."

The only time Katrina didn't miss Reed was while she was performing. Being on stage took all of her concentration and she was thankful that, if only temporarily, the effort blocked him out of her brain. But as soon as the curtain fell, her chest would hollow out again and her stomach would start to ache.

The applause from tonight's audience had barely died down. She was pacing her way along the hall to her dressing room, and her tears were once again close to the surface. She'd picked up her phone about a hundred times in the last few days, longing to call him and hear the sound of his voice. She wasn't ready to let him go. Not yet. Not so soon.

She'd concocted all kinds of wild schemes to eke a few more hours out of their brief relationship. Maybe he could come back to the city for a day or a week. Or maybe she could go to Colorado for another visit. Maybe it wouldn't be so bad there, if she was with Reed.

But deep down inside, she knew none of the plans made any real sense. It would still be temporary, and she'd get her heart broken all over again. Reed was like a drug, and her only hope was to go cold turkey.

She made it to the privacy of her dressing room. But before the door could close behind her, Elizabeth appeared.

"Another full house," she told Katrina, breezing inside, letting the door fall shut, taking one of the two armchairs in the compact room.

Katrina dropped down on the padded bench in front of the lighted mirror, automatically pulling the decorations from her hair.

"That's great news." She forced herself to smile, catching Elizabeth in the reflection.

"Have you heard from Reed today?" Elizabeth asked.

Katrina's fingers fumbled, and she dropped a small jeweled comb. It clattered onto the table and down to the floor.

"From Reed?" she asked stupidly, as she reached down to retrieve it. Could she have misheard? Why was Elizabeth asking about Reed?

"I left a message for him this morning, but he hasn't gotten back to me. That doesn't seem like him."

Katrina picked up the comb, her fingers slightly numb, mind scrambling to find some logic in Elizabeth's words. "You left Reed a message?"

"Yes."

"Why?"

"Just some more paperwork we need to sign. Danielle couriered it over, but I'm not clear on some of the tax sections."

Katrina blinked at Elizabeth. "Tax sections?" she parroted. What on earth would Elizabeth have to do with Reed's taxes? Or what would Reed have to do with Elizabeth's taxes? And what was Danielle doing in the middle of it?

Katrina knew she couldn't let herself be jealous, but she

simply couldn't help it. She wanted to be the person Reed called. It wasn't fair that it was Elizabeth and Danielle.

"Just details," Elizabeth said brightly, coming to her feet and putting her hand on the doorknob. "If he calls, can you make sure he has my cell number?"

"Certainly." Not that Reed would call. For a wild moment, Katrina thought of using this as an excuse to call him. But she dismissed the idea. It would be so transparent.

"So you met Danielle?" she asked Elizabeth.

Elizabeth laughed lightly. "We've been talking every day. Ten million dollars needs a lot of babysitting."

"Ten million dollars?"

Elizabeth stilled. Her expression faltered. Her hand dropped from the knob, and she stared at Katrina. "You don't know?"

Katrina didn't answer.

"How can you not know? Have you *talked* to Reed?"

Katrina swallowed a lump. "Not in a few days. We, well, we left things on bad terms after the gala."

Elizabeth sat back down in the chair, her hands going limp. "The gala? You haven't talked to him since the gala?"

"No," Katrina replied.

"She didn't tell you?"

"Elizabeth?" Katrina tried to tamp down her anxiety.

"Before he left New York. Before… Reed set up an endowment named the Sasha Terrell Fund. It's for us. It's for Liberty. It's ten million dollars."

The breath whooshed out of Katrina's body.

"His only stipulation," Elizabeth continued, "was that we kick Quentin Foster off the board and out of the organization forever."

*"What?"*

"I thought…" Elizabeth gave a helpless laugh. "I assumed. I mean, a man doesn't do something like that for just anyone. And after his performance at the gala. Well, if a man stepped up for me the way Reed stepped up for you…"

Katrina's hands started to shake. What had Reed done? Why had he done it?

"I was embarrassed," she confessed in a small voice. "At the gala. I was mortified by his behavior. I told him to leave, to get out of the city. I told him to go back to his sawdust-covered honky-tonks where he could make a point with his fists."

Elizabeth's jaw dropped open.

Katrina's stomach churned.

Elizabeth cleared her throat. "I, uh, guess he did this instead."

"What was he *thinking?*"

Elizabeth cocked her head sideways. "I guess he was thinking he wanted to protect you. And he didn't appear to care what it cost him."

Guilt washed over Katrina. Ten million dollars? He'd spent *ten million dollars?* "Who does that, Elizabeth? Who *does* something like that?"

"Apparently, cowboys from Colorado."

"I hate Colorado." But Katrina was blinking back tears. "Okay, I don't exactly hate it. But I don't want to live there."

"Reed's there," Elizabeth offered softly.

"I love Reed," Katrina admitted her worst fear out loud. "I *love* Reed. But my life is here."

Elizabeth moved to the bench, tucking in beside Katrina and taking her hand.

"I need to apologize."

Elizabeth squeezed. "I hate to ask this. It seems terribly insensitive. But is there any chance you could do it by phone?"

Katrina gave a watery laugh. "I don't think so."

"We've got sold-out performances for four more nights running."

"I know." Katrina wouldn't walk out on Liberty. "Maybe Monday? Caleb, my sister's fiancé, has a jet. Maybe I could talk to him about flying—"

The dressing-room door swung open. The two women all but jumped up as Reed's form filled the doorway.

Katrina froze, her stomach going into a freefall.

"Hello, Katrina." His deep voice reverberated around her, exactly as she remembered it.

She opened her mouth, but she couldn't seem to make any words come out.

Elizabeth recovered first, coming smoothly to her feet and moving toward the door, pausing beside him. "May I talk to you later on, Reed? About the paperwork?"

His gaze never left Katrina. "Sure. I'll call you."

"Thanks. See you both later then."

Reed moved in as Elizabeth moved out, and the door clicked shut behind him.

Katrina came shakily to her feet, steadying herself on the dressing table. She was still in her costume, her hair half up, half down.

All she could muster was a whisper. She swallowed. "Elizabeth just told me about the endowment."

Reed opened his mouth, but Katrina shook her head. She moved forward and touched her fingertips to his lips to silence him.

"Why did you do it?" She blinked against the stinging in her eyes. "I mean... No, that's not what I mean. I mean, thank you. And I'm sorry."

"I'm the one who's sorry." Reed spoke around her fingertips.

She shook her head again. He had nothing to be sorry about. He'd been right all along.

"I'm sorry I threatened to kill him," said Reed. "Okay. That's a lie. But I'm sorry it upset you. And I honestly would have killed him if he'd come after you. But I outsmarted him instead. And Mandy and Danielle tell me that's a more civilized solution."

Katrina smiled through the tiny tears that leaked out the corners of her eyes. "I can't believe you did that. Reed, you spent all your money."

He reached for her hand, enclosing it in his, pulling her close. "Don't cry."

"But—"

"It's not *all* of my money."

His hand was warm and strong and secure. She moved

against him, closing her eyes and absorbing the feel of his body and the scent of his skin. "I missed you so much."

"I missed you, too." He held her tightly and sighed. "You feel so good."

She fisted her hands into his shirt, voice raw. "I don't know if I can let go of you again."

"I know."

"Oh, Reed," she whispered, then drew a shuddering breath. "What are we going to do?"

"I hope we're going to love each other."

"How?" she sniffed.

He touched his index finger to her chin, tipping it up. His eyes were warm and rich, and his smile was soft. "I thought we'd start with real estate. Maybe a nice place in Brooklyn. Though I could be talked into Manhattan."

"Huh?"

"And after that I was planning to propose to you."

Katrina didn't understand. What was he saying? He couldn't mean what she thought he meant. "You're..."

"Moving to New York City?" He nodded. "Yes, I am."

"You can't do that."

"Turns out I can."

"But the ranch. Your family. Your new house. Your heritage."

"I want you to be my family." He smoothed back her hair. "I love you, Katrina. And I think my mother would love to know she had little ballerina granddaughters going to fine arts school in New York City. I think she would love that a lot."

"Oh, Reed." Katrina's heart swelled. She couldn't believe this was happening. She couldn't believe he would do such an amazing thing for her. She pressed herself tighter into his arms. "I love you. I love you *so* much."

"That's good. Because it turns out I can't wait on this. I'm proposing right now." He drew back again. "Will you marry me, Katrina?"

She nodded. Then she nodded faster. "Yes. Yes, I'll marry you, Reed. And I'll learn to ride horses, and I'll befriend the chickens. And we can spend weekends and holidays in Colorado with our families."

"That's my girl." He kissed her hairline. "I sure wish I had a ring. I shouldn't be doing this without a ring."

"There's a Tiffany's around the corner," she teased. Then she paused. "Or we can go to Brooklyn. Would you rather buy a ring in Brooklyn?"

"Sweetheart." He hugged her tighter. "You can have any ring you want. You can have any *thing* you want. As long as you'll stay with me for the rest of my life."

Katrina stopped in her tracks halfway between the Terrells' farmhouse and their barn. "I thought you said I could have anything I wanted."

"You can," Reed cajoled, taking her hand in his.

She snatched it back. "But I *don't* want *this*."

"That's not the same logic."

"Close enough."

"You'll love her," said Reed, slipping an arm around Katrina's shoulders and urging her forward. "She's twenty-two years old, has raised nine foals. She's as gentle as a kitten."

"She's as big as a house." Katrina complained, trying to shrink back as they approached the dapple-gray mare tied to the hitching post in front of the corral.

"She's maybe fifteen hands. Her name's North Star."

"Can't I start with a pony?" Not that Katrina had any desire to get up on a pony, either, but at least it would buy her some time. Maybe she could hide while Reed was looking for a pony.

"You promised you'd try," he admonished.

"I lied."

He laughed. "I'm not going to let anything happen to you."

"No offense, Reed. You're big and strong and capable, and all. But you're a human being. She's a horse."

"And she knows who's boss."

"Well, it's sure not going to be me."

"Katrina."

"What?"

"Buck up."

"That's your pep talk? 'Buck up'?" They were drawing closer to the mare by the second. She fought an urge to squeeze her eyes shut.

"I don't think you want to hear the alternative."

She wanted to be brave. She really did. Deep down inside, she knew this was an irrational fear. Very few people were killed by horses each year. And those that were tended to be in the rodeo or ride in steeplechases.

But an irrational fear didn't normally respond to logic, and so she was stuck with it. "I think I'm going to pass out."

"Katrina," he told her firmly. "Quit being such a wuss."

"You quit yelling at me."

"I am not yelling."

North Star snorted and shifted.

"You're scaring the horse," Katrina complained.

"So now you care about the horse?"

"Absolutely I care about the horse."

They'd stopped about five feet away from the hitching post.

"You'll make her sad if you don't ride her," said Reed.

"Nice try."

"Just look at those big brown eyes." Reed left Katrina behind and moved around the hitching post to stroke North Star's neck. "She loves teaching new riders."

"She does not."

"Want to bet?" He scratched the mare's nose, and she gave a couple of long, slow, obviously contented blinks.

Katrina didn't blame her. Reed did have magic hands.

"I've had six-year-olds on her back," Reed offered in smooth, honey tones. "She's a mama through and through. She won't let anything happen to you."

North Star was gazing at Katrina now. She did look rather gentle. In fact, she looked quite friendly.

"You want to come closer?" asked Reed.

"Not really." Katrina was tempted, though. When Reed had proposed back in New York, she had told him she'd learn to ride. She wanted to keep that promise. And if she could force herself to get on the horse's back, it would be one less thing to be embarrassed about while she was in Colorado.

And they were definitely going to spend time in Colorado. Reed had been amazing about offering to move to New York City. The least she could do was try to meet him halfway.

She glanced at him.

His expression had turned loving, one of understanding and patience.

She wiped her damp palms across the front of her blue jeans and took a step forward, then another and another.

When she came up beside Reed, North Star swung her head to look. But her movements were slow and calm, not at all threatening.

"Pat her neck," Reed suggested. "Firmly, or you'll tickle her."

"I don't want to tickle her." Katrina reached out. She patted the mare's neck three times. It was hot and wiry under her touch. A small puff of dust came up.

The horse didn't move at all.

"She's all saddled up," said Reed.

"I'm terrified," Katrina confessed in a whisper.

"I'll hold the lead rope. We'll walk her in the round pen."

"Inside the pen?" That would be easier.

"Until you're ready to go out."

Katrina screwed up her courage. She nodded. "Okay. But only inside the pen." It had to be safe enough. Surely to goodness, Reed wouldn't let her die before the wedding.

He kissed the top of her head. "Back here." He moved. "Put your hand around the saddle horn."

She reached up to grab the hard protrusion of leather.

"Foot up in the stirrup. I'm going to grab your butt."

"You're not allowed to enjoy this," she warned.

"I'm allowed to enjoy it all I want. Let me know when you're ready, and I'll give you a boost."

Katrina braced herself. "One, two, three." She pulled and Reed lifted, and before she knew it, she was perched on top of North Star. The mare hadn't moved a muscle.

"See how easy it is?"

Katrina adjusted her seat. "I'm awfully high up here."

"Put your other foot in the stirrup. And relax. You're not going anywhere."

He released the lead rope from the hitching post, and the horse shifted under her. Katrina gave out a little whoop of surprise.

"Go with the motion," Reed advised. "Don't fight it. We both know you have good balance."

Katrina tried to relax. Reed was right. She did have good balance. In that, she was ahead of the game.

He opened the gate to the round pen and led the horse inside. North Star's gait was slow and smooth beneath Katrina. The horse's barrel was warm against her legs. Its breathing was somehow soothing. And having Reed close by certainly helped.

He stopped North Star then moved back and released the reins that were looped around the saddle horn. He reached into the back pocket of his worn jeans and produced a pair of small, leather gloves.

"Put these on."

The gloves were soft against Katrina's hands, warm from Reed's body.

He placed the reins across her palm, showing her how to hold them. Then he backed away, holding a long length of the lead rope while North Star started forward, moving in a big circle.

It took a few minutes for Katrina to realize she wasn't afraid. A little while later, she felt as if she'd found her balance. And when Reed asked if he could take off the lead rope, she found herself agreeing.

He stayed in the middle of the round pen while North Star, who apparently knew the drill, paced around the perimeter with Katrina on her back.

"You're doing great," Reed told her.

She braved a look up from North Star's back. She smiled at Reed, and he smiled back, strong, sexy and confident.

The sun was high in the sky above him, the snow-capped mountains rising behind, a knife edge against the crackling blue sky. Wildflowers fanned out in the field, and aspen leaves blew in a gentle breeze. Even the cattle looked bucolic grazing on the hillside, while robins, chickadees and bluebirds flitted from tree to tree.

Katrina's heart lurched, and for the first time in her life, she felt at home in Lyndon Valley.

A pickup's engine rumbled in the distance, growing closer. The truck pulled into the yard, and North Star glanced over her shoulder, but otherwise didn't pay any attention to the interruption. A few moments later, Mandy and Caleb appeared and moved toward the fence.

Reed paced his way over to Katrina and North Star, stopping the horse with a hand signal and a low word.

"Probably don't need an audience yet," he told Katrina. Then he helped her down from North Star.

She was grateful for his understanding.

Reed took the mare, and she waded her way through the deep, loose dirt, back to the round-pen gate. Mandy opened it, beaming.

"You did it!" She laughed, pulling Katrina into her arms.

"I did it," Katrina agreed happily.

Reed had been right. North Star was gentle as a kitten, but she felt proud anyway. She hadn't been scared, and she hadn't fallen off, and she was actually willing to try it again.

"Caleb and I have been talking," said Mandy, linking arms as they started toward the house.

A stable hand took over North Star, and Reed and Caleb fell into step behind.

"About?" asked Katrina. She pulled off the leather gloves and twisted her new engagement ring back into place. The band was a stylized tension wave, platinum, holding a round diamond solitaire, with two small emeralds embedded in the outsides of the band.

She and Reed had found it at a funky jewelry store in Brooklyn. Katrina had loved it on sight. An hour later, she had her ring, and Reed had bought into the jewelry business.

"Why don't we have a double wedding?" Mandy asked in a breathless, animated voice.

Katrina blinked in surprise at the unexpected suggestion.

"Katrina doesn't want to get married in Lyndon Valley," said Reed.

"It doesn't have to be in Lyndon Valley," Mandy responded.

Reed moved up next to Katrina. He took her free hand and placed a kiss on the back of her knuckles. "I think she wants a New York City wedding. And I've promised her anything she wants."

"We'll be living in New York City," Katrina put in. Not that she wanted to get married in Lyndon Valley. But Reed had certainly made one huge concession. She could do the same.

"What about Chicago?" Caleb suggested. "That's halfway in between."

Katrina glanced at Reed. She kind of liked the idea of a double wedding with her sister and Reed's brother. But Chicago didn't mean anything to either her or to Reed.

"Denver," said Mandy, with conviction. "It's Colorado, but with skyscrapers and beautiful parks and five-star hotels."

"It doesn't have to be a double wedding," said Reed.

"I like Denver," said Katrina, her heart warming to the idea. "It's a nice compromise."

"You sure?" asked Reed, concern in his voice.

Katrina let go of her sister and turned to Reed, slowing to a stop, taking his hands and looking deep into his eyes. Her chest was tight, her heart full. "I'm sure," she told him. "After all, I am marrying Colorado."

"Yes, you are," said Reed, drawing her into his arms, holding her close while Mandy and Caleb got farther ahead. "And I'm marrying the very best thing in all of New York City."

"Our children can ride bareback to the Met," she teased.

"Or wear a Versace dress to a barn dance."

"I can't wait to see that."

He paused and the sounds of the ranch filled the spaces around them. After a minute, he stroked the rough pad of his thumb across her cheek. "I'm an ordinary cowboy, Katrina. As ordinary as they come. How'd I ever deserve someone as amazing as you?"

He had it all wrong. But she didn't know how to explain. "You're the one who's amazing," she tried. "And I love you so much."

"Oh, sweetheart." He leaned down for a kiss, his voice turning hoarse. "I'm going to love you forever."

\* \* \* \* \*

Don't miss the next COLORADO CATTLE BARONS
book by *USA TODAY* bestselling author
Barbara Dunlop, coming in October 2012!

*A sneaky peek at next month...*

# Desire™

## PASSIONATE AND DRAMATIC LOVE STORIES

*2 stories in each book - only £5.49!*

*My wish list for next month's titles...*

In stores from 15th June 2012:

❑ Ready for King's Seduction — Maureen Child

& The Cowboy's Pride — Charlene Sands

❑ A Breathless Bride — Fiona Brand

& Bed of Lies — Paula Roe

❑ The Wayward Son & A Forbidden Affair
   — Yvonne Lindsay

❑ A Secret Birthright — Olivia Gates

& Bachelor Unleashed — Brenda Jackson

Available at WHSmith, Tesco, Asda, Eason, Amazon and Apple

*Just can't wait?*

**Visit us Online**

You can buy our books online a month before
they hit the shops! **www.millsandboon.co.uk**

0612/51

# Special Offers

Every month we put together collections and longer reads written by your favourite authors.

Here are some of next month's highlights— and don't miss our fabulous discount online!

On sale 15th June

On sale 15th June

On sale 6th July

# Save 20%
## on all Special Releases

Find out more at
**www.millsandboon.co.uk/specialreleases**

*Visit us Online*

0712/ST/MB377

# Have Your Say

*You've just finished your book.*
*So what did you think?*

We'd love to hear your thoughts on our
'Have your say' online panel
**www.millsandboon.co.uk/haveyoursay**

- 🌹 Easy to use
- 🌹 Short questionnaire
- 🌹 Chance to win Mills & Boon® goodies

*Visit us*
*Online*

Tell us what you thought of this book now at
**www.millsandboon.co.uk/haveyoursay**

YOUR_SAY